Un-Hitched

By Jillian Neal

Un-Hitched
Written by Jillian Neal
Cover Design by The Killion Group
Edited by Chasity Jenkins-Patrick

Published by Realm Press
36 South Court Square
Suite 300
Newnan GA 30263
http://realmpress.net/

ISBN - 978-1-940174-39-6
Library of Congress Control Number: 2017940512

First Edition

First Printing – April 2017

To Brandi -
Thanks for always listening with your heart

Table Of Contents

Chapter 1

Kaitlyn Sommerville should have been vibrating with fury as she stared down at her phone, but the only emotion she could locate at that moment was abject relief.

Her eyes managed a few quick blinks, making certain she was reading the text correctly. But as her gaze lowered from the cell phone in her hands to the long flow of white satin and lace cascading down her body, the boulder in her throat expanded. What was going to happen to her parents? What was going to happen when she ran? Because she was finally going to give in to the desperate desire to fly that had been threatening to overwhelm her for the last three years.

Another roll of ominous thunder shook the windows of the clubhouse. The storm outside was nothing compared to the maelstrom stirring in Kaitlyn's stomach and the black hatred filling her hollow chest. How could he have done this to her parents?

"Motherfucking asshole," she spat the first curse words that had exited her lips in three long years, before she remembered she was not standing in the bridal room of Hillcrest Country Club alone.

"Kaitlyn?" Her grandmother's eyes goggled.

"Sorry, Nana." Every exit sign in that ridiculously extravagant room where she'd been sequestered glowed enticingly. The walk signal from the crosswalk outside the window gave blurry blinks through the deluge of rain.

"What on earth?" Her grandmother's perfectly manicured hands reached and took the phone from Kaitlyn's grasp. Cringing, Kaitlyn wasn't certain what her grandmother would say to this. It would be easier to escape if she'd been alone.

'Darling, know that I wish it were you in white today, and nothing will change what happens between us. She's nothing more than a business transaction. You are my everything.'

"And to whom did he intend to send this since you *are* the one in white today?" Her grandmother sounded almost as disgusted as Kaitlyn felt.

"Look at the top, Nana. He sent it to me and to Kelsey. It's a group message, but her name is first. Bastard didn't look closely enough at who he was sending that to. Seth's always like that. He doesn't give a damn about anyone but himself and never cares if he gets caught being the asshole he is." For her foul mouth to have been so rusty, the words were flowing rather freely at the moment.

"Kaitlyn, dear, I know you're upset, but do mind your language."

"Nana, I'm standing in my wedding gown, in this stupid country club, and my fiancé has been cheating on me with a girl who has already walked down the aisle because she is one of my bridesmaids. Daddy's going to be in here any minute."

Her grandmother's beautiful face, a product of years of methodic Pond's Cold Cream and Oil of Olay applications, twisted in thought. She stalked quickly to the vase of six perfect white roses, sent a few hours earlier from Seth, situated on the counter along with Kaitlyn's makeup bags. Only someone as tight as Seth would send a *half*–dozen roses. Kaitlyn was surprised he'd sent her anything at all.

Plucking the card from the florist, her grandmother touched a few buttons on the cell phone in her hand.

"This is Katarina Sommerville. Yes, dear, that's right, Chief of Police Sommerville's mother. I was hoping you could help me." Her grandmother smirked. "I had a feeling you'd be more than happy to. There was a delivery order today from Mr. Seth Christensen. I need to make certain it's been received." Kaitlyn had no idea what her grandmother was up to. The roses were sitting before them in all their stupid glory; obviously, they'd already been delivered. "Should have been sent to Kelsey Bennett. Ah, yes I see. Twelve dozen pink roses were signed for by Kelsey herself. How lovely."

So that was why he was always such a tightwad despite his parents' money and his job at the D.A.'s office. He was spending all his spare cash on Kelsey.

The opening chords of Pachelbel's Canon in D were shattered by a lightning strike that split the darkening sky plenty loud enough for even Kaitlyn to hear.

Acrid breath seized in her lungs. *Oh, my God. Oh, my God. I'm supposed to get married. Now.* The room tilted and spun. Her heart refused her another beat. Something inside of her snapped.

What would people say when they found out she'd run away? Her parents paid a fortune for all three ballrooms in the club. The flowers alone were obscenely expensive, not that any of it had been Kaitlyn's preference. It had all been her parents. And the gown. Dear God, the stupid, ridiculous gown she'd been shoved into had cost more than some people make in six months' time.

Some small voice she barely recognized became more audible with each passing moment and each vicious clap of thunder announcing an impending storm. Nowhere in her soul could she locate sadness that Seth didn't love her. What the hell was she even doing standing there in a gown? How had this gone so far? The coma she'd forced herself to live in for the past three years began to unravel. She had no intention of mending it yet again.

The rush of blood in her good ear muted the onslaught of rain as it assaulted the building. Mother Nature took up Kaitlyn's cause as she pummeled the windows with angry fistfuls of water.

An eruption of emotion streamed from her mouth. "Daddy will be here in just a minute to walk me down the aisle. The entire town is out there waiting on me. I have to get out of here." The words bubbled up from Kaitlyn's chest.

"Then we only have a minute. You, my precious child, have always deserved better than Seth Christensen. All your parents have been through in the last few years has made a mockery of their good sense. You deserve more. You know it, and I know it. There is a great deal more to life than living it safely, or even worse, allowing someone else to dictate who you become. Safety can be a vicious bind, Kaitlyn, never forget that. You've never loved Seth, and it will be over my dead body that my granddaughter goes through life with a cheating bastard, never knowing true passion. It is out there my girl, but you must go find it.

"Now, run. I'll explain everything to your parents. You go. Let Seth and Kelsey deal with the aftermath of this bomb they've detonated. You have the plane tickets for your honeymoon, right?"

"Yes, ma'am. They're in my bag."

"Good girl. Go on your trip. Find passion. Come back in a few weeks, and people will have better things to talk about."

"Nana, are you sure about this? Daddy'll freak. And Mama, good grief, if I run away she might … come unglued … again."

"We are Sommervilles, darling. We do not run away. We run *to* things, things that are deserving of our spunk, our smarts, and our sass. You have spent the last three years of your life worrying over your mother and your father. You gave up everything you ever wanted to keep them from falling apart. It's high time you go out and live a little. Just go. I hear Langston coming now."

Kaitlyn's grandmother, an indomitable force, had been born unable to hear in one ear just like Kaitlyn, due to sensorineural deafness. After her brother's death, however, the nerves in Kaitlyn's left ear were deteriorating due to stress.

It took her a moment more, but she did indeed hear, "My little girl's getting ready to walk down the aisle. I do not have time for this today. The storm will have to wait."

"Go," Nana urged.

"I don't know where I'm going."

"You'll figure that out on the way." Her grandmother tugged on her good ear. Kaitlyn did the same. Their good luck gesture. Kaitlyn hoped it worked this time.

Standing on the precipice of a life of misery and no passion just as her grandmother had predicted, Kaitlyn prayed that her parents would understand this one indiscretion—her first since Keith's death—and not dissolve into the abyss they were when she'd arrived home from culinary school that grey afternoon after the phone call.

Gripping her suitcases, she brushed a kiss on Nana's cheek and slipped out the back door just as her father entered the door on the opposite side of the room.

"You ready, baby girl?" She could just barely make out her father's voice.

Kaitlyn slowly eased the door closed before she raced out through the sheets of water spilling over the gutters.

The rain baptized her as she sprinted towards her car. The white dress became almost see-through as it sealed itself to her body. She didn't care. She'd find a hotel somewhere out of town. Take a shower, change, toss the damn dress in an incinerator, and figure out what to do from there.

Through the onslaught of cold rain plummeting from the sky, she could just make out Seth's ridiculous candy apple red Audi R8 parked three spaces down from her Honda. Driven only by rage, both at Seth and herself, she set her bags down on the wet concrete and dug her car key into the hood of his car, leaving slashed scars back and forth. One after another, she cut herself free from every expectation heaped on her by everyone else.

When she was soaked through, and the keys were too wet for her to grip effectively, she grabbed her bags and slogged to her car weighted down by the drenched gown, a vicious bind indeed.

Slamming her suitcases into the backseat, Kaitlyn held her face to the rain letting it wash her clean. Black mascara pooled with the blush she'd applied. It marred her face and dripped onto the bodice of the dress. Good.

Scrubbing her hands over her face, she leaped into the driver's seat, passed the two dozen police squad cars in the parking lot of the country club and flew to the entrance gates.

Nana was right. She'd lost herself when they'd buried her brother. She'd let her parents run her entire life and look at where it had gotten her.

*****

Grant Camden glared at the dark clouds surrounding his truck. Damn it all to hell and back; this was just what he'd needed. He'd left Pleasant Glen two hours ago to escape the leaded clouds there. The storm had chased him East, never letting him out of its clutches.

He worked his jaw and narrowed his eyes trying to see through the deluge of water washing over his windshield. Flipping on his hazard lights, he knew better than to pull over. Some idiotic city-slicker would eat the back-end of his new truck, and that would *not* improve his mood.

Lightning fierce enough to scar the very earth shattered the sky. Grant's gut churned ominously. This wasn't good. There was a green tinge to the clouds, and the air surrounding him was weighted with atmospheric tension. And there was the smell, the distinctive odor in the air every Midwesterner knew meant trouble.

Fishing his phone out from his pocket, careful to keep his eyes on the car lights in front of him every time his windshield wipers flung enough water away for him to see, he touched his granddaddy's number on his favorites list.

"You 'bout here, son? Gettin' bad out there."

"Yeah, I'll be there in ten minutes long as nothing gets worse. I can't even hear my radio. What's the weather report saying?"

"I ain't had power in an hour. Last I heard it was a tornado warning. I'd feel better if you were here."

Grant couldn't help but smile. He was a grown man, owned a massive cattle ranch with his family, farmed enough corn to subset the cows should anything go wrong, and had been taking care of himself for the last decade, yet his parents and his grandparents worried about all the Camden kids like they were still knee-high to a cornstalk. "I'll be there soon. You go get in the storm shelter though, you hear me?"

"Don't go ordering me around, Grant Camden. You ain't out-ranched your granddaddy yet. I'm heading out there. I 'spect to see you in there soon."

"That's definitely the plan. We'll go check on Gran tomorrow."

"I already called the home. They got 'em all down in the auditorium. I told 'em if anything happened to my baby I'd have plenty to say about it."

"She'll be all right, and I'll be there soon."

Taking a moment to feel the consuming loss that always managed to sucker punch him whenever his granddaddy talked about his grandmother, Grant slowed the truck again. They were crawling through the streets of Lincoln. Better than swimming, he supposed, which was the only other viable option.

His grandparents had been married sixty-two years. They'd lived through the great depression, more wars than you could count on one hand, had raised up Grant's daddy and his brother, then helped raise all six of the Camden grandkids, and ranched until his grandmother's COPD needed constant treatment.

According to his granddaddy, he'd known his grandma was the one from the moment he'd laid eyes on her. The way he still called her baby even though she was in her eighties certainly gave credence to the tale.

The winds shifted hard against the truck. Grant gripped the wheel and felt his right front tire lose traction as he collided with a puddle deep enough to drown a good-sized dog. He couldn't even give the country club a one finger salute as he normally did, lest he lose control of the truck and take out the minivan in front of him.

This was yet another reason he despised coming to the city. Three-quarters of the population lost all ability to drive when it started storming.

There was nothing like Nebraska in the spring. She was almost vicious in her beauty. One minute the sun would highlight all her best features, the next a storm would wash it all away. And when Mother Nature had enough, or when she had PMS or something, she'd release a twister meant to show mankind just who held all the power.

From what Grant could see through the rain, the green clouds blended in with the horizon and another roll of thunder gnawed at the preceding lightning. Definitely not a good sign.

Edging his way past the entrance to the ridiculous country club where city-slickers of every variety loved to show off their money, Grant's heart seized in his chest when a tail of water spewed from the minivan's back tires, covered his truck and robbed him of all visibility.

6

He slammed on his brakes and gritted his teeth like that might prevent his truck from inhaling the van.

When the water finally freed his sight, he breathed a sigh of relief just before he was thrown forward into this steering wheel. Searching his rearview mirror he couldn't see the car that had hit him, but the unmistakable thud and screech of folding metal over the thunder said he'd been hit hard.

Chapter 2

"Oh, my God!" Kaitlyn beat back the airbag that had slapped her firmly across the face. Her cough stirred white dust, only making it harder to breathe. What had she hit?

Patting herself down through her soaking wet gown she tried to think of what to do next. For some ridiculous reason that had to have come from being the police chief's daughter, her mind immediately conjured what to say to her dad about the accident. She'd rear-ended … something. All she could see through the rain was black metal and green sky. It was clearly her fault, but really it was the storm's fault, and she wouldn't have even been out in the storm if it weren't for Seth, the asshole extraordinaire.

Yes. This was all Seth's fault. It took her less than two seconds to hate herself for trying to blame someone else for the accident. Allowing herself one moment to stare into the now-cracked rearview mirror, she wondered when exactly she'd lost all track of who she was.

The fissured mirror split her face into three distinctive pieces. Her eyes were a divided hollow of confusion. She barely recognized the whole, much less the disjointed pieces. It took her three blinks and the throbbing ache in her neck and head to remember that she'd just hit someone. Terror took up residence in her soul. What if they were hurt?

Fumbling for the handle, she managed to heave herself out of the car. A river of water swept down the street and sent her reeling. Her heels were soaked, and she fell forward, barely managing to grip the remains of her car to keep from falling.

The hood now far more resembled an accordion instead of an Accord. And there in the center of what had just moments before been the front of her car was a massive trailer hitch, attached to the biggest truck she'd ever seen. From what she could tell, the black GMC didn't even bear a scratch from their encounter. At least that meant whoever was inside probably wasn't hurt.

"Ma'am? Are you okay?" Suddenly, there were hands steadying her. Large, capable hands and they were attached to a drenched button down shirt that clung to forearms and biceps that could never have come from a gym membership. Arms like that came from work, hard work. Her eyes traveled up the wet shirt and the broad expanse of masculine chest, landing on a wide set of substantial shoulders.

She squinted against the rain and took in his pine green eyes shielded by the brim of a cowboy hat that diverted the water away from his angular face covered in a few day's old beard.

Kaitlyn stared at the most gorgeous man she'd ever laid eyes on and wondered if perhaps she'd died in the accident. Was this Heaven? Would it really storm in Heaven? *Oh, my God, I can't die. My parents cannot lose another child.*

Thoughts of her parents jolted her back from the warm hands on her hips that blocked out the cold rain. He'd said something. She couldn't hear over the rain. Concentrate, Kaitlyn.

"What did you say?" She stared at his lips.

"I asked if you were okay," he matched her volume.

"I'm okay, but I have to get out of here, now."

Before he could respond, the rain turned to hail. She cringed against the icy slaps on her arms and face.

"What'd you say?" To her shock, he awkwardly leaned in and held her against his chest, protecting her from the icy bullets striking her skin. His massive body surrounded her in warmth as he took every blow on himself. The pings of the hail played a dirge on the remains of her car.

"I have to leave!" Her car was not going to go anywhere ever again. There was no question. But her father had access to every available Lincoln police officer, and if she was going to escape this horrible day she had to get out of there. Nana wouldn't be able to stall him forever.

The man searched her face. The moment he realized she was wearing a wedding gown, his mouth hung open stupidly.

Kaitlyn rolled her eyes and tried to jerk out of his firm grasp. She only managed to stumble again, and once again he steadied her.

A howl of wind pierced her skin, sending a shiver throughout her body. She was soaking wet and freezing.

"I have to go," she repeated.

"You ain't going anywhere in that." He pointed to the remains of her car. "Are you running away? From your wedding?" Suddenly, his shouts were audible to her. The hail halted abruptly, and the very air surrounding them took on an eerie sense of impending doom that hung in the stillness.

"Shit." The cowboy had a filthy mouth. For some unfathomable reason, a sense of peace washed over her as the air around them heated and a whirl of debris and leaves from the road swirled around them.

"Yes, I'm running away. Please, can you help me? I have to get out of here before my father and every police officer in a fifty-mile radius comes looking for me."

"Get in the truck. This ain't good."

"I'm well aware." Kaitlyn grabbed the bags from her backseat and accepted his hand. He helped her climb up in the truck then managed to separate their cars with one quick shove of his booted foot against her front bumper. He was up in the truck's driver's seat a split second later and flooring the accelerator.

"If I tell you to get out and hit the dirt, do it. We're in for it."

"What?"

"You ever heard of the calm before the storm?" The bed of the truck skidded to the right when he took a sharp turn down a residential road.

"Yes. Is that what this is?" Kaitlyn's brain was still in shock. It couldn't quite keep up.

"You ain't from around here, are ya?"

"I am, actually, but it seems fairly obvious I'm having a rough day."

"Yeah, sorry about that." His gorgeous eyes scanned the length of her body again. She wondered what she must look like. A half-drowned rat, probably. "You sure you're okay? From the wreck I mean?"

"My heart's still racing, and I'm a little sore, but I'll be fine." She gingerly touched a long red scrape on her inner arm from the airbag. A bruise would be visible by morning, but it wasn't her body she was worried about. Her body would heal. She'd been lucky, really. It was her unrecognizable soul that had her concerned. That, and the way she couldn't stop staring at the cowboy who'd effectively become her knight in shining—no, make that dirty cowboy boots. She couldn't quite figure out if her pulse was in overdrive because of adrenaline or because of the cowboy.

His capable hands gripped the steering wheel and drove them out of town like a bat out of hell. She'd always had a thing for hands, and his were masculine perfection. His jaw was tense, creating gorgeous angles. She wanted to run her hands over his slight beard. What on earth was wrong with her? Maybe she'd hit her head in the wreck.

The heater in the truck brought his scent to her lungs. Potent leather, sweet hay, and an elusive undertone of cologne mixed in the thick air and made her mouth water. *Hello, Kaitlyn. You just left your asshole of an ex standing at the altar, totaled your car, and are in the middle of a tornado. Maybe now is not the best time to be drooling over a cowboy.* Her brain tried to save her, but something about this man had her heart thinking things she'd never thought before, not with Seth, or any of the stupid idiots from the club her parents approved of but she did not. Not with anyone, save maybe her vibrator.

Every centimeter of his chiseled body radiated with a profound protectiveness over her, and she didn't even know his name. The way he'd held her close to keep the hail from harming her bare skin spread liquid warmth throughout her veins. It eased the insanity of her day if only for a minute. She couldn't recall the last time anyone had put themselves in the line of fire, or ice as the case may be, for her. No one had ever done that. No one, except maybe Keith.

"I'll call a wrecker about your car when this is all over," the cowboy explained. The rumbled thrum of his low bass voice was commanding and authoritative as if he were giving himself an order.

Since her brain was acting completely irrationally, she wasn't even surprised that it immediately conjured other far more sexy phrases she'd love to hear him say. *'Take your panties off for me, baby. Spread your legs for me. Let me touch you. Let me own you.'* Never before had any man ever affected her on such a primal, sexual level.

In an effort to get herself together, she pinched her own exposed shoulder and winced slightly at the pain. "I'll try now. Not sure anyone can get to it at the moment, but I don't want my car to cause another accident." She looked up a wrecker service on her cell phone and touched the number to call but was directed to some kind of answering machine. In the middle of her message, all sound was vacuumed from the earth. The line was dead. How was that even a thing?

"I don't have any signal … at all." She stared at her phone in disbelief.

"Storm must've taken out the cell towers. Hang tight. We're almost there. You've got a bruise on your … uh … chest there. Might need to take you to the hospital when this passes."

"No. No hospitals. I'll be fine. It's just a bruise." So he was looking at her chest, was he? Kaitlyn couldn't help but grin. There was indeed a light marking at the top of her right breast just above the dress.

And his voice, oh, that deep, throaty voice, vibrated throughout her entire body. She wanted to curl up with it like a warm blanket and let it soothe her.

Before she'd stepped out into the hellish storm, the gown had been a perfect fit. The bodice showed off her cleavage, and the long skirt draped her legs, managing to show off the curvature of her hips but disguise the thickness of her thighs that she despised. It was ridiculous, and the price was outrageous, but it had been beautiful.

Since Seth frequently commented on her needing to lose twenty or more pounds, she wondered what the cowboy thought.

Of course, now the gown was soaked through, torn, dirty, and, just like the rest of her life, didn't have any real hope of returning to its former glory.

Another split-second glance from the cowboy came her way, but he quickly returned his eyes to the water-laden road. The impressive truck split through the racing waters with as much ease as it had bisected the hood of her car.

Another mile flew by as he sped further outside of Lincoln. She managed a few breaths when he finally turned down a gravel driveway and stopped in front of a small, white, brick house built at least a century ago. They'd escaped.

"You see that door in the ground right there?"

Kaitlyn rolled her eyes. "I know what a storm shelter looks like."

"Good. Run." He threw the truck into park, and they bolted for the door in the ground, bracing for impact from the wind.

Her life, this day, her car, her wedding, it was all too much. A storm shelter a dozen miles from the country club would have to do for a hideout until the storm passed, then she could figure out how to get the heck out of Lincoln.

The trees in the front yard bowed with the winds in an effort to knock them off their path. Once again, the cowboy blocked her from any harm, taking on the fist of a swinging branch himself as it bit at his right arm. His capable arms accepted the blow as if it was nothing and then wrapped steadily around her as a whirlwind of fresh fallen spring leaves whipped around them.

Certain the wind itself was going to lift her off the ground, Kaitlyn clung to him as they pushed through the gale force doing its damnedest to keep them back and finally made it to the door.

Granddaddy Camden held the door open as Grant scooted the bride down into the ground. She slipped on the ladder, and his heart leapt to his throat, but she caught herself, and he managed a breath.

"Son, you stop by a bridal store on your way in or some'um?" Granddaddy chuckled as he secured them all inside the tiny shelter.

"Pretty sure they sell them dresses," Grant gestured to the ruined gown, "at bridal stores, old man, not brides themselves."

"Well, how do, Missuss …?"

"Oh, um," her shiver speared Grant's heart, "I'm Kaitlyn Sommerville. I hit his truck. I'm sorry about that. Did I already say that?"

Unable to hide his grin, Grant grabbed a quilt from one of the low shelves in the shelter and wrapped it around Kaitlyn's shoulders. "You did. No harm done to my truck. Take it easy. You've had a hell of a day." He settled her on some old wooden pallets that had at one time held cattle feed bags.

"Thank you."

Granddaddy Camden couldn't seem to wipe the delighted grin off his face, visible in the glow of the Coleman lantern he'd hung from the ceiling.

"I'm Henry Camden, by the way, since you got Grant so distracted he forgot the manners his mama taught him. Let me get this straight, you hit my grandson's truck, and instead of fuming and fussing 'bout it, he's wrapping you up in a quilt. Ain't that interesting? Grant's more rancher than even I was, and that's sayin' something, sweetheart. Most ranchers'd be cursing your name. You know how we are about our trucks."

Grant rolled his eyes just before shooting his grandfather a look that told him to sit down and clam up. "I'm Grant Camden. Sorry, I forgot to make introductions in the middle of a twister. Ignore him. He's an old codger with a mouth the size of the Nebraskan plains. 'Sides, ain't no mortal man ever out-ranched my granddaddy." He winked at her, and her responding grin made his day. "My truck's fine. I'm more worried 'bout you."

Something in Kaitlyn's broken gaze took up residence in Grant's musculature. She triggered protective instincts in him he was never aware he possessed. The way that damned see-through dress clung to her lush curves and showed off a rack that should've had its own zip code had claimed an address somewhere else in his body. Somewhere that was going to make itself known if he didn't quit thinking like this.

He switched his thoughts to how exactly they'd gotten where they were sitting. Whoever she'd been about to marry had done something bad enough to make her run out in a fucking tornado to get away. Bastard was lucky Grant couldn't get to him.

"Oh, don't worry about me. I'm fine. Actually, thank you so much for saving me. I ... uh ..." she took another visual inventory of the remains of her tattered gown, "I had to get away from there. I can never thank you enough."

"Oh, I 'spect Grant could come up with several ways you could thank him," Granddaddy laughed.

"Jaysus, Pops, d'you get into your stash when it started raining or something? How 'bout we let her take a deep breath and relax? She don't even know us, and we've got her down here with a twister beating on the door." Besides, Grant had no interest in her thanks. For some inexplicable reason, he just needed to know that she was going to be okay. His aching arms longed to hold her again, to protect her, to shield her not only from the storm but from all life had clearly thrown her way as of late.

He turned back to Kaitlyn, "Like I said, ignore him."

Her pale cheeks were the color of an autumn sunset after the recent comments. An adorable smattering of freckles made their appearance. She didn't seem like she'd minded his grandfather's teasing too much, but he'd embarrassed her, damn him.

As Grant studied her, his mind couldn't help but come up with ways to get her out of that dress. Thing looked like it weighed more than a bull, loaded down with water and completely ruined.

With nothing better to do than imagine as the storm continued its assault, he envisioned cutting the thing off her with his Stockman, giving her a bath to wash away everything she'd endured, and wrapping her up in him. He wanted to wipe away the inky stains of mascara on her cheeks that might've come from the rain but he suspected had come from tears. Then he could take her to his bed and make her forget all about whoever it was that had done her badly enough to make her run.

Damn, you are hard up ain't'cha? His mind taunted him. He had no business fantasizing about some runaway bride he'd just up and rescued off the side of the road, but it had been far too long since he'd inhaled the warmth of a woman, drowned himself inside the sweet nectar between soft shapely thighs, and buried his every need in perfect, feminine curves. Damn it all, if he wasn't getting desperate, and saving Miss Kaitlyn had done just as much for his hungry cock as it had his bruised ego.

He'd been the love 'em leave 'em king of cattle ranchers not too long ago. Lately, he just wanted someone to talk to, someone to take care of, someone who wasn't afraid to need him, and maybe the same someone night after night wasn't such a bad deal.

If he were shooting straight, which he always tried to do, he'd even admit that he wanted someone to look at him the way his brothers' wives looked at them. Someone to share a life with. Someone to share the ranch with. Sunrises over vast cattle land didn't mean much if there wasn't someone soft and warm in your bed to show them to. He wanted someone to take care of, and it more than pissed him off that his brothers had figured all this out before he had.

And he'd had it up to his earlobes with the likes of cowgirls. All they ever wanted to do was argue and then try to outride him. As much as he loved a woman with fire in her veins, he wouldn't mind one with a sweeter side as well. His traitorous gaze made another return trip to Kaitlyn, seated nearby.

If he wasn't mistaken, there, in the weary fear and tenderness held in the most beautiful blue eyes he'd ever seen, was more than a hint of a brewing wildfire. He wanted desperately to kindle the blaze and then stir the flames.

Ordering his cock to give him a break, Grant settled on the stack of pallets beside her in an effort to keep the bulge in his jeans known only to himself. The stale scent of feed and kerosene stirred in the air. Not a good sign since they were in an enclosed shelter. Grant's body seized in warning. Ever attuned to the atmosphere around him and always someone who trusted his gut, he felt it coming.

And there it was, a shrill howl like an incoming freight train preceded the shelter door shaking violently. The land itself sounded as if it were being severed from the earth as a whole. The earth's protesting groans were bone-chilling.

Kaitlyn screamed, and before Grant could process anything else, she'd leaped in his lap. He was holding her, protecting her.

"Shh, I gotcha. It's all right," he tried to soothe over the howl but wasn't certain she'd heard him. She seemed disoriented. He rocked her gently, keeping her cradled in the vast strength of his body.

Half of him pled for the deafening sound to give them a reprieve, for this part to be over with, so they could go on with the aftermath of cleaning up and starting again. He prayed his family was okay, but another distinctive, divided section of his mind didn't want anything to happen that might make Kaitlyn Sommerville stop burying her sweet self against him, clinging to him for all she was worth. God, he just needed to show her that he'd keep her safe no matter what. He had no idea why that was suddenly his entire life's mission, but it was.

Chapter 3

Kaitlyn pressed her face harder against Grant's substantial neck and gripped his soaking wet shirt like her life depended on it. She was fairly certain it did. The sound surrounded her.

A deluge of thoughts she wanted no part of assaulted her mind. She'd left her family back at the country club. What if they weren't okay? No matter how hard she tried, she couldn't make out which direction the sound was coming from. People who were not hearing-impaired would lean away from scary noises. All Kaitlyn knew to do was to lean *in* to Grant.

What had happened after she'd run? What would have happened if she hadn't? Her mother would have been happy. Her father pleased because marrying Seth, the man just a few notches down from the district attorney, fit right in his plan for Kaitlyn's life.

Ever since Keith's death, what Kaitlyn had wanted for her own life mattered far less than what her parents wanted for her. She'd gone along with it, desperate to erase the hollow emptiness in her mother's eyes that had resulted from her twin brother's last tour in Afghanistan.

She'd tried so hard to be a healing balm. All she'd really managed, she realized as she clung fast to a cowboy who'd offered her more protection than anyone else ever had, was to tear herself into pieces in an effort to bandage her parents' wounds.

Once again, everyone else would have been happy if she'd gone on with the ceremony. They would have even brushed Seth's cheating aside as an indiscretion. She could all but hear the words *boys will be boys* spilling revoltingly from her father's lips.

Nope. Nope. Nope. Assholes would be assholes, and she would not allow her father to quantify all men as such. When this storm was over, she'd put her life back together just like the rest of Lincoln would have to. Seth could go straight to hell. Nana was right. It was high time Kaitlyn decide what she wanted for her life. She deserved some passion, didn't she?

And if that caused her parents pain? She cringed closer to Grant. That was always the unbearable conclusion, the knife that buried itself deepest. The pain she would inevitably inflict was why she'd gone on for the last three years allowing other people to run her life. She couldn't bear to cause them anymore grief. They'd been through so much. Her mother still visited Keith's grave each and every week.

She went on Sundays. It took her until Wednesday to stop existing with the graveside as her constant consciousness and return to some portion of reality. Her mother had never recovered.

Another heartbeat, another cringe into Grant, and in the next moment the awful sound was erased from the air. The thick tension eased as if the air itself was simply too tired to hold it any longer.

"It's over, sweetheart. It's all right." Once again the low rumble of Grant's voice soothed her. The vibration made sense to her, a distinctive difference between hearing and understanding. She tried to order her arms to release him but they, just like the rest of her body, weren't listening. She wanted to demand that he continue holding her and calling her sweetheart. Clearly, she'd lost her mind. Seth's cheating, or the wreck, or the storm—or something—had obviously driven her right over the edge. She made a mental note to find a therapist whenever her life settled down. Only she had no real idea when that might happen.

"You okay?" Grant steadfastly continued to cradle her close even though the twister was gone. He brushed the loosened strands of her red curls that it had taken the stylist two hours to contain behind her shoulder.

"Maybe. I'm not sure." That was the truth, and she didn't want to lie to him.

"Yeah, I get that. You mind sitting here for just another minute and lettin' me go check on everything? If it's still standing, we can go in the house and get cleaned up."

Kaitlyn's already addled mind attempted to process the question. She tried to force her lips to explain that she was fine, and he should go check anything he needed to. What fascinated her most in that moment was that Grant didn't seem to want to let her go any more than she wanted him to. Judging from his tone and the way he continued to hold her, it seemed like *no* was just as viable an answer as yes would be.

"Uh ..." *Find passion, Kaitlyn. Live your life. Stop trying to please everyone else.* Her grandmother's orders sounded in her ears, both of them. "Could I get another minute or two?"

She heard Grant's grandfather try to turn a chuckle into something of a cough, but she couldn't find it in herself to care.

"You got it. Having a beautiful woman in my arms is much preferable to 'bout anything else." He thought she was beautiful? Kaitlyn didn't really believe that. He was just being kind. Currently, she had to look half-drowned, and by tomorrow, the aches and

18

tender spots all over her body were going to bear the markings of their collision. She was going to be black and blue.

"You two sit tight. I'm going to check everything," Grant's grandfather ordered. It struck Kaitlyn how much Grant sounded like his grandfather. She'd always found sounds fascinating. She wondered if she ever sounded like Nana. She hoped so, but thinking of her grandmother brought another round of fresh terror to her stomach. What if the tornado hit the country club?

Summoning courage from the stagnant air around them, she lifted her head and eased her good ear towards Grant so she could hear his responses. "I'm really sorry about this," she gestured to herself. "I don't even know how I got here. I need to get back to the country club, I guess. I don't know if my family is okay."

Panic stirred in Grant's gut. She couldn't go yet, and she sure as hell wasn't going anywhere near the shit-licker she'd run away from, not if he had any say in the matter.

"Take it easy, okay? Like I said, you've had one hell of a day. I doubt the roads are passable and the sun's going down. If I were a gamblin' man, I'd say we're stuck out here at least for tonight. That country club's gotta have a shelter or something. I'm sure they're fine."

Haunted fear turned her eyes a deep navy, but she managed an unconvincing nod.

The creak and slap of the shelter door announced Pops' return.

"How bad is it?" Grant inquired.

"Could'a been worse, I 'spose. Yard's a mess. Got several trees down. Thankfully, none on the main part of the house. One through the front porch, though. Bunch across the driveway that'll have to be moved 'fore we can come and go. Before you ask, your truck survived. Got some hail damage though. No power. No phone. Haven't tried the water yet."

"Mr. Camden, I'm so sorry about your front porch." Kaitlyn offered as she climbed out of Grant's lap, much to his chagrin. "Um, you said porch, right?"

"It's all right, darlin'. I did say porch and porches can be replaced. 'Fraid you two are stuck here with me for a night or two 'til we get them trees moved, though."

"I'll get Austin and Brock out here. We'll get you a new porch put on next week," Grant immediately volunteered. "Declan, Natalie, and Luke can run cattle for a few days. We need to get it put on before calving."

"I ain't worried about it. Let's get you two inside and into dry clothes. I don't want you getting sick on top of everything else. There's more on the horizon than the flu for the both of ya."

Granddaddy Camden's house wasn't quite the way it had always been. There was a broken pile of glass on the tile kitchen floor. Plates had been stacked on the countertop and hadn't survived the twister. The trash can was toppled over as well, and there were a few windows in the small den that had blown out.

Appreciative of the way Kaitlyn kept holding his bicep as they stepped around the shards of glass, Grant reached the kitchen sink and located the flashlight his grandfather kept in the cabinet there.

The light awkwardly illuminated the dusky dark, caught somewhere between late afternoon and early evening. Time itself seemed confused after the tornado's assault.

"It doesn't look like there was too much damage done." Kaitlyn sweetly offered his grandfather. "We can clean this up in no time."

When she reached across the pile of glass to grab the fallen broom that had thrown itself in the floor in surrender to the wind, Grant panicked. "Careful. Don't cut your hands." He grabbed her hand before she reached the broom. The connection of their palms shot a jolt of electricity straight to his chest. Their eyes met. She'd felt it, too. Those cool blue eyes stared up at him. Time measured itself in the blink of her long lashes washed of mascara, painted only in shock. What the hell?

"I'll get the glass up. Grant, son, why don't you take Kaitlyn back to the guest bedroom. I 'spect she'd like to clean up."

"Uh ... yeah ... I'll get your bags outta the truck. Be right back." An odd sting sizzled in Grant's hands as he released hers. His body didn't appreciate the severed connection.

Having forgotten the first part of his grandfather's instructions, when Grant returned with Kaitlyn's suitcases from his truck, he located her in the guest bedroom. Clearly, Granddaddy had stepped up on the tour of his small home in Grant's stead. He'd also lit several candles around the room so she could see.

She was staring at herself in the dresser mirror that had once belonged to his grandmother. The glass had been cracked for as long as Grant could remember.

She seemed to be studying herself like she was a captivating stranger. He didn't question what she found so intriguing. God, she was gorgeous.

"Every single mirror I've looked in since I ran out of that stupid country club has been broken. That probably means something, right?" Her inquisitive eyes sought his.

Did she want it to mean something? Searching his mind for the correct answer, he shrugged. "Maybe. Might just mean you ran out in a twister and drove into my truck. I'm just a cattle rancher, though. Never did too well with deeper meanings and all that."

A slight chuckle eased the tension in her beautiful face. Grant found himself glad of that. A split second later, she'd turned to face him. The dress still clung to her curves and was leaving puddles on the carpet. Challenge was alight in her eyes. "I found out he was cheating on me with one of my friends just before I was supposed to walk down the aisle, and I kind of hated him anyway."

Well, hell. Okay then. There it was. "Then he's a damned fool. You should hate him, and you deserve better."

The rapid fire blinks of her eyes said she was trying hard not to cry again. "You don't even know me. Maybe I'm the fool. I agreed to marry him, after all."

"Hey," Grant sat her suitcases down and edged closer. "I'm sorry he was an asswipe, but him being dumber than a stump don't make you a fool. And if you're a fool, I am too. I volunteered to come out here today in the middle of a storm 'cause somebody needed to check on my granddaddy, but mostly 'cause a girl I'd gotten pretty deep with several months back got married today, too. She married the guy she was cheating on me with."

"I'm sorry, Grant. I'm sorry about all this, and about hitting your truck. And I'm sorry she cheated on you. Probably sucked for you."

"Kinda."

"Kinda?"

"Well, the way I figure it, better to find out 'fore you walked down the aisle than after."

"That's true. I haven't had time to process any of this, but, yeah, you're right. Still feel like I could never take enough showers to make me not feel gross that I was with him."

A sultry image of her standing in a fall of hot water with soap suds dripping seductively over those gorgeous tits immediately formed in his mind. He cleared his throat and tried to think of something to say. His mind scrambled, and the first thing that popped into his head was, "Would it be too forward of me to say that you running away from a big 'ole country club wedding might make you the bravest person I ever met?"

There it was. A grin. A real smile, complete with an adorable dimple in her left cheek and a shimmer of sweet heat in her eyes. "You really believe that?"

Not the smoothest thing you could'a said, Camden. Just go with it. "Hell yeah. That took guts."

"Thanks. I was brave once, a long time ago."

"A long time ago, huh?" What the hell did that mean? What had happened to her? She clammed up before his eyes.

"Thanks for bringing my stuff in. I'll just get changed."

You're not just a cattle rancher, Grant Camden. If he'd stayed staring at her with those kind green eyes any longer, those very words would have tumbled out of her mouth. His single nod when she'd dismissed him had spoken volumes. She had no idea what Grant was exactly, but there was nothing simple about him. What scared the hell out of her was how badly she wanted to know the complex truths of her rescuing cowboy and why she longed to discover just what made him tick.

She scrubbed her hands over her face, ridding herself of the last vestiges of mascara, and retrieved a towel from the adjoining bathroom. When she'd wiped her suitcase dry, she heaved it on the bed and searched for something appropriate to wear for a storm cleanup with two cowboys she barely knew.

Digging through the satin and lace she'd planned to wear on her honeymoon made her want to vomit. Finally, she located her favorite t-shirt and one of the many pairs of yoga pants she'd packed. She'd packed them because it annoyed Seth to no end when she wore what he deemed to be workout clothes when she never worked out, but it would have to do.

Closing her eyes, she allowed herself to really feel for the first time that day. Realizing she'd never loved Seth didn't cool the sting of his betrayal as it whipped through her, decimating her self-esteem right along with the carefully-orchestrated plan for her life.

Kaitlyn used to imagine that she could trade a little of the heft of her breasts for a few inches of Kelsey's enviable legs. Kelsey was always at ease and fun to be around. Sure of herself. Magnetic even. And Kaitlyn was none of those things. Kaitlyn was a business transaction. It had been written in black and white. *Guess what, Seth, you were a business transaction as well. You were what I had to pay to keep my family happy.*

Jerking the engagement ring off her finger, she shoved it in her suitcase. In that motion alone, her breaths came easier. The noose around her neck slacked its deadly grip.

All she'd really wanted was a home and a life out of her parents' watchful eyes. She wanted to cook and create delicious foods. If she were being perfectly honest, she wanted to have babies and raise them. She was fairly certain she was supposed to want more from life, but deep down in her heart where she never allowed anyone else to see, she wanted a husband and a family. She wanted to bake cookies and make homemade Christmas decorations. Nothing more than that.

Her mother had been a high-powered prosecuting attorney before she'd married. Her father had climbed the ranks of the Lincoln County Police Department until he'd made Chief. Her sister was well paid for her expertise in jury consulting. Kaitlyn had been expected to carry on the Sommerville tradition of having a career in law.

She'd refused and had secured a scholarship to culinary school in New York. That was the one and only time she'd ever fought for something she'd wanted and won.

When her brother had been killed, she'd dropped out of culinary school and moved back home. She'd gone on with her pre-law degree at UN to make her father happy, but she had no interest in ever becoming a lawyer.

She wondered if there was one single moment that had erased her own spine from existence or if the life she'd endured thus far had washed it away slowly over the past few years.

When her hands reached for the long line of silk-covered buttons that ran down the back of her gown, the very last remnant of any bravery, spunk, or fire she'd ever hoped to have possessed went up in a puff of smoke.

She fumbled with the first button fruitlessly for the better part of five minutes contorting herself in positions even a master yogi wouldn't achieve before she understood that she was trapped in the damned gown. The wet silk was as unrelenting as a straight-jacket, and the only hope she had of escape was once again a cowboy she barely knew.

Chapter 4

Grant tossed the match in the fireplace as soon as the flames licked at the kindling. The tarp and the carport had managed to keep enough wood dry for them to have heat for a while.

He stepped into the half bath off the kitchen and rid himself of his soaking wet jeans. They slapped at the linoleum when he finally shucked them off his legs. Making quick work of drying off, he was thankful for the extra pair of Wranglers he always kept in his truck. He'd have to make do with the stained Carhartt shirt he'd located behind the seat. At least it was dry.

After tossing his wet clothes over the towel bar, he made his way to the den to see about making some chili over the fire for supper.

"I ever tell you the story of how I met your grandmamma, Grant?" Pops asked as he poured water into the percolator for coffee.

Rolling his eyes, Grant handed him the Folgers. "Only 'bout four dozen times, old man. She fell off a stock ladder into your arms at the Montgomery Ward out at Gateway Mall."

"Well, that's just the middle of the story. It's got a beginning and an end too, ya know. Sit down and oblige me."

The ancient couch gave a cough of dust as Grant settled in, more out of respect for his grandfather than any desire to hear this story yet again.

"I left the ranch that morning 'fore the sun was up. Anxious and stirring, but I couldn't figure why. Ol' buddy of mine from my coming-up years was on a strategic missile squadron that had been housed at the old Air Force base, and I'd told him the next time I came to Lincoln I'd go see him out there."

"Miles Jameson, right?" Grant had heard his grandfather speak of Miles several times before and he wanted to speed the story along so he could get back to figuring out Kaitlyn.

"Nah, now, stop skipping ahead. Best things in life you gotta be patient for. Miles and me were rebel-rousers back in our day, but he was a clerk for the Air Force. I'm speaking of Roy Wagner. Don't believe you ever knew the Wagners. They sold their ranch to my daddy 'fore you were even a thought in yo' daddy's head. Though, Lordy, I tell you once your daddy stumbled up on your mama's broke down car on the side of the road, it didn't take him long to have thoughts 'bout how to get all you kids here."

Grant chuckled. "Yeah, well, Mama and Daddy ain't ever had any trouble keeping their hands all over one another."

"That's the way it's 'spose to be. You just remember that. Anyway, I got to thinking on my drive into town that I might like to have me a table saw and there was one I'd seen in the Montgomery Ward catalog that had come in the mail."

"What'd you want a table saw for? Ain't much use on the ranch."

"Don't I know it, and I got no clue. I had not had a single thought 'bout a saw 'til that morning, but just then I decided I needed one that very day. Fate's a funny thing."

"You think fate wanted you to buy a saw?"

"If you ain't got a better explanation then hush up, boy. You scared of fate?"

Grant didn't reply.

"Mm-hmm that's what I figured. Anyway, I sat in the parking lot of the store 'til it opened then I marched inside, hell bent on a saw I didn't need. That's when I saw her. My God, she knocked the wind right outta me. Purdy as they come, and all of a sudden there was something else in the Montgomery Ward I needed way more than a saw.

"I wasn't paying a bit of attention to anything other than watching her. I walked right up to her and then couldn't think of a thing to say. I didn't even notice that she was stocking women's underthings 'til she turned the color of them tomatoes my mama used to grow in the garden. Anyway, I managed to greet her, and she jerked a stack of … well … you know, stockings, and other things, and what not, behind her back."

"You scared to say panties, Pops?" Grant chided.

"Didn't I tell you to hush? So, there we stood. She got rid of what was in her hands and smiled at me. I was done for. I don't even know how it happened, but next thing I knew she'd up and decided I needed a new suit. Kept telling me navy blue brought out my eyes. I swear to ya, I'da bought a purple pinstripe suit that day if she'd said to. She was climbing up that ladder to get me a pair of pants off a shelf. Her heel got caught on a rung, and my heart stopped right then and there. I couldn't even stand the thought that she might get hurt. That's when I caught her."

"Good catch." Grant tried not to think of the panic that had whipped through him when Kaitlyn's heel had caught on the ladder in the storm shelter.

25

"Best of my life. After I finally stood her up, she kept thanking me and apologizing for falling. I considered myself lucky she'd fallen 'cause that meant I got to catch her and keep her safe. She invited me to a protest that evening out in Omaha. I had no clue what we were protesting, and I didn't mention that Omaha was 'bout six hours from the ranch. I said I'd go. I never made it to the base to see Roy. Hell, after that, I never saw nothing but your grandmamma. She's my whole world. Always will be. It turned out we were protesting the government taking Indian land out in Omaha."

"Native American, Pops."

"That's right. I mean no disrespect, just slips my mind now and again. Anyway, to be sure, I was the only cowboy at the protest, but she was so passionate about the land, and the people, all we'd taken from them, and fighting for what she believed in. She was the kind of girl who was willing to sacrifice for what she knew was right. I swear I could'a proposed right then and there."

"That might'a been a touch fast."

"You're a Camden, Grant. Don't ever take us long to figure who's supposed to be ours forever. You know it. I know it. You heard all the stories from generations."

"Yeah, I heard 'em." He had heard them. He just hadn't believed it had all happened that fast until he'd seen Kaitlyn shiver when it had started hailing. God, that had all but done him in. But was this it? Is this the way it all worked out? The insanity of it was absurd. You didn't just pick a girl up off the side of the road after she rams into your hitch, throw her over your shoulder, and carry her off to your cave. What the hell? Camden meant cattle rancher not cave-man. When he found himself regretting that momentarily, he called himself an asshole.

"You know your great-granddaddy Miller never did like me too much."

"Oh yeah? He mad at'cha for taking Gran out to the ranch?"

"He was mad at the world, Grant, for all it had taken from him, and I was a convenient target. People full of spite are always fighting a war within themselves, and they'll go to battle with anyone they see as trying to take more from them than they think they should have to give."

"Uh, I'm so sorry to interrupt," Kaitlyn's timid voice quaked through the fire-lit room. She had Grant's attention as soon as she appeared. "I ... uh ... I can't ..." she gestured to the back of the wet

26

gown she was still in. "I can't get the buttons undone," flew from her tongue in a jumble of shame. Her eyes closed in abject defeat.

"Sweet Jesus," hissed from between Grant's teeth. He was on his feet in the next heartbeat.

"Boy, you have clearly been living right," Granddaddy Camden was quick to point through his quiet laughter.

Still trying to curb his caveman desires for no other reason than to prove to himself that he could and that the Camden code of falling in love at first sight was nothing but bullshit, Grant cinched his fists to keep from hastening Kaitlyn down the hallway to the guest room.

She seemed half-terrified and every struggled step she made was smaller than the one before. Impatience surged through his blood until he forced himself to really focus on her. The fear in her eyes jerked his thoughts out of the head below his belt upwards to somewhere in the vicinity of his chest. God, she really had been through hell. When she'd woken up that morning, she surely hadn't imagined that some guy she'd only just met would be the one stripping her out of her wedding gown.

Easing the door closed in an effort to preserve what dignity she might've managed to cling to, he swallowed down another round of ardent desire and offered her a consolatory grin.

"Hey, I know this can't be the way you thought this would all go down. I'm sorry."

"You're sorry you have to undress me?" Ire struck her tone.

"Oh, God, no. That ain't at all what I meant. I just figured you didn't want me to be the one doing this."

"Better you than Seth." Her jaw tensed. A spark of fire flared in her cool blue eyes, fiercer than all the candles lit in the room, but it was immediately doused with another round of fear.

Her fists clenched at her sides. Determination resonated from her body to his as she narrowed her eyes. So she did have some spite in there somewhere. Good.

Grant's heart thundered in his chest, part of it desperate to find Seth and pound him into the ground the other half beating out its point – the Camden code of falling in love at first sight was in fact the way it worked. Dammit.

"Just do me a favor. Please don't lie to me. The last three years of my life have basically been a lie, and I can't take it anymore. If you don't want to undress me, be honest. I'll figure out how to get this off some other way."

If he didn't want to undress her, he'd have his head examined. No man in his right mind would begrudge revealing her all for himself. Obviously, she needed someone to show her just how gorgeous she was. Well, he was more than happy to be the man for the job.

"Turn around," he commanded.

The dress slid audibly along the carpeting as she made her hesitant turn. He should have gone for the first button. He told himself to only touch the fabric, but his hands hungered to know her skin. He simply didn't possess enough strength to deny himself.

His index finger slipped over the nape of her neck and slowly traced down the column of her spine until he begrudgingly encountered wet silk. Her slight shiver elicited a half-strangled grunt from the depths of his lungs.

A quick breath escaped her as he worked until he'd loosed the first button from the loop that held it prisoner.

"I ain't the kind of man that lies about anything. Ever. Never seen the point. I always shoot straight." He made it through two more buttons. His eyes drank in her shoulder blades and every inch of soft cool skin he encountered. When he'd opened another few, he eased his palm under the fabric in an effort to bring warmth to her skin, chilled from being wet, and to satisfy his own need to know her.

A heady perfume of fresh cut strawberries with a hint of feminine nectar filled his lungs with every button he unfastened. Most delicious strawberry wine he'd ever smelled, and damn if he didn't want a taste.

Every muscle in his body was poised to take her, to claim her in some small way. He clung to a semblance of sanity. One of his brain cells managed to convince the others to at least *act* like a gentleman.

Another shiver rocked through her when he reached her mid-back, revealing the delicate arch of her spine. His mind instantly registered that she wasn't wearing a bra. Sexy little minx, the picture of virtue in the white gown, had a sinful side. He'd suspected as much and here was his proof.

Seth was not only a douche—he was a dumbass. He'd thrown away what he had. Women like this sure as hell weren't a dime a dozen.

She clung to the bodice of the dress, keeping her breasts covered and the dress from falling. His eyes eagerly sought the last button in an effort to see if she'd forgone panties as well as a bra.

"Thank you for doing this. I know it's probably not exactly what you had on the agenda for the day."

Truth be told, he couldn't recall any other time in his life that he'd taken a dress off a woman without the intent of bedding them. As he revealed the hollow at the base of her spine and a pair of perfect dimples playing peek a boo under a pair of white lacey panties, he decided this wasn't any different. The bedding her part would just have to come later, when she was more sure of herself. But he did know a thing or two about women.

God knew he'd been with more than his fair share. God also knew what He was doing when he made the fairer sex. Grant loved everything there was to do with sex. Loved the flirting, the banter, the dancing, the kissing, the teasing, the touching; whatever it took to access the wild, carnal desires that would make a woman fly in his arms. None of the other women he'd had in his life or in his bed had ever mattered as much as she did at that moment, however.

He shook off the fear of that realization and focused on what he did know. Their gorgeous bodies would speak on their behalf if they trusted you, and there was nothing more beautiful than a highly satisfied female. One quick way to restore a little of a woman's confidence—show them how fucking much they turned you on.

Wrapping his right hand around her, he braced her abdomen and drew her back against him. "Trust me, sugar. The pleasure is all mine." He rocked his hips forward to make his point. He was harder than a steel pipe. Hell, he'd been sporting a semi since the moment he'd wrapped his arms around her standing by her totaled car. He let his denim-covered erection dig into the skin of her back. Through a fucking tornado, he'd still longed for her. Had to be something to that, and she needed to know the kind of power she held.

She whipped around to face him. Heat clung to her cheeks. Her lips were slightly swollen, the shade of an early raspberry, and they looked distinctly kissable. When her tongue darted out to lick them, he all but moaned.

If the dress slipped a half of a centimeter, he could have seen her nipples. Known their lush color, their size, how they tightened and puckered, every auxiliary bump that he could soothe with the heat of his mouth, and just how turned on she was currently. He caught himself praying for an earthquake after the tornado to shake the gown loose.

A harsh swallow contracted her neck. He longed to suck and mark the delicate skin there, and damn if he didn't want to see the round feminine globes of her ass. The dress damn near framed it for his eyes, but he wanted to feel, to massage, to kiss, lick, bite—and spank if she was in the mood.

An intoxicating form of timid innocence was penned in every lush curve of her body. She put on airs of being a lights-out, missionary, once-a-week out of obligation kind of girl. Maybe that's who she'd been with Seth. He hadn't even deserved that. But that sure as hell wasn't who she was. No, the wildfire that had finally sprung to a full blaze in her eyes and the fact she'd forgone a bra on her wedding day told an entirely different story.

Grant liked his sex with more than an edge of submission from whomever he was bedding mixed up with some naughty kink, and preferred a woman who only showed off her dirty side all for him. They all had one. You just had to be a man worth your salt to get them to reveal it, and damn if Kaitlyn Sommerville didn't have all the makings of being the entire package all wrapped up in a white bow, currently.

Sweet, beautiful, kind, seemed smart too, with a hearty dose of spunk that it would have taken to run out on a cheating asshole just in time, and sexy as sin on a Sunday. He was done for, and he knew it. Just didn't quite know how to explain to her that generations of men in his family had a habit of laying eyes on a woman, often by way of some kind of mishap, and then falling head over boots in love with them.

Her eyes glimmered in challenge and a mischievous grin played on her lush lips. "Little forward, aren'tcha?" she sassed. "I appreciate your honesty there, cowboy, but I *just* left a guy at the altar. Not sure now is the time for me to be … *saluted*." She gestured his head to his package still on full display.

Damn it all to hell and back. He'd let his granddaddy and the shit stories about Camden men get in his head. What was he thinking? He'd been right all along. You couldn't just up and decide some girl was going to be your one and only. She did have some say in the matter. More than likely he'd just fucked up the possibility of ever fucking her. Disappointment took a vicious blow to his gut.

Shaking off the rebuke she'd levied, he doubled down in typical cowboy fashion. "I could apologize, but I just told you I hadn't ever seen the point in lying, and I ain't even a little bit sorry about being a man. You're beautiful. Don't let that douchebag fiancé of yours get in your head. He don't deserve your thoughts." With that, he forced his feet to retreat. He had to order every step he made to avoid yet another trip up. One quick drop of her fingers and the gown would

30

hit the floor. His work was done, for now. If she wanted more, the gate was open. He had to play it cool. Stop acting like a green plowboy out on his first row.

"Don't apologize," she managed just as he reached the door. His heart thundered out its relief. "As ridiculous as it makes me, you pretty much just made my day, Grant Camden."

"Ain't a single thing about you that's ridiculous. Now get dressed 'fore I lose the ability to keep from ripping the dress outta your hands and doing several other things to show you exactly how stunning you are and precisely what your gorgeous little body was made for."

Okay, so he was coming on a little strong. Nothing wrong with that, necessarily. He knew what he wanted. No harm in going after it. Maybe he just needed to play it with a little more consideration. She *had* just left some asshat at the altar. Maybe he needed to prove he was worthy of her time and her body.

No. Come back and show me. Please. Her mind pleaded with his retreating form. He filled the entire doorframe with muscle and might, and then disappeared down the hallway. The feeling of him hard and hungry all for her sizzled up her spine. Her body heated until her previously freezing-cold, clammy skin was fevered.

A wave of guilt and panic washed away the sensation almost as soon as she'd allowed it to take hold. Thinking about sleeping with Grant, heck, all but begging him to go on with it, constituted cheating on Seth, didn't it? Even considering kissing him somehow felt wrong.

He cheated first. Her mind was quick to remind her. Did she owe him an official breakup before she considered the cowboy who'd undone her dress and her inhibitions? Could you get more official than leaving someone at the altar?

Another wave of shame slammed through her over the pain she'd inevitably caused and what people must've said or were undoubtedly still saying. Staring longingly at the bed in the room, she wished she had time for a good cry. Currently there wasn't even electricity to watch a tearjerker movie.

For now, she had to buck up and follow her passion just like Nana had said, and if that meant getting Grant Camden to show off his readily-apparent skills then so be it. Seth had Kelsey to lick his wounds, if he even cared at all. If he'd cared, he wouldn't have cheated on her, right? The guilt and confusion were unrelenting. Bile swirled in her stomach. Unable to access any reasoning that soothed her tattered nerves, she turned her thoughts back to Grant and her heart steadied.

Grant Camden positively oozed sex appeal. Kindness exuded from the brim of his hat right down to the tips of his boots, but there was so much more to him. There'd been an intoxicating dark heat in his gorgeous, green eyes when she'd spun out of his arms and away from his hard on. She'd felt his raw hunger in his breath when it whispered over her shoulders. The way he kept staring at her lips. The rough calluses on his fingertips that had to have come from years of hard work as they caressed her tender skin. The fire in his eyes had all but burned away the rest of her dress.

Most of her had wanted him to jerk her back into his arms and kiss the hell out of her, to take possession of her body. His obvious craving to do just that had been more than apparent. Heck, he'd shown it off loud and proud.

She'd been handled with kid gloves her entire life. No one thought her capable of handling anything at all. To her parents and most everyone in Lincoln, her inability to hear properly seemed to mean that she was incapable of having normal human needs. To Seth, she was too stupid and clumsy to bother with.

Well, she wasn't a china doll. She wasn't going to shatter on impact. She'd just walked out from her own wedding because Seth was—what had Grant called him—a douche. Yes, that's it. She'd had guts enough to walk away. She certainly had guts enough to take what she wanted from her rescuing cowboy, someone who had no idea she couldn't hear properly.

What she wouldn't give for a night or two with him. She was beyond certain he could skillfully show her the ins and outs of rough passionate sex, the kind that left love notes visibly in her skin from his teeth and his hands, the kind where she felt his occupation for days after it was over, the kind she found herself wanting more and more with each passing moment.

Heat shimmered over her flesh on a southbound journey down her body. Images of herself on her knees before Grant Camden with her hands bound behind her back blended readily in with thoughts of his low bass drawl demanding that she take more of him in her mouth. Fire sparked low in her belly, a fire she was fairly certain was going to become an inferno if she didn't find someone to help her douse her eager desires … soon.

As she dropped the ruined gown to the floor in a puddle of satin, lace, and water, she let a few of her more recent fantasies enliven her body and soothe her weary soul.

Chapter 5

Dammit, Pops, what are you doing? Grant sprinted out the back door of his grandfather's home.

His grandfather had himself wedged between two downed trees in the backyard. "I would've helped you move 'em, and waitin' 'til daylight would make this easier." Gripping the tangle of branches Pops had been trying to clear, he tore them away and then knelt down to slide the massive trunk out of the way.

"I was trying to give you and Ms. Sommerville a little time alone in case she let you make her day a little better. Slipped on the mud moving that one." He pointed to a third tree he'd successfully pushed to the tool shed that was currently missing most of its shingles.

"Yeah, well, Ms. Sommerville and I just met and I need you to keep them shit stories away from me. I'm putting three carts before the horse."

Before Pops could respond, Kaitlyn made an appearance. "Can I help?"

Grant instinctively spun towards her. Now she was wearing a University of Nebraska t-shirt and some of those tight black pants that clung to every feminine curve between her hips and her calves. She looked good enough to eat. As soon as he rescued his granddaddy, Grant was going to have to go take a long, cold shower. She'd pulled her hair up in a wet ponytail and was running around in flip-flops. He supposed that was better than heels, but only a little.

With another few moves, he shimmied the largest tree out of the way so Pops could lift his leg out. "You okay?"

"Yeah, I'm fine. Rancher's always fine. Let's get you two back inside. I'll save the rest for morning."

"Since we're out here, do you want me to pull them trunks out of the driveway with my truck?"

"Nah, the ground's too wet. That's how I got caught up. Let's wait."

"Looks like you're two for two in the savior department today, cowboy." Kaitlyn gave Grant a grin that he swore was prettier than any sunrise he'd ever encountered. And damn if the admiring tone in her voice didn't swell his ego as much as his cock. What the hell was she doing to him? He resisted the urge to perform more feats of strength or to try to find kittens he could rescue or something, just so she'd keep staring up at him with that look of wonder in her eyes.

Before he allowed a smirk to form on his face from thinking of one little sex kitten in particular he'd like to keep right on saving, he scoffed. "I'm sure as hell not a savior."

"Well, you do kind of have a dirty mouth to be a savior," she challenged with an impish grin.

Pops chuckled to himself. "You hear that, boy? She's gone try to save your sorry soul from yourself."

"Yeah, well, I wish her luck with that. You should'a waited 'til I could help you."

"I hear ya. I could of done it. Just got a little stuck."

"Mm-hmm," Grant rolled his eyes. He worried over his grandfather. He'd moved to the city so his grandmother would be near her doctors and ultimately so she could be moved into a facility to treat her COPD. He still attempted to do the work of a man half his age and there was no telling him not to.

"So, Kaitlyn, sweetheart, where do you work?" Granddaddy Camden inquired as Kaitlyn leaned over a cast iron pot Grant had hung over the fire. At least that's what she thought he'd said. She'd taken over chili preparations when Grant seemed lost.

Unable to focus on his mouth while she stirred, Kaitlyn turned her good ear towards him. "Hmm?"

"I was asking where you worked, darlin'."

"Baylor, Holsten, and Brown," she replied automatically. Regret immediately plunged through her. Embarrassment scalded her cheeks. Living outright lies was difficult to undo.

"You're a lawyer?" Grant sounded offended. Kaitlyn didn't blame him.

"No. I'm sorry. It's just that ... well, that's where I tell people I work. I actually work at the Iron Skillet out in Wahoo."

Sinking her teeth into her bottom lip, she attempted to ignore the concerned glance Grant and his grandfather shared.

"So, you tell people you work for that fancy law firm on the TV, but you really work out at Chully's Iron Skillet?" Grant demanded.

"You know Mr. Chully?" Kaitlyn hoped that would somehow make them forget her first response.

"Yeah, Chully's a friend of the family, but that don't answer my question."

"It's kind of a long story."

"Uh, Chully makes 'bout the best brisket I ever had," Granddaddy Camden vowed in what Kaitlyn assumed was an attempt to rescue her from Grant's interrogation.

"Thank you." Despite the inner monologue in her head assuring her that she was an idiot and just as much a liar as Seth was, it always made Kaitlyn happy when someone genuinely loved her cooking. Since the Camdens had no idea she was the cook for Mr. Chully, the compliment was obviously sincere.

Confusion furrowed Granddaddy Camden's brow adding to the wrinkles on his distinguished face.

"Sorry, I don't mean to be cryptic. I'm actually the cook for Chully's, so ... I make the brisket. It's not hard. The flavor comes from the dry rub I make and a chicory coffee sauce. I could show you sometime if you'd like."

"I ain't much of a cook, darlin', but I'd be more than happy to let you make me some."

"Geez, Pops." Grant rolled his eyes. "She's already making you chili."

"I wouldn't mind at all, Mr. Camden. I owe both of you for taking me in tonight."

"You don't owe us nothin'," Grant vowed.

"That's right. 'Sides, you vastly improve the scenery. Grant ain't much to look at," Granddaddy Camden's wink made Kaitlyn laugh. The sound was so odd. She wondered how long it had been since she'd been genuinely humored.

"Oh, I can't say I agree with that at all, Mr. Camden," she tried. Her gaze wandered to Grant's seated form. She offered him a mischievous grin. God, she wanted to flirt. She missed flirting so much.

The old Kaitlyn, the one who existed fully in her own body, who'd had opinions, and spunk, and soul, the one who still let her parents run her life but at least argued with them about it occasionally made a hesitant showing.

Like she was surfacing from a drowning deluge after far too many years, breath rushed to her lungs. Bliss stirred beneath her skin. A butterfly or two might've even fluttered in her stomach. The new Kaitlyn, the one she'd become to try to give her parents what they'd had with Keith, would never have said that. The new Kaitlyn needed to go.

And if she wasn't mistaken, the glow of the firelight said her flirtatious comment elicited a sexy half-grin from her rescuing cowboy. His grandfather was still chuckling, but she didn't care. Life itself flowed through her veins.

Tapping the wooden spoon on the side of the pot, sweat tracked down her spine as she stood. Whether it was from the heat of the fire or the embarrassment she didn't know. "It's about ready. Just tell me where the bowls are, and I'll make everyone some."

"You kidding me? You cooked supper. I'll fix bowls." The spurs on Grant's boots jangled along the linoleum flooring as he made his way into the kitchen. Kaitlyn's heart timed itself to the metallic beat.

Watching Grant inhale her chili was oddly fulfilling. He had four bowls, continually commented on how good it was, and made no apologies about enjoying eating in general. One of the many tasks Kaitlyn had taken over when she'd moved home from New York was preparing dinner as her mother, crippled with grief, was unable and her father refused. Each night was a practice in playacting, a fabrication of a family meal.

Her father would storm in from the precinct after phoning Kaitlyn three to four times to determine the exact time food would appear on the table. He didn't want to leave work any earlier than he had to.

Making as little noise as possible, her mother would leave the master bedroom and seat herself at the dining room table only to return to her previous post after eating barely enough to sustain her meager existence.

The only conversation was about the upcoming wedding. It was the only topic that successfully jolted Kaitlyn's parents into the present. Seth would come over for dinner once a week or so. In the presence of company or when she was at the club, her mother put on a mask of her former self, never allowing anyone outside the family to know how she was barely surviving. It always slid away as soon as she was back home.

Setting the chili bowl down on the coffee table, Kaitlyn fought the nausea that tidal waved over her. She'd always been pleased for Seth to be there, excited even. In that moment with only the glow of the firelight to navigate her thoughts, she knew she'd been happy to have him there because her parents would make an effort to at least appear normal. She'd allowed Seth to be her savior for no other reason that he was a reluctant barrier between Kaitlyn and her parents' all-consuming depression. He'd become her normal. How sick was that?

"I told you I always shoot straight and I'll say this, that was the best damned chili I've ever had. Much obliged," Grant vowed.

Happiness chased away the impending doom for a moment. Forcefully ripping her thoughts away from dinners at her family's mansion and the terror over what would happen now that Seth wouldn't be coming over and there would be no talk of weddings, Kaitlyn managed a smile.

"Boy, you best never let your mama hear you say that," Granddaddy Camden teased.

"Does your mother like to cook?" The hope Kaitlyn heard in her own voice levied another round of sadness in her soul. How pathetic to desperately need to know that somewhere outside the walls of the home that had become her cage, people cooked, and ate, and enjoyed a simple meal as a family without the weight of grief as the centerpiece of the table.

"I never really thought to ask her if she likes to cook. Probably should'a. She seems happy when she's doing it so I assumed, but that's generally a bad idea. She had six youngins to feed every night and all us had been out working a ranch most of the day so we were hungry. All us are grown now and we still eat up there most every night."

"That's nice." Kaitlyn tried not to feel the sting of jealousy, but she still hadn't regained any control over her feelings.

"Trust me, she loves to cook. My daughter-in-law is a sweetheart and a spitfire. She and my wife used to go head to head occasionally on who was gonna cook what for who. 'Fore Grant was even here on this earth the two of 'em would start bickering over who was gonna cook Thanksgiving supper and Christmas breakfast in July. Got so Ev used to eat six times on both days so as not to get his britches caught on his own pitchfork."

"Ev's my daddy," Grant explained. "I never knew about that, Pops. I always remember Gran and Mama cookin' together for the holidays."

"Yeah, well, see that's how life works. We raise up kids telling 'em to think. Then they get to thinkin' and wanting to change things. Generation that told 'em to think gets to feeling a little bit replaced with their new way of doing things. Like two bulls that go horn to horn, they go back and forth 'til one gains a little ground then the other pushes back harder. Only two outcomes—they either lock each other up and nobody gets nowhere or they both decide it ain't worth losing a horn over. Eventually, they figure there's plenty of pasture for everyone involved. I mighta suggested to your gran that she should go on and admit she was a little tired of cookin' for all us every night and she was just bein' stubborn, and maybe Jessie did know what she was doing in a kitchen. And your daddy mighta mentioned to your mama that *his* mama was feelin' a little replaced. You can make a lotta headway when you try to see something from the other side of the fence between ya."

"Sometimes the fence is more like an impenetrable wall," Kaitlyn commented to herself.

Grant studied the way the firelight danced in those gorgeous blue eyes and lit the flecks of orange in her auburn curls. She was spinning them around her index finger over and over again. Nervous habit she didn't even seem aware she had.

Girl was a puzzle if she was anything at all. Why in God's name did she tell people she worked for a lawyer's office? What was wrong with being a cook? Was that not a good enough profession for her? His gut said that wasn't it, but every word that fell out of those pretty pink lips produced ten questions for every answer.

Keeping the question locked up tight in his mind instead of demanding to know why she lied about her work while they did dishes together proved difficult.

"Just ask me," she finally demanded.

"Ask you what?"

"Whatever it is you want to know. You keep looking at me like I'm a ticking time bomb set to explode."

"That ain't it exactly." It was true, he couldn't seem to keep his eyes off her. Running his hand under the faucet, he jerked back as the freezing cold water splashed on his t-shirt. Damn it all to hell, he had to pay attention to something other than Kaitlyn.

"I am either stupid or I pay so little attention that my fiancé was able to have an affair with one of my closest friends without me noticing. Trust me, I'm paying attention now. *You* want to know something."

"I told you, you ain't stupid for not knowing he was cheating. He's the dumbass for doing it. But fine, why the hell do you lie about where you work?"

"I knew that's what you wanted to know."

Grant didn't respond. She was more nervous than a Junebug in July. If he kept his trap shut, she'd keep talking. He would have bet the profits from half his stalks on it. Silence ticked between them.

A huff of hot breath preceded, "I lie about where I work so my parents won't know I quit the job at the law firm."

Interesting. "So, why did you quit?"

"One, I don't want to be a lawyer. Two, one of the partners informed me on my first day that I would get further faster if my skirts were shorter and I showed off more of my *assets*. He also wanted me to extend my hours with him. Three, I don't put up with stuff like that. Four, I want to be a chef, but I can't, so being a cook is as close as I can get."

The white-hot rage that bubbled in his gut had Grant white-knuckling a dish towel like it was the lawyer's neck in his grip.

"I'm sorry," he finally managed, though he barely recognized his infuriated growl as his own voice.

Skepticism hardened her gaze as she shrugged. "Thanks. I used the sexual harassment in my favor. Threatened to go public and tell my dad. The lawyer agreed to have his admin assistant tell people I was with a client if anyone ever calls there asking for me in exchange for me keeping my mouth shut."

"Yeah, well, you shouldn't have to trade your silence for his piss-poor behavior."

Setting a bowl down she'd been drying, she offered him another one of those genuine smiles, the one that made that sexy little dimple appear on her left cheek. The anger in his gut mixed oddly with the heat sizzling in his veins. What the hell was this girl doing to him? He'd never wanted to beat the shit out of some asshole while laying her out and showing her how real men treat women simultaneously.

"You really believe that?"

"Believe what?"

"That I shouldn't have had to make a deal like that?"

"Hell yeah, peaches."

"Seth said I should just keep quiet about it. Told me that was the way it worked in law. He said I was stupid to have quit and that I should have considered his offer. But since I didn't, he told me I should keep my word and never say anything."

"Am I allowed to ask why you can't just be a chef?" *If I ever meet your ex, I'll shove his own head so far up his ass he'll be able to lick his own tonsils.*

"No." She shook head and tried to hide a harsh swallow. "Thank you for everything you've done for me, Grant. I know I keep saying that, but it means more than you know." Well, that was a subject change if ever there was one.

"Pops thinks there's something to all this." He gestured between them using the wet spoon he was holding in his hands. Water splattered all over the linoleum floor.

Laughing at him, Kaitlyn knelt to dry the flooring. Grant stared unabashedly at her plump ass caught up in those yoga pants. His heart thundered out its adamant approval. Damn. Damn. Damn. She was gonna kill him before the night was over.

"Your grandfather is so sweet. I guess it is a little crazy how we ended up here, but I probably shouldn't be ready to date or whatever. I haven't even spoken to Seth yet. Not that you asked me out. I'm a mess."

An irritated grunt vaulted from Grant's throat. Every time she spoke that fucker's name he wanted to level somebody. The sheer number of asses he wanted to whip on her behalf was concerning. He hadn't even known her twenty-four hours. He cursed himself for alluding to them going out sometime even if he had blamed his granddaddy for it. However, she hadn't said she wasn't ready to date, just that she didn't think she *should* be ready. Interesting.

"You ain't a mess," was all he offered.

"Trust me, I am. Would you mind if I took a shower?"

"Water heater's electric. You're welcome to bathe, but it's gonna be colder than a witch's tit." *Course, I could always get in with you and keep you nice and warm.* Grant tried unsuccessfully to order his thoughts from that idea.

Do not look at her tits. Do not look at her tits. She's been surrounded by nothing but assholes lately and you acted like a horny plowboy on his first root with the dress. Show her how cattle ranchers treat a lady.

Rather proud of himself for following his own directives, Grant fought not to verbally congratulate himself.

"Oh," she wrinkled her adorable nose. "Maybe I'll wait and see if the power comes back on soon."

Sinking his teeth into his tongue to keep himself from offering to heat her up after a cold shower, he managed a slight nod.

Suddenly the air between them lost a little of its heat. His eyes tracked her fingertips as they rubbed over the delicate column of her neck. When the collar of the t-shirt shifted under her caress, he saw the red burn from her seatbelt and the bruise that was forming around it. Regret filled him.

"You hurting, sweetheart? I can find you some aspirin or something. It might help."

She stared up at him. Several slow blinks of her long eyelashes revealed what appeared to be confusion.

"Do you call everyone sweetheart and peaches and all that?" Heat bloomed across her features. It slowly edged down her neck, painting the burn mark with her embarrassment. Another swallow worked her throat. He longed to brush his lips right there, flood her body with heat that had nothing to do with the wreck or her being embarrassed.

"No, I don't."

"Oh." She managed a half nod of understanding. "Um, I think I'll just go on to bed. I'll see you in the morning." With that she whisked from the room.

It took Grant a full minute to realize that she was about to cry and had been trying to escape. He debated going after her, but it was him she was clearly trying to get away from. Damn, he really was a dumbass. She'd been through hell that day, had the battle scars to prove it, and every single time they were alone he came onto her. *Dumbass.*

Chapter 6

"What is wrong with me?" Kaitlyn asked the ether in the room around her, wishing for a response she knew wasn't coming.

She'd been having fun at dinner. She'd even flirted. For a moment, she'd felt like the girl she'd been so many years ago. Why was she crying now?

Scrubbing her hands over her face, she tried to summon the courage she'd had back in the living room, but it had abandoned her. She'd been the new version of herself for so long. It apparently wasn't going down without a fight.

Every cell in her body ached. Muscles she didn't even know existed radiated with pain. Her head felt like someone had put it in a vice. Even her teeth ached, and she could barely turn her neck without wincing. The fury and adrenaline from Seth and the wreck had clearly worn off. Now she got to deal with the aftermath.

Staring at her blank cell phone, she willed the signal to come back on so she could call her sister just to find out what had happened after she'd left. The phone was no more cooperative than her courage.

It couldn't have been much past eight, but the darkness was oppressive. The candles Granddaddy Camden had lit for her when he'd shown her the guest bedroom pierced the blackness but they were losing the fight against the night.

Going back into the living room and facing Grant wasn't an option. He made her feel things she had no business feeling. Just the tone of his voice stirred some kind of delicious bliss inside of her.

Timing was everything, and theirs just sucked. He was clearly interested, but he deserved someone whose life wasn't currently a circus sideshow.

The room felt foreign and they were too far away from the city lights she was accustomed to seeing outside her bedroom window to ground her. Every single thing in her life felt variable. Like standing on a sandy shoreline while the tides washed away her footing.

Creating a new Kaitlyn after Keith's death had almost been easy. The task had numbed the pain better than any drug in existence. She'd put herself in a kind of coma. Focusing only on how to repair her parents made her able to ignore her own feelings. The only things that mattered were doing what Keith would have done. Keith had been the perfect son. Straight A's, captain of the football team. He'd climbed the ranks in the Army faster than most. Her parents never even tried to conceal that Keith was their favorite child. Kaitlyn and her sister Sophie hadn't even minded. Keith had been their hero, too.

Kaitlyn had gone as far as reading books on football and golf so she could watch them with her father and understand what was going on. Every Sunday afternoon she was able to succumb herself in the safety of the way things used to be. Football was on the television and her father wasn't yelling at her. It was something.

She'd traded her soul for normalcy and had sought redemption by sacrificing herself for moments of almost-happiness from her parents. Almost-happiness. Was there any sadder phrase?

Shedding the t-shirt and yoga pants she'd donned, she dug through her suitcase until she located the most conservative nightie she'd been given at her lingerie shower. It was still entirely too revealing to be sleeping in a stranger's guest bedroom. Pulling on the matching robe at least gave her slightly more coverage.

Before she crawled into bed, she gathered the ruffled lump of wet silk that had been her gown and heaved it into the bathtub. She didn't want it to ruin the carpeting, and she couldn't stand to look at it anymore. Tomorrow, she would either ask Grant if there was a large trash bag anywhere in the house or she'd throw the damn thing in the fire.

Easing under the covers, the pills on the old sheets agitated the burn on her neck from the seatbelt. Her heart tripped over the next few erratic beats inside the hollow ache of her chest. Her breaths hurt far more than they should've. Maybe she had a broken rib or two from the airbag, or perhaps her heart had been so anxious to escape the traps she'd forced it in, it had shattered the cage on its own.

Hot tears tracked out the side of her eyes. She wiped them away before they reached her hairline, but a moment later there were too many to contend with. Turning into the pillows, she sobbed; not for all she'd lost that day, but for all she'd willingly given up three years before.

"Shouldn't we do some'um?" Granddaddy Camden demanded of Grant yet again.

"Pops, I barely know her. As much as it tears me up to hear her in there crying I got no idea what to say to her to make her fiancé cheating on her not hurt. I'd go clobber the fuck-whistle if I knew where to find him, but that ain't really my right either." He continued pacing in front of the fire. "I've already made an ass of myself with her anyway."

"What's that mean?"

"I came on too strong. I gotta let her be."

"Camden men don't back down when they know something's right."

"Yeah, well, that ain't exactly the way the world works."

"I'd bet my left boot on the two of you. I seen the way you keep looking at her, and she up and told me she don't mind you none at'all. Maybe you ought to stop thinking of reasons to leave her be and go in there and see if you can't make her stop crying."

"You are more stubborn than a mule with a purpose." Grant had no idea what to say to Kaitlyn that wouldn't make this worse. Surely, she didn't want witnesses to her misery. The woman deserved whatever parts of her dignity she was managing to cling to. She'd been through enough. *She deserves someone who will cherish her and worship her.* His mind took up his Granddaddy's banner, but that didn't mean he had any idea what to do with a crying woman.

Keeping his eyes on the flickering fire, he willed the universe to give him something to say that would either shut his granddaddy up or help Kaitlyn. Coming up empty, he sank back down on the couch, calling himself a coward.

Completely unable to sit and listen to her cry any longer, he sprang back up just as quickly and marched to the guest bedroom. He raised his fist to knock but couldn't seem to force a connection with the door.

Leaning in, he listened instead. Her sobs had lessened in volume. Maybe he was right and he should leave her be. Maybe she'd finally found a little peace. No amount of his granddaddy thinking she was meant to be his made that so. Yet for some unfathomable reason, she affected him. Watching her cry would be his undoing. His entire body responded to her on a cellular level he didn't even understand. He knew men couldn't and weren't supposed to fix everything, but dammit he wanted to make her feel better. He had no clue how to go about doing that, however.

Shaking his head, he stomped back down to the living room. Kaitlyn was in the only guest bedroom in the house. He was more than happy to sleep on the couch, assuming he slept at all.

Chapter 7

Pressing the heels of his palms against his eyes wasn't helping. Grant's head pounded. Assuming he'd tensed up when his truck was hit, he cursed himself for being weak. He was a fucking rancher. Pain was part of the job. What the hell was wrong with him?

He poured another glass of his granddaddy's Crown and willed the whiskey to take away the dull ache in his muscles and the heavy weight in his head so he could sleep. It had to be two in the morning. He reveled in the burn as it centered in his chest, slightly easing the strain as he took another sip.

Slinking down on the sofa, he'd just pulled his hat over his eyes when he heard someone stumble in the hallway. Bolting upright, he barely had time to register Kaitlyn gently easing along the wall before his muscles protested his quick movement.

"Jesus," escaped his mouth in a hiss. His body tensed in approval and his mouth went drier than the Sahara. His cock leapt to attention despite the pain radiating throughout him.

Her hair had dried in a soft halo of red curls framing her delicate features, but his eyes zeroed in on the softness of her abundant cleavage on display in a short, crystal-blue, satin nightie that barely covered the plump globes of her ass.

Delicate lace slightly obscured her nipples. She had on a matching robe but it did nothing to cover her. Blinking rapidly, Grant wondered if he was dreaming. He couldn't recall any other wet dream he'd ever had that had included lingerie. His dreams were far kinkier than the sweet little nightie she was wearing. Maybe if she was bound to his bed in the nightie he would've believed this wasn't reality.

"Grant!" leapt from her mouth in a shocked gasp. "Uh ..." she wrapped the damned robe tighter, only managing to draw a deep V at the collar, creating a map for his eyes straight to the swells of her tits. "What are you doing in here?"

Far too much blood was on a southbound trip to his cock for him to have responded intelligently. He willed a few of his brain cells to sort through what she'd just said. His heart timed his silence only serving to irritate him. "Sleepin'. No, scratch that. Drinkin'. Definitely drinkin'."

She couldn't manage to keep the top of the robe closed without the bottom giving away more information than she was clearly comfortable sharing ... yet. His eyes drank her in like a parched man offered a long cool drink of water.

"You ... uh ... you okay there?" There, that was marginally polite.

"Kind of. My whole body hurts. I just thought I might come in here and see if I could find some aspirin like you said earlier."

Managing to stand without leaping over the coffee table between them, dragging her into his arms and drugging her with his kisses instead of painkillers, he cleared his throat, hoping his mind would clear as well. No such luck.

His hands longed to climb under that sweet little gown and see just how innocent she was. He wanted to track kisses up and down the injuries on her neck and chest, leave a few markings of his own. He wanted to make her forget she was in any pain at all.

Her beautiful mouth twisted in consideration before she glanced down at the gown and rolled her eyes. Like waving a white flag of surrender she dropped both of her arms and let the lingerie flow free. "You've already seen most of it anyway. Might as well go ahead and flash you," she sighed.

"Well, I'm sure as hell not gonna try to stop you if that's what you've got a mind to do." He winked at her, feeling himself steady slightly.

"Such a gentleman," she teased.

"Never a gentleman, darlin'. Always a cattle rancher, though. I'll give you a little time to figure the difference. You do know you're driving me outta my mind in that, right?"

"I'm sorry."

"Don't apologize."

"But I am sorry. I only have the stupid things I packed for my stupid honeymoon. This covers more than anything else in my stupid suitcase."

"Trust me, ain't nothing about what you're wearing that's stupid." He willed his mind to stop conjuring what else might be in her bags. "Uh, I'll get you the painkillers. Think they expired about two decades ago. Pops ain't much on ever throwing anything out."

"Actually, I'm pretty sure *that* would work better than aspirin anyway." She pointed to the whiskey. "I mean, if anyone has a right to get drunk after everything that happened today it seems like it's me."

"Agreed," Grant chuckled. "But you ain't getting drunk on my watch so you can get that thought right on out of your pretty head."

Retrieving another tumbler from the kitchen he poured her a half shot.

She accepted the glass and considered it before drinking. "You always so bossy, cowboy? Is that what makes you not a gentleman?"

"Sure as hell part of it."

Drawing another hesitant sip, she puckered up a little but then seemed to settle in to the Crown. "I've never had this without Coke, and I guess you're right, being sick on top of being sore wouldn't be much fun. Part of me wants to get drunk just because it would be so unlike me. I did once when I was in New York. Unfortunately, the memories linger." She shuddered.

And if you do it again I'll paddle your sweet little ass. Grant slung the last of the liquid in his own glass down his throat letting the whiskey burn away that particular thought. "That back when you think you were brave?"

"Yeah."

"Seth the reason you don't think you were brave lately?"

"No."

"You ever plan on giving me more than a one-word answer?"

"Maybe," she smirked and giggled through another sip.

Arching his left eyebrow, Grant shook his head. "It's a good thing you ain't mine."

"Why is that?" Mischief played in those cool blue eyes and the slip and slide of the satin gown as she seated herself beside him made him ache in frustration for all it revealed and all it kept covered.

"'Cause I'd find some way to make you talk. I'd get all them secrets you're keepin' outta your head."

"Trust me, you don't want to hear my sad, ridiculous story topped with how pathetic it is that my fiancé cheated on me with the kind of girl my parents would much prefer I actually was."

The thunder of his pulse in his veins made it difficult to hear her excuses. The firelight surrounding that sky blue nightie painted her in a thousand shades of a sunset. Every shade from burnt orange to dark crimson played in her hair. Her alabaster skin was dotted with hundreds of tiny freckles and merciful Christ if he didn't want to drag his lips and his tongue over every last one of them.

She'd said something about Seth, and Grant wanted nothing more than to wipe his existence from her memory.

"Darlin', he's an asshole of the highest caliber, and if your parents really think like that it don't sound like they're much better."

"I keyed the hell out of his car before I drove into yours."

Unable to halt his chuckle, Grant had never been more pleased. "I figured there was a hefty dose of hellcat in there somewhere. Bastard deserved it."

"He *loved* that car," she sighed in what Grant sincerely prayed was not regret.

"He should'a loved *you*. I bet he didn't even know how kiss a woman like you." No turning back now. He had no hope of retreat anyway. The whiskey drowned any inhibitions he'd been clinging to. The entire world seemed distant, erased in the blackness of the night as it enveloped them. Nothing could touch them. No one outside of his family even knew where they were. And he wanted to know the taste of those pale pink lips more than he wanted to draw his next breath.

Awareness shadowed her eyes. So she knew she was being baited. He could almost tell the moment she decided to go on and swallow the hook. "And how should a woman like me be kissed, cowboy?" Line ... *and sinker.*

Leaning closer, dominating her space, he stared into those deep blue eyes. Hunger swam in their crystal depths. That intoxicating scent of strawberries and woman filled his lungs. She licked her lips, taunting him. His eyes focused there.

"There are rules for how a country boy kisses a lady," he explained.

"Oh yeah? I don't think I've ever been kissed by a country boy. Tell me these rules." Her voiced was perforated with breathy lust. The crackling fire was nothing compared to the current running between them.

"Kiss oughta make a woman crave. Make her hungry, damn near needy for more. Oughta prove to the woman that she belongs to you and make her damned happy about that fact. Like a hot brand, needs to let her know she's yours. Needs to make her want more. Needs to show her that you're gonna take good care of each and every single thing she requires. And most importantly ..." he studied her. Her chest rose and fell in anxious pants. Her eyes were at half-mast in preparation for him to get on with it. Grant paused amplifying her desire.

"What's most important?" she finally pouted in frustration.

"Every damned kiss needs to make your panties so wet you ache. Make you so nice and hot and creamy a man can sink himself balls-deep in your heat because he's undone you so thoroughly."

"Oh, my God," she breathed the words over his lips as he traced his thumb along her cheek.

Another heartbeat. The anticipation between them took on its own pulse.

His left hand wound through that mass of red curls, drawing her closer. His right toyed with the lacey edge of the nightie positioned at the top of her thigh as he staked his claim. He sank into the soft sugar of her mouth. Too impatient to stop himself, he licked the seam of her lips. She parted for him and his growl of approval stirred the very air around them.

A quick gasp of breath. Dammit, what was he doing? Taking advantage of her made him almost as much of an ass as her ex. He forced himself to talk. "Tell me to stop, Kaitlyn." If she didn't want this, she needed to speak up now.

"No."

"I'm about to take exactly what I want, baby, tell me to stop."

"Please don't stop."

The frayed rope on his restraint snapped. He devoured the heat of the whiskey as it lingered on her tongue. She tasted like liquid sin and the sweetest sunshine. The combination sucker punched him. God, he needed more and he'd be damned if she was going to control this kiss.

The sweet little whimpered moans she made zinged straight to his cock. He edged his hand higher and deepened the kiss, sucking, biting, licking until she melted fully into him.

Her thighs parted. Oh hell yeah. Fire burned in his bones. She came alive in his arms. Her hands traced down his chest on a direct path to his crotch. A low hungry groan spilled from his mouth into hers.

The cracks and pops of the dying fire had nothing on the sounds of her voracious hunger.

He hadn't expected another shocked gasp however. "My God, you're hung like a horse."

"You have that affect. Now, hush up and kiss me some more." The constant, mounting pressure in his cock erased any pain that lingered from the wreck. Now, all his body demanded was more of her.

"So bossy." She leaned in sank her teeth into his bottom lip. The pain registered instantly and unadulterated pleasure. Oh, fuck yeah.

"You have no clue just how bossy I can be, peaches," he managed as he jerked away, turned his head and kissed the hell out of her. Her arousal perfumed the air. He longed to demand that she ride him.

Desperation to see her stripped bare and dripping ignited in every muscle in his body.

His hands accepted the invite her thighs had extended. Wet heat greeted his fingertips and welcomed him further. "Kiss doing its job, baby? Making you nice and creamy for me?"

A frantic, carnal cry of hunger was his answer as she writhed for him.

Greed seized him. He painted her neck with tender, suckled kisses. Brushing his tongue over the markings and burns where her seatbelt had marred her beautiful skin.

She arched her body, begging for him. Restless, he stroked his thumb along the scrap of wet satin he located at the apex of her thighs.

"Guess it is working." He continued to explore her. "Nice and wet all for me."

Another breathless gasp worked up from her lungs. Suddenly, she threw her right leg over him, straddled him and thrust her ample breasts in his face. He gripped her lush ass and drew that wet satin against his crotch.

"So, do you have rules for sex too, cowboy?" She whimpered as he brought his mouth to the lace covering her nipples. The robe tumbled down her arms. He'd get to that later. Currently, he was drenching the lace of her gown, making her nipples raw with need as they pulsated against his tongue.

"Oh, fuck yeah, peaches, most important one is for you to understand that I'm in charge."

Another slow grind against him and he was certain he was going to come in his shorts like a green kid. Gritting his teeth, he ordered himself to get it the fuck together.

"And if I want to be in charge?" she challenged as she laid the left side of her face against his shoulder, cradling into him. Using her new position to his advantage he nipped her right earlobe. She jerked her head away but still seemed into it so Grant continued his dirty talking.

"When I show you just how high I can make you fly, darlin', when I prove to you that I'll make you feel better than you ever have you'll have no desire to be in charge. You'll find that being at my mercy is a pretty damn good place to be."

"You sound awfully sure of yourself, cowboy. You really going to show me all the naughty things nobody ever wanted me to know?"

She lifted up onto her knees and sank down in another slow grind that was going to end him.

"Oh, hell yeah. You can be a sweet girl for me and everyone else until I get you in bed. Now, lay back for me. Spread your legs, peaches. You're so nice and wet and I'm so damned thirsty for you."

"Yes," she cried in what sounded distinctly like relief.

His cock throbbed against her.

Suddenly, a spark of electricity lit a low hum throughout the house. The kitchen lights and lamps in the living room ripped away the covering the darkness had provided. The refrigerator groaned back to life and the television blared at deafening decibels.

Furious at the interruption, Grant attempted to keep his mouth on Kaitlyn's chest while locating the remote to turn the blasted thing off.

"Oh, my God!" Kaitlyn scrambled out of his lap, much to his chagrin. He leapt to steady her when she fell forward, almost crashing into the coffee table.

It took him another full second to see what she was seeing. A recent picture of her was on the television screen with the letters BOLO underneath what Grant immediately noticed was not a sincere smile.

"Police Chief Sommerville's youngest daughter, Kaitlyn, has been listed as missing after her car was found totaled outside the Hillcrest Country Club today during the storm. Charges of felony vandalism have been brought against Chief Sommerville's daughter and she is suspected to be on the run. Cell towers all over the city are still down, but if you have any information on Kaitlyn's whereabouts and are able, please call the number at the bottom of the screen here and on Channel 8 Eyewitness News' Facebook page. Police Chief Sommerville has set up a direct line to his office."

"Did that just say what I think it said?" Blood was still pounding in her good ear from the heady sensations Grant had offered her and shock muted any other noise.

Grant was staring at the television screen. Shock resonated from every chiseled plain of his body. "Your daddy's the chief of police?"

Kaitlyn managed a slight nod. The movement made her dizzy.

"And he's going to arrest you for wrecking your car?" Stunned disbelief bordered on fury in his tone.

"No. I mean, I don't think so. It said vandalism, didn't it? I watched the reporter's lips. That's what she said. So, that means Seth is pressing charges for his car. Oh my God. What am I going to do?"

Grant's grandfather stalked into the living room. Kaitlyn had forgotten she was barely covered until Grant quickly wrapped her in an afghan he grabbed off the back of a chair.

"I'd apologize for interrupting whatever ... was going on here, but I'd dare say we need to figure just how much trouble you're in, sweetheart," he offered apologetically.

"I need to call my sister." That was the only possible next step. Sophie could tell her just how much trouble she was in. "My cell phone won't work."

"Your sister got a house phone? We can use the landline." Grant pointed to a cordless phone that had come back to life with the electricity.

"I don't know her number. I always just touch her name on my favorite's list."

"Okay, deep breaths, darlin'. Just cause it won't make calls don't mean you can't get to your contacts, right?"

"Thought you hated cell phones?" Granddaddy Camden quizzed.

"I do, but that don't mean I don't know how to use 'em. I hate entering all the stats on my steers on my computer too, but I do it. Ain't no good in doing things the way we used to do 'em just 'cause that's how we used to do 'em."

Kaitlyn didn't have time to listen to them bicker. Guilt ravaged her. What must her parents have thought when they saw her car? How could she have been so selfish? Even if she refused to be new Kaitlyn anymore, old Kaitlyn was still considerate of her parent's feelings. Speaking of things even old Kaitlyn wouldn't have done, what was she thinking, daring Grant Camden to teach her all the finer points on dirty love-making? That was one hell of a first kiss. The magnetism between them quelled a little of her guilt, but nothing else mattered other than making certain her family knew she wasn't missing.

When all this was over and she'd paid Seth back for his ridiculous car, then she could think about a second and maybe a third kiss with Grant Camden.

Chapter 8

Please answer. Please answer. Please answer. After she'd changed clothes, Kaitlyn listened to her sister's cell phone ring. There was no answer. Not even her voicemail message. Sophie didn't have cell service either.

If her family really believed she was missing they were probably all down at the precinct, but Kaitlyn absolutely could not speak to her father currently. Unbearable wouldn't even cover the way he would react when he figured out nothing was wrong with her, she'd just stupidly decided to leave her wrecked car on the side of the road.

The tornado would be no excuse to a man who was a formidable hurricane.

With another fervent prayer, Kaitlyn dialed her sister's home number into the old phone.

"Hello?" Sophie's frantic voice took another vicious blow to Kaitlyn's psyche. The guilt increased its death-grip.

"Soph, it's me. I'm not missing. I'm fine."

"Oh, my God! Kaitlyn! Thank God. Wait, are you really fine? Or is someone making you say you're fine when you're really not fine?"

"Sophie, I swear, I'm fine. I found out Seth was cheating on me with Kelsey. I ran into this guy's truck when I was running away from the church. Then the storm and tornado and I'm with him and he's ... very nice. Really." That didn't come close to covering the things Grant Camden made her feel, but the cowboy himself was looming ever closer, pacing as he listened to her talk, so *nice* would have to do.

"You're lying. I always know. Okay, if you're still in Nebraska say *'I'm fine, really.'* If your kidnapper has been driving for a while say ... uh, say ... hmm ... okay, say, 'the blue bird lives in the nest with seven eggs.'"

"Oh, my God, yeah, because that wouldn't be obvious. I swear to you I'm completely fine."

"But are you saying that because they still have you in Nebraska or because you're really fine?"

"I'm going to hang up if you don't believe that I am fine."

"Answer the following questions correctly and I will consider believing you. When we were kids, what color were those God-awful comforters Mama put on our beds?"

"Sophie ..."

"Answer me, Kit-Kat, or I'm calling Dad to tell him you're being held captive and that you're still in Nebraska."

Her sister's nickname for her dampened her resolve. "Mine was orange and pink and yours was rose and green."

"Okay, good. I think. Uh, how old was I when I lost my virginity?"

"Sophie."

"Answer me."

"You were nineteen."

"And who was the cherry picker?"

Kaitlyn scowled. "Marty Jensen."

"And besides the fact that he came before I was even in the bed what else made the experience revolting?"

"Are you *trying* to torture me?"

"Are you *being* tortured?"

Grinding her teeth, Kaitlyn was ever aware of Grant's presence in the room. Clearly privacy was not the cowboy's forte. "Please do not make me say this."

"I'm getting in my car and driving back to the precinct. This is the perfect question not to answer if you are in any danger."

"He had gross ass-pimples." Kaitlyn cringed. Grant's scowl matched her own. "Now, I am fine, but I can't come home just yet. There are trees down everywhere."

"If you really are fine, Kit-Kat, you can't come home for a while."

"What? Why?"

"Seth was beyond furious when he figured out he'd texted both you and Kelsey. Kelsey high-tailed it out of the church screaming that she was sorry and his tiny dick wasn't worth hurting you over. So, then he was really livid."

Kaitlyn huffed. "Yeah, well, she wasn't lying. He was definitely not gifted."

"Yeah, I gathered by her sincerity. Anyway, the tornado passed by us on the south-side. After it stopped raining, he went outside and saw his car. I knew he was an asshole, but I had no idea he was this much of a crapbag. Anyway, he got the club to release the security footage of you ... let's go with 'penning your frustrations in the hood of his beloved douche-canoe'. And he's pressing charges. And our father, in all his stubborn stupidity, agreed to allow him to do this as he feels like that will teach you not to run away from your problems, which he says you've always done. He also feels that if you had been kidnapped, having an escaped felon as your captor allows the police to be more aggressive in locating you. His words. Not mine. You know he's just freaking out because we didn't know where you were, but I swear I've never seen him so mad."

"I'll pay for Seth's stupid car. I'll pick up more shifts at Chully's or something. Why can't I come home? Surely, he's not mad I didn't marry Seth."

"He is, actually. You know, Dad. Family dignity before everything else. The fact that everyone knows about this is killing him. *I am the Chief of Police. This makes me look weak, like I have no control over my own daughter.*" Her sister mimicked their father's stern tenor to perfection. "And there's more. Guess who good-ole Seth has representing him in your case?"

"Why isn't he representing himself? He works for the D.A."

"Conflict of interest. He's already hired himself some help just to stick it to you."

"Oh my God. Are you seriously telling me that he hired ..."

"Yep. Resident ambulance-chaser with a huge grudge since you've had him by the balls for the last year, Morris Holsten, your old boss. When Dad found out you weren't working at Baylor, Holsten, and Brown, he lost his proverbial shit. Said some pretty awful things."

Holsten was known for convincing judges to give no lenience for any reason, and he'd love nothing more than to make Kaitlyn's life miserable.

Simply unable to stand any longer, Kaitlyn slunk down the paneled wall seeking steady ground. Her heart refused her another beat. "What am I going to do?"

"Let Dad simmer down. I'll tell him you called and that you're fine. As soon as we have cell service, could you call Mama? I don't know how to handle her like this."

"She's back in bed and refusing to eat or speak, right?" Kaitlyn already knew the answer.

"Yeah, so call her and call Nana. She'll talk to Daddy. As for Seth, just make sure the Lincoln police department doesn't find you until Daddy calms down and comes to his senses."

"How exactly do I do that?"

"Can you stay where you are? You don't have to go back to work for a while, right?"

"I have three weeks off, but I can't stay here, and don't you think disappearing for that long will only make Daddy angrier?"

"I don't think that's possible. They're pretty hurt, and they'r. scared. I don't know how to deal with them like this. This is your job."

"I know. I'm so sorry. I just ... Maybe I could go to Hawaii tomorrow like we were supposed to. Figure everything out and let Daddy calm down."

"Uh, do you seriously think Dad doesn't already have uniforms along with Bailey and Stevens camped out at the airport?"

If her father's third-best undercover detectives had been dispatched to the airport, that meant his best detectives were out and about looking high and low for her.

The all-too-familiar desire to run and never stop surged through her. "I have to get out of here."

"Uh, yeah but don't stay gone too long. Nana told me what she told you. I guess I kind of agree with her. You lay low and so help me, Kaitlyn, figure out who the hell you are now, and then you come home and deal with Daddy. As soon as he talks Seth into dropping the charges, you can come back. But Seth is too furious, and Daddy's letting him run the show."

"I seriously cannot believe any of this is actually happening."

"Kit-kat are you certain you're safe? I know this all sucks, but I'll come rescue you myself if I need to. We can run away together just like when we were little."

"I'm safe. I'll be okay. I'll figure something out."

"I love you and I'll talk to Dad again, but listen, I just thought of something. You can't call Mama or Nana, even when the cell towers are fixed."

"Why not? You just told me to call them." As soon as Kaitlyn asked she knew the answer. "He wouldn't."

"He would. The machine thing is already set up awaiting your ransom call."

"Good Lord. There is not going to be a ransom call because I was not kidnapped. I was ... *rescued*." And in that moment she knew she had been. Rescued from a life of misery with Seth. Rescued from her own delusional attempts to be someone else for the sake of her parents. Rescued from her own stupidity. And if he was still willing after she got all this sorted out, maybe Grant Camden could rescue her from her own naivety.

"You know how Dad is. Hang on a sec." Kaitlyn heard the phone crackle and then Sophie was back on. "I'm going to erase this number off my caller ID. It says Lincoln on here. You need to get out of Lincoln."

"Yeah, I heard you the first time. How do I know if Daddy drops the charges if I can't call?"

"I'll call your cell when I get through to him. I love you, Kit-kat, but I can't do all the things you do for Mom and Dad."

With that, her sister ended the call.

Stunned. There was no other word for what she was feeling other than absolutely stunned. Squeezing her eyes shut she refused more tears. She'd cried enough and that wasn't going to solve anything anyway. Anger swept away the liquid emotion. Fury pulsed at the base of her spine. Anger at her father, certainly, but she knew the person she was really mad at was herself.

She had to figure out some way to get out of Lincoln, and currently, she couldn't even get out of Mr. Camden's driveway, and she still didn't have a car.

"What'd she say, peaches?" Grant demanded.

With her breaths as shallow as her resolve, Kaitlyn tried to think what to tell him. "Maybe, I could walk to a car rental place." She hadn't intended to state that out loud, but talking herself through things helped her think. They weren't that far outside of the city limits. If she left now, it would still be dark for several hours.

"Why in God's name would you do that?"

Lifting her eyes to Grant's concerned gaze, she debated what to tell him and what to keep from him. "You have to understand that my father is very ... he's very by the book. Strict. Military. And he's been through so much. He probably isn't doing this to be awful."

Grant seated himself beside her. "What's he doing exactly?"

Shame mixed with her anger as it swirled into a maelstrom in her stomach, radiating out to her limbs. "Seth has the security video from the club. The one of me keying his car. I apparently did enough damage to make it a felony offense. Daddy knows I'd pay for it, and he could get Seth to drop the charges, but he found out today that I've been lying to him about working for that law firm I told you about. He's furious, so he has his detectives out looking for me and if they find me, I'll be arrested. I need to get out of Lincoln. Locked up safe in a prison cell is pretty much how my father would prefer me to be. He'd know where I was and in his mind it's an appropriate punishment for running out on the wedding and embarrassing our family."

"What the hell? I'll pay for the damage you did to the jackwagon's car. You ain't getting arrested." Grant's infuriated growl sped Kaitlyn's heart. "Not on my watch. I don't give a damn what your daddy has to say about it." Before she knew what was happening, he lifted her off the cold linoleum and seated her in his lap. "Not. Gonna. Happen."

Intense protectiveness radiated from his musculature. Fervency burned in his pine green eyes. Whatever the hell this magnetism was between them, it was inexplicable. Kaitlyn longed to bury her face against the breadth of his substantial shoulders, curl herself against his chest, and pretend her life was entirely different. No cheating fiancé. No father who was the chief of police with a grudge. No mother who'd lost the ability to exist in reality. None of that. Just him and her. The way it was before the electricity had rudely ushered reality back inside.

"You barely know me. You're not paying for my mistakes, Grant. Thank you for all you've done, but Sophie thinks I need to try to get out of town until Daddy calms down. Now that he'll know I'm safe, hopefully, my Nana can get through to him."

"Now, where on the good Lord's green planet could she go stay where the city of Lincoln police department and the rest of Lancaster County's finest would have no hope in either heaven or hell of finding her for a few days?" Granddaddy Camden looked oddly pleased. His tone was almost goading.

"I hear ya, Pops, but I still can't get my truck outta the driveway."

"Where there's a will there's a way, son, and where there ain't a way there's a rancher with a chain and a truck hitch that could pull them trees outta the way."

"I don't understand. Where are you going?"

Chapter 9

Grant searched for the irritation or the fear he knew he should feel. He'd gone from having her ram her city-girl car into the hitch on his new truck to harboring a fugitive, which would get him in a heap of trouble if they got caught, and yet all that mattered was getting her to the ranch and keeping her safe.

Usually a rancher who much preferred not to offer trouble a seat at the table, he had no hesitations. She might not know it yet, but she was going to be his. And he always took care of what belonged to him.

Her daddy was obviously a real piece of work. My God, no wonder she went running off to marry some piece of shit that was cheating on her. Girl had no one who cared about her at all, save maybe her sister, and Grant wasn't giving anyone in her family any allowances at this point.

Daughter of the chief of police. He grunted to himself. If they'd met on any other day under any other circumstances, he would've sized her up as a spoiled little rich girl—and he would have been summarily wrong. Not spoiled. Not at all. And not a little girl either. She was all woman, and damn, if he didn't still want to prove that to her. Her family surely had money enough for a country club wedding, but that wasn't Kaitlyn.

"I'm taking you out to my family's ranch. It's two hours due west. Long as we get out of Lincoln without getting caught, no one will know where we are. You can stay as long as you like."

"Stay ... with you?"

Trying desperately to gauge her question, he noted the hint of fear coupled with a hearty dose of hope in her eyes. Did she want to stay with him or did it frighten her? Jesus, what the hell was he doing? This looked a whole lot like dragging her off to his cave.

"You ... uh ... you don't have to stay with me. You could stay with Mama and Daddy or you can stay in the cottage. My cousin rebuilt most of it last fall. It's warm now. Little closer to the entrance off the road than I'd like you to be, but I ain't gonna make you do anything you don't want to do. I'm just trying to help."

"I know you won't. Thank you so much for everything. If you don't mind me staying with you, I think I'd like that. Maybe I could ... help out on the farm or something. Or cook. I'm a good cook."

Grant bit back a chuckle. Poor girl had clearly been raised on asphalt. "It's a cattle ranch, sweetness. It ain't a farm." Maybe he could show her how country boys made life work. Hell, maybe she'd like it. He'd donate his left nut to see her bobbing up and down in King's Creek nekkid beside him with her toes in the mud. Or maybe wearing nothing but a pair of them lacey panties and some cowgirl boots. Ideas of her spread-eagle in the bed of his truck sizzled under his skin. He reached out and grasped her hand, needing to touch her skin again. The way she gripped his palm said she desperately needed something to cling to. Well, he was the man for the job.

Shaking himself, he tried to mentally prepare for what had to happen. "They ain't set up roadblocks or anything like that, have they?"

"No. Well, I don't think so. Sophie's going to tell him I'm not in Lincoln anymore, I think."

The sister moved up a few notches in Grant's book.

"Then let's get."

"Are you sure you don't mind doing this? I feel terrible causing you all of this trouble."

"Oh, now, some trouble's worth having. Very rarely in this life will you find that the right path and the easy path are one in the same. Paths still gotta be hoed," Pops explained to Kaitlyn. Grant had been told that very thing all his life. His daddy and his granddaddy, and hell, even his great-granddaddy had been quoting it forever.

One thing Grant had noticed in his thirties that never made it into the adage: the easy path might not be the right path, but that didn't make the right path any smoother to forge.

"Let's go see 'bout moving them trees," Grant commanded.

"How are you going to move tress in the dark?" Concern and shame still dominated Kaitlyn's tone.

"I'd go with very carefully." He winked at her, rather liking the way she always grinned involuntarily at him when he did that.

"What happened to 'the ground is too wet to drag the trunks out the way with my truck?'" Grant demanded of his grandfather as they slogged out towards the end of the driveway, following the flood of light from their lanterns.

"Well, now, see, I figured having you two locked up here a few days would help things take to root a little easier. But circumstances changed and getting her in the ground and growing out on the ranch is an even better idea."

"You are aware she's a woman not a corn stalk, right, Pops?"

"I ain't ever seen you groping a corn stalk in my living room, but I'd dare say she does need tending. You can look in her eyes and see she's lost and ain't been cared for. She needs to be taken care of, and she needs it from a man who knows what it means to work for something, even when the going gets tough. Somebody who's going to love her and protect her. Somebody she can count on. Somebody who's aware of her value and who knows the cost of losing a woman like that and vows never to let that happen. You won't never convince me that fate didn't have her driving her car up on your truck. Your grandmamma always says there are no accidental meetin's. You can't argue with her or with fate."

"Mama'd tell you I could argue with most anything, and we ain't talking vows yet. And we ain't going to be talking like that for a damn long while. She just left one shit-whistle at the altar. And I wasn't groping her. I was … doing something else."

"Mm-hmm. You had your hands so far up that nightgown get-up she was in, you embarrassed the stuffing out of my sofa. Taking advantage ain't exactly what she needs right now."

Agitation roiled in Grant's gut. That was far too close to the truth for his liking. "I wasn't taking advantage of her. She came in there and …."

"You decided to help yourself to the pickings."

Too frustrated to keep going and refusing to have this conversation with his grandfather, Grant rolled his eyes.

"I ain't saying I blame you. I'm just saying you kids get right to the dessert 'fore you've ever had time to enjoy the meal these days. Feels better if you've earned it 'fore you spend it."

"We gon' move these trees or not?"

"Yeah, we're gonna move 'em. Get that chain wrapped around that tree trunk. You need to get out of here 'fore sun up, but just think about what I said. When you get her to your house with miles of ranchland any direction, maybe take some time to get to know her mind and her heart 'fore you get to know the rest of her. It'll make the getting to know the rest of her even better."

Grant gave his customary, non-committal grunt.

"Easy now. Watch the mud," Pops called as Grant slowly pressed the gas. The metallic click of the chain feeding itself between his hitch and tree timed the turning of the tires. He felt the truck pull and pressed the accelerator harder.

The branches gave several hisses as they dragged across the gravel. Soon enough, Grant had eased the tree away from the others that blocked their escape. Hopping out of the truck, he pulled on his gloves and helped his grandfather guide it off the driveway.

"One down. One to go," he brushed the dirt from his gloves.

"That's assuming you ain't stuck now." Granddaddy gestured to the back tires of the Sierra swamped in mud.

Grant had to give it to his Granddaddy's old Ford F-100. This time the chain was between the trucks and it was the Sierra that was being dragged out.

Eventually, the trees were moved enough for Grant to get the truck out, but they'd lost precious time. Sun would be up showing off things that might not want to be seen all too soon.

"Grant," Granddaddy halted his path back in the house to hurry Kaitlyn along. "You mind your business out there. Keep your wits about you. Any man with enough hurt to lock up his own daughter for not wanting a life it sounds like he dictated to her wouldn't think a thing of doing even worse to you."

"I'll be fine, Pops. I'll get her to the ranch and we'll go from there. 'Sides, her old man don't sound hurt to me. He sounds meaner than a striped snake in a handling-church. I ain't having her around that anymore."

"I hear ya, son, but listen to your Pops for just a second 'fore you go off trying to outrun whatever may be coming. Angry people always want you to see how powerful they are and they'll stop at nothing to show you that. And meanness ain't nothing but hurt's most trusted pistol."

"I can't believe I'm actually a fugitive," Kaitlyn finally spoke. The silence was getting to her. How did Grant ride like this? No radio. Nothing to distract them. Just quiet.

His response was once again a grunt. The tension in the cab of his massive truck felt like concrete bricks stacked around her. The air was disappearing. She couldn't stand it anymore.

"So, do all cowboys grunt like you instead of using actual words? What do they even mean? I'm freaking out over here. I'm going to get you in trouble. If we get caught, Daddy will probably have both of us arrested. I ran into your car and now I'm making you hide me from my own stupid family. Why don't you yell at me or something? Can you do anything but grunt?"

She squeezed her eyes shut. Nice job, Kaitlyn. Your temper decides to make its triumphant return, not in front of the people who actually deserve to be on the receiving end of it, but on the one man who's willingly risking his neck for you. "Sorry," she managed dejectedly.

He held his right hand out to her palm up.

"Why are you doing that?"

"Hold my hand," he instructed calmly.

Simply because she'd just chewed him out for no good reason, she obeyed.

"Good girl. Now, you want me to pull the truck over so you can get out and do the whole bit, stomp your feet and everything, or you about done with that little fit?"

"I said I was sorry. The quiet gets to me. Makes me think too much."

"Mm-hmm, and what is it you don't want to think about so bad, peaches?"

"Why do you keep calling me peaches? I get darlin', or sweetheart, or baby, or whatever," she tried to mimic his low western drawl but only succeeded in making him chuckle. "But why peaches?"

Glancing towards her, he smirked. "You really want me to tell you why I call you peaches, *peaches*?"

"I wouldn't have asked if I didn't want to know."

"'Cause you look damned good enough to eat, and it's taking most of my thought-processes to keep from taking a bite. Might be why I'm grunting instead 'a talking. But I 'spose sometimes I do it 'cause I'm processing what you said and deciding on how to best answer. Also trying to decide if that cop car is following us or if he's just making his rounds. Might need to get off 80 and on the state roads for the time being. Soon as we get to rural routes, I figure we got it made," he supplied without missing a beat. Heat flooded her cheeks.

It took her a moment to process the comment about the cruiser. "Dammit, Daddy, I swear, one day I'm going to stop taking all your shit," she spat to the air around her. Spinning in her seat but trying to remain hidden she narrowed her eyes to make out the number on the car. "Can you see the black numbers on the side? Maybe I can tell who it is."

"Not unless you want me to let him get closer."

"No. Don't do that, but also don't speed. Don't give him any reason to pull you over. Are your tags current? Your mirrors aren't cracked, are they?"

"See, this is why I grunt. Keeps you from flipping your lid. Somebody needs to simmer you down, sugar. Give you somewhere

64

to put all that crazy. Take it easy. I ain't gon' let anything happen to you. And weren't you chastising me about my filthy mouth a few hours ago?"

"New-Kaitlyn didn't cuss." Never before, even after the day and night she'd endured thus far, had she ever wanted the ability to vacuum words she'd just spoken back into her mouth. Clamping her teeth together she willed Grant not to have heard her. For once in her life, couldn't someone else have a hard time hearing?

"New-Kaitlyn?"

Well, so much for that hope.

"I take it you think there was something wrong with Old-Kaitlyn?"

Perceptive cowboy, wasn't he? "Never mind." She slunk further down in her seat in an effort to disappear both from the cruiser that was coming up on Grant's side and from Grant himself.

To her dismay, he slowed the truck.

"What are you doing? He's going to be able to see in here."

"Talk."

"What?"

The cruiser gained ground. Kaitlyn's heart leapt to her throat and beat out some kind of tribal cannibalistic ritual dance before a feast. "Please, just drive faster."

"Fine." He sped up. "But we're gonna talk. You got all huffy about me being quiet, so talk. You leapt in my arms when we were in the shelter. I undressed you, and sugar, forgive me for being frank, but you climbed up on me while we were kissing like you wanted me to answer all them questions your body was asking of mine. I'm taking you home and we're gon' see where this goes because I ain't gonna sit here any longer pretending we ain't got something going on. You know we do. No matter how fast it's been. And I tell you something else, this crazy thing we have going on is damned good, and I intend to keep it that way and see where else this road's gonna take us. I told you I shoot straight. Never done it any other way. But I expect the same from you. Now, tell me what the hell all this is about New-Kaitlyn and Old-Kaitlyn and anything else I need to know about you."

Abject panic throbbed in her chest. Her hands went numb. She couldn't tell him. He'd never understand any of it. She didn't possess the courage to explain how incredibly weak she was. How she'd changed most everything about herself to make her parents happy. She couldn't tell him about Keith because if she stated what had happened to her twin brother out loud that would make it even more real. For that one moment in time, she desperately needed it not to be real.

She needed her brother to be out there somewhere, rooting for her even if she couldn't see or touch him, even if she would never hear his voice again.

"Kaitlyn?" Grant's voice took on a tender tone much different from the one he'd had a moment before when he was explaining to her how he thought this was going to work.

Before she could open her mouth to supply him half-answers enough to keep him driving, blinding blue lights pulsed in the rearview mirror.

Chapter 10

"Shit," Grant growled out in far more syllables than was probably necessary.

"Oh, my God. Grant, I'm so sorry. I'll get you out of this. Let him arrest me. If he cuffs you, just don't say anything. I'll talk to Daddy. I'm just so sorry."

"Would you hush up a minute, sweetness? I said I wasn't gonna let anything happen to you. I don't go back on my word."

"Wait." Kaitlyn spun and scooted up on her knees to lean closer to the back windshield. Grant resisted the urge to grab a handful of her sweet little ass, both because he'd wanted it back in his hands ever since their little impromptu grind session had been so rudely interrupted and to jerk her back into her seat. "That's Josh!" she declared like this was somehow great news.

"Josh is in uniform so I'm gonna go ahead and assume he's still a cop. Did you forget cops are bad in this particular situation we've got going on? There's a blanket in the backseat. Duck down and get under it. I can talk my way outta this."

"Yeah, because hiding from the cops *always* works." She rolled her eyes. "Sorry, cowboy, this time I'm saving both of our asses. Roll your window down."

"Who is this guy, Kaitlyn?"

"He was my brother's best friend."

"Sir, are you aware a vehicle matching this description was involved in an accident outside the country club this afternoon?" Josh spoke before he stepped fully into view, and he knew far more than Grant would've guessed.

"Josh," Kaitlyn leaned across Grant's lap. "Please, for me, just don't tell him you saw us."

"Kit-kat? Are you okay?"

"I'm fine. I couldn't marry Seth. I just couldn't. For me, please. For Keith, just don't tell daddy you saw us. I ... need to get away from here. Please. I can't do this anymore."

"Who is this guy? Does your dad know him?" Josh thrust his finger in Grant's face.

Grant promptly moved his arm.

Fury flared in the cop's eyes. "Kaitlyn, get out of the truck."

"She ain't going anywhere with you," Grant countered.

"Josh, please. I am better than I've been in years. If you take me in, Daddy will get his way. Seth will get his way. Keith wouldn't have turned me in. He would've helped me get away. You know he would've. Please help me. You'd be my hero." She played the bastard like a fiddle. Grant hid his grin.

He noted Josh's expression falter. Consideration eased the tense set of his shoulders and his right hand moved away from his holster.

"So, you are running away then?"

"I don't know. Maybe. Seth is impossible and you know it. Daddy's no better. I gave up everything when ... well when I had to come back from New York. Just this once let me have this."

"Where is he taking you?"

"I'm not going to tell you that because I don't want you to get into trouble if this all blows up in my face, but I promise it's better than here. Anywhere is better than going back to that mausoleum I've been living in."

Well, damn. Girl was vehement when she wanted something. Clearly what she wanted was to go with him. Still couldn't quite figure out who Keith was or what she was talking about with the mausoleum.

"Sophie knows I'm okay and that I'm running away for a little while," Kaitlyn continued to plead.

"She does? Was she okay with it?"

"It was her idea. I swear, Josh. Call her, or go by her house. She'd like that."

"She would?"

Grant's brow furrowed. He was exhausted and it took him a minute to understand that Josh had a thing for Kaitlyn's sister. Well now, wasn't that useful information?

"Yes. And the two of you can help me. Call my cell phone when Daddy calms down and makes Seth drop the charges against me. It would mean so much to me."

"You're sure you're safe? He isn't taking you against your will? I'll keep you safe, Kit-kat. Always. You know that. I could rescue you."

Scratch that. Maybe it was Kaitlyn Josh had a thing for. Grant huffed out his indignation at the very idea. Jealousy slithered over his skin and took up residence in his muscles. "If you think for one blasted minute that I'm gonna let her go anywhere near you ..."

Kaitlyn's hand landed softly on his chest. It distracted him from his fury. Hell, the girl's smile would distract the devil himself. "It's okay. He has to check. Don't you think if I didn't want to be right where I'm sitting I would be clawing and scratching and screaming to get away?"

"Few years ago I'd agree with you, but I don't know about now. You lost your fight when Keith died."

Kaitlyn's eyes closed as if they could dam back the words Josh had just spoken.

After an audible breath she blinked and stared Josh down. "My fight is back. I'm right where I want to be. I just need to get out of Lincoln. Please. I'm begging you."

"All right, fine," Josh sighed. "But listen to me. Your dad lost his shit when we found your car. He scraped your front fender himself and we got a tiny bit of the metal off this guy's truck hitch. He drove out to the lab and paced outside for hours while they ran it under his orders. Made them push every other case they were working on aside. He was like a man possessed. He loves you, but you know how he gets. So, everyone is out looking for a 2017 GMC Sierra 2500 with a custom Curt hitch. Nice truck, by the way," he offered Grant.

Grant gave him a single nod. He didn't like this guy, and he wanted him far, far away from Kaitlyn. But he wasn't above using the idiot either. "So, how the hell do I get her away from here? I stuck to the interstate because I figured there was storm damage on the backroads."

"Yeah, there is. It stayed away from the main streets in Lincoln. I called in when I pulled you over. I had to. It's the rules."

"I ain't ever been big on rules," Grant explained.

"Yeah, you have that look about you. I'll tell him it wasn't your truck and spin something about seeing another truck matching the description heading the other way. That'll buy you a little time. I don't know how far you're going, but if you're staying west, 1ˢᵗ Street is clear. Maybe take it to Rosa Parks and cut across 77. The interstate isn't a good place to be."

"Nice try, but I ain't telling you how far we're going or if we're staying west."

"Grant," Kaitlyn huffed. "He's helping us."

Grant offered her another grunt.

"You know, I could take both of you in now. I'm not sure you can take care of her."

"I much prefer to prove my intentions than to argue about them. Much as I might agree that she needs someone lookin' after her, I think every single shitlicker in her life, yourself included, needs to realize that she ain't a little girl anymore. She's more than capable of seeing about herself and doing whatever the hell she wants to do. Now, I'd be much obliged if you'd go get back in your car so we can leave. We got places to be. Places you ain't."

"Kit-kat, are you sure about him? I got a bad feeling. Does he know you can't hear well?"

"I'm sure, Josh. More sure now than I was five minutes ago. I'm fine. I'll come back when Daddy calms down."

Grant wondered what he'd said that had elicited her claim of trust, and what the hell was all that about her hearing?

"Just be safe, Kit-kat. Call me if you need me. I'll come anywhere to rescue you."

"I know you would, but I'm going to be okay."

"You could've been nice to him. He doesn't even know you," Kaitlyn smarted. Irritation kept her on edge. Stupid, stubborn cowboy could've ruined everything being a jackass. Seth desperately wanted to be someone's hero. He had since he was a little boy. With a deep breath, she reminded herself that the stubborn cowboy was rescuing her.

"You aware he's got a thang for you? I just told you we got something going on. I don't share."

"He has a *thing* for my sister. He always has, just like he's always looked out for me. I told you he was my brother's best friend. You didn't have to be a jerk."

"So, Keith was your brother."

"Yes."

"I'm sorry, sweetheart."

"You're sorry he was my brother?"

"God, no. I'm sorry for whatever happened that made it so we keep having to use the word *was* instead of is."

The sadness Kaitlyn had fought so hard to keep at bay nipped at her heels. She wasn't going to be able to escape it much longer, not if they kept talking about Keith. "You should get off the interstate like Josh told you. He wouldn't lie to me."

She noted a single nod from Grant in the passing flashes of car lights. It was distinctly odd to have driven away from downed trees, roofs ripped from their structures, destruction on every side and to now be on a road that appeared never to have seen the tornado. Just a few miles the other way lay havoc and ruin. Grant kept the truck moving quickly the opposite direction.

70

"That's gonna add another hour to our trip, but it's fine. I got two sisters myself. Got two brothers, too. Most of the time growing up we'd fuss, and fight, and try to get each other in trouble. But let me tell you something, anybody else ever did anything to any one of 'em, I'd clobber 'em good. And if you messed with my baby sisters, God himself couldn't save you. I know your brother loved you like that, too. It's an automatic thing."

No. No, they were not going to have this conversation. Swallowing down the pain for what had to have been the thousandth time in the last few years, she nodded. "He did."

Seeming to sense that she couldn't bear to talk about Keith anymore, Grant squeezed her hand. He'd placed it in his own as soon as he'd started driving again. "You'll get to meet all of 'em when we get to the ranch. We all run it together."

Kaitlyn had been aware her entire life that just outside of Lincoln, thirty miles west, just beyond the borders of the life she'd been instructed to live, there was a great deal of corn and a great deal of cattle. It just hadn't been part of her existence. "I don't know anything about cows or ranches or anything. You don't all live in the same house, do you?"

That elicited another one of those chuckles that she swore she would remember for as long as she lived. It soothed her. She wished she could have the chance to hear him talk and laugh with both ears. The sounds pervaded the marrow of her bones. She longed to lay in his lap and just listen to him talk.

"Hell no, sugar. It's a big ranch. Bigger than I figure you can imagine 'til you see it. You could get lost out there, and if we ain't got cattle out in a nearby pasture we wouldn't find you for days. I moved out into the house on the land that's mine when I was seventeen."

"You figure if you keep talking to me about your life I'll eventually tell you about mine?" Kaitlyn knew what he was up to. Her temptation to do just what he wanted grew with every word he spoke. Why did he have to be so easy to talk to?

"Figured that was preferable to me demanding you talk. I'll get demanding later, after we get to know each other a little better."

Heat fluttered in her abdomen. Her nipples tightened against the slight bra she was wearing. The UN t-shirt she'd put back on was tight against her and did nothing to conceal her cleavage. Why did the very idea of him making demands sound so utterly appealing?

"Cold, peaches?" He turned up the heat in the truck, but the cocky smirk on his face and arrogance in his tone had her crossing her arms

_ chest. She didn't require any more heat. There was enough _ charge the sun currently residing in her cheeks. And he knew it.

"You just notice everything, don't you?"

"See, that's another reason I call you peaches. When I say something that makes you blush you turn that cute shade of pink and orange and all of them freckles glow. Makes me damned hungry."

"Would you shut up and just tell me why you moved out when you were seventeen or whatever you were talking about?"

"Well, I can't really shut up and tell you why I moved out now, can I? And I hadn't finished answering your first question."

"Which question was that?" The way he kept her constantly off balance juxtaposed with the calm steady feeling she felt when she was holding his hand made no sense. What was he doing to her? No one had ever had this effect.

"You asked me if I noticed everything, and the answer to that is if it's about you, hell yeah, I do. Never doubt for a moment, sweetness, that I intend to learn every single thing there is to know about you. What makes you smile, what makes you laugh, and most importantly what makes you moan. This whole manure pile with your daddy and your ex might keep me distracted for a minute, but soon as I know you're safe, we're gon' spend a whole lot of time getting to know each other."

"I don't suppose after what happened on your grandfather's couch I could really pretend I'm not interested in all of that."

Another grunt preceded him easing his hand out of hers so he could squeeze her thigh. *Higher. More.* She shook herself again. Now was not the time to let him distract her so thoroughly. Apparently, she was going to get to stay with him for the next few days. He could distract her all he wanted then.

"You can suppose anything you want, sugar. I never mind working hard for what I want. You can give chase. I'll sure as hell catch ya."

Refusing to give him any other indication besides her nipples—which were practically standing at attention and saluting him—that he was affecting her, she tried to remember what they'd been discussing. Anything but Keith's death was fine by her. "So, you were saying you moved out when you were seventeen."

"We still playing that game? All right, I'll allow it for a little while. Mom and Dad's rule was you could move out of their house when you either had a degree or were running your own herds. I sure as hell wasn't getting a degree. Got caught with Macey Davidson in my bedroom. Got mad and mouthed off to my old man. My daddy's 'bout as even-keeled as any man could possibly be, but you don't get mouthy with him. After a week of him working my ass harder than I'd ever worked, I decided I didn't need him and Mama nosing in my business no more. I figured I was smarter than Mama and Daddy combined. Hell, I figured I was smarter than Jesus Christ himself.

"Hellbent on moving out, I told Daddy I wanted some of my money out of the family ranch business trust. He let me go on thinking I was a genius and buying cheap stock in the fall which is 'bout the dumbest-ass thing any rancher living in Nebraska could possibly do."

"Why?" Kaitlyn was genuinely fascinated. Deciding to contemplate why she was interested in cattle all of a sudden much later, she tried to guess what the explanation might be.

He turned to stare at her. His brow furrowed. "You really want to know that?"

"Yes. I like learning things. I was stuck at UN getting a law degree I didn't want, bored out of my mind. This is interesting."

Seeming pleased at that, he gave her another one of those panty-melting half grins. "Well, you gotta figure out how to feed 'em all winter. There ain't no grass to eat, and Dad and Luke, that's my big brother, owned all the hay from the ranch since they'd worked the hay all summer. Meaning I had to buy hay and feed on top of what I'd spent on the stock. For about a week living in my own house, I thought I had it made. That was the week before the first snow. When I ran outta money, Dad saved my sorry ass. Shame's a real good teacher. Take it from me. He supplied the feed and the hay, but I had to do all the work. Also had to keep up the house I'd taken possession of. The one that had no furniture. Turns out a sleeping bag ain't all that great for long term usage. But I 'spose I learned my lesson. Mama finally took pity on me and fed me meals again."

"Macey Davidson must've been some girl." Kaitlyn couldn't believe she was giggling. Another layer of the shield she'd erected around herself the day Keith died fell away as they drove further out of Lincoln. Teasing him felt so good. Almost as good as flirting with him had. But nothing felt as good as being in his arms. She willed the miles to go by quickly.

His warm laughter filled the cab of the truck. "She's married to Trenton Weber now. They got like five kids of their own. I swear to you, I have no idea what it was about getting caught with her that drove me to pure idiocy. I can't hardly stand to be around her when I see her and Trent in town. God, she bitches 'bout everything. Women are nothing but trouble."

Chapter 11

Having no clue as to why he just kept right on talking other than that smile that brought out that sweet little dimple in her left cheek when she looked at him, Grant sighed. "Like I said, I learned my lesson. Had to drop outta school few months 'fore graduation because I refused to admit I couldn't do it all and ask if I could move back in with mom and dad. They would'a let me, but I'm sure you've noticed I'm kinda stubborn."

"I might've noticed that," Kaitlyn assured him with another one of those dimpled grins. "I can't believe your parents let you drop out of high school." She continually spun her curls around her index finger over and over. Grant changed his mind on it being a nervous habit. Maybe she also did it when she was thinking.

He shrugged. Dropping out wasn't something he was proud of. He still couldn't figure why he'd up and admitted that to her. He hadn't even thought about it in years. "Ranching's probably easier with some business learnin', but it can be done without it. Camdens have been ranching since before the Civil War, so it wasn't like I didn't have people who could tell me what to do if I didn't know. And I did know. I'd been on horseback since I was weaned. I'd just gotten impatient to get out of the house. Deep down I knew I was setting myself up for heartbreak. Ranching's a crap-shoot, even with the odds in your favor. But most important rule of thumb is to be patient, and work hard, and let things work out. Never take nothing for granted 'cause it might not be there tomorrow."

"At least you got to do what you wanted."

And once again Miss Kaitlyn spoke volumes in just a few words. There was still so much he wanted to ask, but she'd clearly been burned and clammed up every time he touched on something raw. But he wasn't going to let her off the hook either. He considered his words. She didn't want to talk about the past. That was more than obvious. Didn't take a genius to figure that the past held all of her pain. Besides, he was much more interested in her present and in their future.

"And what do you want, Katy Belle?"

"Ka-ty Belle?" She sounded appalled.

"I'm trying out a few different things. Josh gets to call you Kit-kat. I want to give you a name, too."

"Everyone who's known me since I was four calls me Kit-kat. Keith and I were Heath and Kit-Kat to most everyone. Like the candy bars. Get it?" She rolled her eyes.

"While I agree you do taste like candy, other than that, I don't get it."

"Keith was my twin. Sophie is two years older than us. She couldn't quite pronounce our names when we were born. Her K's sounded like H's. So Keith was Heath and she only managed Hat-Hat out of my name. A few years later we had our first Halloween candy. There are pictures of me covered in chocolate because, well, I love all things chocolate and I always have. I ate it all as soon as I got it.

"Even when he was four Keith was perfect, so he saved all of his candy and never ate more than one piece a day. Heath bars were his favorite because my dad told him stories about how they used to be in soldier's ration kits in World War II, so he saved those for very last. I guess it just stuck. It even makes sense if you think about it. He was tough and hard to break. I was fragile, already mostly broken."

Grant swore right then and there if he ever got the chance to meet her shit-stick of a father he'd put his fist through the asshole's face. What the hell kind of man let his daughter go on believing she was fragile?

"That's a bunch of bullshit right there," he huffed. "You ain't fragile, and you sure as hell aren't weak. Takes a whole lot of strength to walk out on some ass-kisser just before you're supposed to walk down the aisle. Takes a hell of a lot of guts to run away with some dimwitted cowboy you barely know, too. And just thinking about you keying that shit wagon's car makes me want to figure out how to draw your little hellcat side out in the open 'cause it sure is right there under the surface. Has to take a heap ton of guts to face up to losing your brother and not let it end you. I stand by what I said, you're probably the bravest person I know. So, tell me this, what is your favorite chocolate bar, Katy-Belle? 'Cause it sure as hell ain't a Kit-Kat."

She stared at him like he'd just sprouted an additional head or had suggested they turn around and head back to Lincoln. Silence extended between them. Grant couldn't quite figure what was going on in her head.

"You're the only person who has ever asked me that. Everyone always just gets me Kit-Kats."

"I told you. When it comes to you, I pay attention."

"I don't want to pick just one. Sometimes I like Butterfingers. Sometimes I'm craving 3 Musketeers. And if I'm really PMS-ing, I dunk Reese's cups in peanut butter. Now that I think about it, can we just pretend I didn't admit that out loud?"

Chuckling, Grant shook his head. He wished he could snap his fingers and get past this ridiculous introductory stage. They had enough heat and enough lust between them to go on and get the awkward shit out of the way. She had no reason to be embarrassed with him. "Because you figure I'm dumb enough to think you're the one magic female on the planet that don't PMS? I still got that old knapsack I used to sleep on when I first moved into my house. I can take it out to the barn if it gets too bad."

"Very funny, but you're not dumb, Grant. I just can't seem to keep from saying whatever pops in my head when we're talking. The whole thing is insane. I'm crazy attracted to you, but I still haven't officially ended it with Seth. I'm going to stay at your house. We haven't even been on a date yet. Now, I'm telling you about PMS, but as long as I'm going to keep talking, you might as well know, if you keep me supplied in Reese's you probably won't need your knapsack."

"Good to know."

"It's just strange how we talk like we're going to date seriously."

"Some reason we ain't?" He didn't like her thinking like that, not at all.

"We just met."

"Have I done something that's a deal breaker or something?"

"No. You've been completely amazing. Stubborn, but amazing. You might get me out to wherever we're going and decide you don't like me. I'm not much of a cowgirl."

"That ain't how the Camdens work." Well, shit. Clearly, she wasn't the only one who said stuff they'd intended to keep to themselves for a little while longer at least.

"How do the Camdens work, then?"

Now was definitely not the time to go off announcing that the Camden men—and women, according to his sister Holly—met their one and only and knew it from the moment they laid eyes on them.

"I don't want nothing to do with a cowgirl so you can forget about that right now." Mildly impressed with his ability to dodge, he waited to see if she'd let it go.

Her bottom lip slipped between her teeth as her brow furrowed in debate. He held his breath and nudged the accelerator a little harder, desperate to get her to the ranch and to escape this particular line of questioning.

"I take it the girl who cheated on you, the one who got married yesterday, is a cowgirl."

Relief raced through his veins. "Don't matter what she is or was. Someone else has all of my attention and I don't think that's gonna change."

"How are you so sure about me? Assuming I'm who you're talking about. Otherwise I'm extremely self-centered."

"You're sure as hell who I'm talking about and I know 'cause I know. I live by my gut. Always have. Always will. Gut's never steered me wrong."

"What about your cheater?"

"Yeah, well, I was listening to another part of my anatomy with her. My gut didn't like her from the start. Probably why I didn't really let it sting too bad when I found out somebody else was warming her sheets. Same problem with Macey, I expect."

"I'm oddly jealous and a little put off that the other part of your anatomy isn't as enthralled with me."

"Oh, trust me, sugar, that part likes you real good. Believe you felt that when we were on the couch. I'm happy to show you again anytime, though. You just say the word."

"And what word should I say, cowboy?"

"'Saddle up' works just fine. 'Take me. Make me wet. I want you. I need you.' Let's see here, oh, how 'bout 'fuck me so hard I can't walk, Grant'. That's 'probly my favorite."

God, he loved making her blush. Streaks of heat painted her face and neck, settling in seductive roses in her cheeks. Those adorable little freckles that played peek-a-boo most of the time made an irresistible showing.

Every fiber of his being needed to see her naked in his bed. Exposed all for him. He gripped the steering wheel tighter, lest he pull the truck over, the police be damned. He'd show her just how enthralled he was with every part of her. She had nothing to worry about. He'd never wanted anything the way he wanted her.

He longed to show her just how wild and dirty good girls could be when they were with a man who knew how to guide them, knew how to strip away any pretenses that made them believe they didn't deserve the pleasure he could give.

Those baby blue eyes narrowed. Her cheeks were still ablaze. "Think I'm going to go back to the way the Camdens work for that comment."

"Get used to hearing all of that, peaches. Plan to make you say it quite often. And how 'bout we go tit-for-tit on the Camden thing. I'll tell you what you want to know when you tell me something I want to know."

"I believe it's tit-for-tat." She giggled.

"Yeah, but I like tits way better than tats, so I like it my way."

"Very funny."

"I thought so."

"I told you about why people call me Kit-Kat so you tell me the Camden thing," she tried negotiating.

"Nah, see, that ain't how tit for tit works. We didn't make the deal 'til after you told me about you being as sweet as a candy bar so it don't count."

"How about if you tell me how the Camdens work, I'll let you play with my tits."

"Tempting as sin, sweetness, but I figure you'll let me play with 'em anyway."

"And how do you figure that?"

"'Cause, baby, I seen the way you lit up in my arms, remember? And I know how to give you what you're needin'. I'd dare say you ain't been with a man who can show you and teach you what you're really wantin'."

"But you're sure you know what I want." Her scoff irritated him, but not half as much as her eye roll. Redhead through and through. Oh, he'd show her. Come hell or high water or whatever might be headed their way, he'd prove himself right on her account.

"Try me," he challenged.

"Tell me how the Camdens work."

"Tell me what happened to your brother."

"No."

"Then no."

"My God, you're stubborn."

"Right back 'atcha, peaches."

Hesitant sunlight danced just behind a windmill in a postcard scene. Kaitlyn started to snap a picture with her phone, but was certain Grant was accustomed to seeing sunrises like this and would think she was silly.

She'd never been so far west. Before that moment, she'd been certain sunrises over the skyline of New York City were the most beautiful thing she'd ever witnessed. She'd loved the energy of the city, but this was entirely different. Contentment pervaded the prairies, turning them from indigo to a dusty orange. As if the land had been awaiting the sunrise after the storm and was finally assured it was on its way to ease the turbulence of the day before. When it made its way into the cab of the truck, she saw Grant ease back in his seat. An involuntary smile formed on his features.

His ease calmed her frayed nerves. Her entire body responded to his. Before she allowed herself to think thoughts about him being her sun, or perhaps the moon to her ocean, she called herself stupid and turned her cell phone off instead of snapping a picture. She had no reason to believe that her father wouldn't call in favors to have her tracked. She'd check to see if her sister had called her later.

They had to be almost to Wyoming. Maybe. Geography wasn't her best subject, but she felt like they'd been driving for hours.

Popping the crick out of her neck, she watched for other hallmarks of ranch land, anxious for reassurances that they were far away from Lincoln and everything the city held. His ranch had to be close. All markers of city life felt foreign to this untouched landscape. An entire lifetime away, she wished. The last small town they'd passed had been at least twenty miles back.

"Are we almost there?" Her curiosity was getting to her and he'd gone quiet again, back to communicating in grunts, after her refusal to tell him what had happened to Keith. Maybe one day she could find the words to explain to him that talking about Keith's death made it real and she simply couldn't allow it to be real again until life settled down.

"Anxious, sugar?"

"Kind of."

That earned her a genuine grin. She caught herself staring at his lips again. They were flawless. She'd been reading lips since she was a toddler. Everyone's were a little different. Some thin and almost non-existent, others full and lush. His were the perfect shape, masculine and full. Another hungry rush surged in her belly. Thoughts of kissing him still made her weak with need. The remnants of guilt over not yet officially talking to Seth released her with every mile Grant put between them. Seth was the asshole who was pressing charges against her for his car. Grant was right. He'd deserved much worse.

"We got a few miles yet 'til we're in Pleasant Glen. Ranch's 'bout five miles down a dirt road off the other end of Main Street. We'll cross the tracks in another mile or two."

"I've never seen so much land. It's beautiful out here."

When he grunted his agreement, she giggled.

"What are you laughing at?" he teased.

"I'm learning to distinguish your grunts. Not sure if I'm speaking cowboy-language or just Grant-language, but I'm proud of myself."

"You should be. And you've been speaking my language ever since you ate my hitch with the front end of your car. I don't want you learnin' any other cowboy's speakin'."

"Possessive and stubborn. Interesting."

"Interesting good or interesting bad?"

"I'm not sure yet, and for a girl who's had her whole ridiculous life planned out for her from the moment she was born, I can't tell you how freaking exciting that is."

There. He wanted honest, wanted her to tell him something she'd never tell anyone else. Well, that was more honest than she'd been in years, with anyone including herself.

"You still not gonna to tell me about your brother, are you?"

"You going to tell me how the Camdens work?"

This time there was a grunt of consideration. "Maybe if I let out a little rope while I ride I'll catch a filly."

"I don't know what that is."

"A filly's a female horse, sugar. First thing we're gonna do when we get there is give you ranching lessons."

"So, I'm a horse?"

"I don't know. Gotta see how you ride, first."

"Do you ever think about anything but sex?"

"Not when you're sitting two feet away from me smelling like strawberry candy and looking even sweeter. I'm strung tight, sugar."

Still unable to believe that he would readily admit whatever he was thinking, Kaitlyn was certain her cheeks were going to be permanently stained red. "It's my lotion," she babbled to try and cover her embarrassment at his admission. "I wear a different flavor every day. Seth hated the strawberry scent. Probably why I wore it yesterday."

"Interesting."

"Interesting good or interesting bad?"

"Both. Good, in that you clearly couldn't stand him and looked for most any way you could to annoy him. That makes me happier than

81

a bull in a field full a' heifers in heat. Also means you probably won't lose much sleep over him, and he sure as hell don't deserve you suffering on his account. Also good, 'cause I don't much like other men thinking they have some kind of claim on my girl and it remains to be seen how much of a pecker-sore Seth's gonna be. Bad in that somebody or something convinced you to go on with the engagement, and I don't like whatever or whoever did that at all. I'd say it's 'bout six in one half dozen in the other."

Kaitlyn found herself giggling again. "You have a very colorful vocabulary, cowboy."

Another grunt.

"And I like the way you sound when you talk." Okay, Kaitlyn not a normal thing to say. People who hear properly do not say things like that. She needed to get the hell out of his truck or to locate some kind of tape to stick over her own mouth. "So, I'm your girl already?" There, surely that would cover up her bizarre assessment of the tone of his voice.

"If you wanna be. I don't mind courtin' you either, though."

"Courting me? Apparently, your truck is some kind of time machine, which makes hiding out from the cops way easier."

"If you don't hush your sassy mouth, I won't be able to say welcome to the Glen 'cause we'll be out of it in about another two shakes, seeing as it's gotta be the smallest town in the great state of Nebraska."

Kaitlyn turned to study the shops they were passing. Railroad tracks ran along the left side of the truck. She noted trees down along the road. The storm had tracked through this town as well.

The church on her right was larger than the grocery store nearby, but didn't appear to be able to hold more than 200 people. One of the large windows of the grocery held a poster of a silhouetted bull rider. 'PBR Champion Austin Camden to ride in the Western Nebraska Stampede Rodeo' was printed at the bottom of the sign. "Is Austin Camden related to you?"

"If you meet a Camden in the Glen, peaches, they're related to me. Austin's my younger brother."

There was a CVS, a feed store, and an old gas station after that, and then something called The Cut 'n Curl. If Grant had confessed that his truck was indeed a time machine she probably would've believed him. The little town didn't appear to have changed much in the last sixty years.

The weakening glow of neon lights as they sun rose alerted her to a decent sized bar on the other side of the tracks. The sign in the parking lot declared that Saddlebacks Honkytonk Bar and Grill had live music on weeknights when they could get a band. Kaitlyn's brow furrowed. The brick surrounding the sign had the Pleasant Glen United Methodist Church insignia on it. "Is it a church or a bar?"

"Oh, that, yeah, that's the bar. Church is across the street. See, the preacher belly-ached just fore they passed the plate each week 'til we all up and bought them a big enough sign to get a bible verse on. Ed Olsen, he and his wife Eliza, own Saddlebacks. Ed's so cheap he's still waiting on the bible to come out in paperback, so he up and decides he's gonna use the church's old sign to advertise for the bar since they were throwing it out. The Ladies Aid society 'bout gave birth to four bulls a piece, horns and all, when he put the original slogan for the bar on the church sign so he went back to advertising the music."

"What was the slogan?" Kaitlyn swore then and there she would love nothing more than to spend hours just listening to him talk about life in this tiny town.

"It ain't all that original. He probably stole it from some bar in Dallas or Sheridan or somewhere."

"Well, I still want to know what it was."

"Liquor in the front, poker in the rear."

"Sounds like something you would say," she laughed.

"Definitely two things I'd do, not sure if I'd say 'em or not. Depends on if you like dirty talking or not, peaches."

Before she could think of a comeback, they turned down a long dirt road. Trees were down along either side and the gravel appeared to have been scattered in several places. The buildings in town hadn't suffered any damage that she could see, but the winds here must've been bad.

"That ain't a good sign," Grant sighed.

"Have you talked to your parents? Is your family okay?"

"Pops called 'em and told 'em we were on our way. I was trying to get you out of town quick-like. If anybody had been hurt, they would'a told Pops, but I don't know how the corn or the cattle did."

She detected a low murmured sound in the distance but couldn't quite determine what it was just yet. Rocks pinged the underside of his truck muffling the sound, so Kaitlyn gave up and tried to prepare for meeting his family.

"You said you have two brothers and two sisters?" Why hadn't she asked more questions before? She was about to meet these people.

"Yep. Luke, Austin, Natalie, and baby Holly."

"How old is baby Holly?"

"Twenty-four."

"Bet she's sick and tired of being called baby, then."

"Well, you two'll surely get on just fine."

Slowing the truck, Grant turned left off of the road. Tension mounted in Kaitlyn's head. What if these people didn't like her? What the hell was she doing here? Yesterday, she was supposed to become Mrs. Seth Christenson. A repulsed shudder worked through her. Today, she was with Grant on a ranch in the middle of nowhere. A low hum sounded in her good ear. *Relax, Kaitlyn, just relax.* Panic made hearing even more difficult.

Suddenly, a tall, wrought-iron sign came into view. *Camden Ranch ~ Est. 1868,* with what she guessed was some kind of cattle brand on either side. But it was the wording underneath the sign that brought breath back to her lungs and silenced the hum in her ear. *Set your troubles down. You are home.*

"That ain't a good sign either." Defeat resonated in Grant's low drawl.

"What isn't?"

He gestured beyond the sign where a cluster of beasts stood munching on grass. Having never actually seen a cow in real life she instinctively slid closer to Grant. Were they supposed to be that massive?

"They're … very … large."

"Them? Nah, they're just over yearlings. They're Dec and Holly's. Problem is they're not behind a fence. Best get you in the house so I can go to work."

"How do you know they're Holly's?"

"That's her brand on their back ends there. We all have our own brand. Makes things easier. But I bet I got some out and about where they ain't supposed to be, too. My land's on the back side of the ranch so mine run away from the entrance when they get spooked."

Before Kaitlyn could think of more questions, they'd driven by the cows and were passing what looked like barns and a few other buildings.

84

The rapid rhythmic clicks of the emergency brake alerted her to a large farmhouse nearby. She'd been so busy taking in the sweeping plains and outbuildings she missed the house.

People spilled out the side door and down to meet Grant. A few of them had to be his brothers. They all looked similar, though he was by far the sexiest, more rugged with that intoxicating determination that resonated throughout any space where he existed.

"Let 'em love up on you for a minute then I'll take you to my house," he offered apologetically.

Attempting to swallow down her nerves proved unsuccessful. Her voice shook. "They don't even know me. Why would they love me?"

"'Cause they figure you're here to stay." He offered no further explanation before his booted feet landed in the muddy grass.

Chapter 12

"Finally," Grant's mother Jessie forced a hug on him whether he wanted her affection or not. "You scared me to death."

"I'm sorry, Mama. I couldn't call. Uh, this is Kaitlyn Sommerville. Well, she is 'til I convince her to let me call her Katy Belle."

Jessie rolled her eyes. "Well, come here, sweetheart. We'll call you Kaitlyn until you tell us otherwise, since I know my son is a smartass. Cute, but occasionally obnoxious. Now, it sounds like you've had quite a night. Come on in. I've got breakfast on the stove."

"So, she drove her car into your hitch?" Dec, Grant's brother-in-law, inquired as Kaitlyn was ushered in the house.

"Yep. Right as she was running away from her wedding. Found out her fiancé was a cheating sonuvabitch. Hitch has a scratch on it, but don't mention it to her. This'll be a hell of a story if I make this all work out right." Grant was tired of pretending away the Camden legend. He wanted to make it happen. He just hadn't quite figured out how.

"Ah yes, well, I believe it was Mr. London himself who said the most beautiful stories start with wreckage." Dec's British accent spilled heavily into his tone.

"I'll take your word for it." He didn't want to ask who Mr. London was. Dec was the genius psychologist on the ranch. Grant was perfectly happy just being a rancher. "You know you got stock out by the entrance gates?"

A solemn nod preceded Dec scrubbing his hands over his eyes. "Holly and Summer are out rounding them up. Wind took down most of our fence. I say this with all of the sympathy I can muster, grab some food and then hop in the skid steer. Austin just hooked up the auger."

"Yeah, I hear ya. You been over to my side yet? Bet I got stock *and* corn to deal with."

"We went after your stock first. Didn't want them getting in what's left of the corn. They're penned up at Luke's. Fences over there managed to stay upright for the most part, but we've got to get them back on your side soon. The hail was not kind to the corn. I'm sorry, man. Looks pretty rough over there."

Defeat sank through Grant. He swore the earth itself drew his boots deeper into the wet ground. "I figured that."

"No one's got power and we're welling it."

"No water either?"

"Supposed to be fixed tonight or tomorrow."

"Jay-sus." Grant shook his head. "I brought her out here to try and convince her to leave all her misery in Lincoln, not so she'd have to haul in buckets of water."

"Don't give up yet." Dec slapped Grant on the back. "Could be romantic. Candles, firelight, the whole deal. Women generally like that. They're all perfectly capable of taking care of themselves, but most of them rather like being cared for as well."

"'S'pose you would know, being a sex doctor and all." Grant tried to feel encouraged, but exhaustion took a mighty blow to his weary frame.

Dec laughed. "Glad my work prior to becoming a rancher can help a brother in need."

"In need don't even begin to cover it. I can't even think straight."

Still chuckling, Dec nodded his understanding. "She agreed to come out here with you. That's a good sign. Now, just wow her with your wild cowboy ways."

"Yeah, I'll get right to that after I clean up four dozen acres of corn."

It would take them a week or more to get the ranch restored and him another two to clean up what was left of his corn—if he was even able to salvage it at all. So much for knee high by the Fourth of July. He hoped he had enough to replant next season. His family thought he was crazy when he'd wanted to diversify half of his land. Row crops always yielded more cash, especially corn, unless Mother Nature had a bone to pick with you. But a few years back, he'd tripled his money and had managed to add quite a sum to the family business accounts several years in a row. The past two hadn't been as good, unfortunately.

"You know we'll help you with that, right?"

"Ain't your job."

"The twister didn't touch down here so it was just wind and hail damage. We lost a few early calves who got bogged, and several heifers. Luke's trying to get all of them paired with other mamas. There's plenty of work for everyone. Holly and I never would've gotten up and running as quickly as we did if you hadn't helped me learn how to do all of this. I can help you clean up downed crops," Dec informed him. He sounded mildly pissed off. "For now, you might want to rescue your newly-minted one-and-only from your mother, lest she begin planning *your* wedding."

Grant grunted at the thought, but Dec was right. His mother being overzealous could have Kaitlyn running before he got a chance to tie her down. She was already skittish.

"Uncle Grant," bellowed from Austin's five-year-old son, J.J. "You're back." He tore off across the yard with Luke's dogs, Bella and Bailey, running at his flanks.

"Hey, little man." Grant caught him in mid-flight. "You helping Daddy fix fence this morning?"

"Yeah, it's a mess. Mama and Aunt Natalie got most'a our calves. Aunt Holly's rounding up the rest'a hers. Mama says you were bringing a *girl* back to the ranch. She says you're gonna marry her. I told her you ain't getting married 'cause girls are gross, and they just boss you around all the time, and they ain't good for nothin'."

"Did your Aunt Holly hear you say that, J.J.?" Dec scrubbed J.J.'s sandy blond hair. "I'm betting she didn't since you aren't tied to a fence post."

"She did hear me, and she and Mama yelled at me and made me clean out the horse stalls all by myself, and I didn't get to go on the Gator neither. And now I have to help Memaw and Papa watch the *babies* instead a' watchin' the fight with you and Daddy and Uncle Luke on next Friday night." J.J. sounded as if his list of punishments had included hot coal walking along with tar and feathering.

"Good. Now, let that be the last time you ever say girls ain't good for nothin', you got that?" Grant demanded.

"Are you two gonna yell at me, too?" J.J.'s huff of disdain had Grant and Dec hiding their grins. "I won't say it no more, just please, tell Mama not to make me watch them babies."

"I ain't telling your Mama nothing. You talking like that, you better thank your lucky stars your daddy didn't do more than keep you from watching the fight. He might'a tanned your back side."

This had J.J. wiggling down out of Grant's arms. "Did you bring a girl home or not?" He demanded as he sank down on the grass and let Bailey lick his face.

"I did bring a girl back to the ranch with me and you, mister, better be on your best behavior when she's around."

"What's her name?"

"Kaitlyn."

"There's a girl in my class named Kaitlyn. She screamed when I tried to show her a lizard I caught on a tree by the slide. Girls scream too much."

"Well, do your Uncle Grant a favor and don't show this Kaitlyn any lizards just yet, okay? And don't show her any of them bullfrogs you keep catching from the lake either."

"She don't like lizards neither?"

"Probably not."

Popping up off the ground like a kernel of popcorn in a hot skillet, J.J. shook his head, "And you don't think girls are good for nothin'."

Before Grant could catch him, he scooted up the stairs and inside the house.

"You know, he's probably got a frog in his pocket so if you don't want him surprising Kaitlyn with it you better catch him." Dec nodded towards the house.

"That boy is his daddy through and through. Austin deserves every one of his shenanigans."

"Yeah, but Summer doesn't."

"Ain't that God's truth." Grant headed in the house to locate Kaitlyn before his nephew gave her a lesson in pond creatures.

Bliss once again danced just under the surface as Kaitlyn sank down on the living room floor of what she assumed was Grant's parent's home to play with two adorable baby girls just managing to sit up on their own on a blanket. *Twins.* In that moment, Keith felt just a little closer. The fire roaring in the fireplace warmed her soul.

"You're welcome to pick them up, but you have to pick both of them up. They don't like to be apart. Luke and I had to put them back in the same crib." Luke's wife, Indie, explained.

"I think that's probably normal. My mom used to say I was like that with my brother. I used to go everywhere with him. When you're together from the first moment, it feels strange to be apart."

"You have a twin brother?" Indie grinned. "My little sisters are twins, and they're still always together like that."

"Had. I had a twin brother."

"Oh. I'm so sorry."

Kaitlyn wished the shake of her head would rid her of the pain of her loss. "What are their names?"

"Dakota and Savana."

"Oh, like the cities?"

"Nope, like the cars. Dodge and Chevy," Indie pointed to each child in kind.

"Oh, uh, that's … interesting." Who named their kids after cars?

"For a while, we were worried she was gonna name 'em Axle and Rod." Grant's deep voice stirred inside of Kaitlyn. Her focus immediately honed in on him leaning against the door jamb. "Indie's Pleasant Glen's own resident wrench-head."

Kaitlyn started to scold Grant for calling Indie a name, but she sank her teeth into her tongue instead. She didn't even know Indie, and she had no right to get on to Grant. This wasn't her family. Grant wasn't even her boyfriend. She just couldn't shake the feeling of belonging here.

"You know it, and from what your woman was just saying, Grant Camden, it sounds like you need to offer to babysit so I can pull the hitch off of your truck 'fore you go getting yourself arrested for kidnapping."

"You told 'em about all that?" Grant reached down and managed to scoop up both of his nieces at once. All of Kaitlyn's reproductive organs performed some kind of country line dance she wasn't even aware existed before that moment.

"Your grandfather told them everything he knew, but of course he didn't know about Josh pulling us over."

"She was trying to apologize to us for being here of all things." Grant's mother came into the living room drying her hands on a towel. "I told her not to worry about a thing, and that oddly enough, this is not the first time we've harbored a fugitive for one of our boys."

"Damn, I nearly forgot Summer was on the run when they showed up here," Grant sighed.

"You're not 'posed to say that word, Uncle Grant. Mama makes Daddy put a dollar in the cussin' jar when he says it." A little boy Kaitlyn hadn't met yet appeared at her side. He turned to her with a mischievous grin. "And if he says fu …"

"Jahan James Camden, so help me, son," Grant's mother clapped her hand over his mouth. Kaitlyn couldn't help but giggle. Grant just shook his head and gave her another one of those winks that she swore lit sparklers in her stomach.

"We call him J.J. when he ain't in trouble," Grant explained.

J.J. managed to escape his grandmother's grasp. "You wanna see what's in my pocket?" He leapt back to Kaitlyn's side.

"J.J.," Grant bellowed.

"It's just a rock." True to his word, J.J. produced a decent sized rock and dropped it in Kaitlyn's palm.

90

"Thank God. I thought he was about to hand you a frog." Grant brushed a kiss on one of his niece's heads and Kaitlyn fought not to swoon.

"I used to catch frogs in the water traps at the country club when I was a little girl." She told J.J. "Maybe later you can show me where you catch them."

J.J. studied her speculatively. "You like frogs?"

"Of course," Kaitlyn rather enjoyed the shocked look in Grant's eyes.

"What about lizards?"

"I like them, too, but you have to be careful catching them. We don't want to hurt them. They're important, just like frogs."

With a broad grin, J.J. turned to Grant. "Okay, Uncle Grant, I guess you can marry her, but you have to promise to still let me drive the Gator with you and we sometimes leave her at your house."

Marry her? Certain she'd misunderstood the little guy, Kaitlyn fought to hear over the pounding of her own heart. "What did he say?"

"Nothing. He's … being ornery. I need to get over to my house. Apparently I got fence to fix and corn to get off the ground. You hungry?"

"Oh," she didn't care for the irritated gloom in Grant's tone. "I can fix us something at your house. I want to help." Desperate to wipe the frown off of Grant's face, she debated what to offer next.

"Nonsense. Breakfast is ready. Go make your plates. I'll bring you all lunch wherever you're working," Jessie commanded everyone standing in her living room. "And Grant, let your brothers and your daddy help you."

Chapter 13

Several hours later, Kaitlyn stood holding Grant's hand as they surveyed the acres and acres of land that ran along the back of the ranch. Kaitlyn didn't know much about farming or ranch work, but she was fairly certain the short stalks laying in rumpled heaps on the ground were supposed to be standing up.

"You gon' fuss if I curse for about the next ten minutes?" he finally asked.

"No. That was New-Kaitlyn remember?"

"Right."

"I'm so sorry, Grant. I didn't know you had corn and cows. I never knew so many people's lives depended on the weather." She'd already watched him help his brother Luke dig graves for a few of his cows who hadn't survived the storm.

"I got the bright idea to diversify a few years back. Thought if something ever went wrong with the stock we'd have a backup. Like I said, ranching's a crap-shoot on a good day, and row crops usually turn a nice profit."

"That's really smart," Kaitlyn offered feebly.

"Don't look too smart from where I'm standing right this moment."

"I can help you clean it up. Just tell me what to do."

"Thanks, sugar. I gotta fix the fences before I mess with this. Gotta get my stock outta Luke's pastures 'fore they eat all his cattle's grass.

Unable to hear him fully, she kept constant watch on his lips to understand him as he spoke. The wind robbed her of another opportunity to hear the low gravel of his tone, the tone she was becoming more and more addicted to hearing with every word he spoke.

"Will you look at me?" She prayed he wouldn't ask why. It made reading his lips so much easier.

"Anytime, peaches. You're my favorite thing to look at." He turned to study her. "You okay?"

"I want to help. I know I'm completely useless. I've never been on a horse or even seen a cow before today. I don't know why you all keep talking about Gators, but I'm assuming you aren't referring to alligators. I have no idea what to do with corn that won't stand up like it's supposed to, but I want to help."

To her surprise, he cupped her chin forcing her to focus on him as he narrowed his eyes. "This is your one and only warning, Katy Belle. I ever hear you say you're useless again, I'll turn you over my knee and paddle your sweet little ass 'til it's as red as your hair. You think I won't do it, try me."

Rebellion fed the fire he'd just ignited in her blood. He could not have just said what she thought he'd just said. He couldn't have because that fantasy only lived in the dark. It only existed when she was alone with her most carnal thoughts, when no one else was around and she could finally be herself. "What did you just say to me?"

His jaw tensed and his hands clamped to her hips. Acrimony flared in those gorgeous green eyes, darkening them. Before she could steady herself on the softened dirt he jerked her forward, layering her body to his. His left hand cradled the back of her head and forcibly laid her bad ear against his shoulder.

The stubble of his beard rasped at her cheek. "This is the ear you hear best in, right?"

The tender sweep of his lips along the top of her ear juxtaposed with the fierce grip he kept on her body. It melted her thoroughly. "How did you know?" Her voice vibrated to the frantic rhythm of her heart.

"I told you, when it comes to you I *fucking* pay attention." His infuriated growl shot another inexplicable jolt of pure lust up her spine. "You turn your head a little when people talk to you. You said something last night about reading the newscaster's lips when we found out your asshole of an ex was pressing charges against you. You jerked your head away from me when we were getting hot and bothered on the couch when I nibbled your right ear but you seem fine if I do your left. Then Josh asked you if I knew you couldn't hear well. If it involves you, I'm on it. But you can hear me better than them can't you? You heard me when you couldn't always tell what Pops was saying at his house without reading his lips."

"It's because your voice is so much deeper." He'd figured her out. No sense in denying that she was broken.

"Then listen to me, sweetheart, I can't explain this any way that would possibly make sense, but I'm crazy about you. And I know we just met, and life don't work out like this, and your daddy's an ornery SOB or whatever the hell else, but you make me think and feel things I ain't ever felt and I ain't even gotten you in my bed yet. But I will. Believe me baby, I'm gonna have you every possible way I can think of and then a few more. But it makes me nuts when you say shit like that about yourself. I can't stand it, and I won't have it. I don't know who the hell convinced you that you're worthless, but if I ever find them I'll drive my boot so far up their ass they'll be lickin' cow shit off the leather.

"And I'll tell you another thing, too, I'm sick of you hiding from me. Sick of you keeping stuff from me. I told you I don't see any point in lying about anything, so I'll stand right here and tell ya, you're in my every fucking thought. Not all of 'em are dirty, but I'll readily admit for the moment most of them are. Turning you over my knee, watching that gorgeous ass of yours jiggle and get nice and pink for me goes through my mind every time I lay eyes on you, so it sure as hell wouldn't tax me to do so. But if it helps you remember that you're about as far from worthless as the Earth is from the Sun then so be it. That works just as well. Now, tell me what happened to you and then tell me what I can do to make it easier for you to hear me."

Everyone had moments, markers in their life, when everything they thought they understood about the way the world worked changed. Kaitlyn had several. When she was five and finally began to understand that there wasn't anything anyone could do to help her hear. She remembered the sterile odor of the doctor's office, and the cold metal of the silver handles on the otoscopes lined up far too perfectly on the wall. The sorrow in her mother's eyes, and the way her father kept checking his watch even though there was a ticking clock on the wall so loud she could hear its impatient charting of time. And the powdery sweetness of the warm piece of bubblegum Keith had given her from his pocket, the one he'd been saving for later.

When she was eleven and had been invited to Lori Caruthers spend-the-night party. Lori was the most popular girl in her class and had never even spoken to Kaitlyn. She'd been thrilled until everyone in attendance wanted to play that stupid Telephone game. The haughty laughter that stabbed through her soul when she'd turned her good ear to the girl seated beside her only to discover that the entire game had been suggested for the purposes of proving that she was completely deaf in one ear.

When she was fourteen and cooked Beef Bourguignon with pasta from scratch, complete with a four-layered Napoleon for her and Keith's birthday. Her father had raved about the meal. His praise was a rarity. The pride she'd felt had forever altered the way she saw herself. If she just tried hard enough and did things perfectly, she would receive more praise. If she just followed her father's orders without any mistakes, she could make him happy.

And this moment when a man who she was fairly convinced she'd already fallen in love with, despite the few hours she'd known him, had discovered her hearing impairment and asked what he could do to make it easier for her all while making it perfectly clear that he wasn't going to allow her to think less of herself any more than he was going to treat her like she was feeble and weak.

Dirty thoughts about even dirtier sex spoke volumes about what he believed her capable of both wanting and giving. Thoughts of him turning her over his knee somehow strengthened her.

Another wave of rebellion coupled with the thrill that enlivened her. A heated cocktail of need surged through her. She lifted her head and narrowed her eyes. Life, once again, sprang anew inside her. "I'm pretty sure when it comes to ranching, I am worthless," she challenged.

So, his sassy little redhead wanted to see if he'd make good on his word, did she? Keeping her plastered against him with his left hand he drew his right hand back and smacked the soft globes of her ass caught up in the yoga pants. For good measure, he gave her two more quick taps, taking on the brunt of his own strength since she was against him. Then he shoved his hand down the waistband, connected with the supple skin he'd just fevered, and massaged away the sting.

His cock swelled its adamant approval as he groped handfuls of her flesh. A fact she couldn't possibly have missed any more than he could have somehow not noticed the rush of wet heat gathering just below her lush ass cheeks. Damn, but she was going to be his undoing. "Do I need to keep going, peaches, or did I make my point?"

Suddenly her hands tunneled through his hair. She sure as hell wasn't gentle. In no time at all, he found her lips with his own, inhaling her like his life depended on it. He fed on the sweet confection of her mouth, melted into her. She drew on his tongue, sucking it, hungry for him.

His right hand dove lower. God, he couldn't go on without owning her. The fact that some shit-whistle had been the last man to occupy her drove him insane. She was his and he'd damn well make sure her body knew it.

Unable to help himself, he pressed her abdomen against his erection, so fierce he hurt with it. She rocked her hot, wet pussy against him with nothing more than an insubstantial pair of pants and satin panties between him and what he wanted.

"Fucking hell," he panted before he went back in for more of her kisses. He wanted her drunk on him. She pressed harder and shuddered as his cock brushed just the right spot.

A growl Grant barely recognized as his own tore from his lungs. He adjusted his head so he could speak into her good ear. "Let me tell you something, peaches, you rock your little pussy hot and swollen against me or you rub your sweet ass against my cock like that, you're getting fucked hard. Fair warning."

"Oh, my God, yes, now!"

"I don't do nothing in half-measures, Katy. You hear me? You want to be with me like this, we're doing it my way."

"Please, Grant. I want you any way I can have you. I've never wanted anything like this. I've dreamed of being with someone that could show me ... what I've been missing out on."

What she'd been missing out on? What the hell did that mean? Before he could contemplate further, the distinctive sound of someone clearing their throat ripped him from the moment. "Shit," escaped his lips as he jerked his hand out of her pants.

Holly shook her head at him with a gotcha grin that he knew would come back to bite him somehow. "Hi, I'm Grant's little sister, Holly. I wanted to meet you, but thought maybe I would wait until my brother wasn't gagging you with his tongue." Holly giggled as she stepped closer.

Kaitlyn's fair complexion was streaked with pink heat. The sunlight caught the strands of orange and gold in her auburn hair. His little peach, indeed.

"Oh, um," Kaitlyn gnawed on her lip, not helping Grant's current efforts to quell his erection. One quick scan of the downed corn proved far more useful. "Sorry. I didn't hear you coming. I was ... well, I guess you saw. So ... you're Holly. That's right, I met your husband. He's the one that looks terrifying and is British, right?"

Grant bit his lips together as Holly doubled over laughing. So, she was a little distracted. That just meant he was doing his job. He wrapped his arm around Kaitlyn giving her a place to hide. Unable to help himself, he brushed another kiss on her overly-pink cheek.

"Holl, come on," he ordered.

"Sorry. Yes, Dec is my husband. He is British, but is not actually terrifying, despite the tats and all of his piercings and the extreme muscles. I promise. I'm not completely crazy about the gauges he had done, but I'll get over it. I just wanted to say hi and see if you wanted any help with the corn."

"Got to get the fences up first. This'll have to wait a day or two."

"I'm going to go fill up one of the fire trucks and bring them around to everyone's house. Figure that's easier than everybody hauling water in to flush toilets," Holly explained. Grant had to give it to his baby sister—she was a hell of a lot smarter than he was.

"That's a good idea. I'll get some buckets. Any idea when the water'll be back on?"

"Hope took Brock's truck into town to pick up some extra feed for your stock and said the water company trucks were down there, so hopefully soon."

"You have your own firetruck?" Kaitlyn looked genuinely fascinated.

"We burn the fields back each spring," Grant explained. "Gets rid of all of the dead grass that we don't want the cows eating. Keeps 'em healthier and fattens 'em up better. We use the fire trucks to control the burn. I'll show you how they work after we get all of this cleaned up." He didn't want her to think there was any part of life there that he wouldn't explain to her. She was capable of most anything and he was going to prove that to her.

"I'll be back up here in a little while. As soon as Dec and I finish with our fence, we'll come help you. Brock and Austin are already on their way over. Luke's still working on the cows that got bogged, but after that he'll be up here, too. It was nice to meet you, Kaitlyn. If you ever need any help dealing with his stubborn ass, call me. I'll take him down."

Grant rolled his eyes and grunted his disbelief over his baby sister doing much of anything to him as she hustled back to her truck.

"Don't grunt like that. I'm pretty sure at some point I'll need her help." Kaitlyn smirked.

"This is probably all kinds of the wrong thing to say, but it sure gives me a big head that you can hear my grunts and tell what they mean and that you can hear my voice and not everybody else's. Not that I ain't sad you have to deal with … this." He gestured to her right ear, permanently cementing himself as not only a dumbass but also a possessive shit-sack, he was certain.

To his relief, she laughed. "That was all kinds of the wrong thing to say, but I'll let it slide this time. I love how honest you are. And I'm sorry I was keeping things from you. I don't mean to. Still figuring out life moment to moment at this point. I was born deaf in my right ear. My grandmother also has hearing issues. It's hereditary nerve damage. The hearing in my left ear was perfect. The wind out here makes it a little harder for me to hear, but your voice is so low and so deep I can hear you over it as long as you're standing in front of me and not speaking into the wind. I couldn't make out everything Holly said, and I cannot believe I said out loud that her husband is terrifying looking."

This time Grant couldn't halt his chuckle. "She wasn't offended. I sure as hell wouldn't want to meet him in a dark alley if I didn't know him. No harm done, sweetness. But tell me why you said the hearing in your left ear *was* perfect."

"Damn, you really do pay attention."

"I think you'll find that you like that once I get you in bed."

"I think I like it now. No bed required."

"Talk, peaches."

"When Keith was killed, the stress of it all and dealing with my parents, the hearing in my left ear diminished. The nerves reacted poorly to the sheer amount of stress. So far, it hasn't improved, and I don't know if it will continue to deteriorate. There's no way to repair damaged nerves in your ears unless your body heals them on its own, so I could eventually be completely deaf. Sometimes that terrifies me. Most of the time it terrifies me, actually." The earnest honesty she offered him swelled his heart until he swore it was in his throat.

He drew her back into his arms and cradled her in his strength. "Bravest woman in the whole damn world."

"What's brave about being deaf?"

He held her tighter. "You have any idea how brave you have to be to admit to someone what scares the shit out of you? Like I said, you're the bravest fucking woman in this world."

Chapter 14

"All right, sugar, wrap the chain around it just like I showed you," Grant called from the seat of the tractor.

Kaitlyn had no idea what she was doing, but she tried to wrap the chain around the bent fence post just the way he'd taught her.

"Keep it steady," he guided. Keeping the chain pulled taut, she watched him slowly raise the bucket on the John Deere where the other end of the chain was attached. Accomplishment had her grinning as the post slid out of the ground.

"Good girl." He winked at her as she tossed the post in a nearby heap. This was actually kind of fun. She wondered what he would say if she asked to learn to drive the tractor.

When all of the bent posts were gone, Austin, Grant's younger brother, drove the auger into the holes with something called a skid steer and Grant set new posts. He'd shooed his brother Luke away and leveled them himself as well. Stubborn through and through.

When the sky held only faint traces of glowing orange against the indigo dusk, Grant ordered everyone home. "I'll get my stock out of your pastures first thing tomorrow morning," he told Luke, who'd returned despite Grant swearing that he could handle everything.

"I ain't in any rush. We can let mine feed over here a couple of days later on if the grass gets short. They're fine where they are."

"Still though, just let me get a little shut-eye and I'll get 'em."

"I ain't gon' argue with you. You want Indie to pull the hitch off your truck tonight?"

"Nah, not yet. If I just have to leave here, I'll take one of the old trucks. I'll put the tractor up, too. You go on home and rescue your wife from your rug-rats."

"Mama's got the girls. Indie's stringing fence over at Dec and Holly's."

"Then go rescue Mama."

"If I didn't know better, I'd say you were trying to get rid of me. You got plans tonight?" Luke harassed.

Kaitlyn grinned. She certainly hoped he had plans that included her and his bed. She'd been so busy helping Grant and thoroughly enjoying the work she'd somehow managed to forget that she was a fugitive from her own father. Seth hadn't crossed her mind in hours. The relief of that soothed her soul. Existing in a world entirely outside of Lincoln had given her a peace she'd been certain she'd never have again.

"Fuck off, man. Like I'm gonna discuss 'em with you."

Kaitlyn loved the way his entire family existed as a unit. They were a force unto themselves, which she supposed could only come from owning half of a county's worth of land and working it. They depended on each other. Even when Grant resisted help from everyone, they still showed up and did their part. This was the way a family was supposed to be.

Having no desire to think of the dysfunction that pervaded her own home, she shut those memories down. That life was wonderfully inaccessible. She wished it would stay that way.

"You two have fun. Kaitlyn, it was nice to me you, sweetheart. If you need anything while you're here, come find me or Indie and we'll set you to rights. And for all that is good on this earth, promise me you won't take any shit offa him." Luke waved as he headed back towards his truck.

Grant was still seated in the tractor, and Kaitlyn had no idea what came next. She was hungry. Dinner sounded interesting, but nothing sounded as good as being in his arms and listening to him tell her what he wanted to do with her, to her, for her, or any other dirty thing that might come to his mind.

"If I didn't know better, I'd say you think my tractor's sexy, peaches," he goaded.

Kaitlyn laughed. "I kind of, sort of think you're sexy. The tractor is just okay."

"That so? Just kind of, sort of?"

"Yes," she lied and he knew it.

"Get over here."

"Why?" She edged closer anyway, unable to resist his summons or his cocky grin.

"Hop on up." He patted his legs. "I'll teach you to drive it."

"You want me to sit on your lap on the tractor while you teach me to drive it?" That couldn't be right or safe. Her mind conjured a million things that could go wrong because she had no idea how to work a tractor.

"Can't think of a better way to teach you, and I saw you staring at it curious-like while we were pulling posts. Besides, I got a bulk feeder down on the back forty I got to clean up before I can get my stock back in here. You can help me."

"What's a bulk feeder?"

"Climb up here and I'll show you."

"I'll probably wreck your tractor," she protested.

"Katy-Belle," he warned. "I can turn you over my knee right here."

Rolling her eyes, she accepted his offered hand and let him hoist her up into his lap.

"All right, put your feet on top of my boots."

"Won't that hurt if I'm supposed to press the pedals?"

This time she received a grunt of disdain. "You ain't gon' hurt me. You couldn't if you tried."

When she placed her feet over his boots, he maneuvered so his cock was centered between her butt cheeks. She tried with all of her might not to blush but came up short. He chuckled in her good ear.

"Now, you know why I wanted to teach you like this."

"I think I showed you that I like your less civilized side."

"Once we get all the feed off the ground, I'll show you just how uncivilized I can be, sugar. All right, this here's the throttle. Press your right foot on the brake while you press your left foot to the clutch. Turn the key right there and drop the throttle just a little. It's already warm so it'll go right off."

"Okay," Kaitlyn reviewed everything he'd told her. "Brake, throttle, key, got it." She grinned when the tractor roared to life. The rhythmic whir of the motor shook her backside against him. A hungry grunt filled her ear this time.

He released the parking brake. "Can you hear me as long as I talk right here?"

She nodded, afraid to take her eyes off the machine.

"All right, ease off the clutch real slow like and steer. You got it."

The tractor lurched forward and she stomped on his foot, ramming the clutch back to the floor, bringing it to a hard stop again. "Sorry. I told you I couldn't do this."

"That's two," he informed her.

"Two what?"

"Two strikes."

"And am I out on three?"

"That ain't the kind of strike I'm talking about and you know it. Now, settle in and try it again. You're doing just fine."

On the next try, she managed to ease the tractor forward and out into the field where he directed her. She turned it too hard once, but he just grinned and caught the wheel before she dumped them on the muddy ground.

Every bump and shake of the motor hardened his cock against her. Every capable plane of his body cradled her against him in a cage of masculine protection. The vibration of the machine made her weak. She was desperate and more than distracted by the time they reached a large, overturned metal bin that had at one time been tall enough to drive a truck under. The smell of cattle feed, scattered in heaps on the ground, filled her lungs but she couldn't quite find it in herself to care.

"I swear I'm about to come in my Wranglers," he groaned.

"I'd rather you come in me." Her words were breathy and laced with desperation. Pleading utterances wrenched up from her soul. Desire burned away any of her rationale or good judgment leaving only a flash fire of need in its wake.

"I ain't got a condom out here with me, but I swear to you if I did, I'd already be so deep inside of you, you'd feel it for days to come."

"Grant, please, can't this wait until tomorrow? I don't care if it's reckless. I don't even care if it's wrong. I just need you."

"It might be reckless, sugar, but it sure as hell ain't wrong. Nothing about us is wrong."

She spun in the seat, abandoning the wheel. Working quickly, Grant shut down the motor, his mind full of nothing but her. Unable to help himself he thrust his hips, driving his denim-trapped cock against her hard and fast.

A high-pitched keening plea fell from her lips, "Please, Grant. Take me."

"Damn, I love you begging for me. Drives me wild."

"Please," she whimpered readily. Lifting up on her knees she made one hell of a presentation of her tits.

"Careful, peaches, I might take that as an invitation," he warned in a half growl.

Biting her bottom lip seductively, she whipped off the t-shirt she'd been wearing all day. Her luscious tits bounced in his face caught up in a lacy black bra. His hands slipped up from her waist to cup their heavy weight. "Sweet Jesus, you're fucking gorgeous." His cock surged against her. Too damn many clothes between them.

Before he could do away with their barriers, a distinctive gallop echoed in the distance. He studied her. Given the way she continued to grind against him, pushing him closer and closer to the edge, she couldn't hear the only horse Grant would delay this for.

"Put your shirt back on, sugar. Quick-like for me."

"What? Why?" Mutiny stormed in those blue eyes that he swore had turned to lakes of fire in that moment.

He grabbed the shirt and hoisted it back over her head. She struggled with him, doing nothing but kicking his rampant craving into overdrive. "I'd love nothin' more than for you to get scratchy and hissy in my bed in a little while, peaches, but right now, listen."

That got her attention. Watching closely, he noted everything she did to try to help herself hear what he was hearing. A quick swallow. She settled back down in his lap, easing her head out of the incessant wind, using him as a buffer. Her brow furrowed in concentration.

The thunder of hooves grew louder and suddenly she stood and hopped down off the tractor. "Is that a ...?"

Grant joined her on the ground just as his father, mounted on his jet black stallion, Busco, came into view. In other teams of horses a mare might be dominant, but on Camden Ranch, Busco called the shots. At 18 hands high no one wanted to take him on.

Another few long strides and his daddy was dismounting with an all-knowing grin. "You teaching her to drive the tractor, son?"

Making no effort to hide his eye roll from his father, Grant grunted his impatience. This at least made Kaitlyn grin. "Katy, this is my daddy, Ev. He rules the roost around here."

Ev laughed outright at that. "You believe I have any say about what any of my kids do, darlin' you'd be more wrong than right. It's nice to meet you, though. I'm sorry I wasn't up at the house when you got here. I saw this bulk feeder down when I was checking his cattle early this mornin' and I knew Grant wouldn't let tell his brothers about it 'cause he wouldn't want them to help him with it. Your mama's bringing the old Dodge up here. We'll get it cleaned up and get y'all settled in."

"I got it Dad. Don't worry about it." Irritation settled squarely between Grant's shoulder blades, an itch he just couldn't scratch. He was more than capable of handling his part of the ranch.

"I know you can do it, son, but occasionally it's nice to have a little help, and pardon me for saying so, but you two look like you were ridden hard and put up wet. I know neither of you slept last night. Your mama's got you some supper. 'Sides, it makes me feel useful." He winked at Kaitlyn.

"That's so nice of you both. Trust me, I'm of no help. I'm still not even sure what this was before it fell over," Kaitlyn beamed at Grant's daddy, only adding gall to his irritation. She was plenty helpful. Why did she keep saying shit like that?

"That's three, peaches," he whispered in her ear. She promptly turned every shade of a bright pink sunset.

"You not get around to explaining what a bulk feeder was?" His father laughed at him outright. "Can't imagine what you were doing instead."

"We keep cattle feed in these, sugar. We drive the feed trucks under 'em, load 'em up, and then take the feed out and scatter it. That's how they eat 'til the grass is full in. I can't get my stock back over here 'til this is cleaned up. If they stumble up on it, they'll be all over it. Surprised a few of 'em didn't get into it before Luke drove 'em over to his fields."

"They were all pretty shook up this morning," his father explained. "And we got to 'em quickly. Handy to have someone else lookin' out for you when you're out lookin' after your granddaddy and Miss Kaitlyn here. Nothing wrong with relying on other people."

Grant had received that particular lecture more than a few times in his life. He didn't want his family to have to look out for him. He wanted to be the one looking out for them.

Another minute passed and Grant's mother pulled up in his father's first Dodge Ram.

"So, what do we do? How do we clean it up?" Kaitlyn asked him quietly.

Scrubbing his hands over his face and willing his brain to think straight in her presence, he tried to order his night. Clean up the feed. Thank his mama for supper. Take Katy back to his house. Show her around. Fuck her senseless. No. Dammit, he had to do this right. She was different. She was innocent, relatively speaking. She wasn't used to being with demanding ranchers who'd put a lover through her paces before turning her loose. And he had no intention of letting her go, anyway.

"We'll get back on the tractor, scoop up the feed, and put it in the back of the truck. I'll tarp it tonight in case we get any more rain. Tomorrow, I'll take it out and shovel it to the cattle once I get 'em back over here. Then we'll put the rest in another one of my feeders 'til I can get this one replaced. So, hop on up and we'll get started, sweetness." He winked at her, knowing exactly what she was about to say.

"Grant Camden, I am not getting back up on that tractor and sitting in your lap with your parents watching us." The alarm in her eyes proved just as satisfying as he knew it would. He couldn't help but chuckle.

"All right, I'll let you do it yourself, just watch it. Don't turn the wheel while it's loaded or you'll flip it over."

"No! I would either wreck the tractor or wreck your father's truck or both. In fact, knowing me, I'd probably kill all of us."

Dammit. "Come here to me." Grasping her right hand, he jerked her into his arms, caging her against him and nuzzling her head until his mouth was against her good ear. "First off, you would be just fine. You can do anything. Second, I ain't gon' ask you to do something I haven't helped you learn to do first. I was teasing you. And third, claiming you'd kill everyone's gotta be worth ten strikes minimum."

She gave no verbal response, but her left hand trailed up his chest, her fingers landed on his nipple, and she twisted through his shirt rather hard.

He caught her hand with an irritated grunt. "We'll get to all that later, peaches. Damn, I like this feisty side."

"Good," she challenged with an impish look in her eyes.

Clearly having heard a little of the conversation, Grant's father shook his head. "When Grant was about twelve, I taught him to drive a stick so he could pull the hay trailer. He was doin' all right 'til Austin backed one of the Gators into my truck. That's that dent right there." He pointed to the driver's side door. "You can't hurt this truck. If you want to try and load the feed, darlin', one of us can help you. Ain't no better way to learn than by doing."

Kaitlyn jerked out of Grant's arms. "Thank you, sir, but I'm good right here. I'll just watch."

"Let's get it done," Grant commanded. He was more than ready to send his parents on their way. He'd been trying desperately to extend his fuse of patience all damn day. Every time they were alone, she offered him more of herself, gave him more honesty, and showed him what she needed to feel her own worth. In doing all of that, she set him on fire. His composure was gone, burned up in craving her. He was tired of waiting. His pulse double-timed through his veins as he climbed up in the tractor to make quick work of the feed on the ground.

Chapter 15

Caught up in watching Grant expertly maneuver the tractor like it was something he'd been born doing, Kaitlyn missed what his mother had said. She'd barely heard Grant's name over the whir of the tractor and the incessant wind.

"I'm sorry, what?" The endless debate began in her mind. When do you tell people you can't hear properly? If you tell them too soon, it makes them uncomfortable. They usually respond by reaching a decibel just under a shout making Kaitlyn want to melt in to the ground.

If you waited and told them after they'd gotten to know you, you risked hurting their feelings. For some reason, people seemed to believe if you cared about them you would have told them sooner. Of course, no one could actually define *sooner* for her, and Grant Camden was the only person who had ever figured out she was deaf before being told outright.

"I was just saying that no one works harder than Grant." His mother smiled and scooted closer to Kaitlyn, saving her from having to explain why she was struggling to hear. "I hope we all haven't completely overwhelmed you, sweetheart. We're just so thrilled to meet you."

Why? The question danced hesitantly on the tip of her tongue, but she couldn't produce the word. The sensation that she was missing out on something gnawed at her psyche. "I'm thrilled to be here. That probably sounds odd, though. You couldn't have been expecting me."

"Oh, I wouldn't say that. Maybe not expecting, but definitely hoping for you. Never know what fate has in store I guess."

"You believe in fate, Mrs. Camden?"

"I didn't when I was your age. Believe me, honey, I've been right where you're standing. When Ev first brought me to the ranch, I'd never seen so much land, and I'd surely never set eyes on a pack of heifers. But you can't live in the middle of all of this, and see life here, and not believe in fate."

"But what about when bad things happen? Do you think that's fate, too?" Kaitlyn had no idea why she desperately needed Grant's mother to answer her inquisition. "I'm sorry. That's probably a rude thing to ask." She needed some kind of explanation, but had no right to demand it from this woman who'd been nothing but kind to her.

His mother offered her a tender smile, and suddenly she drew her in to a motherly embrace, the kind Kaitlyn hadn't felt from her own mother in years. "You can ask me most anything, anytime, sweetheart. Doesn't mean I'll always have an answer, but here's what I do know: there are people who will tell you everything happens for a reason, and I think that might just be one of the cruelest things you could ever say to someone. Now, mind you, they call themselves being kind, but how you look someone in the eye and tell them that the pain they're existing in was meant to be I will never understand.

"Sometimes life is just downright mean, and there isn't any explanation that can make it different. We don't get a say. But sometimes life reaches out its hand and makes us take a step we'd never planned to take and it ends up being the very step we so desperately needed to help us heal from the pain it served up previously. The only thing we don't get to do is stand still. We have to keep taking steps and hope we somehow learn the dance. I can tell you this too, an awful lot of things in my life had to go terribly wrong for me to end up being in the right place for me, and it might be the same with you."

"Thank you for not saying bad things happen because of fate. People kept telling me that when my brother died." The words stung the back of her throat. Their weight took another vicious blow to her weary frame. This was why she hated to say it out loud.

"People don't know what to say because somewhere deep in their soul they know there are no words that can erase the pain and that is what most people want to do. Every now and then, sometimes only once in a lifetime, fate offers us someone who figures out the right things to say or the right things to do to ease the pain. Sometimes they love you enough to just go through it with you, and there's nothing better than that."

Kaitlyn had no idea how to respond. Did Grant's mother think he was willing to go through this with her? And perhaps more importantly, shouldn't she already have gotten over her brother's death? When did time heal the wound? Wasn't that a thing? Grant didn't even know what had happened yet. She'd just met him. She didn't even know how to tell him anything beyond the fact that Keith was no longer alive.

After the feed was loaded into the back of Grant's father's Dodge, Kaitlyn found herself clutching a covered pot of vegetable soup and a plate of cornbread, supplied from his mother, as she once again climbed up in Grant's truck.

It struck her as odd they'd been working in his fields most of the day but still weren't close enough to his house to have walked. The sheer amount of land soothed her. Nothing could touch her there. No one could find her. Nothing bad could happen. She could exist entirely alone with him. Nothing had ever been more appealing.

She just needed a night or two to really live before she would be forced to reconcile everything she'd done in the last twenty-four hours. The impending conversations with Seth and her father weighed on her mind, but she forced them away. The blank board of vacant despondency that was the result of every conversation she tried to have with her mother was more difficult to ignore.

"You're mighty quiet over there. You okay, peaches?" Grant spoke through a half-yawn. His sleepy drawl once again quaked in her blood. Suddenly, all she wanted was to curl up with the smoky warmth of his voice and let it absolve her. That husky gravel that rumbled from his lips was the healing balm to any problem she could ever have.

"Thank you for teaching me all of that. It was fun."

"You're one hell of a sexy ranch-hand. The pleasure was all mine." He winked at her as the last vestiges of sunlight were finally vanquished in the evening sky. "Well, it ain't much, but it's home." He pulled up beside a ranch house that sat low to the ground, tucked safely into a slight roll in the relatively flat prairie land. It was twice as long as it was wide and decks ran the length of the front and back. Substantial stone fixings secured the home on each corner and held the decks in place.

"It's perfect."

His lips formed a half-smirk that brought another flood of heat to her cheeks, though she couldn't explain what about their exchange had elicited her reaction. She cursed her bright red hair and fair complexion for showing off her every thought.

"Might want to see the inside 'fore you decide that. It's unlocked. Give me this," he lifted the food from her hands, "and scoot on in out of the wind. I'll get your bags."

Easing inside the dark house she tried to imagine what Grant's days must look like. The ranch still had no power and the moon was slightly obscured behind another layer of clouds. When she bumped into something hard she stumbled forward, but once again he was there. Dropping her bags to the floor, he caught her in his arms. She hadn't heard him come in. "I gotcha, sweetheart." Someday, she hoped she would be able to explain to him what those three words did to her, how they affected her, how much it meant to know it was somehow true.

"Sorry," she offered. "It's my hearing. Makes me a little clumsy sometimes. I get dizzy."

He brushed a kiss along her forehead. Her eyes closed in contentment as she grasped his biceps, letting the feel of his sizeable muscles steady her. "I imagine it has more to do with the fact you ain't ever been in here, that I'm kind of a slob, and that it's so dark you couldn't see your own hand in front of your face. Stay right here. Let me light some lanterns and get a fire goin'."

Begrudgingly, she pulled her hands from his arms. "Hurry," slipped from her lips without her permission.

She received another grunt, one she hadn't quite heard before. Hunger and impatience were communicated in that quick, frustrated sound. Her pulse sluiced through her veins far too quickly, as if her heart couldn't quite keep up.

Kaitlyn instinctively turned her head to hear the strike of the match and the pop and hiss of flame. It was one of her favorite sounds. When he touched the fire to the wick on several lanterns and then blew out the match, she inhaled deeply, reveling in the smell.

"What are you grinning about now, beautiful?" What the hell? Grant had no idea how her every smile threatened to bring him to his knees. God, he couldn't help himself. His body responded to her every breath. Every cell, every muscle, every hair was honed in on her like she directed the beats of his heart.

"It's my favorite smell and it used to be my favorite sound." Her grin expanded the width of her beautiful face.

"What is?" Surely she wasn't talking about him. He had to smell like cow shit, hay, cattle feed, and sweat at this point. Certainly nothing worth wanting to inhale. He had to figure out how to bathe before he could make good on his promises to her.

"The smell when you blow out a match and the sound when you light it."

"How come they're your favorite?"

"Because it means something good is about to happen. Like lighting the candles on a birthday cake or lighting candles for a romantic night." She shrugged. "Something like that."

Her body was silhouetted in the lantern light, and he swore in that moment he'd set himself on fire to have her ... forever. He'd set the whole damn world on fire for her. They could sit and watch it burn.

"How come it's not your favorite sound anymore?" He knew the answer. He just couldn't believe he could ever be this lucky.

"Because I heard your voice and," she stared down at the hardwoods like she wasn't certain they would continue to hold her upright, "now it's my favorite."

Beside her in a heartbeat, he gently tilted her head up so he could stare into those gorgeous blue eyes. "Look at me."

"I am," she barely managed the words.

"I know this is quick and makes no damned sense at all, but this means something. Do you understand what I'm saying?"

"I can hear you. I can always hear you."

"That ain't what I meant and you know it. I know you can hear me, but do you understand that this, us, together, it means something."

"I know."

"Good."

"It scares me … a little. I'm still not very brave."

"Hush." He captured her unnecessary fear and worry with his mouth. He'd starve them until they vanished from her in entirety. He wouldn't allow anything to scare her ever. He'd feed her dreams and show her that she was capable of anything she ever wanted to do. She never had to be afraid. He would never let her fall. He would never allow anything to hurt her ever again.

Her lush lips moved in rhythm with his. Her hands wound around his shoulders, clinging to him. He cradled her tighter, deepening the hot, open-mouthed invitation she extended. He drank her in.

She rocked her sweet little body against his. God, he needed more. She tasted like the sweetest sin and the most seductive angel he'd ever known. Hot breath tempered with a soft hunger filled his mouth. Craving greed surged through his veins. She was his and every fiber of his being longed to explain that to every intimate part of her thoroughly and repeatedly.

Her sexy curves melted into him. His heart thundered in his chest. She was so soft and so damned beautiful. His entire body vibrated against hers. The marrow of his bones shook with need.

She pulled away with a gasp of breath. "Grant, what's wrong? Why are you shaking?"

Incoming regret taunted him on the periphery of the all-consuming greed that had taken up residence in his cock. *Dammit, get it the fuck together, Camden. This is different. She just told you she was afraid.* His muscles flexed anxiously. His cock staged a revolt against his better judgment.

"Grant?"

"I'm sorry, sugar. Jesus, I'm trying not to rut on you like I've lost any damned sense I ever hoped to have. Just give me a minute." He tried to draw deep breaths, but only succeeded in bringing her sweet scent of strawberry seduction to his lungs. He grunted in frustration. "I ain't feelin' too fucking gentlemanly right now, and you deserve a helluvalot better than the way I want to take you."

"How do you want to take me?" She trembled against him, but he'd succeeded in building that wildfire in her eyes once again, the one he swore was going to be his undoing. Her bottom lip slipped between her teeth, and her hellcat side made an appearance when she ran her fingertips along his zipper line, taunting him. "Tell me."

He growled out his warning. "Hard, fast, rough, fuck you so hard you ache and the only thing that makes it feel better is more of me. I want to use you, which I ain't gonna do. I swear I could own you all night and still not get enough."

Her eyes closed and a choked moan escaped those perfect pink lips. Dammit all to hell and back. She was going to kill him.

"But that's exactly what I want. My whole life people have treated me like I can't do anything. Like I'm too delicate to get dirty. I can't hear so I'm already broken. Everyone has to be careful with Kaitlyn. Maybe I want it rough. Maybe I want to be fucked so hard I can't walk. Maybe I want you to show me exactly what you want. Maybe I want to be used. Maybe I just want to be taken dirty and rough and all those other things you said. You ever think of that?"

"Filthy words from such a pretty little mouth. I'm gonna make you wrap those lips around my cock and suck me dry and that will just be the beginning."

"Good."

"And I call the shots. Where I want you, how I want you, and when I want you. Whatever I say goes."

"Yes." Her vow was a half-strangled breath. Her eyes darkened in the lantern light. Her nipples were drawn so tightly they strained against her shirt, so tight she had to be in agony.

Beyond any ability to reason with himself, he gripped his cock and tugged against the denim, desperate for relief. The single stroke did nothing to help.

"I could do that for you. Just show me how."

"You telling me you never had your hand on your shithole of an ex's cock? Don't lie to me, Katy."

"I did, but it was never like this with Seth. I never ...."

"You never what?"

"I never wanted him the way I want you. No one's ever made me feel the way you make me feel. That's why I'm scared. But I used him, too, you know. It wasn't just him using me."

"Good. But I ain't finished with my warnings. There won't be one part of your gorgeous body that won't belong to me. Understand that I'll push you. I'll take what I want."

"That's what I'm asking for."

"One more thing you need to know, you remember me telling you I don't do nothing in half-measures?"

She gave him a single nod.

"I meant that. I work damned hard. I do the work of ten men and I like it that way, but I play even harder. I like sex. I like *a lot* of sex. And I know sex with you will feel so fucking good I won't be able to think about anything else. It'll be better than anything else I've ever felt. And I'll make it so good for you, baby girl, I swear to you, but know this, I'll want you morning, noon, and night and I won't back down. This might make me a possessive shitlicker, but I told you I'd never lie to you so here it is, you don't get to change your mind and walk away. I don't do too well being told no. You're mine. You understand that?"

Chapter 16

Holy mother of all of the saints. Kaitlyn had never even in her wildest dreams imagined there was a man anywhere who could make her entire body throb just from speaking. The words he said. The honesty in his graveled tone. Like he'd picked a script out of her darkest fantasies and brought them to life with the rasp of his voice.

A single brain cell attempted to reason with the rest of her body. It tried to inject panic over allowing someone else to tell her what to do, letting someone else order her around. That was how she'd spent most of her life, after all, but everything about Grant said this was different.

Besides, her reproductive organs reasoned, *this* was exactly what she wanted, and she was so tired of denying herself the very things she craved.

"I want you more than I want to draw my next breath, Katy Belle, so if any of that ain't gonna work for you, speak up now."

Another gush of wet heat soaked the crotch of her panties. She shuddered, hyperaware of every sensation he brought her. Her skin was raw with fever. She longed for his touch. "Grant?"

She got a half grunt of impatience in response. "I'm so wet it hurts. Take me. Please."

Like a wolf capturing his prey, he conquered her, bringing her down to his couch in one quick movement of muscle. "I ain't fucking you until I've at least had a shower. This ain't the kind of filthy we're gonna be tonight. But I sure as hell won't have my baby needy and wet, hurtin' for me. I'll make it feel better, sugar. I'll make everything better."

"Yes," hissed from Kaitlyn as he overwhelmed her senses. His eyes were dark pools of liquid heat, scorching her as he ravaged her mouth with a kiss that she swore sent jolts of electricity down to her pussy. His hands flew over her like he couldn't quite decide where to touch her first. She bucked against him and a predatory growl shook from his lungs.

His muscles flexed and rippled under her fingertips as he stripped the yoga pants down her legs. When he tossed them to the side, Kaitlyn tried to think only of how good his hands felt on her bare legs, but she couldn't. She spread her legs voluntarily as his fingertips teased along her inner-thighs making her weak, but her brain wouldn't get on board. "Grant ... my pants ... they're going to catch fire."

"What?" He jerked away and saw the dangerous proximity of the black cloth to the nearest lantern. "Shit." Rectifying the situation seemed to temper him. He stood and started pacing.

"No, please, just come back. Do more of that," she whimpered.

"Dammit, no. You deserve more than this, and I'm sure as hell not saying that because I think you're delicate so get that thought right on out of your head." His right hand rubbed the back of his neck like he could somehow massage patience into his head.

Mutiny stormed through her. "Why is it *you* get to decide what we do and *when* we do it?"

His eyes narrowed and a wicked half-grin formed on his features. "Believe I just told you that's how it works when you're with me, sugar. And I believe you just gave me the go ahead. No backing out now. But sweetness, you've got marks on your legs and neck from your seatbelt. And I know you got bruises on your chest. I saw 'em when you whipped your shirt off on the tractor and I nearly embarrassed myself. I'm filthy. And you're cold. Just let me do this right."

Her body seemed determined to take up his banner. She shivered involuntarily. "Ugh, believe me you were doing a hell of a job of heating me up."

"Baby doll, I'm gon' keep you nice and hot for me, and we'll get plenty dirty, but we're gon' do this right. Let me get a fire going. Let me feed you. You worked your ass off today. Then I'll figure out how to get cleaned up, take you to bed, and I ain't ever gonna let you leave. I have half a mind to go get some rope from the barn and tie you to it have my way with you over and over again."

Grant had only made the last comment to try and prove to her that he wasn't calling this off because he believed for one moment that she was weak, but the flash of excitement in her eyes and slight purse of her lips said she was intrigued.

His cock gave another hungry pulse. Clenching his jaw, he damned the mental imagery of her tied up in his bed straight to hell before he located some rope.

Fire in the fireplaces first, then they could go about setting his bed on fire. He ordered his steps to the massive, four-sided, stone fireplace that sat in the middle of his home, dividing the living room, kitchen, and dining area.

Impatience still agitating his resolve, he made quick work of stacking enough logs to heat half of Lincoln county. "I need some kindling," he commented to himself as he grabbed a lantern and searched his kitchen counters. A stack of papers shoved in the corner of his desk in the kitchen caught his eye. Grabbing them he headed back to the fireplace.

"Wait. What are those?" Kaitlyn, still wearing nothing but a t-shirt shredding any lick of determination he'd managed to summon to keep from taking her hard and fast, leapt to his side.

"Some ridiculous things the city keeps sending me."

She jerked them out of his hand.

"Katy, I'm looking to get a fire going, get you fed, and then get you to bed. Give me them."

"No. Grant, are you serious? These are certificates thanking you for being a youth football coach for the past ... five years. You cannot burn these. I didn't know you coached football."

"They needed a coach for the peewee league. I like football. I don't need awards for helping out." He held out his hand for the certificates.

"You are not burning these. Did you used to play football?"

He fought not to roll his eyes. None of this mattered. "Yeah, in school. I left Coach Chalmers high and dry when I dropped out. I always felt bad about it so when he asked me if I'd coach two of the city teams, I said sure. Give me the damn papers."

"No." She spun out of his reach.

"Katy, what'd I tell you about telling me no?"

"You are not burning these. Were you the quarterback? Keith was our high school quarterback."

"Nah," Grant sighed. "Luke was the star quarterback when he was there. My cousin Brock played receiver. He could'a gone pro if his daddy wasn't such a piece of shit. He ain't fit to shoot at when you want to clean your gun. Austin's the big time rodeo star, PBR buckle and all. I was just a running back. So, see, no big deal. Give me them papers."

"Running backs take the ball from the quarterback and run, and you also catch the ball, and you sometimes protect the quarterback. You can't play the game without them. They're very important. And coaching kids is an amazing thing to do."

"You like football?" Sweet girl was full of surprises.

"Kind of. It's a heck of a lot better than golf. It's fun to watch sometimes."

"I won't make you watch it with me." He still hadn't determined what she meant when she talked about Old-Kailyn and New-Kaitlyn, but he didn't want her doing anything that she didn't want to do.

"I don't mind. Here," she scooted carefully to one of her suitcases that he'd stacked by the kitchen door, "Burn these. I would really love to watch them go up in flames."

Furrowing his brow, he accepted a stack of envelopes and napkins. Stepping closer to the largest lantern he read the inscription—Seth and Kaitlyn. Bile singed his throat. "Gladly."

"Those were extras they shoved in my suitcase."

"You wanna do the honors, peaches?" He offered her the match.

"Oh, hell yeah." She gave him that sexy-as-sin grin and struck the match against the box. The audible friction seemed to delight her. "See, I told you good things almost always happen after you strike a match." She touched it to the napkins, which caught fire immediately. They melted through the invitations and ignited the wood.

Chuckling, Grant headed back into the kitchen. "I'm gonna start calling you my sexy little arsonist."

"I'm already in trouble for keying his ridiculous car. Burning his house down might sound appealing, but I should probably limit my felonies for a while. Plus, I just don't care. I never want to see or hear from him again. It's like you said, I'm glad I found out *before* I walked down the aisle. It's the best thing that ever happened to me."

Kaitlyn didn't care anymore that she was saying too much or pushing too hard. She knew what it was like to live in your brother's shadow. How Grant ever believed that he was somehow not as important as his brothers was incomprehensible. He was the living embodiment of her every fantasy, and he'd rescued her from a life she'd orchestrated right to hell.

She refused to believe he would only be her getaway ride and rebound lover, but if that was all he ever wanted, they were still worth it. If he was nothing more than the person who taught her the difference in boys and men, that was more than anyone else had ever given her. And somehow she knew he was so much more than that. Perhaps there were boys, and there were men, and then on an entirely different plain, another existence altogether, there were cowboys.

She also refused to put her yoga pants back on. Never having been a fan of her pudgy thighs, she tried to ignore the visible dimples that

116

came from tasting far too much of the food she loved to prepare. Grant couldn't seem to keep his eyes off of her legs and if she had to continually tempt him to get him to give in and give her what they both wanted, so be it.

He was definitely stubborn, but she suspected there was some other reason he kept stopping himself, and whatever that reason proved to be she wanted to incinerate it quickly.

A wave of warm air spilled into the house from the height of the flames. He toed out of his boots and carried the cast-iron pot of soup to the fire. He set it on the hearth and then added the foil wrapped cornbread nearby.

"So, how do we shower if you don't have any water? Or is that what Holly was filling all of those buckets for?" Checking off his things that had to be done before they could have sex was her singular goal.

"Nah, that ain't good for bathing unless you want to boil it and then let it cool, and that'll take too damn long. When we were kids we used to tell Mama we'd bathed when all we'd really done was dunk each other in the stock tank."

Kaitlyn grinned. "I don't know what a stock tank is, but it sounds like you shouldn't bathe in them."

"Big huge basins out near the pens we fill up for the horses to drink out of, and the cows if the lakes are frozen over, so the water's probably not real clean. Didn't matter to me so much when I was eight, but you sure as hell don't want to crawl in bed with me 'fore I bathe now."

"I'd crawl in bed with you no matter what you do, Grant Camden. I just can't quite figure out how to convince you of that."

"You're either crazy or your city-girl side's showin'."

"You're either being stubborn or you're scared."

"I'm covered in cowshit, sweetness."

"Or you're full of it."

"I ain't scared. What the hell would I be scared of anyway?" Oh, she'd struck a chord.

"What you said. That this means something. I don't think I'm the only one who's a little afraid of it all and how fast it's happening."

"That ain't it ... exactly," he admitted, proving his vow that he wouldn't lie to her. Unable to resist his magnetism, she edged closer to him.

"Then what is it *exactly*?"

"There's more to it than you know." Stirring the pot of soup, he refused to look her in the eye.

She seated herself beside him on the stone hearth. "Look at me, please."

His cool green eyes lifted to hers. She took his hands, needing his strength, needing his bravery, because she could locate precious little of her own.

"My brother was killed in Afghanistan. He was in the Army, just like my dad. All they really told us was that it was a road-side bomb, and he was trying to save some kind of make-shift orphanage that had been set up near their base."

"Baby, I'm so ..." he started to apologize but she shook her head.

"There's more. Just please, let me tell you everything. I want you to know. It's not like how it is in the movies exactly. You know, where you see this black car pull up and some old guy in his dress uniform comes to your door to tell you that your brother won't be coming home. And then they hand you this folded up flag thing, and that's supposed to make it worth it somehow. It does happen that way, but you just sit there and you can't process it and they try to help you, but no one can help you.

"It changes your whole life. I was in New York so no one came to see me. I've spent the last three years wondering what would have happened if I'd just never picked up the phone. That's the worst part, I think. When they're killed overseas you'd already kind of gotten used to them not being around. It's so surreal. Sometimes, if I try, I can pretend that he's just still over there fighting. That one day he's going to walk back through my parent's front door and be perfect just like he always was."

Grant dropped the spoon in the pot of soup and stood. Before Kaitlyn knew what he was doing, he'd lifted her gently into his arms, seated them on his sofa, and cradled her in his lap. "Keep talking, sweetheart. I've gotcha."

"You have to understand how Keith was. Like I keep saying, everything he did was perfect. My parents couldn't seem to wrap their heads around the fact that he was gone. They'd built their entire life around him. His achievements were everything to them. Everything was about him following in my dad's footsteps, training in the Army and then becoming a cop. I quit culinary school and came back home to try and help them. My mother didn't speak for three months. My dad just worked all the time. He still does. Everything is broken. I tried so hard to fix it, to be the things Keith

118

had always been, but I can't. That's the whole reason I was with Seth in the first place. My father thinks he's great. He set us up. That's why he's so mad I ran away."

"And that's this whole business with New-Kaitlyn and Old-Kaitlyn. You figure you changed who you were for your parents when Keith died"

"I did change. Keith always got perfect grades and did exactly what Daddy told him to do. That's why he went into the Army to start with. Dad always wanted me to go to law school. I never wanted anything to do with it. I'd wanted to be a chef since I was a little girl, but I signed on for a pre-law degree at UN. I hated every moment of it but it made my parents happy so I just did it.

"Keith was so serious about everything, and I always had my head in the clouds so I made myself be more serious all the time. He was analytical. I was more creative, especially with food. Now, I only cook dinners for my parents that I know they like and they only like things that remind them of the way our lives worked before Keith died. Nothing new. Never anything new. Life stopped moving forward the day we found out he wasn't coming home.

"Before that, I was so sick of being treated like a baby my whole life, when I got to New York I was determined to figure out who I was without my parent's input. I never got into too much trouble, but Keith never did anything wrong. He never drank too much, never partied too hard, he even dated this one girl that my parents adored because she was just as driven as him for most of his life. When I got back here, I'd already given up that whole self-discovery thing. Running away from that ridiculous ceremony yesterday is the first thing I've done in three years that actually made me happy. It's the first thing in a long, long time that felt like me. And walking into your grandfather's living room last night, kissing you, and climbing up on you is the second." Every word she spoke eased the noose of tension from around her neck. Why hadn't she told him sooner? The weight she'd carried for so long somehow eased its strain.

"Trust me, sugar, you doing that made me damned happy, too. Most everything about you makes me happier than a pig in mud."

"Grant, I haven't ever told anyone else how Keith died. I mean, most people know, if they know my family. It was in the papers, and on TV, and everything because of my father's job, but I don't talk about it because it hurts more when I say it out loud, or it used to. We never say anything about it at home because everyone is afraid of what my mom might do. But I told you, and for some reason I feel a little better. So, please tell me why you're scared. It might help."

"Scared ain't *exactly* the right word."

"Then what is the right word?"

"I don't know. I told you I'm not a scholar. I'm just a rancher."

"I don't think there's anything wrong with being a rancher. I don't want a scholar. I just want you."

Well, hell. Grant had no comeback for that. He could keep feeding himself the line of bullshit that he wasn't afraid, but the rubber had just met the road. He wasn't so much afraid to say the words to her. He just had no idea how she might respond. She said she wanted him, and if it was in his power to give her anything in the world she wanted he'd do it.

"Did you think it was a little odd that my whole family treated you like you're here to stay, like we're already a permanent fixture or something?"

"Kind of, but when you haven't felt welcome anywhere except the little diner where you work the breakfast and lunch shifts you just appreciate acceptance anywhere you can find it. Your family is great. Everyone was so nice."

"Yeah, well we have our moments, trust me."

"You said in your truck that if I told you about Keith you'd tell me about how the Camdens work. I sense that's where you're going."

"Yeah, but I'd be much obliged if you'd give me another minute or two to be a complete coward, if you're willing."

That elicited another one of those adorable giggles.

"How'd you get to be so damn brave anyway?" It was a question he honestly wanted the answer to, but he was still stalling and she knew it.

"Just tell me what you Camdens do that you think is so odd."

"For generations—I'm talking longer than this land where we're sitting has been Camden land, and that's been a long damn time— when a Camden sees the person they're supposed to be with they know, somehow. It was like that with my parents, and my grandparents, and my great-grandparents. Both of my brothers, and even Holly with Dec. It's apparently ... the way we're wired or something. I know that sounds nuts, but that's why everyone figures you're here to stay."

She shifted against him and he caught himself holding on to her tighter, afraid she was about to take to her feet and run. "When you say 'be with,' what does that mean exactly?"

"Be with for a long, long time, kinda." The word *forever* would not breach his lips if he had any say in the matter.

"And that's why you haven't slept with me yet? Because you think this is for a long, long time?" The fervency in her questioning eyes robbed him of breath. "You swore you'd never lie to me."

"Yeah, maybe. I just need to do right by you, Katy. I need to do this right even if I'm the Camden that's not gonna get a long, long time."

"Why wouldn't you get that?"

He shrugged, refusing to give credence to the fact that he wouldn't get forever if she decided she just wanted him for a getaway ride and a rebound fuck or two. He had no say. It was all up to her.

"Because of me? You think it's all up to me?" She sounded astonished, and how the hell was she already reading his mind?

"I never said that."

"You didn't have to. Nothing has ever been entirely up to me in my whole life. I don't even know what to do with that, but Grant, I've spent the last three years being what someone else wanted me to be. And I spent every year before that battling my parents for control of my own life. I'm still not over my brother. I'll eventually have to deal with Seth, and my dad, and everything. At this point, I'm not entirely sure I would even recognize myself in a lineup. We met by a total accident, literally. I don't know anything about ranching, and I have no idea what's waiting on me back in Lincoln. I really just need to take life moment by moment for a while. Is that okay with you?"

"Do I get to be in those moments with you?" He barely recognized his own voice strangled with fear.

"Yes."

"As something more than a casual fuck?"

"Definitely. As crazy as it is to think that your family's stories are true, and that you think I'm the one, I'm pretty excited to see if that's true."

"Then yeah, I guess that's okay with me." He'd just make for fucking sure every moment they spent together made her want to spend more time in his presence. He'd pull out every stop if she was the prize. And most importantly he'd help her figure out exactly who she was. He just prayed the girl she'd been was also the woman who wanted him.

Chapter 17

"Your kitchen is really nice."

Grant was pleased she seemed taken with his house now that she could see the main living areas in the glow of the roaring fire. Maybe the ranch wouldn't be as hard a sell as he'd worried it might be. He watched her delicate neck contract as she swallowed down another bite of soup-drenched cornbread.

"This is so good." When her eyes closed and a contented moan sounded from her, another round of desperate anticipation crashed through him. He ordered himself to be patient. God knew she was more than worth the wait.

"This was Mama and Daddy's house back in the day. When Mama got pregnant with Natalie they were worried if they put Austin in the room with me and Luke, we'd tear that half of the house from the foundation. There's only three bedrooms. Gran was more than ready not to have the big house to take care of, so they moved into what's Holly and Dec's house now. Mama and Daddy moved up to the farm house since it has eight bedrooms, and left this one empty. But you heard Pops talking about how Mama likes to cook. Dad redid the kitchen for her when we were little. Probably needs to be updated now, but if I eat here, I just pop a Hungry Man in the microwave."

"It doesn't need much updating. Trust me, eight-burner double Viking ranges never go out of style, and I can't believe you eat microwave meals if your mom makes suppers like these."

"I eat up there a fair amount, but sometimes I need a break from the house full of kids and all of my siblings."

"I can see that, I guess. I'm usually so lonely when I'm home with my parents I think I'd give my right arm to have a house full of people just for the company. Plus, your nieces and nephews are adorable."

"They're cute and I love 'em more than 'bout anything else, but my brothers seem hell-bent on seeing which one can repopulate Western Nebraska with Camdens the fastest. Austin was pissed Luke got two in on one go. Mark my words, Summer'll turn up pregnant any day now."

"You ever plan on getting in on that game?" Her question rang with a note of hopefulness. Her blue eyes turned navy in the firelight. She gnawed on her bottom lip like she was bracing herself for

123

something. Disappointment, if Grant had to guess. So, she wanted kids, did she?

He smiled to himself. "Hell yeah, peaches, but since I didn't have anyone ready and willing, I let their harassing each other annoy the shit out of me. Not like I could cowboy up and either beat 'em *or* join 'em so I just let it piss me off."

Her grin was brighter than the fire. It lit a low flame in his gut. Warmth spread throughout him as she rubbed her hand along his thigh. Come hell or high water, he was going to make this work.

"I know I probably say this too much, but I really love how honest you are with me. It means more than you'll ever know."

Lifting her hand off of his leg, he brushed a kiss along her knuckles. Clichéd? Hell yeah. Something he'd done with other women? Hell no. But this was all kinds of different. "Do something for me, sugar."

"What?" She grinned at his gesture.

"Stop second-guessing everything you do. You don't say anything too much 'cept maybe claiming you're no good at things, which is total bullshit. Having a man be honest with you is what you deserve. And I already told ya I'm gonna show you how a country boy treats a lady."

"You also promised to do some less-than-gentlemanly things to me, cowboy, so which is it? I told you I'm not looking for you to be polite and gentle with me."

"You keep thinkin' ranchers are gents, darlin', and that just ain't the truth. No reason you can't be my sweet princess when we're out and about and my naughty little vixen when you're in my bed. Same way I'll always treat you right, but that includes indulging your dirtiest fantasies along with several of mine. I swear to you there's nothing sexier than a good girl who knows how to misbehave."

Still not moving fast enough for her liking, Kaitlyn watched as Grant grabbed a bar of Lava soap from the master bathroom and stalked back to the kitchen.

"What are you doing?"

"Going to bathe." He peeled off the dirty Carhartt shirt he'd been wearing since the day before and flung it into the laundry room. She paused for a moment to drink in the firm muscles of his chest and biceps and the perfect disks of his nipples.

"I thought the water wasn't running?"

"It ain't."

"Then how are you going to bathe?" Wrinkling her nose, she sank her teeth into her tongue to keep from reminding him that she was very much a city-girl who was disgusted to think that he was going to bathe in one of those stock tanks he'd talked about.

"We got lakes all over this ranch, peaches. It'll be cold, but it's better than nothing."

"So, you're going to skinny-dip?" Hopeful anticipation sizzled under her skin.

"You sound mighty intrigued with that idea."

"I'm filthy, too. Just how cold are we talking?"

"Baby, you ain't even begun to get filthy yet, and too cold for me to let you join me right now. There's a shallow creek a few miles from here that'll warm up quick if we get some sun. If you want me to pop your skinny-dippin' cherry, I'll take you up there."

"What makes you so sure I haven't ever skinny-dipped?" Probably the fact that her cheeks were glowing pink once again. She fought the urge to hide her face in her hands. Truthfully, she couldn't even doggie-paddle. Her mother had been convinced swimming would further damage her hearing and she'd never been allowed to do it.

In two long strides, his long legs ate up the distance between them. His right hand cradled her face. His thumb stroked her cheekbone. "Because, baby doll, you are all kinds of sweet and innocent. That's another reason I'm gonna make damn sure I do right by you. I know I'm about to take all of that away from you. I'm about to make it all mine."

"I'm not all that innocent," she protested, but his index finger landed lightly on her lips.

"Don't."

"Don't what?" She attempted to speak through the barrier.

She swore his dark half-chuckle reached through her skin and settled between her thighs. "Clearly gonna have to fill your mouth with either my tongue or my cock to hush you up. Don't pretend with me. Don't try to be something you're not. I want you just the way you are. Not New-Kaitlyn, not Old-Kaitlyn, just my sweet Katy Belle the way she is right this moment, and the moment after that, and the one after that, whatever version of you that might be, even if it changes second to second. Stop being ashamed of what you have or haven't done. I told you, I'm possessive as hell, sugar, it's a damned turn on that what you're willing to share with me you haven't done with some other guy."

Suddenly, his finger was replaced with his lips, warm and hungry. This kiss was different. The perfect mix of soft and demanding with a raw edge of pure craving need. His body vibrated again.

Desperate for more, she pressed her tongue between his lips, wanting his taste to fill her. Unable to resist, her hand skated down his bare chest, feeling every rippled plane of muscle as they bunched and flexed, pulling her closer. The firm pillows of his abs, chiseled from manual labor, tensed as she neared the waist of his Wranglers.

"Keep going, sugar. Grab me," he grunted as he trailed kisses down the sensitive skin of her neck.

She immediately complied, palming the hardened bulge of his cock. He throbbed in her hand. Heat spilled through the denim into her hand. She needed more. She wanted his flesh against hers.

His greedy growl drew a whimper from her lungs. "See what you do to me, honey? See how fucking bad I want to own you?"

Frustration lit through her. "Then stop putting me off and take me." Popping the snap on his jeans, she took what she wanted. Diving behind the waistband of his briefs, her fingers encountered the slick, satin-covered steel of him. She ran her fingertips through the pearly essence of need spilling from the head and circled his crown.

"Jesus Christ, you trying to kill me?" Another rumbled growl grunted from his beautiful lips. Somehow his decadent voice lowered even more when she had him like this. It took up residence in her veins. Desperate craving flooded her bloodstream. All she wanted was for him to talk and then to rid her of any innocence she might still have.

"You feel so good. Grant, please." He said he wanted to hear her beg. She'd beg willingly, as often as he might like.

"I know my cock feels good, sugar. I'm gon' make it feel so damn good. It's gonna feel even better when I claim you. I'm gonna bury it so deep inside your sweet little snatch you never forget you're all mine."

"Now," she ordered. Impatience had her grabbing him with more vigor.

"No." He eased her arm out of his jeans. "You're already forgetting who's in charge, peaches. When I say. Where I say. How I say. Remember?"

Damn him, why did that have to sound so fucking sexy when he said it like that? His voice when he was giving her orders somehow rendered her unable to dispute his demands.

"I'll be back quick." He brushed another tender kiss across her lips and then two more on the seatbelt markings on her neck. "Gonna be kissing those constantly 'til I've made 'em all better."

"Wait just a minute. If you're going to take your clothes off, I'm going to watch," she informed him as soon as she managed a breath of air that didn't contain the pure musky scent of him that was far too intoxicating.

"I was hoping to cool off a little. Your sweet ways, those little noises you make, you grabbing me like you hadn't ever quite felt a man before makes me way too quick on the trigger. Plus, all I've been thinking about all damn day is how good you're gonna feel when I'm balls-deep inside of you making your ass jiggle for all that shit you said today about not being able to do stuff."

A little tired of the reminders of her perceived innocence and beyond frustrated, she felt like arguing. "Too bad, cowboy. I'm coming with you."

"I'm walking."

"Good. Lead the way."

He flung open his front door. "Get then, and that's gotta be good for five more strikes."

"Little tired of all of your talk, Grant Camden. Let's see some action." She whisked by him, marching out onto his expansive front porch. The cold air bit at her bare thighs, distracting her. She still wasn't wearing pants and somehow she'd forgotten.

So taken with the cold, she hadn't really expected the *snap* that followed his hand smacking her ass any more than she'd expected him to follow the first strike with a second. But the most unexpected thing of all was the rush of wet heat that immediately dripped from her lower lips. She trembled and started to plead for him to give her more. The rush of slight pain made her woozy as it coupled with her desperate desire.

"You wanna go back in and put some clothes on? I ain't too keen on my brothers seeing what belongs to me and only me, and I told you it was cold out here. We'll get to more of that after I've bathed."

"You are awfully bossy." She spun back to face him, refusing to admit she was freezing.

"Guilty as charged." That stubborn smirk both irritated and enlivened her.

"Bet if I sat on your face, I could wipe that smirk off of it."

This time a voracious growl echoed in the cool air. "Oh, don't worry, peaches, I'll get you up there and let you see if it works. Go get some clothes on, and here," he ushered her back inside and wrapped her up in one of his thick winter coats. When she'd pulled her yoga pants back on, he grabbed a towel, took her hand, and led her out into his fields.

"I thought you liked my talkin'," he finally asked as they headed towards an expansive pond.

"I do, but I also like you doing what you keep promising to do."

"Do me a favor and remember you said that." He slid out of his boots at the water's edge. The cattle on the other side sipping the cool water distracted her until Grant shucked off his jeans and underwear in one quick move. It struck her that he was completely shameless; not that he had anything to try and hide. Her eyes coasted down the muscles of his back to his firm ass that she longed to touch. When he turned to face her, she immediately honed in on his cock, standing at half-mast after their walk. Only partially aroused, he was still bigger than any man she'd ever seen.

"Like what you see, darlin'? I can keep standing here if you want."

"Shut up and get bathed."

"Shit," he grunted as he stepped into the lake. His muscles rippled faster than the water. She watched his jaw flex as he lowered himself to his waist. The scent of him clung to the coat he'd wrapped her in. She inhaled deeply, wishing she were wrapped up in his arms instead.

"Cold?" she teased.

"Than Witch-tit-istan. You're gonna have to warm me up when I get out."

"Gladly."

He sank into the water, submerging himself. Her heart thundered so loudly in her chest she could barely hear over it. Anxious to see him, she stalked closer to the muddy bank. The wind whipped over the water making her shiver despite the warmth of his coat.

Rivulets of water tracked down his face and trailed down his chest when he reappeared. She watched him haphazardly run the bar of soap over his chest and under his arms.

"Hurry," she begged.

He gave her another cocky smirk as he proceeded to stand in the knee deep water, lather his right hand, and run it over his cock. The freezing water had robbed him of its impressive length, but she had no doubt his erection would return in a moment's notice once he was out.

When he'd finished washing, he climbed back up on the bank and scrubbed the towel over his wet skin. Wrapping it around his waist, he gathered his clothes and boots and headed back towards his house.

"You're walking all the way back like that? You'll freeze."

"I told you it was your job to warm me up when we get back."

"Well, yeah, but … aren't you cold?" She hurried to catch up with him.

"Fucking freezing, baby, but it's gonna make it feel so damned good when I'm up against your fever hot skin and have my cock inside your warm wet pussy."

Geez, Camden, you wanna maybe shut your mouth every now and then? Grant tried to clamp his jaw shut. He never mouthed off like this to a woman, but every time he spoke that greedy little fire he lit in her eyes drove him crazy. And he was ten country miles past any sign of sanity. She was no longer a want. She was way past a need. This wasn't even a craving. His very existence depended on owning her so thoroughly she forgot any other men even walked the face of the earth.

His fingers itched to know how wet he'd made her with all of this buildup that was clearly about to drive both of them up a wall and over four hay bales.

If he didn't have her pussy juices all over his tongue in the next sixty-seconds, he swore he'd find some way to end it all and put himself out of his misery.

Dropping the towel somewhere on his porch, he scooped her off of her feet, making her squeal as he rushed them inside.

"At some point, peaches, I'm gonna take my time with you, but I'm all out of patience. Tell me you want this."

"I want this," her voice was a breathy plea.

"Tell me you're gonna be a good girl and do what I say."

She paused. "I will." Hesitance threatened her vow.

"What? What is it?" He searched his body, the room, the entire house for patience and came up empty. The leash on his lust was frayed beyond repair.

"Please, just fuck me."

"Filthy mouth and ornery to boot." He stood her on her feet outside his open bedroom door. "Tell me why you hesitated."

"I don't want to tell you that."

"Katy, now."

"I can't always hear very well in the middle of having sex. Everything gets overwhelming, and I can't concentrate enough to hear. And with you it's going to be even more overwhelming. So, I guess I'd make a pretty terrible submissive, or are submissives not supposed to do what the other person says because the punishments are part of the whole deal? I have no idea how that works." The heat between them cooled enough for Grant redirect a little blood flow back to the head above his belt buckle.

"Baby, I like to do things my way and only my way, especially in the bedroom, because I know how to take you places you've only ever dreamed of. I know how to make you feel so fucking good all you want is more of me. You don't have to be able to hear me for this to be incredible. And I'm sure as hell not some surly-assed sex-club Dom any more than you're going to play my sub. I may not have a degree hangin' on my wall, but I do know the difference in dominant and domineering." God, she was so sweet and she was trying so hard to have this experience with him, but now he understood why her family was so protective of her. In one quick moment, he decided he could give her everything she wanted in his bed and still be the man who protected her above all others.

"But now you're thinking that I really am weak and you're not going to *do* all the things you promised because of my hearing."

The fire roared. The heat licked at his back, drying him off as it continued to heat the entire house. She stared up at him with expectation and disappointment pinned in her deep blue eyes. "If you can't hear me at any point, speak up, sugar. There are a thousand other ways we can communicate." If she needed him to prove himself, he was all in. "Now, take them clothes off for me. I don't need a fucking striptease, I just need you as nekkid as I am in the next five seconds."

"Are you serious? All the things you said we'd do you'll do them?"

"I said get nekkid," placing a demanding emphasis on his orders wasn't even difficult. Her hearing had nothing to do with him wanting her and it had nothing to do with what she needed to feel when she was with him. There was a power in giving yourself over to a lover. There was power in submission. He just had to show her that.

She pulled the t-shirt off, revealing her tits still trapped in that damned black lacey bra, obscuring what he was desperate to see. When she reached for the waistband of her pants, a frustrated grunt spilled from his mouth without his permission. Rampant desire rocketed up his spine. Reminding himself not to back off with her, he went on with precisely what he wanted.

"Bra next. Show me them titties, baby. I'm gonna spend a long damn time getting my fill of them first."

Her bottom lip slipped through her teeth as she popped the back clasp. Her breasts spilled forward, beautiful mounds of flesh that swayed with her frantic breath. Returning his right hand to the hard strain of his cock, he tried to tamp down the hot greed filling his erection. Her nipples were drawn into diamond-hard beads of raw need. Pale, pink, and flawless by his estimations. He followed the arch of her spine down to the swells of her ass, plump and full, feminine perfection.

"You're so fucking gorgeous, darlin'. My God, do you even know how beautiful you are?"

"But I'm n ..." she protested.

Beside her in a second flat, he ground his teeth, ordering himself to remain in control. "Don't you dare say what you were about to say."

He caught her slight eye roll and smacked her ass again. "Keep it up. I'll make you count 'em for me." Damn, that was addictive as hell. Good thing his innocent little city-girl liked it. Another quick moan escaped her. Letting his impatience run the show, he knelt down and jerked the yoga pants and her panties down her legs. He used the advantage of his position to stroke his thumb over her mound covered in scant amounts of delicate auburn fuzz. She shuddered from the sensation.

She'd waxed recently. "Something your ex wanted, I'm guessing?" he snarled.

A quick nod was his answer. Her body trembled at his touch. Standing, he lifted her back into his arms and settled her in his unmade bed. "No more. You're not hurting yourself for anyone's jollies, you got that? I want you natural, my perfect little peach. I want to see those sweet red pussy curls. I want to feel 'em wet all for me. Feel 'em with my fingers and my cock. Spread your legs for me, sugar. I'm gonna make it all feel better."

Chapter 18

Still surprised that he wasn't backing down after her confession about her hearing and sex, the wet rasp of his tongue up and down her slit stole the breath from her lungs. She wasn't certain, being a cowboy and all, if he knew that the pain of getting waxed didn't last much past the appointment, but she decided to mention that later. Much, much later.

He moved his ministrations to her inner thighs, sucking and nibbling along her tender flesh. Another swirl of his tongue at her crest sent a jolt of pleasure throughout her nervous system. Her entire body shook. She spread her legs wider in a silent plea for more.

"You showing me where you want my mouth, peaches?" Denying her what she most craved, he crawled up her body like a stalking lion moving in for the kill. "Think you need to remember who's in charge. I'll let you fuck my tongue 'til your juices are running down my throat in a little while. Right now there are other places I want my mouth." He layered his body to hers. The weight of him against her skin, the connection sizzling between them, it was more than she fully understood. Why was this so different?

His hands scooped the heft of her breasts. The calluses on his fingers pricked at her skin. He soothed the burn with his mouth, laving the underswells with his tongue.

"More," she begged readily.

"That's it. Let me hear you beg for it."

"Please."

"Good girl." His lips latched onto her right nipple, drawing it into the velvet heat of his mouth as he sucked. Her world spun. Winding her fingers through his thick brown hair she arched her back, desperate for him to take more.

He spun his tongue around her once more and trailed kisses between her breasts. "You're so damn hungry for it, baby. Clearly nobody's been taking care of my sweet girl for way too long. No more. From now on I'll make certain you know who you belong to, and I'll give you every single thing you need."

As he worked his mouth to her left nipple, his right hand trailed slowly down her body. A tide of desperate need followed in its wake. She tensed her belly, praying he'd continue the path between her legs.

Suddenly, his mouth was beside her good ear as his fingers danced along her slit. He pressed in slightly, drawing a strangled moan from her mouth. "You're so wet for me, sugar. It's a damned turn on." That low rumbled tenor speared through her, decimating any hesitance she'd ever had. She wanted this. Wanted everything he could give. Her body required the reckless abandon he held in the palms of his capable hands.

Mercifully, he dipped a single finger deep within her. "My God, you're so damned tight. I can't wait to feel your hot little pussy around my cock. I'm gonna open you wide." His deep drawl took on a tunneled effect as he heightened her pleasure with every stroke of his finger.

"Then don't wait."

"You're so wet I could, you know, I could take you hard and fast right now. Make you ache."

She detected warning in his tone. His skin glided against hers making her burn.

"How many times do you need to hear me beg?" She had no sense of how loud she was, but it must've worked. He advanced.

"I swear to God, someday soon I'm gonna run my tongue over every single one of your adorable freckles, here," he brushed kisses on the patch of light brown dots in the center of her right thigh, "and here," he swirled his tongue where her leg joined her torso, right beside where she so desperately wanted his mouth, "and right here," he suckled at her mound covered in tiny freckles, "but I'm flat out of patience tonight. I need this."

The calluses on his fingers rasped along her thighs as he spread them further, exposing her.

"Oh, God," whimpered from her as his thumbs separated the lips of her pussy. The hot air from the fire taunted her vulnerable skin.

"All for me," he growled plenty loud enough for her to hear as he spun his tongue around the hood of her clitoris. Her entire body seized. Just like everything else he did, he set to work with rapt focus.

The spicy flavors of her filled his mouth. Holy hell, if he spent the rest of his life getting high on her he'd die a happy man. Craving greed drove him. He whipped his tongue back and forth between her folds. Her moans reached fever pitch. He suspected she'd lost a little bit of her ability to decipher her own volume. Smiling against her, he continued his teasing licks. He liked her loud and the sounds she made when he was between her warm, willing thighs drove him wild.

Studying her every reaction he used the few brain cells still functioning to memorize her preferences. Circling her clit, he taunted and teased until her fingernails dug into his scalp and she called out his name.

He dropped lower, gauging her reactions as he tempted her perineum with his tongue. She clenched and begged for more.

"Feels good, doesn't it, sweetheart?"

She hadn't heard him, but she spread her legs further so he continued his explorations. When she was thrusting in the air, he moved back up her pouty little pussy and gave her what she'd been begging for.

Drawing her timid little pearl into his mouth, he suckled gently while he dipped two fingers deep within her channel. The musky perfume of her arousal filled his lungs. He gorged himself on her juices. Next time, he'd see to it that she came repeatedly before he took his own, but not tonight. He was too far gone.

Her thighs clamped around his jaw as she tried to close herself to him. Oh, hell no. Using the strength of his left arm he held her left leg open and his right shoulder took care of her other leg. There were a thousand other ways to communicate during sex. And this was one of them. Her harsh cries of ecstasy said he'd made his point.

Keeping his fingers moving constantly, he increased the suction of his mouth until she shook. Her pulse pounded in her clit. It throbbed against his tongue. Heat streaked her gorgeous curves. Her entire body seized as he pulled his mouth away and loomed over her once again.

"Just let it go, baby. Come for me." He made certain she could read his lips. "Like a good girl." And with the next stroke of his fingers, she sprang free on a desperate cry of his name. Returning his mouth to her, he drank everything she gave up for him.

When she stilled, he made one last suck and reached for a condom in the next second.

Her eyes were still closed as she came down from the high. Tossing the condom on a pillow, he called himself an asshole for rushing her and joined her on the bed, cradling her against him.

"Can you hear me, sweetheart?"

She shook her head making him chuckle. She'd clearly heard something. When her eyes fluttered open, he grinned at her. "Most beautiful thing I've ever seen. You taste like candy made all for me. A mix of sweet and spicy, just like my girl," he kissed her, needing her to taste their flavors combined. "Perfect," he breathed the word across her lips. She grinned. "Mm-hmm, you heard that."

"I'm just a little dizzy."

"Dizzy's good, but I'm dying over here. I need to be inside of you. I want to feel you, Katy. You're gonna feel so fucking good on my cock."

With that little hellcat grin she kept hidden far too often, she eased closer to him, sliding her pussy against his cock. A shuddered moan wrenched up from his chest. She continued grinding against him, slicking him with the cream of her release.

He shuddered against her. Dammit, he was trying to take his time, and then he realized that wasn't at all what she wanted.

"What'd I tell you about rubbing up against me like this?"

"That I'd get fucked hard," she cooed.

His approving growl was so loud his brothers probably heard from their houses so he knew she'd heard him. "Naughty girl, you want it rough?"

"I thought you were in charge," she challenged.

"On your knees, grab a'holt of headboard, and don't let go."

She complied instantly. Stretching out in a stunning display all for him. Wasting no time, he rolled a condom on and impaled her with one fluid thrust to his hilt.

She gasped. Her body shuddered from his girth. Jerking her hips back, he took with unrelenting greed coursing through his veins. Pistoning his hips as she opened, he pounded inside of her, listening to her all-consuming moans of pure pleasure.

His eyes rolled back in his head. He'd been with dozens of women. Hell, he was probably registered as a man-whore in several surrounding counties, but this, everything about her, about *them* was different. He drove harder until she melted around him.

Her pussy milked every twitch of his cock. Somehow she tightened with each thrust. He wasn't going to last. Dammit, she was too good, too tight, too wet, too hot. Every gasped breath was filled with her scent. Her moans out-roared the fire. Every stupid mistake he'd ever made burned inside of her. Her juices dripped down his thighs. She called out for him like a hymn of redemption.

He groaned out her name like a prayer. Absolution his only goal.

"Feels so good. More, please," came out in broken syllables of carnality. Her thighs quivered and she bit into the pillow under her face. Fucking hell.

He felt like a god. He craved her surrender as streams of liquid fire surged through his shaft. He was going to lose it all.

Leaning forward, he prayed she could hear him. He didn't fully understand it, but he knew his voice stirred her. Positioning his head at her ear only deepened their connection. His climax barreled through him, soaking down the condom. "Come baby, please. Ah, Jesus Christ," he groaned as it drained him of everything he'd ever hoped to be. But at his command, she released again.

She collapsed to the mattress, quivering around him as spurts of hot cum continued to fill the condom.

Blinking the cloud of rapture from his eyes, he eased away from her and disposed of the condom.

Her right hand reached back where he'd been a moment before.

"I'm right here, sweetheart." He settled back beside her, not certain she'd heard him. He tried to arrange her on his chest, but she shook her head so he held her back to him instead.

A full minute later she turned and cuddled into him.

"You okay?" He stroked his fingers through her long copper curls, wondering if she was comparing him to Seth. He couldn't drive the thoughts from his mind. What if their connection hadn't been to her what it had been to him? And then he'd gone and blown his rocks before she'd gotten off like some teenager in the back of a truck on a Friday night.

"Did you ask if I was okay?" Her voice was barely a whisper.

"Yeah," he raised his volume slightly.

"Much better than okay."

"Listen, I'm sorry about that. I uh, usually have more staying power. You sorta … undid me."

Confusion set in her eyes as she leaned up to study him. "What did you say?"

Fuck. Making that apology had been hard enough the first time. Apologizing for anything made him feel weak and stupid. It wasn't something he relished doing ever. "Uh … I'm sorry I didn't last."

"I don't understand."

He squeezed his eyes shut and debated making up some story about needing to go, somewhere, anywhere that wouldn't have him needing to apologize for being quick on the trigger.

Man up, Camden. You're the one that fucked up. "I'm sorry I …"

"No, I heard you, I just don't understand why you keep apologizing. That was the most amazing thing I've ever experienced."

136

"It was good for you?"

"Grant, you were everything. I've never felt like that. My whole body is still throbbing. I was a little sad to think about having sex with you because I knew I wouldn't be able to hear you as well and I really love the sound of your voice, but it was still amazing. That's the only word I can come up with. Amazing. I loved it."

"So, it was … better than … with …"

"Ugh, I don't want to think about him. Why did you bring him up?"

"Sorry. Just not feeling like I did right by you, which was my whole fucking plan."

"I think you did perfect, but we can try it again and again if you want to up your game." That sweet, sleepy giggle righted most everything in his world.

"Oh, honey, there's still so much more we're gonna do. I'm still keepin' a tally of your strikes, remember?"

"Maybe I'll just keep earning them."

"Damn, you're making me hard again, woman, thinking about spanking you. You have one fine ass."

"It's huge."

He swatted the curves in question, rather hard. Her quick gasp was followed by a naughty grin. "Every time you say something like that. And if you get too ornery with it, I will turn you over my knee."

"All of a sudden, I understand why submissives might not do what they're told."

"Killin' me, woman."

Settling the sheets and blankets around them, he proceeded to massage the sting out of the ample curves of her backside, seeing how she might respond. She wiggled even closer, giving him better access. He grinned.

As their collective exhaustion took over their afterglow, she sat up. "I only have lingerie to sleep in, and I don't have any ranching-appropriate clothes, I don't think. I only have sundresses and yoga pants."

"Works for me if you just stay nekkid."

"Funny." When she started to crawl out of bed, he caught her arm.

"We'll figure out you some clothes tomorrow, but tonight you're staying nekkid in bed with me. My bed my rules, remember?"

"You sleep naked?"

"And so do you when you're with me."

She narrowed her eyes. "What if I get cold?"

"I'll fuck you again, make sure you're nice and hot."

Shaking her head, she wiggled back up on his chest.

"You have my permission to wake me up if you get cold or if you get horny."

"If I sleep on your chest, I'll be fine."

"Consider me your personal pillow, sugar."

"Oh, I consider you a whole lot more than that."

Sweet perfection poured out in gorgeous female form and laying in his arms. Now, he just had to keep her there.

Chapter 19

A good two hours before sunrise, Kaitlyn shifted against him. Her seductive scent roused him from his slumber. Blinking repeatedly, Grant tried to determine what that sound was. A low, shuddered groan and then a hum shook the house. The water was back on.

Rubbing his face, he finally determined that the hum was the refrigerator. The overhead light in the living room was on. He'd left in such a hurry two days before he must've forgotten to turn it off.

He had to get up and get his cattle out of his brother's fields in a little while, but first there was something else he needed to take care of, and the light spilling in the room showed her off in all of her feminine perfection. He owed her better than blowing his wad before he got her off, and that fact had driven him crazy most of the night.

He had to have another fix of her. She was tucked beside him in a sexy little ball, her hair a halo of messy red curls. His beautiful angel. Brushing kisses on her cheek, he avoided her bad ear. She still jerked away whenever he got too close. Vowing to himself that he would earn her trust, he ran his hands down the descent of her spine and over the thick globes of her ass. Plying her warm flesh, hot-leaded desire took him over yet again. He wanted her just like this, warm and natural, safe in his arms.

She groaned and turned over in her sleep, pressing her ass to his cock and her back to his chest. The movement also revealed her good ear. Perfect.

"I need you again, peaches."

Her whimper made him chuckle.

"I need you bad. I'll never get enough."

He tunneled his right arm underneath her and circled her nipple with his thumb. Her back arched, pressing more of her breast into his hand. Now, they were getting somewhere. His left hand tracked to her pussy. He teased at her mound, making her eyes blink open hesitantly.

"You're wet, sugar. You dreaming about me?"

"Your voice is even sexier in the morning," she spoke through a deep yawn.

"Oh yeah? Well, I'll have to take advantage of that." With his middle and ring finger he circled the crest of her slit. Her breath caught as she reached her hand back between them and stroked his cock.

"Wow," escaped her lips. His ego swelled as well as his hard on.

"It's all for you, sugar. You make me so fucking hard I ache."

"I need you, too. I did dream about you, about all the dirty things I want you to do to me."

"You tell me every single one of 'em, I'll make 'em happen." Her ample breasts spilled through his fingers as he gave a greedy thrust against her backside.

A shiver shot through her. "Feels good right there, doesn't it, sweetness?" He positioned his cock between the lush cheeks of her backside and was worried momentarily he was going to lose it all once again before he'd even gotten her started. He gave another thrust, determined to show off his skills this time.

"Yes." Her whisper was lost in a quick gasp.

"So many naughty things I want to do with you. Make you feel things you ain't ever felt before." Abandoning her pussy, he skated his left hand up her soft belly to join his right on her breasts. Cupping them in his palms, he groaned as her nipples responded instantly to his touch. "I love your tits. So soft. So round and heavy. So responsive to me. They fill up my hands, fill up my mouth. Someday I'm gonna lay you down, bury my face in 'em and suck on 'em for hours 'til you come for me. Then I'm gonna leave my mark all over 'em."

"Oh, my God," she panted.

"You like my talkin' 'bout the things I'm gonna do to you or you like what I'm doing?" He rolled her nipples between his fingers before returning to grope the heft of her breasts.

"Both."

"Good. Now reach your hand down and touch yourself. Get them fingers nice and creamy. Show me exactly how you like to be touched and then feed me that sweet honey."

Her entire body went rigid. "I can't ... do that ... with you ... here."

"You can and you will. Show me. I'll be on horseback all damn day working my ass off. I want a taste before I go and I'll have another as soon as I get back, so be ready."

She tried to turn to face him but he held her still. "No ma'am. I'm gonna have you just like this. Now show me."

Mechanically, she touched somewhere in the general vicinity of her mound. He grunted his impatience. "Come on, peaches, when you think about all them things you want me to do to you, what does it make you want to do? Show me. I'd say it'll be the sexiest things

I've ever seen, but I've seen you nekkid, watched you whip off your shirt on my tractor, and watched you come for me, so it'll have to be after all that on the list."

"Keep talking." The tender request shattered the edge of his ego.

"Spread your legs for me, sweetheart just a little," he began his instruction. She complied. "So damned beautiful. Perfect pussy wet and hungry for me. When you ain't worried about what anyone thinks of you, when you're all alone, show me what you do. Touch your thighs with your fingertips real easy like. That's it." He brushed a kiss on the nape of her neck, nuzzling her hair. "I know what you want, sweetheart. We're gonna explore every single one of your fantasies. Now, touch your pussy lips gentle like. Up and down. Good girl." He shifted his left thigh, widening her legs yet again. "I'm gonna own every wicked little thought you've ever had about what a real man can do. They all belong to me. Nothing's off limits. When you're ready, I'm gonna tie you to this bed and take you hard and fast then soft and slow. Fill you so full you feel hollow when I'm not inside of you."

She trembled as her fingertips circled ever closer to her clit.

"Makes you wet to think about me taking exactly what I want, doesn't it, sugar? I know." Easing his left hand from her breast, he trailed it down to her plump backside. Positioning his hand between them, he ran his fingers up and down the crack of her ass.

"Keep going. Let me see that cream you make so sweet for me." As she eased her lips apart he stroked the puckered rosebud of her backside back and forth, gently.

"Oh, my God." Her breathing disintegrated into frantic pants.

"I'm gonna make it feel so good. I'm gonna take it all. Make your ass all mine. I told you nothing is off limits."

She tensed, clenching against him and circling her clit faster.

Certain she had to be caught up in some kind of fevered dream, Kaitlyn felt a part of herself give way. The coaxing rumble of his voice dripped with sexual prowess. It was a drug and she was woefully unable to resist, a remedy to everything wrong in her world.

"Get them fingers nice and slick for me," sounded in her ear. She didn't even have to concentrate to hear him. His entire being consumed hers. The rasp of wiry hairs on his legs abraded the backs of her thighs. His cock burned like a hot brand against her ass. Pillows of firm muscle cradled her back to his chest. His hands cupped and massaged her breasts, propelling her closer and closer to the point of no return. The heat of his breath whispered across her cheek and stirred her hair. His scent filled her lungs with every breath she managed. And his voice reached deep inside of her, decimating any fear she'd ever clung to. No part of her was left untouched. He reduced her entire world to him.

"That's it. Driving me fucking wild, you know that? Look how you're dripping for me. Give me a taste."

Anticipation tangled her in knots. Trembling, she lifted her fingers to his lips. Drawing them into the silky heat of his mouth, he sucked them clean and groaned like he'd never tasted anything better.

"So fucking good. Now it's my turn."

"Yes, please." The parts of her he was readily stripping away, the fear, the worry, the belief that she wasn't capable of much needed to be filled and restored with him. He slicked his fingers with the liquid heat he coaxed from her with ease. They plunged deep in her opening hard and fast. In and out with constant pressure, each stroke building her higher.

She cried out for him and for more. Her body trembled against his. The steel-hard, hot length of him pressed harder between her cheeks. She rocked back against him, tensing her ass around him.

"Jesus Christ, that feels good." His words kept her spellbound. She soared. Every fervent stroke deep within her pushed her closer and closer to the edge. Pulsing pressure built behind her mound. She begged for release, and the last thing she heard before she spiraled over was, "Come for me."

Her body flexed rapidly against his fingers and then they were gone. She was coming around nothing. Before the emptiness could register and she could protest, he filled her full, thrusting to his hilt, amplifying the current of pleasure he'd given her.

His raw heat filled every hollow. The waves of excruciating pleasure began again.

A string of expletives flew from his mouth in a reverent groan followed by, "So ... damn ... tight."

His satisfaction sated her soul.

This was more than she'd ever fathomed. He was more than she could ever possibly deserve. It felt too good. The air between them stretched so thin she couldn't breathe. The depth of his position drove his quick shallow thrusts right where she so desperately needed them. When his fingers honed in on her clit as he pounded with unrelenting force, she gave herself over. *Too good*, the words

142

echoed in her head. The overwhelming masculinity surrounding her muted all other sound.

Too good. Oh, God. Too good. Wait! "Grant," she gasped. "Condom." But she was too close. She couldn't fight the tide he drowned her with. She shuddered and felt her muscles seize around him.

"Fuck," he jerked away and splashes of hot cum soaked down her ass. Again and again. The man was nothing if not potent.

Willing her hearing to return quickly, she felt the sheet he'd wadded up scrub away his seed. Some devious part of her, the part of her he accessed far too easily, wished he'd asked her to wear it. She turned over, swallowing before making her apologies.

"Some fucking time I'm gonna fuck you and not have to fucking apologize afterwards. Damn, I'm such an idiot."

"Stop it," she demanded with enough force she shocked herself. "You are not an idiot, and I'm on the pill. It's just ... I should be the one apologizing to you."

Scooping her up in his arms, he cradled her in his lap. "Why in God's name would *you* apologize for *me* forgetting the condom?"

"Because the only reason we need a condom is Seth. I ... well ... he and Kelsey and all of that. I might have something, I guess. I'll go get checked ... somewhere."

"I ever meet the motherfucker, I'll skin him alive just before I turn him out with the bulls, fair warning."

"I'm so sorry." Unwelcomed regret ate at her. She didn't want to think about Seth or Kelsey or anything but Grant and what they'd just done.

"I ain't gonna kill him for you thinking we need a condom. I'm gonna kill him for being a Grade A asshole who hurt you and made you have to go get checked out."

"I've known Kelsey most of my life." Her voice caught. Dammit, she would not feel any feelings about this. She had no time for any feelings other than the all-consuming ones she felt for Grant. "I would know if she had something. It's just ... I don't know if she was the only other girl." Bile flooded her throat. She never wanted to think about being with Seth again in her life. That had been sex— boring, obligatory, rare, and unsatisfying. This was none of those things. This was something else entirely. This was everything.

"Hey," Grant's fingertips gently stroked her jaw as he lifted her chin. "I don't give a damn. I want you just the way you are. I told you that, and I meant it. I also told you I'd never lie to you, so listen up. This afternoon when I get back from driving cattle and clearing out crops, I'm gonna have you again, and this time I'm gonna watch my cum drip out of your swollen pussy, ripe and raw from how hard I take you. And that is the only thing I want you to think about while I'm gone today."

Never before in her life had she understood how the truth could set anyone free. In her experience, the truth hurt. It was occasionally too much to bear. But with every word Grant spoke, every unguarded truth that flew from those flawless lips of his, she felt her soul make another attempt to break free from the shackles of expectation other people had placed upon her life.

"Want me to say all that again, peaches?" She got another one of those winks that she swore quaked in her soul.

"No. I heard you."

"Good. Now, the water's back on. Let it run for a few before you try and use it. Probably muddy. I'll grab breakfast up at Mama and Daddy's. You go back to sleep. Got another hour before the sun's even up."

"I feel bad sleeping while you work."

"Don't feel bad. You need your rest. I told you, sugar, I'm relentless." Laying her back down in the bed, he spread her legs again and brushed a kiss along her swollen folds.

"What are you doing?"

"Getting a fix before I go." He swirled his tongue inside of her and then immediately rose up and gave her a no-less decadent kiss on her other set of lips. "Damn, I'm gonna miss you."

"You won't be gone long, right?" She needed him there with her. Why did there even have to be a world beyond them? That made precious little sense at four-thirty in the morning after being taken so thoroughly twice in the last seven hours.

"I could be gone less than five minutes and still miss you like crazy, peaches."

Being missed wasn't something she was used to experiencing either. Seth had never once told her he missed her, even when they would go weeks without seeing each other. Depending on how long he'd been seeing Kelsey on the sly, she assumed he didn't care. At the time, she'd told herself it was because he was so laid back. He never cared about much of anything other than his car, his bank accounts, and his laptops.

On full display, naked before a demanding, hot-blooded, eager cowboy whose craving stare rendered her weak assured her that laid-back was no longer an appealing quality.

144

Grant slid into a pair of clean Wranglers he located in the closet, and Kaitlyn slunk back down in the soft coverings on his bed. She enveloped herself in the remnant of heat from his body and his heady scent. Reminding herself to wash the sheets later, she watched as he buttoned up a starched shirt and pulled on a pair of thick wool socks.

When he finished, he seated himself on the bed with another pair of his socks. Fishing her feet out from under the covers, he put the socks on her.

"How did you know my feet were cold?" Being thoroughly taken care of wasn't something she'd been accustomed to either.

"Because you had 'em up against my feet all night, sweetness. I ain't gonna be here to keep you warm. It's my job to take good care of you even when I'm out working."

"You're the best thing ever."

"You just keep telling yourself that. I'll be back quick."

Still reflecting on his vow that he would miss her, Kaitlyn tried to recall if her parents had ever missed her. Her mother used to say it occasionally when she was in New York, but usually their conversations revolved around what Keith was doing and when they'd last had contact with him. The 'miss you' had become almost as habitual as the 'love you' at the end of their phone calls.

Insubstantial words that held no more weight than the emotion they carried, spoken far too often and somehow, not often enough.

Chapter 20

The sun was high in the sky the next time Kaitlyn awoke. In those moments between being fully asleep and fully awake, in the twilight of consciousness, before her body fully understood why she was waking up in an unfamiliar bed, her heart knew precisely where it wanted to be. She never wanted to leave his arms. No matter what happened outside of the ranch, she wanted to stay right where she was. She'd never been more certain of anything in her life.

A smirk creased her features as she recalled the first time she'd been awoken. Refusing to open her eyes just yet, she recalled every single delicious thing Grant had said during their morning session and then every wicked thing he'd done with his body.

When her stomach grumbled out its complaint at her lack of nourishment, she slid her arms along the cool sheets and stretched, reveling in the tender ache between her legs. He was right. She did feel hollow without him. Lusciously hollow and ready for him to fill the empty spaces again.

Pleased with her own naughty thoughts, she climbed out of bed and oriented herself to the bedroom and the noises around her. Shower first? She considered but then shook her head. Coffee first.

Pure happiness drew a broad grin across her face as she slid into one of Grant's t-shirts. The soft fabric teased at her nipples, erect from thinking about him.

Heading into the kitchen, she discovered a yellow notepad propped on the counter by the coffee maker. "Just press On. It's ready to go. Hope you like it strong, peaches. Cream in fridge. Sugar in cabinet. Be back soon for a taste of your cream and sugar." There was even a hastily scribbled jagged heart drawn at the bottom. It was clearly not a shape he drew often. She wondered if he'd ever written a note like this before. Telling herself he hadn't, she beamed. As it so happened, she did like it strong.

If she'd had any idea that men like Grant existed or life could be like this, she would have dumped Seth's sorry ass two years ago and told her father he was crazy if he thought Seth could ever make her happy.

Her father. Nope. Not going there. Her father and Seth and everyone she'd ever known before could just stay in Lincoln. She deserved a break.

After her shower, she dug through her multiple makeup bags until she located her new favorite scented lotion, peaches and cream. She spent the next half hour trying to achieve the coveted I-woke-up-like-this look and then decided to wash the sheets and the clothes she'd worn the day before. Still chilly despite the heat being on and wearing his socks, she traded his t-shirt for one of Grant's starched button-down shirts and a lacy pair of boyshort panties she'd found at Victoria's Secret at Gateway Mall. She rather enjoyed the fact that Grant would get to see her in them when Seth never had.

Boredom set in after that. She stalked around Grant's kitchen searching for something to cook. She'd eaten a bowl of cereal she'd located behind the sugar in the cabinet. She wasn't hungry, but desperately needed to create something. Not thinking about life two hours East was much easier when she was busy or when Grant was there.

Recipes she could impress him with flipped through her mind as she opened the freezer. A dozen Hungry Man meals stared back at her. Shaking her head, she opened the fridge. Eggs, three packages of some kind of meat wrapped in butcher paper, milk, a dozen bottles of Killian's Red, four six-packs of Dr. Pepper, a half-pack of bacon she was pretty certain should have been thrown out a week ago, and a half bottle of ketchup.

The cabinets didn't reveal anything more helpful, though she did locate a little salt, an old bottle of lemon pepper seasoning, and a spice jar of cinnamon. Even she wasn't that creative.

The notepad and pen Grant had used to write her the note caught her eye. Doodling out a few hearts and a sunflower, she considered.

Turning to a fresh sheet of paper, she scripted Katy Belle Sommerville. Wrinkling her nose, she crossed that out. Next she wrote Katie Sommerville. Something was still off. She wrote it with a Y instead of an IE. Not bad. Maybe instead of New-Kaitlyn or Old-Kaitlyn she could figure out exactly who Katy was. Katy Camden played on the fringes of her imagination, but she couldn't write that. Grant might see it and tempting fate seemed like a terrible idea. Plus, she needed to figure out Katy Sommerville first.

When the wind whipped into the house and lifted his shirt from her legs, excitement zinged through her. He was back. Attempting a sexy come get me grin, she spun only to discover his mother standing in the doorway.

"I'm sorry, sweetheart. I knocked. I got worried when you didn't answer," Mrs. Camden immediately apologized.

147

"It's fine. Don't worry about it." Kaitlyn tugged at Grant's shirt while cursing her stupid un-hearing ear. "I just didn't hear you knock."

"No problem. Grant mentioned that you needed some jeans. You're about Natalie's size so she sent me over with a couple of pairs you can borrow. She's out helping Holly fix fences."

"Oh, thank you. Uh … tell Natalie thanks, too. I really appreciate it. I'll just … go … put these on." Spinning back into the master bedroom, she shut the door and prayed the jeans would fit. She'd met Natalie briefly the day before, and Kaitlyn wasn't certain she'd be able to snap them.

Arching her back and sucking in her stomach as much as she could, she held her breath, flung herself back on the bed, and got the button through the hole, cursing her love of food right along with her lack of hearing.

Victory! She even managed breath, though the waist was rather tight. Doing a few deep knee bends, she tried to stretch the denim a little before she remembered she'd left Grant's mother in the living room.

Ordering herself to leave the bedroom, she debated. This wasn't her house. Certainly his mother had been in the house far more than she ever had. They used to live there, after all. Playing it by ear was a phrase she generally abhorred, but that was precisely what she was going to have to do.

"Can I do anything to help out, Mrs. Camden? I feel kind of useless in here. I know there has to be a ton of work to do." Discreetly she turned her left ear towards Grant's mother. She had a hard time hearing her speak.

"Oh, honey, one thing you'll learn real quick is that there is *always* work to be done. Nobody on a ranch has time to watch grass grow, but working constantly don't make much of a life. That's something Grant needs to learn. You'll also discover that there's plenty of work to go around. You'll figure out just what you can do to help in due time. Besides, it sounds like you've had a time of it lately. Why don't I make us some coffee and we'll talk?"

That sounded nice. Pleasant, even. Only Kaitlyn wasn't certain which version of herself she was supposed to be with Mrs. Camden. How pathetic was that? She didn't know herself well enough to communicate.

Disgusted with herself, she forced a smile. "Sure. But let me make the coffee. I was looking for something to cook anyway. How about a cinnamon latte? I don't have a way to whip any cream, but it should still be good."

"Sounds delicious, sweetheart. Do you like to cook?"

The tension knotting Kaitlyn's shoulder blades loosened. "Yes, ma'am. I love to cook. Other than spending time with Grant, it's my very favorite thing to do." Clamping her mouth shut the knot returned. "Sorry. Probably shouldn't have said that. I don't know what's wrong with me lately. I keep saying whatever pops in my head."

Inwardly lecturing herself, she concentrated on making another pot of coffee.

"You telling me you like spending time with my son isn't something to apologize for. Makes me happier than you could ever know. And I 'spect you've been trying for an awfully long time to keep your thoughts to yourself. Caged birds most often sing the songs of whoever holds the key, but you should hear their song when they're finally free." His mother joined her at the coffee maker. "All right, now, tell me what you're doing because I'm always on board for new coffee."

Grinning, Kaitlyn decided maybe it wasn't only Grant that would allow her to exist however she wanted. Maybe here on the ranch she could take off the mantle of grief that kept her confined. If she could just set it down for a few moments, draw a full breath, have a few thoughts that were all her own, that weren't poisoned with what someone else wanted her to be, then she could pick it all back up and live with it again. She just needed a break.

"If you layer the cinnamon between the scoops of coffee and then put a little bit of salt on top of the coffee grounds it helps the flavors of both to bloom fully. It will be delicious. I promise."

"I believe you, sweetheart."

The simple phrase slipped into Kaitlyn's one hearing ear and pricked tenderly at her heart. She didn't have to prove anything to his mom, not even that she could make a great cup of coffee.

"Here, let me wash these. I know my son probably hasn't done dishes in more than a week." Mrs. Camden located two travel mugs with an AFR Insurance logo beside the sink. When she turned on the water, Kaitlyn busied herself with the coffee maker. She couldn't hear much over the fall of water so she prayed Mrs. Camden wouldn't talk until she'd turned it off.

"Would you like to have our coffee outside? Turned out to be a beautiful day." Mrs. Camden gestured outside.

"What?" Kaitlyn asked almost reflexively. Defeat took another stab at her.

The way his mother studied her made her feel exposed, but her kind smile covered Kaitlyn like a warm blanket. "Right ear or left?"

"You Camdens are really good at figuring things out."

"Well, that might be because we care about you, or it might be because on a ranch you have to pay attention to every little thing to keep the cattle safe so we're trained to do that. Or it might be because my husband needs to get over his stubborn self and wear hearing aids and he won't, so I recognize a few of the signs."

"My left ear is my good ear. Did you say something about outside?"

Mrs. Camden eased closer to Kaitlyn's left side. "I did. Thought you might want to have our coffee out there." Her voice rose only a decibel or two, allowing Kaitlyn to hear her.

"Thanks for not screaming that at me. Most people do once they find out I don't hear properly."

"Well, most people haven't figured out that the solution to the problem is usually a lot smaller than the problem itself."

Unable to help herself, Kaitlyn threw her arms around Mrs. Camden's neck. "Thank you for saying that."

"Come on," she patted Kaitlyn's back and squeezed her harder. "Let's go outside."

"The wind makes it a little harder for me to hear."

"Not much wind today, but I'll speak up. Just ask the boys, Mama can make certain she's heard when she needs to be."

They settled out on Grant's front porch with the coffee. "It's so beautiful here," Kaitlyn sighed. Expansive fields painted in the colors of the mid-morning sun as far as the eye could see. She wondered where all of the cows were at the moment, but then remembered that Grant's cattle had been moved to Luke's fields, wherever they were.

"That it is, and this is delicious." Mrs. Camden lifted her coffee in exultation to Kaitlyn. "I might stop by here on the regular."

Smiling, Kaitlyn wondered if she was just teasing or if his family did pop in often. She wouldn't mind at all, unless she and Grant were busy doing something they wouldn't want an audience for.

"I'd love that. Grant was telling me that you and Mr. Camden used to live here when he was little."

"Yep, it all started right here. Somehow it seems like that was both yesterday and a hundred years ago. Oh, that reminds me, the back far left burner on the stove is ornery. You have to start it a few times before it lights. Ev never got that fixed before we moved out, and Grant Camden loves to eat, but ain't much in the way of a cook."

Grant's hesitant confession that his family thought she was here to stay for a lifetime swirled in her mind once again. It just couldn't be that easy. Nothing was ever that easy. "If I get a chance to use the stove, I'll remember," she assured Mrs. Camden.

Kaitlyn caught a quick furrow of her brow. "Some reason you wouldn't get to cook here?"

"Oh, I don't know." Downing a long sip of coffee kept her from telling Grant's mother that nothing in her life ever worked out the way she wanted it to.

"You know, when I first moved out here, Ev's mama was a little wary of me. I loved to cook, too. Only thing at the time I thought I was any good at. She resented me a little. I promised myself back then if I ever had kids and one of my boys ever brought home a girl that could do the things I pride myself on that I'd help them. I'd invite them in. Two sets of hands are always better than one. If you love cookin', sweetheart, you just come right on up to the house and we'll make all the cattle ranchers deliriously happy with what we whip up."

"That would mean the world to me, Mrs. Camden. Thank you."

"Believe me, it's my pleasure."

Inventorying the surrounding prairie lands again, she couldn't help but grin. "It feels like the whole rest of the world is so far away from here. It's so peaceful."

"Do you wish the rest of the world weren't right outside the fences, sweetheart?"

"Maybe. That's a dumb wish though, right?" Heat blossomed across Kaitlyn's cheeks once again. Even his mother made her blush. That couldn't be a good sign.

"Not at all. We all need a place to hide away every once in a while. But at some point you might find that the problems outside the fences only get bigger when we pretend they aren't there. I've been sitting here telling you about the time after I got here, but did Grant tell you how Ev and I met?"

"No ma'am."

"I'll keep it short, but it's a good story so scoot over here closer so you can hear it."

Laughing, Kaitlyn did as she was told.

"I was about your age, and just out of a spider's web."

"A spider's web?"

"That's what I like to call it. I came up in Denver, and I'd just broken up with a man who wouldn't be fit to lick the manure off Ev Camden's boots. My wings were all but broken. I had a good job, but traveled more than I cared for. And one day my traveling brought me out here when I was supposed to be somewhere between Lincoln and Omaha, not between Cheyenne and Lincoln. Fate gets her way when she wants it. I ran outta gas. Everett and two of his buddies came up on my car and that was that. Or at least that's what I tell the kids."

A rush of delight filled Kaitlyn. "Does that mean you're going to tell me more than you tell your kids?" She couldn't believe that. Her parents never told her anything. She felt like a little girl being let in on a secret.

"Figure I might as well. I feel like talkin' and you need to hear this. When I finally relented to Ev and let him convince me that he loved me and wanted me forever, I let myself pretend that Denver and the spider were just too far away for me to worry over. This ranch and Ev's arms were my sanctuary, and if I pretended hard enough the entire state of Colorado ceased to exist, which was just the way I preferred for it to be.

"But life don't much like to be erased from existence. Can't have a future if we never had a past. If you erase all the things that hurt you, you also erase all the things that were so good they made the bad times hurt. Can't have the sunrise if it never sets, so to speak.

"While I was busy pretending I'd just appeared in Pleasant Glen and that I didn't give half a hoot or a holler about the twenty-four years before that, my daddy was busy working himself to death. For as much as I resented him never being there for me when I was growing up, always working all the time, I never got to say goodbye. And I can't ever have that moment back. Even if I get to see him again when I get to those pearly gates, I can't undo that. So, don't let life outside of those fences go on for too long without you. It never stays still. It keeps right on marching along."

"We'll be fine. It'll work itself out. You're still showing a hell of a profit from a few years back," Luke was trying to sound reassuring, but Grant could tell he was worried. He stared down at the ancient adding machine in the dimly lit office willing the negative sign in front of the painfully large number off of the damned machine.

"Can't believe we lost thirty-seven steers, a dozen heifers, and 1500 acres of corn." Austin shook his head.

"I lost the corn. You lost a few cows," Grant couldn't help but argue. Complete and utter failure chaffed his bones. His brain throbbed with it. Both of his brothers rolled their eyes.

"I don't know, man, cattle's up, corn's been down for two years now. Tempting for us to tear them fields up, burn 'em back, get some grass growing, and buy spring stock to run on the land," Austin stated what everyone else was thinking.

"Don't mean cattle won't be down next year and corn'll be up," Luke tried to ease the blow.

"Yeah, only problem with that thinkin' is that wheat's heading down too, meaning cattle's likely going with it and we're screwed six ways from Sunday." If Grant had to be the realist, so be it. His entire body ached. Tension mounted on his shoulders like four tons of concrete brick. All in the world he wanted was Kaitlyn. If he could just go home and hear her voice, he swore he could leave the numbers in the office. And if he could take hold of her, feel her in his arms, feel her breath on his chest, he figured he could forget about commodities, and stock, and downed crops altogether.

"You know, I didn't get myself thrown off of bulls just for the glory of it," Austin tried.

"Bullshit," Grant and Luke bellowed simultaneously.

"Fine, so I did, but there is a shit ton of money sitting in the Camden family business account. We're gonna be okay."

"We ain't touching your winnings. We'll figure something else out." Luke started to pace.

"If I burn it back and then run cattle on that land, I can't go back to corn for a year or more. If corn goes back up, we're out," Grant considered the possibilities.

"You lost over $40,000 last year when the markets crashed," Austin took three large steps backwards as he said this, as if Grant wasn't already aware.

"You think I don't know that?"

"Looked to be a bumper of a crop this year, though. He would'a made it back."

"Not if the markets never turned. I'm so fucking sick of rich men spreading their shit around to get richer off 'a my work and me never seein' a fucking dime of it."

"Ranching's a crap shoot on a good day. Don't mean I wanna sit behind a desk taking orders from some asswipe. If I'm gonna sit anywhere, it'll be on my horse," Luke huffed.

Unable to sit there and stare at that damned number any longer, Grant stood. "All I know is I need a beer."

"We got beer right here." The jangle of beer bottles filled the dusty air as Austin opened the small refrigerator they'd put out in the office when both the corn and cattle market had been up and they'd had more than enough money to spare.

Gall pricked at his sunburned neck. "I don't want *that* beer."

"Um-hmm," Luke chuckled. "Let me guess, the beer that's in the house that also contains the cute little red head you brought home yesterday should hit the spot, right?"

"That a problem?" Grant bellowed.

"Easy there, slim, you might want to cool it before you go scaring off your city girl with your ornery-assed mood," Austin warned. "She ain't a cowgirl. She probably doesn't understand how much a good hard fuck can ease crashing corn commodities."

"Shut the fuck up, Austin," Luke scolded. "My God, you ever use your boots on the ground or do you always got one stuck in your mouth? Indie's anxious to get out of the house. I'll see if Mama and Daddy'll watch my girls. Let's head to Saddlebacks. I could use something stronger than a beer."

"I was just calling it like I saw it, but Saddlebacks sounds good to me," Austin agreed.

"Yeah, fine, but not right now," Grant couldn't argue that a night out might do a lot to improve his mood, and Kaitlyn had to be getting bored up at the house.

Debating as he slammed his truck door, he scooted up the front porch. He didn't want to startle her. She could usually hear his voice, but he'd bet what little was left in his bank accounts she couldn't hear him coming in the house.

"Katy Belle," hung on his tongue, but he never called. She was sitting on the sofa looking good enough to eat in one of his shirts and a pair of blue jeans that appeared to have been painted on. Only problem, his mama was sitting right beside her.

"Hey, Mama." He nodded to the woman who'd given him birth but marched straight to Kaitlyn, leaned down, and plastered her mouth with his own. Her taste teased at his lips. More. He just needed more. So fucking much more.

But he of all people knew you almost never got what you wanted. Shocked with his vehemence, she pulled back.

"Grant," she hissed quietly.

"I ain't near done."

154

"He is more stubborn than a mule with a purpose. Gets it from his granddaddy. Don't worry, son, I'll leave you two be." His mother smacked him on the ass as she passed him. "Behave."

Kaitlyn erupted into hysterical giggles that eased a little of the tension from his day. Not as much as another kiss would've, but he thanked the Lord for small favors.

Chapter 21

"Hi there." A heady mix of bliss and relief worked through Kaitlyn. She'd enjoyed spending the afternoon with his mother, but what she really wanted was to be back in his arms.

Another one of those sexy as sin grunts was his response as he fell to his knees in front of her, threaded his fingers through her hair and guided her lips back to his.

The heat of his body and the now-familiar scent of hay and leather coupled with his musk filled her lungs. Where most of his kisses were demanding and hungry, this one held notes of desperation, like he needed something only she could provide.

A quick moan escaped her mouth as he worked his lips over the markings on her neck from the wreck. His fingers set to work on the buttons of the shirt she was wearing.

"So fucking sexy having you in my shirt, sweetness, but I want you nekkid."

"These are Natalie's jeans."

"Jay-sus. What the hell?" He jerked back like he'd been struck. "Did you have to tell me that?"

Another round of giggles overtook her. "I thought it was sweet she leant them to me."

"Yeah, well Nat can be a real sweetheart when she wants to be and as long as you don't stand in the way of most anything she wants to do, but you lookin' good enough to tempt a eunuch and them being my little sister's jeans confuses a man. Take 'em off. That'll solve everything."

"But your mom told you to behave." God, she loved the wild intention that radiated from his eyes. Grant Camden could be an absolute saint, and he was most certainly her savior, but his sinner side was more appealing than just about anything else.

Determination perforated his low greedy tone. It wouldn't take much and she would succumb to that voice all over again. "You can ask Mama later 'bout how well I behaved coming up. Not much has changed. I need you, sugar."

"Well, she also said we should come up to their house for supper, and that I can help cook since I didn't do anything much this morning."

His grunt of frustration came next.

She loved flirting with him. She loved being in his presence. She loved where this would inevitably lead as soon as she ran out of made-up excuses. She loved … no. No, no, no. Regret vanquished the desire coursing through her veins. The only man she'd ever said that to had been Seth. She'd been certain she was supposed to say it to the man she was engaged to, but it had all been a lie. Empty words in an effort to make herself believe them. She'd never much cared if Seth had.

"What?" Grant demanded.

"I told your mom I'd help with supper."

"Nah, not that. You were coming up with some'um else to say to put me off 'cause you're wanting to be chased and then all of a sudden you started thinking about him again, didn't you?"

"How did you know that?"

"'Cause you get this look on your face. I can't figure out what it is exactly, not mad or sad, just … I don't know … lost maybe. Kinda scares me when you get that look in your eye, to be honest."

"Grant, I know it's only been a few days but please believe me, I've never felt more *found* than I have right here with you. It's just that it *has* only been a few days and I still don't know what to do when I leave here. I mean, I do have to leave here at some point, don't I?"

"Not if you don't want to. Fact, I'd much prefer you didn't."

"Pretty sure that's just wishful thinking."

"Only thing I'm wishin' is that you'd stop thinking about your shithole of an ex and get nekkid for me. Bet your sweet little pussy's feelin' neglected, ain't it, peaches? I bet it's needin' to be licked, and I'm powerful thirsty for it. I won't have you needin' and me not providing, but I might be willing to just hold you and we could talk about what happens when you leave here if you're damned and determined to go at some point."

Seating himself beside her, he scooped her up into his lap, and just like that he swept away her regret and her confusion. "Talk, baby. I ain't at all sure how long I'm gonna be able to sit here holding your sexy self without my cock wanting some attention."

"You really are relentless, aren't you?"

"When it comes to you? Hell yeah. That a problem?" Concern darkened his pale green eyes. Kaitlyn wanted nothing more than to erase it from their depths.

"Not even a little bit. I don't really want to talk about leaving here because I don't want to think about that yet, but I also don't think we can have sex again right now."

"Why the hell not?"

"Because your daddy is heading this way." Disappointment doused the fire she'd been trying to resurrect between them as she pointed out the windows by the front door.

"Wonder what he needs?" Grant lost a little of the frustration in his tone. He patted her backside as he hugged her tighter to him before he settled her on her feet. "Fair warning, the longer it takes me to get between your sexy thighs, the harder I'm gonna be when I get there."

"Mmm, maybe I'll put you off a little longer."

"Naughty little vixen with an innocent angel face. You're danger with a capital D, sugar."

Kaitlyn sincerely wished she were a naughty vixen or even knew how to behave as one for Grant. That's what she'd set out to become in New York. So much for that plan. "There is absolutely nothing dangerous about me at all."

"That's an outright lie and probably good for another few strikes."

"No, it isn't."

"Woman, quit arguing with me. Turns me on when you get stubborn, and I think about paddling that ass. Dad'll be in here in a sec, and I ain't got time to prove you wrong."

Before she could respond, his father was standing at the door. She wasn't certain if his knock was just very light or if he hadn't knocked at all before Grant opened the door. Either way she hadn't heard it.

"I'm sorry. I know I'm interrupting."

"It's all right, Mr. Camden. Come on in. Can I make you something to drink?" Manners had been preached, lectured, and branded into Kaitlyn from the time she was a small child. It was an automatic response.

Grant smirked and his father appeared astonished. "Darlin', if you can get some of that good breeding into him, we'd be much obliged. Did you hear that, son? You better take good care of her. I wouldn't mind a beer, and I know my son has some cold."

"I intend to, Dad. You need something 'sides a beer?" Mentally thanking his lucky stars that Kaitlyn was comfortable enough in his home to play hostess, Grant grabbed a beer from the fridge, popped the cap, and handed it to his old man.

"Well, I was thinking about your downed corn and the money you lost, and I wish you'd let me help you."

"Dad, I'll be fine. I ain't takin' money out of the family accounts for my losses."

"Yeah, I knew you were gonna say that, but I went into town today to see about ordering you another bulk feeder and I ran into Wes Ablekopp."

Ignoring his irritation that his father was trying to purchase him a new feeder for a moment, Grant tried to remember who Wes Ablekopp might be. "From Scottsbluff?"

"Yep, that's the one."

"What the hell was he doing all the way over here?"

"Does it bother you if he curses in front of you, darlin'?" Grant's father asked Kaitlyn. Once again her sweet giggle eased his annoyance.

"No, sir. I like how honest he is. Trust me, it's refreshing."

"If he gets too big for his buckskins, you let me know."

Kaitlyn shot Grant a mischievous grin that he swore reached through his chest and gripped his cock. "I promise I will, Mr. Camden."

"That'a girl. Anyway, Abelkopp's selling off all of his land, his equipment, and all of his stock. Got 350 head. More'n most ain't calved. Got a dozen prize bulls, too. Be hell getting 'em over here, but if you want 'em, he ain't asking near what they're worth."

"Why's he selling off cheap?"

"I asked that. He's in a bad way. Marital troubles. His wife never quite took to ranching life. He's moving her back to the city trying to save the marriage. He says he don't have much hope. I feel for the guy. I really do. I'd like to help him out if we can."

"I don't know, Dad. It's like I told Luke, if I burn it all back and run cattle on it I can't go back to corn. We're out if the markets change."

"Yeah, I know that, too, but keeping your stock outta your corn keeps you working round the clock. Diversifying is great, but so is settling down … maybe takin' a load off now and again … maybe making me some more grandbabies, if that's what's in the cards."

Gall surged through Grant. If his daddy didn't shut his mouth, he was gonna scare Kaitlyn off. Five minutes ago, she was talking about when she had to leave the ranch. "You got any more plans for my life I oughta know about?"

"Take it easy. I wasn't trying to ruffle your feathers. I just wanted to tell you about the sale. He says he'll sell 'em to you before he calls the auctioneer if you want 'em. I ain't trying to plan your life for you. I'm trying to help."

"When's Abelkopp want an answer?"

"I'm sure he'll give you a week or two. I got his number."

"I'll think on it. Still don't know which ends up just yet."

"Well, when you get it figured, let your old man know. We'll help you move 'em."

"All right, fine. Thanks, Dad."

"Your brothers said you all were thinkin' about going to Saddlebacks."

"I ain't even gotten a chance to ask her if she wants to go."

"Go where?" Easing beside him, Kaitlyn laced her fingers through his. A steady calm washed through his weary veins as soon as their skin connected.

"Remember the bar with the church sign? My brothers think a few drinks and a few dances with you would do me good tonight. You interested? If you don't wanna go, we can just stay here. Either way suits me fine."

"Dancing sounds like fun, but I'm still kind of a fugitive, aren't I?" As soon as her teeth sank into that bottom lip Grant knew she was nervous.

"I was just about to say the same thing," Ev sighed. "I doubt anyone all the way out here knows who she is, but you know I don't care for any of my kids to invite trouble to supper."

"We'll do whatever she wants, Dad."

"Let me know what you decide about the stock. Your mama's got supper on. I'm gonna go eat. If you need us for anything, call us."

"Will do," Grant noted the wistful look Kaitlyn's beautiful blue eyes as he saw his father out.

"I doubt anybody from the Lincoln police department has even heard of Pleasant Glen, sugar. Your daddy included. But now that I think about it, I have a better idea if you're wanting to get away from the ranch for a little while."

"I have a really hard time hearing in bars, so I've never actually been to a honkytonk before, as lame as that probably sounds to you."

"You grew up on an asphalt farm, peaches, why would you not going to a honkytonk make you lame? Ain't nothing about you that's lame."

"Dancing with you sounds so sexy. I'd love to go, but I am a little worried someone might see me." That intoxicating heat painted swirls in her cheeks once again.

"Sexy, huh?" Jerking her into his arms, he brought her lips back to his and ravaged her mouth like a man possessed.

Her inquisitive little fingers stroked over his chest. She trembled in his arms. God, she was exquisite. He had no idea how to explain that to her. He only knew how to show her. "Damn, I need you," he grunted.

"I thought we were going to a bar?"

He caught the note of curiosity in her tone. "Maybe later, or some other day. Tonight I'm gonna take you out dancing, and then I'm gonna take what I've been wanting since the moment I walked out this door in the morning."

"How are we going to dance if we aren't going to the bar?"

"Let a man give you a few surprises. I can be damned near romantic when I put my mind to it, and when I'm hard up enough to drive fence posts with my dick."

She dissolved into hysterical giggles while he located clean clothes to wear and packed a few supplies. "When we get back will you also tell me what all of that was about corn and cattle?"

"I'll tell you anything you want to know, sweetness. Ain't a real pleasant conversation so I'd much prefer to have it after our date, if it's all the same to you."

"Should I change for this date? I have a few sundresses in my suitcase."

"Sugar, if you take them clothes off now, I make you no promises we'll ever make it out to the truck. Just don't mention to me again whose jeans those are. 'Sides, I like you in my shirt."

Chapter 22

"Where are we going exactly?" Kaitlyn asked him for the third time in the last two miles. Not taking any chances with her, he'd driven one of Luke's old Fords instead of his new truck.

She was twirling those curls around her index finger over and over.

Holding his hand out for her to grasp instead, he grinned. "You nervous or excited about where we're going?"

"Both, I think. I don't know much about country life, so if we're going out to gather eggs or feed cows or something I'll be terrible at it, and you keep driving further and further away from town."

Chuckling, Grant shook his head at her. "You're the cutest thing I've ever laid eyes on. Have I told you that today?"

"You told me I was beautiful, which I much prefer to being cute."

"You are beautiful, but you're also cute. Just have to get over it, peaches. And by the way, you saying you'd be terrible at feeding cattle, three more strikes. First off, egg gathering usually takes place in the mornings, so I'm told. I wouldn't know because chickens are evil and I don't want nothing to do with 'em unless they're fried and on my supper plate."

"How are chickens evil?" He earned himself another giggle.

"Just trust me on it, they're evil."

"So, just cows for you then?"

"Used to be cows and corn, not sure that's how it's gonna be anymore though."

"Am I allowed to ask more about what your dad said now? I wish I could hear your mom as well as I hear your dad."

"Believe me, if Mama needs you to hear her, she'll get your attention. And you're allowed to ask anything you want, sugar. I'll always shoot straight with you. You know that."

"I know. I love that. So, are you going to buy that man's cows?"

"Not sure," Grant sighed. "Sounds like I could get them cheap and the corn markets took a huge dive two years ago and they haven't recovered. Been rough being a corn farmer lately. Family wants me to burn back the downed corn and run cattle on the land instead."

"What do you want to do?"

Drive you to Vegas tonight, marry you, fuck you constantly for the next several months, put babies in that sweet belly, and grow old with you. Nothing else even matters. He sank his teeth in his tongue to keep from voicing any of that. "Not sure. Dad was right, it was a mighty effort to keep the cattle outta my corn. Beef market's been up for a while, but it'll fall at some point. It always does. It's like I told you, ranching's a crap shoot on a good day."

"Well, what does your gut say? I thought you always went with it."

"I do, but there's a good bit at stake. I have to do right by everyone that depends on me."

Kaitlyn considered his words. His deep graveled tone pricked with tension. She knew what it felt like to be the one stone in the dam keeping the water from drowning your family. She knew it and yet she was sitting there in his truck pretending her family didn't exist. Promising herself that the next day, or maybe the next, she'd ask Grant to take her home just long enough to make certain her parents weren't coming apart at the seams, she laced her fingers through his.

"What was that about the man's wife, the one who's selling the cattle? Why didn't she like ranch life?"

Grant glanced her way. Concern shadowed his eyes. He worked his jaw almost like he was considering not answering despite his promise that he always would. "Ranching … it just … it ain't an easy life I guess. People get in it not realizing that every animal depends on you. When it's hot as hell like it was today, twisters, rain, when there's three feet of snow on the ground, when you're sick and tired, you still don't get a day off. Plus, living out in the country can get kinda lonely. There ain't a coffee shop on every corner. Not a lot of places to go if you get stir crazy and sick of looking at steers. Closest neighbor's miles and miles from your homestead. Just ain't always easy."

"Do you ever wish you hadn't been born into a ranching family?" She already knew the answer. She'd spent hours in his truck the day before watching his eyes light up every time he discussed being a cowboy and growing up on the ranch. He needed to say it out loud so he'd be reminded of how much he loved it.

"Nah, never. I love it. Cattle rancher through and through. Never even considered doing anything else. Never even want to."

"Then there's your answer. When you talk about the cows, your voice sounds passionate, like even when the weather's terrible or something else is wrong it still makes you smile. When you talk about the corn, it just doesn't sound that way. Plus, you said cattle rancher through and through, not corn farmer."

"You're beautiful and smart."

"Thank you. Not sure how smart I am, but believe me, I know the difference in having a job you do because other people think you should and having one you love."

"Do you love working at Chully's, baby?"

"I love to cook. If I'm in a kitchen, I'm usually happy, unless it's my parent's kitchen, and there's no happiness anywhere in that whole huge house. But restaurant work can be weird."

"Weird how?"

"Like one time this woman ordered the country fried steak burned. So, the waitress hands me the ticket, and I just assumed she wanted it really well done. She sent it back because it wasn't black. I put it back on the fryer. She sent it back again, still not burnt enough. By the fourth time, she stood up in the middle of the lunch shift and started screaming at me. I took the plate, put it on the fryer and burned the hell out of it. Then Mr. Chully walked in and got huffy because he saw the steak and thought I'd overcooked it. I tried to explain. The waitress finally just took it back out to the lady. She ate the entire thing, like it was delicious."

"Next time I'm in Chully's I'll have a talk with him about letting morons yell at my baby. I won't have that."

"Thank you, but it's not his fault people are insane. It's all part of the job. I could tell you dozens of stories. But I have another question."

"What's that?"

"Do you ever get lonely, like you said?"

"Yeah." His one word answer spoke volumes. Another truth revealed itself to her. She never wanted him to be lonely again.

When he threw the truck into park, she forced herself to be present in this moment with him. He'd never be lonely on her account, not if she had any say over her own life, which she still wasn't certain she did.

They were parked in front of a tiny watering hole barely bigger than the swimming pools at the club. "Oh my gosh, are we really going to skinny dip?"

"Like I said, if you've a mind to strip for me, sugar, I ain't gonna try and stop you. But the sun is gonna set over them hills in about ten minutes and you said you wanted to dance. I figured the radio on this old truck would work a little better than the juke box at Saddlebacks and the back of a pickup's as good a dance floor as any.

164

I brought some quilts and we can go for a swim afterwards if you want."

"I don't know if I can skinny-dip. I've only been in a pool twice in my whole life. My mother would never let me go. But this is the most romantic thing in the world. I love it."

"I told you I'm a regular Redneck Romeo. How come you weren't allowed to swim?"

"She was convinced it would make my hearing worse."

"It won't, will it?"

"No. People who have eardrum damage can't get their ears wet. The problem with my ear is a nerve issue. Swimming won't hurt me. I just don't know how to do it."

"I'll teach you. I'd never let anything happen to you, sugar. You know that, right?"

"I know, but can we dance first?"

Chapter 23

"All I could think about all damn day was having you back in my arms," Grant grunted as he lifted his lips from hers, turned his head and went back for more. They'd gone from dancing to Tim and Faith to making out in the bed of the truck. Didn't get any better than that if you asked him.

That shiver that he swore shook him to the core whipped through her when he worked the buttons of the shirt she was wearing open. The sun sank low on the horizon bathing them in the last of its fiery glow.

"I missed you, too." She wriggled in the back of the truck trying to get even closer to him.

"I'm right here, sugar. I'll always be right here. Jesus, just let me touch you."

She made quick work of the buttons on his shirt as well, pressing her palms to his pecs, spinning her thumbs around the disks of his nipples, rendering him weak with needing her. Dispensing with her jeans took him precious little time. His hands sought her creamy thighs and the wet heat he knew he'd find there.

"Look at you in nothing but my shirt and a naughty little bra and pair of panties, so damn gorgeous."

"These aren't naughty," she teased.

"Says the woman who could tempt a saint. They're sweet and innocent. Remind me exactly what I'm taking from you and keeping all for myself. It's like I told you, peaches, ain't nothing naughtier than a good girl who knows how to misbehave."

"I definitely want to misbehave."

Thankful they were miles from the nearest human being, Grant's approving growl scared a few birds out of the nearby trees. "You want to be a bad girl for me, baby?" He tempted her mound through the lacey panties.

"Don't stop. Please," she whimpered.

"Want me to touch you? Want me to take what I want?" Running his fingertips under the crotch he hissed at the slippery connection. "So wet for me. So fucking hot and sweet." The lips of her pussy were creamy and fevered.

She spread her legs further. Her hands landed on his cock, still trapped behind his zipper. Before he could stop her, she had his fly open, freeing his steel-hard strain.

"So fucking hard for me. Drives me wild," she came right back.

"Christ almighty," he shuddered as she dipped her hand down his briefs.

Stroking up and down her slit, he felt her bloom for him. Pressing two fingers in her gently, he longed to stretch her again with his cock.

Remembering what he'd learned that morning, he kept his fingers moving inside of her and slicked his thumb with her honey. Tenderly he swept it over her clit, making her cry out his name.

"It's all for me. All mine." He knew she didn't need the reminder but dammit, he needed her to have no doubts. There was no going back.

"Feels so good," she gasped. Her body cantered against his hand. She abandoned his cock, lost in the pleasure he provided. Perfection.

"I'm about to fuck you in the back of this truck, sugar. If that ain't okay with you, speak up now." He spoke directly into her left ear.

She gave no verbal response. Instead, she sat up, scooted the lacey panties down her legs, flung them out of the truck, and threw her leg over his, centering herself against his cock.

"I think making love in the back of a pickup truck means I should get some kind of honorary country girl status, or something," Kaitlyn sighed. She was still mostly naked and plastered to his body as the darkness tucked them away from the world around them. Grant was rubbing her bare ass, back and forth, tenderly over her cheeks and she was loving every minute of it. Relaxation and contentment filled her so fully she had no room for worry or stress.

"Just give me time, sweetness. I'll make you a real country girl." He brushed another kiss on her cheek.

"How do we do that?"

"First thing we have to do is get you nekkid in the creek. Think of it as a country baptism."

"You promise not to let me drown."

"I can't even believe you just said that."

"Sorry. I know you wouldn't. Just a little nervous. How deep is that creek?" She studied the waves of white moonlight as they danced across the surface.

"You promise you trust me?"

"Yes."

"Then come on." He patted her backside.

Before she could protest, he'd leapt out of the bed of the truck in one adept movement. Shucking his jeans, he stood naked before her and offered her his hand. She allowed him to settle her on her feet on the muddy shoreline.

"So, I just take off my bra and your shirt and get in naked?"

"That is the very definition of skinny dippin', peaches."

"Smart ass."

"Don't get sassy. Paddling your wet backside would sting, but that don't mean I won't do it."

"Well, then don't laugh at me."

"Why? You're cute."

Rolling her eyes, Kaitlyn shimmied out of his shirt, reveling in his hungry grunt. He was nothing if not relentless.

As she slid out of her bra, he stalked to the water. With no hesitation, he stepped in and dove forward with a splash. Irritated with her case of nerves, Kaitlyn forced herself to the water's edge.

He resurfaced a moment later.

"Is it cold?"

"Not nearly as cold as the ones on the ranch. It's shallow and it's been blistering hot all day. Come here to me." He held out his hand. "I ain't gonna dunk you or do anything you're not comfortable with. Just come here."

Keeping her eyes locked on his she stepped into the water and sank an inch or two. Readjusting, she made it two more steps and had his hand.

"That's it."

Five minutes later he'd coaxed her in to her waist. The cool water felt nice but not nearly as good as having his hands holding her steady.

"I'll teach you to swim in the daylight and once the lakes at the ranch warm up, but for tonight why don't I teach you to float on your back?"

"Okay." A shiver of nerves worked through her. "What do I do?"

"Relax for me. I'm right here. Ease back in my arms."

She tried. Arching her back, she settled in his capable arms and ordered her body to stop tensing up.

"I'd never let anything happen to you. Ever. Just relax." Suddenly, his wet lips were on hers, giving her a dose of the best medicine. She eased.

"That's it. Now let your head fall back. Get them pretty red curls wet."

"Promise you won't let me go."

"Honey, I ain't ever gonna let you go."

168

Ordering herself to trust him completely, she relaxed in the water. His hands stayed under her back and her ass. A minute later she was floating. Her teeth sank into her bottom lip. She tried to grin without sinking.

"Look at you. And just so you know I'm a good guy, I ain't even sucking them nipples standing straight up, staring at me, tempting the hell outta me. I deserve some kind of prize or something."

When she started laughing, her rear end sunk, but he never let her go under. And she knew he never would.

Chapter 24

The next day, Kaitlyn asked Grant if he'd mind taking her to his parent's house while he was out working. He'd seemed pleased with that, and she was having a ball in his mother's ginormous kitchen helping prepare lunch.

"Can I ask you something else, Mrs. Camden?" She'd been peppering her with questions all morning.

"You ain't gotta ask to ask, sugar. Just ask me."

"Yesterday, Mr. Camden came by Grant's house and was telling him about the man who's selling off all of his cattle."

"Wes Abelkopp."

Kaitlyn nodded. "And he said that his wife hated ranch life. I asked Grant about that and he said it was hard to live out here. Do you think that's true, too?"

She considered while she added another four hamburger patties to the iron skillet. "I suppose if you love the city, love the people everywhere, love the shops, it's certainly a change to come out here. But I just don't really believe life is perfect anywhere. Problems in the city. Problems in the country. Problems in between. If you're depending on your surroundings to make you happy, you're real likely to end up sad. On the other hand, it is important to know yourself well enough to figure out what you want in life and how to go about getting it. But you have to bloom where you're planted. Even in the city, dandelions spring up between cracks in the cement. Might not be where they hoped to end up, but they still go on and bloom."

The ever-expanding weight in the pit of Kaitlyn's stomach grew again. She had to talk to her family. She had to go back home. She couldn't keep running. She couldn't keep using the Camdens hospitality. As much as she was certain she loved Grant, she had to figure out what it was she wanted out of life and how to go about getting it the right way, just like his mother had said.

By that evening, Grant's brothers and sisters were adamant that everyone was going to Saddlebacks.

"We don't have to go," Grant commented again as Kaitlyn applied her favorite peach-shimmer lip gloss.

"It'll be fine. I kind of want to see a little more of the town."

"There ain't all that much to see."

"I know, but it would make them happy for us to go."

"Yeah, but doing something because it makes someone else happy ain't a great reason to do it."

"I know, but this is no big deal. I liked dancing in your truck last night. Now, I can do it at a real honkytonk."

"All right, fine, but if you want to leave, you just say the word and we're out."

Mentally preparing herself for a few hours of intensely concentrating to hear anyone speak at all, Kaitlyn gave Grant a forced grin as he held the door to Saddlebacks Honkytonk open for her.

The whoosh of warm air taunted her cool skin. She gave the gravel parking lot another quick scan. Why had she agreed to come here? Crossing her arms over her chest, nervous tension crawled up her spine. Her stomach flipped and suddenly she wasn't certain she could eat at all. What if somehow someone she knew saw her there? What if she couldn't hear well enough to get away? What if they called her father?

Immediately assaulted by the drone of conversations she had no hope of understanding, the shrill tones of the ancient jukebox, the sloshed bubbles of beer hitting glasses coupled with the hum of the tap, and the scrape of barstools along the hardwood floor, Kaitlyn relaxed slightly when Grant wrapped his left arm around her and kept her tucked by his side. "I've got you, sugar. You want to go back, just tell me. All I want is to be with you." He spoke directly into her good ear and then brushed a kiss in her hair like that was the only purpose of him holding her so closely. She hadn't said a single word. He'd proven yet again that when it came to her he was always paying attention.

Tucking her into a large booth near the back, he positioned himself so he could play interpreter for her if she needed him to and kept his arm around her. His brothers and their wives took the seats on the opposite side.

"If all the Camden brothers are in here it must be bad," a bartender covered in tattoos and piercings approached the table. Kaitlyn scolded herself for the ping of fear that pricked at her stomach. She hadn't quite made out what he'd said other than something about the Camden brothers, and her judgment for his tattoos was something her father had taught her. Even when all of Keith's Army buddies had gotten a few after bootcamp, Keith hadn't because their father hated them.

Summer, Austin's wife, wiggled out of the denim jacket she was wearing. Kaitlyn caught the edge of a tattoo under her black tank top.

Luke was talking to the bartender. She couldn't understand much of the conversation. Luke's voice wasn't quite as low as Grant's, so she discreetly studied Summer's tattoo.

It looked like the Camden brand she'd seen on the entrance gates. "You okay, sweets?" Summer reached over and placed her hand on Kaitlyn's.

"I'm sorry, what?" she startled.

"She asked if you were okay." Grant spoke directly in her left ear again and made it look like another tender kiss.

"Thank you, but I should tell them. Um, I'm hard of hearing. Actually, I'm completely deaf in my right ear, and the hearing in my left isn't great either. It's a little difficult for me to hear over all of the ambient noise in here."

If there had been any remnant of doubt left as to how much she loved the Camdens, it disappeared when none of them appeared shocked.

"Well, Austin's hard a' listening, so we'll figure it out. I'll just speak up." Summer winked at her.

"Probably work out all right for ya, that way you ain't gotta listen to him bitch quite as much," Luke gestured to Grant. He spoke just loud enough for his voice to slice through the noise surrounding them.

"I ain't hard 'a listening." Austin smirked.

"Bullshit," Grant, Luke, Indie, and Summer all chimed in. Kaitlyn doubled over laughing. That she'd heard loud and clear.

"I was just admiring your tattoo," Kaitlyn confessed as the laughter died down.

"Oh, well here." Summer jerked the tank top up, and there on full display wasn't the Camden brand, it was Austin's. Trying to imagine having Grant's brand on her body sent another flood of heat throughout her. Suddenly, she completely understood the appeal of a tattoo. Being branded by Grant was precisely what she longed for.

The bartender returned with a pitcher of beers for the table. "You gonna introduce me, Grant?" He gestured to Kaitlyn.

"This is Katy Sommerville … my girlfriend."

Like she'd been doused with the cold beer, Kaitlyn's mouth hung open in shock. Girlfriend. Had they discussed that? That sounded supremely official. Another round of nerves twisted in her stomach. It sounded a little *too* official. Her mind made no sense. A moment before she'd wanted to tattoo his brand somewhere on her body. She'd spent the entire day mentally preparing herself to live out on the ranch with him. Now, she was nervous about being called his girlfriend. *Grant really should just dump me and find someone who isn't insane.*

"Did you tell her that 'fore you up and decided to tell Aaron that?" Luke chided his brother.

Aaron chuckled. "I'm gonna hand you a shovel and let you dig yourself outta that one, but I will promise to keep it to myself, which might ease the blow. Natalie coming in tonight?"

"I'm beginning to think the only reason we get such good service in here is 'cause you got a thing for our sister," Austin harassed.

Kaitlyn could just barely make out his words. The panic in her mind drowned out most of the racket in the bar. The only other time in her life she'd been someone's girlfriend was when she'd begrudgingly started dating Seth. She'd snuck out once in high school under the encouragement of Trenton Miller, the boy she'd had a crush on, and had tried to go to a party where she was certain he was going to ask to be her boyfriend. Keith managed to catch her at the end of the fairway and made her go home.

In New York, she went to a party with Ollie Shelton, a guy she briefly dated from culinary school, but she'd hated it as much as she'd ended up hating Ollie. Drunk college kids out of control and random hookups that took place all over someone's parents' Fifth Avenue apartment wasn't something she was interested in participating in.

Girlfriend wasn't a role she was all that accustomed to fulfilling, and somehow not one she was entirely certain she was rid of. She still hadn't officially talked to Seth. That ridiculous ring was still shoved in her suitcase.

"I'm sorry. I shouldn't have said that. I told you I'm no good at half-measures," Grant sighed. Disappointment and fear clouded his eyes.

"It's fine."

"It ain't fine. Don't lie to me."

Ordering her thoughts, Kaitlyn landed on the real reason it had upset her. "I'm sorry. I don't want to lie to you. Could we just talk outside for a minute? I want to be your girlfriend. I just need to do this right."

"Move," Grant ordered Austin out of his way. Dammit, why couldn't he just figure out some way to stop fucking up on Kaitlyn's account? He was sick of apologizing and half-terrified she was going to ask to be taken home at any moment.

Stalking through the sea of ranchers and cowgirls clogging up the dancefloor, he let the chilly air slap him in the face as he led them outside, blocking her from the wind.

"I'm sorry," he began as soon as the door slammed shut and he had her out by the truck he'd driven them in.

"Please, don't apologize." Cementing the notion that he would never in this life or the next understand women, she stood on her tiptoes and threw her arms around him. Embracing her automatically, he had no idea where the hell this was going.

"Sugar, I ain't sure if we're washing or hanging out. You wanna tell me how bad I fucked up so I can go 'bout tryin' to fix it?"

When she settled back in front of him, she was grinning ear to ear. "You didn't fuck up at all. I just never, ever want to be a girl that cheated on you. I don't want to cheat on us. I couldn't. You mean too much to me. I don't want Seth to have anything to do with us. The past two days I've been going along, half-pretending that we're already a couple and that we live together, but in the back of my mind I knew I was just playing house. I don't want to do that. It's like I told you, I pretended to be someone else for so long. And you," she shook her head in disbelief, "somehow, you convinced me to at least attempt to be me. Well, I have to deal with Seth and my father. I have to deal with whatever is waiting on me in Lincoln before I can have a relationship with you. And I want to have a relationship with you more than I want to take my next breath. I just have to do it in the right order. It's the only way I won't feel like I cheated on us."

Well, hell. All right then. "So, you're saying after you tell the shitwhistle to go fuck himself sideways, then I can call you my girlfriend?"

Her entire body shook with her laughter. "I would really like that, but I also have to face my dad and whatever hell might come with that."

"You ain't facing any of 'em alone, sugar."

"Thank you, but I think you better take me back to Lincoln tomorrow." He swore the stars above them couldn't outdo the fervent sparks of determination in her eyes. The moonlight played in the auburn of her hair.

His chest ached. His entire body ached for her. She wanted closure. He couldn't deny her that, but dammit, he wanted to. He wanted to make her forget life before they were together even

174

existed. Her life before had been some kind of twisted shit of making her parents happy. It had hurt her. That was more than he could stand.

"Tomorrow, huh?"

"It could maybe be late tomorrow after we spend the day together if you want. Do you understand why I have to do this? Please know I'm not trying to hurt you. It's like my heart, that never ever belonged to Seth, already belongs to you, but my brain wants the closure. Probably my stupid lawyer side and the fact that I was raised by the chief of police. Just please tell me you know that when I'm with you, it doesn't even matter what we're doing, it's all my heart. Does that make sense?"

"Kinda."

"How about I really never want to leave, but I want to do right by you always?"

"Pretty sure that's my line, peaches."

"Yeah, and you're not the only one who's hoping that Camden legend is true."

Desperate to hold her, he drew her back to his chest and nuzzled his face in her hair, inhaling her scent. It was the same today as it was the day before. He'd been so hell-bent on taking her back at his house he hadn't noticed. Now, he wanted nothing more than to slow down time so he could memorize every detail about her. "How come you smell like a ripe peach in summertime all the time now?"

"I decided I don't want to wear a different scent every day anymore. I want one that makes me happy, and I thought you might like it because I really like you calling me peaches."

"You really mean that when you said you hope the legend's true?"

Lifting her face from his chest, she stared him down. "Yes."

"Promise me something," he commanded.

"Anything."

"Promise me you ain't just saying you want to be my girlfriend because you know I want you to say that. I won't be another man in your life who tells you how to feel. I don't want you doing things just 'cause you think they make me happy."

"I promise, Grant. This is me, the real me. Not old-Kaitlyn or New-Kaitlyn, just maybe Katy with a Y," she laughed.

"I can handle with a Y. Just no more of that broken Kit-Kat shit."

"Never again."

"Fuck." Terror bolted through him as soon as he saw the squad car approaching slowly. Blue flashing lights blinded him as it pulled into the parking lot blocking the entrance. "Get in the truck," he ordered.

Chapter 25

"Oh my God!" Abject panic blistered out from Kaitlyn's chest, scorching through her limbs. She trembled. Grant steadied her as he opened the truck door and tried to lift her inside. "No. I am not broken. I am not weak, and I am not going to be bullied by my father anymore." Something deep inside of her snapped in that moment. Her heart beat against her rib cage, certain now was the moment it was going to make its escape.

She clung to Grant but stood on her own two feet.

"You get your hands off of her now," Josh shouted across the parking lot. Suddenly, Sophie bolted from the car.

"Oh my God! Kit-kat." She raced towards them. "Are you okay?"

"I am fine. Better than I have ever been. What are you doing here?" Kaitlyn's voice shook, but she stood her ground.

"I've been calling you for two freaking days! Josh got his tag number when he pulled you over and I made him bring me out here. I'm going to kill you. How could you just run away?"

"You told me to run away!" Kaitlyn matched her volume.

"I also told you to keep your phone on. Daddy's going crazy. He's being awful, yelling at me, yelling at everyone. Mama won't come out of their room. I got Seth to drop the criminal charges against you. How could you be so irresponsible?"

Incensed rage burned away any trepidation she'd felt a moment before. Jerking out of Grant's arms, she glared at her sister. "Is he, Soph? Is he being awful? Demanding and hateful and Mom's so depressed you can't even exist in the same house because the air is too heavy to breathe? Why don't you tell me what that's like?

"I've spent every single day of the last three years living with them like that. You're never there. You go see Dad at the station where he has to act civil, and you call and coax mom to go shopping with you or to have lunch at the club because that's easy. They put on a show for everyone else. But you aren't there when a commercial for the Army comes on and she bursts into tears again and sits in Keith's room for days at a time. Or when Dad hurls the mashed potatoes you just made against the wall and shatters the bowl because I told him again that Mom needs some real help. Or when he screams at me for no reason at all. Or takes your cookbooks out to the garbage can and sets them on fire because you're a lawyer now, not a cook, and he doesn't like it when you make foods we didn't eat before Keith died.

Tell me what it's like to have to hide where you work because it's not the law firm Daddy mandated. Tell me what it's like to have to date a guy you can't stand because dating him is easier than sending your own parents further into the hell where they exist.

"That's exactly how I ran away and how I'm *that* irresponsible. And you know what, I deserved to run away. I deserve a fucking break. I should have been irresponsible a long, long time ago, but I had to hold everything together. No one else knows what it's like to live there, walking around on pins and needles trying to make sure you never accidentally do or say anything wrong. And then there was Seth, whose favorite thing to do was to act like he was some kind of show piece that I should be proud to be with. That was when he wasn't telling me how stupid he thinks I am or talking over me when he had time for me at all. I am so sick of him and his passive aggressive shit.

"So don't you dare stand there and tell me I'm being irresponsible, or selfish, or anything else you came here to say. In fact, just go. I'm not leaving."

Her sister stood before her speechless.

"You're telling us that you're just gonna stay here with him?" Josh accused on Sophie's behalf.

"No, I'm telling you I'm going to stay here because it's where I want to be, and for the first time in my life, I'm giving myself a chance." With her own declaration, a little of her fury cooled. "I am sorry I never turned my phone back on. I should have, but, my God, Soph, I needed a break."

"Your father isn't going to just let you stay here, Kit-kat. He's got the whole force out looking for both of you. I told him you were with some cowboy. I didn't tell him I had the tag number. I wanted to check on you first, but as soon as I do he'll have you both arrested. Now do as I say and get in the car."

"Or you could crawl outta her daddy's ass and keep your trap shut. Let her come home whenever she fucking well pleases, seein' as it's our life and not yours." Indignation perforated Grant's threat, but still his voice steadied her. She reached back and he was right there. His hands in hers and then his strength right beside her.

"I'm going to tell Seth you're out here with some other man, Kaitlyn. You're cheating on him. He made a mistake and this is how you're going to treat him. Keith would be ashamed."

"Don't you dare! Don't you dare even say his name to me!" Kaitlyn screamed.

178

"What the hell is going on out here?" Luke, Austin, Indie, and Summer took position on either side of Grant.

"I could arrest all of you for harboring a fugitive or a runaway, you know," Josh's tenor voice lost a great deal of its earlier confidence.

"You could but you ain't," Austin challenged.

"Bring it city-boy," Indie drawled. "Cow*boys* around here aren't the only ones who know how to skin a live snake."

"Ain't nobody tellin' Kaitlyn to do anything she don't wanna do," Summer menaced. "Just where the hell do you get off, thinkin' you're in charge of her? I have plenty of experience letting whiny little bitches just like you and her daddy know what I think of 'em."

"Believe I heard you say something about somebody dropping the charges. Meaning, she ain't a fugitive, and she's a grown woman not a runaway. I gotta tell ya, son, we don't much like uppity city-police who think they can drive into town and start ordering people around." Luke upped the ante and all of the Camden family looked like they had no issue using their fists to drive home his point.

Suddenly her sister located her voice. "Kit-kat, you don't even know what you're saying. You don't even *know* these people. They are clearly insane. I never should have told you to run. I'm sorry. You're not thinking straight. You're not strong enough to be out here with people like this. Do you even hear what you're saying? Just get in the car and let us take you home."

"Oh my God! Did you actually just ask me if I heard what *I* was saying?" Kaitlyn demanded vengefully. "I may not hear a lot of things, Soph, but I do know my own thoughts. I can't believe you said that to me. I'm not a child and I'm not an invalid. I am perfectly capable of doing what I want *when* I want. And I don't care anymore what Keith might think or what you think. He isn't here and neither of you get to have any say over me anymore. I know these people a lot better than you think, and what's more, they know me a lot better than you do."

Her entire world shifted like the turn of the kaleidoscope she'd had as a kid. Everything around her was different. Aware of the world outside of her own misery, she noted numerous cowboys and cowgirls shifting and lurking in the shadows of the blue lights. Their eyes were all trained on Josh. Eager and edgy, they eased ever closer.

"Fair warning, cityboy, you go after Grant or any of the Camdens, you'll answer to us all. If I was you, I'd git for you git gotten good," a man Kaitlyn had never even seen before spit in the gravel between

Josh's feet. "Ain't a man standing out here that wouldn't beat the shit outta you on Grant's behalf, even if we do end up in jail. Fact is, we all owe him a helluva lot more than that. Camdens are the backbone of this entire town."

"Well, Miss High and Mighty just when are you coming home?" Sophie huffed.

"She'll be home by noon tomorrow or I'm putting out a warrant for his arrest," Josh thrust his finger Grant's direction, accepting his own defeat. "Get in the car, Sophie. We're leaving."

Kaitlyn's heart frantically leapt to her throat when Josh's cruiser almost collided with a truck attempting to pull into the parking lot as he made his getaway.

Several rapid blinks did nothing to blur the memory of her own sister standing in the shadow of flashing blue lights asking her if she'd heard her own voice. She wasn't backing down now. "Grant, I'm so sorry about all of this. I will not let my father arrest you. If you never wanted to see me again, I understand." Of all the things she'd just screamed at her sister, that was the moment she choked. The words were putrid ash on her tongue. She fought not to gag.

"Come here to me." He guided her back into his arms, wrapping her up in that sanctuary of muscle and heat. She buried her face in his chest, desperate to hear the gruff rumble of his voice. He didn't hate her. He should hate her for all of the trouble she'd caused him.

"Bravest woman I have ever met." He rocked them back and forth in the parking lot. With that, she knew nothing about her life before was ever going to be the same, but she had to figure out some way to mend the fabric of Old-Kaitlyn and New-Kaitlyn with the woman she actually wanted to be. She couldn't start a new life while trying to bury the old one.

Having absolutely no right to ask him for anything at all, the plea still sprang forth from her lips, "Will you just keep talking to me for a minute? Please."

She could have asked him to saw off his own arm after all of that, and he would've done it. All she wanted was to hear his voice. My God, had he known years ago that she existed nothing would've stopped him from finding her, from rescuing her from the hell she lived in. Her declaration that she was there because she wanted to be erased any remnant of doubt he'd had.

180

Not certain exactly what to say, he just spoke the first words that came to mind, "I've got you, sugar, and I ain't ever letting you go back to that. I'm right here."

"Grant," Dusty Sullivan nodded as he passed by. "You let us know if we're needed. I got no time for some sonuvabitch that wants to tell a woman to go somewhere she don't wanna be, cop or not."

"Much obliged, Dusty." Grant wished they would go, but they'd been all but promised a fight and were high on testosterone and stupidity at the moment.

"Your daddy sounds like a real piece 'a work, sugar. You let any of us know if you need us, we'll be there. We take care of our own," Wes Kilroy vowed as he passed by. The only indication Grant had that she'd heard him was her strengthening her grip on him.

"Grant, you know where we'll be if you need us," was echoed from several ranchers lookin' to throw in.

"I'm much obliged to you all, but it ain't gon' come to blows. That don't never fix nothing, and you all know it," he gave his decree hoping everyone would find something else to do. "If they'll shut the fuck up, I'll keep talking to you." He lowered his head and spoke directly in her left ear. The smile he felt against his chest righted most every wrong the night had held. "Pretty sure the whole town wants to adopt you."

"I might let them," she tried for a joke but missed the mark. "And I'm pretty sure it's you they love. Would you mind if we went back to your house? I have a few phone calls I need to make."

"Sure, sugar. Hop on in."

Luke was waiting on him at the end of the truck after he got Kaitlyn up in the seat. "She okay?"

"She sound okay to you?"

"Sounded like *she* didn't even realize what hell she's been living in 'til just then. And I'll tell you this, we are lucky fucks Holly and Nat didn't make a show just then or that cop'd already be tied and quartered with my wife holding the whip."

"Don't even pretend thinkin' about Indie with a crop don't make you hornier than a three-balled tomcat."

Luke chuckled. "Trust me, I stay hornier than a tomcat, and she's dangerous enough without a crop. Listen to me, though, he wasn't shitting you. He'll get that warrant if you don't show up in Lincoln tomorrow. Might get it even if you do."

"Yeah, I'm aware."

"What are you gonna do?"

"If she wants to go face 'em, I'll take her back. I'm sure as hell not leaving her there, but I'll take her back and let her tell 'em all what she thinks of 'em. If she wants to stay on the ranch, that's where we'll be. Tell you the truth, I've a good mind to take a crop to her daddy and her ex just 'fore I get after 'em with a tire iron."

"Yeah, well, Indie could loan you a few of those, too."

"You caught that her daddy is the chief of police, right?"

"I figured he was some kinda power-player in all this. But in my experience the best things in life never come easy, and some things are sure as hell worth fightin' for. What I can't quite figure is who Keith is."

"He was her twin brother. Killed a few years ago in Afghanistan."

"Jesus, poor kid." Luke shook his head.

"Yeah. She's tried so hard to keep the rest of her family from falling apart she ain't even really had a chance to deal with it yet. Whole thing's pretty fucked up."

"Then you gotta get the herd up two hills and across a river. Will you do something for me?"

"What's that?"

"For once in your life, will you not take this fight on by yourself? Let us help you."

Gall singed Grant's throat. The vow he'd made to himself when he was seventeen reverberated against his skull. He swore he'd never have to be bailed out again. Glancing at Kaitlyn huddled in the truck, already sitting in the middle waiting on him, he prayed to God he wouldn't have to break his promise.

Chapter 26

"I cannot believe I just screamed all of that out at a parking lot at a honkytonk bar," Kaitlyn whimpered as Grant made the turn off on the dirt road that would eventually lead to the ranch. "Your friends probably think I'm one of those crazy daytime television reality stars or something."

Sinking his teeth into the side of his cheek to keep from laughing, Grant shook his head. "Sugar, the Glen is the kinda town everyone always swears they can't wait to leave but then no one ever does 'cause you'd just miss it too damn much. That was Wes Kilroy that told you we take care of our own, and that's the truth. His daddy is the mayor, by the way. None of them thought anything bad about you. Now, your daddy and Josh on the other hand ..." He refused to elaborate further.

"Did I embarrass you?" Devastation weighted her tone.

"Hell no. I've never been more proud of you."

"You've only known me three days."

"Yeah, and in the past three days I could name you a hundred dozen things I love about you, so I don't really see how that matters."

"You could not."

Ire already resided just under the surface after their run in with Josh and her sister. It quickly surged through him again. "One, I love the way you purse your lips when you stare up at me when you first see me after a while, and you've forgotten that you don't have to concentrate so hard to hear me. As soon as I start talking, you grin when realize you can just relax and look at me. Two, I love the way you get fascinated with things like the tractor or how the ranch works. Three, I like the way you loop and twirl all them curls around your face with your fingers when you get a little nervous or when you're thinkin'. Oh, and I like how you bite your lip, too. Four, I love how brave you are. You look life right in the face, call it a bitch, and dare it to come at you again. Five, I love how gentle you are, and this definitely makes me a bastard, but I love how innocent you are, too.

"Six through about twenty, I fucking love the way you come for me, love the look on your face, love the sounds you make, the way you taste, how rosy pink your nipples get when I suck 'em, that you love it when I suck 'em hard. I love that little sex kitten purr you have when I rub your ass, and Jesus Christ in Heaven, the way you groan out my name when I bring you.

"Twenty-one, I love the way you'll argue with me even when you don't want to just 'cause you know I like it when you're stubborn, which I'm counting as twenty-two, by the way. I love how hard you fought to keep your family from coming apart at the seams. I love how hard you love your brother, and I said love not loved. I ain't that much of an idiot. I love how sweet you are even when you are bein' stubborn. It's like I love how you're a fighter when you're fighting and a lover when you're loving.

"I love that you want kids and you ain't afraid to admit that. Most chicks won't come out and say what they want 'cause they think they gotta play games. I hate that and I love that you don't do it."

"I didn't admit that, exactly."

"See, there you go, fightin' even though you know I'm right. Now, what number was I on? I lost count, but I also fuckin' love the way you feel in my arms, like the whole world could be going straight to shit in a basket and if I can put you in my lap everything feels like it's gonna be all right.

"I love how you ask me to talk to you when that's what you need. I love how we never run out of things to talk about, but even if we do, I like just being quiet with you. I love the way you cook and that you love *to* cook. I love how smart you are. As weak as it makes me, I love that you need me. And your ass. Fuck, and your tits. The way they bounce and swell when I'm pounding into you. I love pounding into you. Oh, and them sweet little squeaks and moans you make when I've got my head between your legs. The way you shiver. The way you taste, spicy and sweet on my tongue. Your whole damn body. I love them curves, darlin'. They drive me wild."

Suddenly, she leaned up in the seat and planted a tender kiss on the stubble of his jaw. "Hey Grant," her sweet breath teased at his lips, "I'm pretty sure I love you, too."

Until the words left her lips, he wasn't aware that's what he was after. She supplied them without him even knowing they were his end goal. "Oh yeah?"

"Yeah."

"What's a guy gotta do to make you damned sure?" He clamped his jaw shut tight enough for it to ache. That couldn't have been the right thing to say.

"He has to let me officially end it with the idiot I was engaged to, and he needs to let me figure out how to make it up to him because I also said those words to that fiancée, and now I'm not sure what they mean at all."

"He could probably let you do all of that. Might even help you figure it out if you wanted him to. He, uh, might'a said it a time or two when he didn't really mean it either." Grant eyed her cautiously, wondering what she'd make of that.

"Grant, I'm so sorry about Josh. I will not let my father arrest you."

Well, that came outta left field. Disappointment crashed through him, but he kept his game face on. "I ain't worried about it."

"I'm still processing you telling other women you loved them. I'm trying not to act like a jealous bitch since I just acted like a crazy person in a parking lot."

"You're too damned good at figuring out what I'm thinking. I told you, you were smart, and you could never be a bitch or a crazy person."

"Your face gives away your thoughts. Being deaf makes you pretty intuitive, and it's weird that I automatically hate whoever you said that to. I don't even know them."

"I hate that SOB you were engaged to, so let's call it even for now."

"This is just really fast. Everyone's going to think I was just on the rebound, but I swear to you I'm not."

"You can't run cattle on another man's opinions."

"What?"

"Something my daddy always says. It means who gives a flying shit what anyone else thinks. This is our life. Fast. Slow. Somewhere in between. Shouldn't matter to anyone but us."

"Yeah, but I do have some kind of a life two hours from here that I have to deal with, and there are several people there that are going to care because they think they know what's best for me about everything. I tried to pretend they weren't there and look where that got us. Your mom was right. I can't wish that life away."

"Mama's pretty much always right, but what'd she tell you exactly?"

"Basically, that it was okay for me to take a break on the ranch and just pretend nothing existed outside of these gates," she gestured to the Camden Ranch sign as they made their approach, "but that if I let life go on too long without me it can spin out of control."

"She hit the nail on the head with that one, didn't she?"

"I'll figure out a way to get Dad to back off and to get rid of Seth. If it weren't for his stupid car, I bet he wouldn't even care."

"I got a feeling this ain't gonna go down easy on any front."

"Yeah, I have that feeling, too."

As soon as they were in the vicinity of Grant's front door, Kaitlyn scooted out of the truck and headed inside. Determination armored itself in her march, quelling just a little of her fear. Digging through her suitcases she located her phone. Her heart hammered in her chest. She had no idea what to say or what Seth would say. Somehow he always managed to make her think every issue they ever attempted to deal with was her fault. Not this time. She would get this formality over with so she could really make a commitment to Grant.

Before she could make the call, he stood in front her commanding her attention. "You don't have to call him, sugar. I'm pretty sure leaving him at the altar and writing your breakup note in the paint of his car let him know what you think of him."

"I know, but I don't want to leave any room for error. He's a dirty lawyer, Grant. I won't give him any ammo to go after either of us with. I have to do this right. It's the only way to convince my family that I know what I'm doing."

"Makes me fucking crazy to think about you talking to him. If he's a douche, Katy Belle, I swear I'll feed him his own sac for breakfast."

"He's always a douche, but I still have to call him."

An annoyed grunt preceded Grant's hand tangling in her hair and his tongue diving past her lips. This kiss was somehow more than all of the others had been. It was a claim of ownership. If he'd tattooed his cattle brand on her backside it couldn't have been any clearer. She was his. It was a demonstration of how he always made love to her: hot, dominating, and all consuming.

Being consumed was all she really wanted. Her body longed to melt into his and forget everything else she needed to do. His right hand cupped her breast through her shirt. His thumb centered over her nipple. A shiver shot through her, one of the things he'd said he loved.

True to his word as always, a frustrated growl sounded from him when she eased out of his hands. "Don't."

"I have to do this."

"Fine, but will you do something for me?"

"Anything."

"Don't fucking apologize for anything. He don't deserve it."

"Sit down, cowboy, and let me do this my way, okay?"

He obeyed with a huffy grunt this time. When she climbed in his lap with her phone, his scowl softened however.

"When I'm on the phone, I have to use my one good ear so I may not be able to hear you if you talk to me," she warned him.

"Not making me hate this less, darlin'. If you're hellbent on calling his sorry ass just get it over with."

"Impatient much?"

"For you? Always." He leaned forward and grabbed the notepad he'd written the coffee note on that morning.

Willing a dose of courage to somehow be in the breath she inhaled, she turned the phone back on and cringed at the fifty-seven missed calls. There were sixteen texts from Seth. Every one of them was basically the same, all demands that she give him the engagement ring back. She touched Seth's name on her contact list.

"Six-hundred and fifty dollars to replace the hood of my car and that doesn't include a new paint job," was Seth's greeting. "And what the hell is Josh talking about you being with some other guy? That's low, Kaitlyn. I don't even know who you are anymore."

Righteous indignation ignited in her blood. "Actually, I'm pretty sure you never had any idea who I was. And are you seriously not intelligent enough to see how insanely hypocritical you're being right now? Just how long have you and Kelsey been in love, Seth?"

Grant wrote 'That's my girl' on the notepad and she couldn't help but grin.

"Kelsey has nothing to do with this."

"Actually, Kelsey has everything to do with this. I'm pretty sure she saved my life. I should really get her a gift."

"You are going to come home and explain your behavior to everyone. I was standing up at that ridiculous altar, Kaitlyn! Waiting on you. Looking like a complete fool. You ruined everything. If I lose my job over this, I'll make you sorry."

"Of course, your car and your job. Nothing else matters. I never want to see you again. You will never order me around again. I'll pay for your stupid car, and I hope you and Kelsey are *very* happy together. Other than that, you can go straight to hell."

Grant beamed.

"When are you coming home?" Seth demanded.

"We are done. You don't get to ask me that. It's none of your business anymore."

"Who are you with?"

Kaitlyn ground her teeth. Grant gently ran his fingers through her hair, giving her some semblance of peace.

"I asked you who you were with. Did you hear me? I want an answer."

"You don't have to keep repeating yourself. I ignored you just fine the first time."

Grant's low bass chuckle surrounded Kaitlyn. For a quick half-second, it soothed her.

"Oh, so he's there with you now. I somehow don't think I was the only one who had someone on the side. I had to stand there in front of the mayor, in front of my boss, in front of the entire police force, in front of Mr. Holsten, the commissioners and council members, and in front of my *father*, Kaitlyn, when you decided to walk out on me and forget the life we were supposed to create. You're the one who chose your side job over me. I won't be the one going down for this disaster you created. Even your daddy won't be able to save you this time."

"But I didn't ..."

He ended the call. Something inside of her snapped. She was certain the sound had to have been audible. The force of it vibrated through her. The last tie to her life in Lincoln didn't fray and unwind slowly. No. Seth's threat severed it completely with a sharpened blade. No amount of mending would ever resurrect her the way she was. All she could do in that moment of realization was smile.

"What didn't you do, honey?" Grant's soothing tenor brought oxygen back to her lungs.

"What?"

"You were about to tell him you didn't do something."

"I didn't cheat on him with you. He has to know that. He's just being a jerk. He's embarrassed. Seth is never more of an asshole than when someone has embarrassed him." She shook her head. "Last year, we were at a party at the club. It was this thing for my dad's thirty years of police service or whatever. My mom had been getting ready all day and then at the last minute refused to go. Dad was furious. I was a mess. But anyway, towards the end of the reception I noticed that Seth's fly was down. I pointed it out discreetly, and he yelled at me for not noticing it earlier. He'd rather keel over than have the D.A. or the mayor think he's less than perfect. He's a ridiculous excuse for a man, and I don't want to think about him anymore."

"Seems the fuck-whistle is always struggling to keep his pants zipped. Suits me just fine for you not to think about him ever again. What would my girl like to think about instead?"

Feeling the heady surge of new life course through her, she slid off of Grant's lap to her knees on the floor.

"I want to think about you." Her voice trembled, but she set to work sliding her hands up his powerful thighs, feeling every rippled muscle tense as he realized what she was after. She traced an outline around his denim covered cock. "I want to think about doing something dirty ... with you."

"I'm betting your definition of something dirty and mine are two very different things."

"Then tell me yours. Show me."

"That really what you want?"

"More than anything."

A hungry growl rumbled from him. She swore the sound took up residence in the marrow of her bones. His gaze raked over her. Her pulse flew frantically. She licked her lips, keeping her gaze transfixed on his. She had no idea what would happen tomorrow, but right then she wanted to feel alive.

"Fucking hell, you're just too damn much," he grunted. His right hand cupped her cheek, stroking her skin with his callused thumb. The friction set her on fire. His Adam's apple bobbed as he swallowed hungrily. His eyes were full of dark need and white hot fire.

"Tell me what to do," she begged.

"Unbutton that shirt you got on. Nice and slow for me. Make me burn for you. Leave it hangin' open."

Fumbling with the first button, she drew a steadying breath and tried to concentrate. Somehow she wanted more and less, faster and slower, to be fully at his mercy and to have him at hers. Her brain scrambled as he watched her attempt to sort through the onslaught of desires. "Take it easy, baby. I ain't gonna do anything you don't want. We're gonna go nice and slow, but tonight, I'm making you all mine, my perfect little sweet, dirty girl."

His voice became her foundation. Grant Camden was the first person in her entire life that understood what she needed, what she wanted, every dirty thing she craved, every experience she longed to have. Somehow he understood every side of her and knew how to cater to each and every one of them.

She was gonna kill him. Sweet innocence melting away before his very eyes, on her knees before him. He was a rat bastard for giving her orders and taking advantage, but she robbed him of any control he ever prayed to have. The words crawled up his throat and damming them back was as pointless as it was fruitless.

"Nice and slow. That's it. Show me," he commanded as she revealed her body inch by agonizing inch. He burned with every button she loosed. Her plump cleavage peeked out of the lacey silk cups of the bra she was wearing. His eyes zeroed in on the front clasp with scope-honed precision.

As she reached the last button on the shirt, he unhooked the closure. The weight of her heavy breasts eased the fabric aside, revealing the tender valley between her luscious tits.

A possessive grunt she had to have heard flew from his lips. The silky lace hung on the tightened beads of her nipples, and he throbbed. Running his fingers under the fabric, he freed her flesh, forcing the garment to release her.

That delicious little shiver she always gave him worked through her. It robbed him of breath momentarily. "Christ, you're so fucking beautiful. Take them jeans off for me."

Her breasts hypnotized him with their rhythmic sway as she stood. His swore his cock burned so fierce for her it was going to set fire to his Wranglers, a fire his naughty little vixen was going to put out with her mouth.

She shimmied out of the jeans and the black flats she'd worn to the bar. "Now turn around for me nice and slow. Let me look at you in them naughty little panties." His eyes roved over the blue satin and lace thong that revealed far more than it covered. Her plump ass cheeks jiggled, begging to be gripped and spanked. He longed to turn them as pink as her pussy.

"Fucking gorgeous. Them panties oughta be illegal." She still didn't believe him, but he was determined to prove it to her. Completing her turn, she gnawed on her lip. His eyes tracked from her face over the lush hills of her breasts, down the slope of her abdomen and landed on the wet patch of satin in her panties.

Another growl thundered from his lungs. "Already wet for me. Such a good girl. You look like a walkin' wet dream, peaches. Get back on your knees and undo my belt." The flash of her eyes revealed a flicker of nerves, but she complied.

The heat of her hands through the denim taunted his already aching cock. He gritted his teeth, ordering himself to take this slowly and enjoy it. Her palm covered his cock as she worked the buckle. He thrust against her touch.

Unable to keep his hands off of her, he traced her face and neck as she worked. He longed to erase the fading bruise from her seatbelt, to replace it with a claim of ownership from his mouth.

When the metal buckle sprung free, he arched his back. "Now take it off and hand it to me."

A quick gasping moan sprang from her lips. The leather strap slipped audibly from the fabric. He wondered if she could hear it.

She folded the belt over and placed it in his hands. "Good girl. Now, undo my jeans."

She made quick work of the snap and then lowered the zipper slowly, like she was opening a Christmas package she wanted to relish. Perfection. Damned fucking perfection. "You see what you do to me? You see how fucking hard you make me?"

A puddle of pre-cum from watching her undress darkened the cotton. Keeping her timid gaze locked on him, she licked her lips again. He gripped the leather in his hand, attempting to cling to his own sanity.

"Pull them down and clean that up for me."

Tugging at the elastic band, she worked the briefs and his jeans down his legs. His cock sprang free, strung harder than a railroad spike. She spun that sweet little tongue on his abdomen, cleaning him while those red curls caressed his strain and her tits played at his inner thighs.

"I love the way you taste. Salty and manly. Perfect."

Certain he was going to lose his mind, he growled out his next command. "Put your hands on me. Really touch me. You look at me like you ain't ever seen a man before. Take what you want, then you're gonna give me mine."

His eyes closed in ecstasy. His body shuddered as she set to work. Her fingertips traced the thick veins running the length of him. "Jesus, that feels so damn good."

"When I do this?" This time she spun her index finger around his thickness, working her way to his crown.

He roared. His body demanded more.

"Tell me what feels the best."

"You. Any damned thing you do feels like heaven, sugar. Good God. Put your hands around me. You're killing me."

Letting her curiosity drive her, she did as she was told, placing one hand around him and then used the other to cup his sac.

Her fingers teased at the thatch of hair at his base. Fire shot through his groin. And then she leaned down, her breath whispered over him, her tongue traced from his crown to his base, and then her lips connected with his sac with a suckling kiss.

Rocketing up off of the couch, all sanity gone, the long fuse of patience he'd been trying to extend for her exploratory session scorched in a blaze. He tried not to frighten her, but he was too far gone to stop himself. Stepping around her, he panted for breath but only managed to bring the heat of her arousal to his lungs. "Put your hands behind your back, now."

"What are you doing?" She followed orders but stared up at him cautiously.

"I don't want nothing but your mouth on me. Hands just get in the way." Making quick work of the belt, he looped it twice through the buckle, effectively snaring her arms behind her.

"*OhmyGodyes.*" Her breaths dissolved into a string of indecipherable approval. Returning to his seated position, he tangled his fingers in her hair until he had a firm grip, then he guided her head to his strain.

"Lick my head, get me nice and wet."

She spun her tongue around his engorged tip. The makeshift tie-up pushed her breasts forward. The soft flesh cradled his sac and her nipples scraped against his inner thighs, making him shudder in need. "I'm gonna fuck that sweet mouth, baby. You like how I taste? I'm gonna make you swallow it all."

"Yes," she whimpered as she went back for more, leaving a wet sheen at his tip from her mouth.

"Lick me up and down like you were doing with your fingers a minute ago."

His blood ran hot and thick with greed as she complied. Kissing and licking up and down his shaft, then spinning her tongue around his crown. "Jesus, that's good. Take more. Take me deep." He had no idea how long she might be able to hear his instructions. Her moans slipped through his veins, rendering him weak.

"Suck me," he growled. Her lips latched tight around his shaft drawing him in. He guided her head in rhythm, trying not to thrust and choke her.

"Can you hear me, baby?" he managed through a desperate groan.

She pulled her mouth away with a wet pop. He grunted his frustration. "I can hear you." With a wicked smirk, she returned to her work.

"Relax your throat muscles and milk me. Let me feel 'em around my head. Take it all."

Again she complied immediately. His mind spun. His vision blurred. She was too much, too good. She sucked like a dream. He lost himself in the heat and soft suckles of her mouth. Gritting his teeth, he walked a knife's edge of arousal. There was still so much he longed to do with her.

She pulled away, needing a break. He watched her lick the pre-cum from her lips. Gasping for breath, he tightened his grip on her hair, keeping her from returning to his cock. "Let me fuck them titties, baby. Lean forward. Present them to me."

Her deep blue eyes burned indigo with lust, a lightning strike over a warm summer lake. Her belted hands lifted her breasts upward, she added to the effect by arching her back in a stunning presentation. Gently, he drew them together and slid his cock, wet from her mouth, up and down between their soft supple weight. "Jesus Christ," he cursed. "So fucking good."

Chapter 27

Potent desire flooded through Kaitlyn. She'd never felt more wanted. Somehow having her hands bound and being at his mercy set her free. Using her upper arms and shoulders, she pressed her breasts tighter together. His responding growl delighted her.

He was slack-jawed, leaning back on the couch with his eyes closed in ecstasy, and she'd done that to him. Raw power catapulted through her.

Leaning her head down, she managed to lick the tip of his massive cock as it crested her cleavage. His flavors saturated her tongue once again. A moan of pleasure worked up from her lungs as his scent filled them.

She made another lick. A hot gasp of air blew from between his teeth. "Dammit all to hell, finish me. Now," his growled demand made her fly. Easing back, she drew him into her mouth and sucked hard.

His right hand threaded through her hair once again. Every nerve-ending on her scalp rejoiced as he took control, thrusting gently in and out of her mouth. His entire body drew taut. Another moan took up what little space was left between her lips.

"Drink me," spilled from his lips as hot cum filled her mouth. She swallowed, not certain she was doing this right. He certainly seemed to be enjoying it, so she continued.

A full minute later, he stopped her. His momentary look of bone-deep satisfaction was quickly replaced with his customary expression loaded with undiluted intent, the look that said he was about to fuck her senseless.

Reaching behind her, he unlooped the belt, freeing her arms. "Fucking hottest thing I have ever seen. Come here to me."

He cradled her face in his right hand, drew her upwards, and then his mouth was on hers. She swore the kiss reached through the fear that had defined her entire life. It sank slowly beneath her skin, electrifying her until her lips were steeped in his kiss. He fed her on his tongue, drugging her, owning her thoroughly.

"I taste myself in your mouth. Damn, you drive me wild. You taste like mine, sugar, all mine, all for me."

"I am yours," she vowed readily.

"And I ain't near done with you." He joined her on the floor after shedding his jeans. Crowding behind her, his index fingers traced from her shoulders down her arms as he removed the shirt and bra, leaving her in nothing but the thong.

"So damned gorgeous," preceded his thick fingers sliding the crotch of her panties aside and tracing her slit.

She writhed between his chest and the couch cushions. "Lean forward," he commanded as two fingers slammed into her hard and fast.

"Oh, God," she cried out as he pumped in and out without reprieve.

"Come on my fingers, peaches. Made you hot and wet to suck my cock, didn't it?"

"Yes," the word echoed in her mind.

"Such a good girl. So nice and tight for me. It's right there ain't it, sugar? I can feel it coming." He spoke directly in her left ear again. The rasping rumble of his voice carried her higher and closer to the point of no return. Every pulse point in her body timed itself to his strokes.

All sound was muted but her own moans. His mouth kissed a trail of sweet fire between her shoulder-blades. His other hand cupped her left breast.

Suddenly, his teeth sank gently into the sensitive spot between her neck and shoulder. His mouth punished and forgave, constantly skirting the edge of pain that bordered on pure bliss. Warmth licked at her spine. All thought left her. She was capable of nothing but feeling. When he twisted her nipple back and forth between his fingers, she broke on a scream of his name.

She was wrung out and trembling in his arms. Still, Grant wasn't even close to being ready to quit. Not if he had to take her back to that hell she lived in tomorrow. He'd make damn sure she existed in heaven all night long.

Laying her head back on his shoulder he kept them on their knees, running his hands tenderly over all of her beautiful curves. "Can you hear me, sweetheart?"

She managed a half nod. Chuckling, he cradled his cock between her ass cheeks, feeling the slip of satin abrade him. "I'm about to make it hurt so good again, baby. You ready?" He couldn't quite translate her moan that time. "I told you I'm relentless and you drive me wild."

"Fuck me," came out in a timid plea that he swore made his blood sing.

"Filthy mouth, darlin'." Grasping thick globe of ass, he massaged and then swatted rather hard.

"Oh, God, yes, more," she whimpered. With that, all semblance of gentlemanly behavior he'd ever managed to cling to disappeared. Jerking the panties aside yet again, he impaled himself on her with another smack of her backside.

"Count them for me. That was two."

With his every quick retreat, she cried out for more. With every hard thrust he brought his hand back to her ass until it glowed pink, driving him wild. "Three," she moaned.

"You feel your greedy little pussy nursing at my cock, naughty girl? You feel how wet you are for me? Dripping down my thighs."

"Yes," hissed from her as she arched her back, offering him more. Raw need blazed through him. Impatience surged through his veins. Every strike made her wetter still. "Four, five."

The panties were drenched. Another gush of wet heat dripped around his cock and his groan of adamant approval shook the windows. His hand connected with the thick globes of her ass again and again, and she cried out for more.

"Six, oh, God, yes. Seven."

He abandoned her backside, moving his hand to her satin covered clit instead, watching his cock disappear deep inside her folds. Tugging on the panties, he slipped the slick fabric back and forth over her sensitive little pearl. Her cries reached deafening decibels.

The longing to fill her full decimated his resolve. Every silky ripple of her pussy spiked his blood. When she cinched so tightly around him he could barely withdraw, he jerked her body closer. Her climax drove his.

Barely managing regular breath, he eased out of her, watching his seed drip out of her of her pussy, shiny and red with the mix of their juices. With what little strength he had left, he lifted her up into his arms and carried her to bed.

God only knew what tomorrow would bring, but tonight he'd sated her thoroughly. Fucked her so good and so hard she was almost out by the time he arranged her tenderly on his chest.

"That was amazing," in her sweet sleepy tone were the last noises he heard that evening.

By one AM he knew sleep was never coming. Josh would follow through on his threat. If there'd been any money in Grant's bank accounts, he would have bet it all on that fact. And that pissed him off thoroughly.

He refused to be afraid, but getting arrested didn't sound like a precious lot of fun, and he didn't have time for it. Taking Kaitlyn back was equally as despicable. Turning her over to low-life asswipes that treated her like shit wasn't happening, not on his watch.

Repositioning himself so he could cradle her closer, he watched the silvery moonlight dance in her hair. Brushing a kiss on her forehead, he prayed she'd awaken.

God must've been in a good mood, because her eyes blinked open and a gentle smile creased her beautiful face. "Hey there, gorgeous. I need another fix. I told you I'll never get enough."

Her smile expanded as he drew her closer.

At 5:00, after another slow gentle session, he eased away from her sleeping form. He had shit to do. He had to decide what he was going to do about the corn and the cattle, and no pansy-assed cityboy was gonna keep him from his duties.

Josh could lick the shit off his boots. Nobody was going to have to bail Grant Camden out. He'd work his ass off before that would happen.

Chapter 28

The sun was far too high in the sky the next time Kaitlyn awoke. She blinked a few times and then ordered her eyes to close once again. It was easier to remember every single detail of the love they'd made that morning before he'd left when her eyes were closed.

That morning had been a gentle answer to the rough passion he'd given her the evening before, their session in the middle of the night a mix of the two. She'd loved every single moment of all three.

She had never felt more powerfully desirable. It was a heady sensation.

"Oh, crap," she jerked upright in bed. They had to leave. What time was it? Stumbling out of bed, she cupped her breasts in her hands to keep them from bouncing when she ran to the living room wearing nothing but the warm wool socks he'd put on her once again before he'd left that morning.

Ten minutes later, she found her phone buried deep in the couch cushions. Her heart located a steady beat. It was only 8:30. They still had time. Part of her longed to believe that Josh was just being an ass, that he was bluffing and would never get a warrant for Grant's arrest, but another part of her knew she just wasn't that lucky. If Josh wanted a warrant, her father would issue it.

A profound sadness washed through her as she turned on the coffee maker. What happened when they arrived back in Lincoln? Grant had become the single most important thing in her life in just three days.

It made no sense to think about him being two hours away on his ranch while she sat miserably in her parent's home on the golf course.

She'd never really dated anyone other than Seth, and most of the time she didn't want to see him so she never worried about the time in between their dates. Not seeing Grant for days at a time sounded inhumane.

Scolding herself for being overly dramatic, she poured a cup of coffee and let the warm liquid sate her soul. They would figure it out. She just had to get her father and Josh to calm down first. After that feat, most anything was doable.

Noticing the slight rub marks on her wrists from his belt, she wrinkled her nose. Hopefully no one else would notice those.

As each moment of the night before replayed in her mind, she casually strolled to the bathroom, pretending to be unaffected, play-acting for no one but herself. Flipping on the light, she turned and cringed at the deep purple markings on the back of her neck and shoulders from his mouth.

Biting her lip, she stood on her tiptoes and made a quick note of the slight pink heat still clinging to her right butt cheek in the distinctive shape of his hand. Damn. At least that would be easier to cover.

Her father had been a detective for the better part of his career. There wasn't much he didn't notice. That's why Kaitlyn and her siblings rarely put so much as a toe out of line.

Borrowing another one of Grant's shirts, she relaxed. The collar more than covered the hickeys and the sleeves came down to her knuckles. She just wouldn't roll them up, keeping the leather markings on her wrists concealed. And she'd have a talk with her cowboy about his claims of ownership, even though she'd loved every moment of them.

Loathing the process, she went on with packing her suitcases and gathering her belongings. At least going back home meant she could get more suitable clothing and dispose of most everything she'd picked out for the ill-fated honeymoon.

By nine-thirty she was panicked. Where was Grant? He'd heard Josh the night before. Pacing in his living room, she debated. In what had to be the most insane part of this whirlwind relationship was the fact that she didn't yet have his cell phone number. They were almost always together. There'd been no need to have a way to contact him.

Slipping into her black ballet flats, she marched out onto the front porch, squinting her eyes, praying he'd come galloping up on his horse. She saw no one.

The ranch expanded for miles and miles on every side. She had no idea which way would lead her to another human being, but she had to find Grant.

Trying to remember the way he'd driven home from the bar, she thought the main road from the entrance was to her left so she headed that way. She passed fields full of cows, but most of them had the NC brand on their hides. They were Natalie's. Doubting Grant was working with Natalie's cows, she stayed on the path.

Suddenly the whir of a motor was upon her. She hadn't heard it coming. Spinning around, Dec grinned at her from the seat of a

Gator. He killed the motor. "You making a break for it or looking for Grant?"

"Looking for Grant. Did you hear about what happened last night with Josh?"

"I did. Not much happens around here that everyone doesn't hear about. Hop on in. We'll go find him. I'm betting he's the opposite direction, actually."

Kaitlyn slid into the passenger seat, hating herself for feeling wary of Declan. He seemed like a nice guy. Doubling down on hating her father for teaching her fear, she drew a deep breath. Manure mixed with sweet corn didn't do much to bolster her courage, however.

"He knows we have to be in Lincoln by noon. I don't understand why he's not back," she sighed.

Concentrating as Dec cranked the motor again, she watched his lips to see his response.

"Oh, I bet if you really think about Grant and how he does life, it wouldn't really surprise you that he's not back."

Odd response. Kaitlyn considered.

"Sorry, I'm a psychologist by trade. I tell Holly you can take the man out of the therapist's office but you can't take the therapist out of the man."

Laughing at that, she nodded her understanding. "Grant doesn't want to take me back." The answer had been right there in front of her all along.

"As you Americans say, *Bingo*, but that's not all."

She considered everything she'd learned about Grant Camden in the past few days. "And he's stubborn and refuses to let Josh affect what he does."

"So, not in any way shocking that he hasn't come to pick you up."

"I will not let him get arrested because of me."

"I've seen the way he is with you. Trust me, he'd throw himself in front of his own hay-baler for you. Getting arrested isn't something that concerns him."

"Well, it concerns me."

"I've been arrested. Not a particularly pleasant experience, so it concerns me as well. Let's go find him."

Kaitlyn was dying to ask what Declan had been arrested for and how all his extensive tattoo work and piercings matched with his career as a psychologist, but knew that would be impolite. She went with her alternative question instead. "You said you were a psychologist?"

200

"Still am. Holly and I run the free psych center here in town."

"Oh, that's so nice. Um, could I ask you a kind of question I've wanted to ask a therapist for a long time?"

Dec turned his head to study her. "That most definitely depends on the question. You can make an appointment, though it might be better if I didn't counsel Grant's girlfriend. I have several colleagues I can recommend back in Lincoln."

"It's not about me. It's about my mother."

"That's probably doable."

"Thanks. My twin brother was in the Army and he was killed a few years ago in Afghanistan."

"I'm so sorry for your loss."

"Thank you. I'm getting better at saying that out loud. That might be a good sign, right?"

"Maybe, but I thought this was about your mother."

"Fine. So, after Keith was killed, my mom sort of came completely apart. She'll go days without speaking and cries all the time to this day, unless she's at the club or with anyone but me and my dad. I keep telling my dad she needs to see a therapist, but then he just goes into this fit of rage. I don't know what to do."

Declan offered her a sorrowful glance. "This is why therapy sessions on the Gator aren't a great idea. Here's what I can tell you, the grieving process isn't what you see on television or read about in books. It's very unique to each person experiencing it. Anger is a very common part of grief, and it's usually most frightening for the person who is the angriest. The anger is usually a result of guilt. That's a bitter anger.

"Your mother *should* seek a therapist, and no therapist in their right mind would attempt to diagnose without ever having seen the patient, so everything I'm saying is an unprofessional opinion as your friend. Your mother's inability to cope currently might not be solely about your brother's death, and your father might need one more than your mum. Your mother's behavior outside the family indicates that she probably doesn't want to feel and act the way she's acting when she's only with you. She's clearly struggling. There may be more at stake that continues to wrench the process they both need to go through to grieve. And the worst part of it all is that we don't get to decide when we're finished grieving. Grief lets you know when it's finished with you and never the other way around."

He drove the deeper into Camden land while Kaitlyn let that tumble around in her head. "That just sucks," she finally summed.

"It does. And I'm very sorry you have to go through it. I'm sorry anyone has to go through it, but it seems to be a part of life."

"Is that a …?" Kaitlyn couldn't believe her eyes. On the left as they passed, she found herself staring at a small graveyard, neatly trimmed, each headstone bearing a bouquet of wildflowers or a small wreath.

"Generations of Camdens are buried right there. We all take turns keeping it cleaned up and tended. This ranch means everything to them. Luke once told me that he intended to work this land all of his life and then return to it when his work here was through. They all seem to understand that death is a part of life, just like grief seems to be. What I wouldn't have given to grow up understanding that.

"Now, Grant is out in that field on Blaze trying his best to forget that he's supposed to be taking you back to Lincoln today." He gestured his head to the small field in front of them.

Grant was seated on a massive copper quarterhorse. He appeared to be counting the nearby cattle. "Blaze? Does she ride really fast or something?" Kaitlyn wasn't certain if she should get out of the Gator. Cows were much larger up close than they appeared from the safety of Grant's front porch, and his horse looked to be several stories high.

"Jessie names all the horses, and her delightful sense of literary knowledge always comes through. Blaze is German for unwavering protector. Sounds like Grant, doesn't it?"

"Yes, it definitely does." Hoisting herself out of the Gator, she marched onto the field, ignoring the hulking masses of the grazing cattle. Cupping her hands to her mouth, she summoned courage. "Grant Camden, you get your ass off of that horse. We have to go!"

Declan, at least, doubled over laughing.

"Shit," spat from Grant's mouth as soon as he saw her. Her hollering across the prairie was about the cutest thing he'd ever seen, but that didn't make taking her back to her asshole of a father and anywhere in the general vicinity of her ex any easier.

If Josh wanted to arrest him, he could just come get him off of his horse, and Grant wished him a helluva lot of luck with that.

"Grant, please," she sounded frantic.

"Damn it all to hell and back." He couldn't turn her down, no matter what she asked of him. He'd gone and fallen in love with her. Clicking his mouth, he edged Blaze forward at a slow canter. "It'll be a cold day in hell when I take you back to them sons-of-bitches, sweetness," he explained as he slung his leg over Blaze and landed right in front of her. "I told you last night you were mine."

"I think I'll just leave you with the Gator while I walk away rather quickly," Dec chuckled. "But I wish you both luck. Be interesting to see who gets their way. A word to the wise, Grant, keeping her here if she wants to be there *is* actually kidnapping."

"I don't want to be there, but I have to be there," Kaitlyn corrected.

"You ain't gotta be anywhere you don't wanna be, which is precisely why I ain't taking you back there."

"But I do have to go back. I have to face them. I have to figure out everything, and I really want to figure it out with you. I refuse to let you even possibly get arrested because of me, and Josh likes to show off his power as often as he can. He's kind of a jerk really. He was Keith's best friend so I think I always gave him a pass."

"I'll make you a deal." In the moments when he'd been able to reason with himself that morning, he'd come up with a somewhat tolerable solution.

"I'm listening."

"I'll take you back. You tell your daddy to take a long walk off a short pier. You get your jackoff of an ex, and Josh, and whoever else has their hooks in my baby to back the fuck up, and then you come back out here with me."

She gave him that grin that always turned him inside out, the one that lit her entire face, pinked her cheeks and made those adorable little crinkles appear by her beautiful blue eyes. When her dimple appeared, he was done for. "You really want me to come back with you that quick?"

"I don't want you to leave at all, peaches."

"I would love to do that, but I probably should see if I can pick up some extra shifts at Chully's. I have to pay for Seth's stupid car, and I have to buy a new car."

"If you come back out here with me, you don't need a new car, and I'll figure out some way to pay off that lowdown shitsucker." He was stubborn enough to ignore the already mounting debt he was accumulating for the moment anyway. "I ain't taking no for an answer."

"All right, fine." She beamed. "I have some money saved up. Maybe I could sell that stupid ring and pay for his car or just get him to agree to use the money from the ring on his car, or something. I'll just go back, apologize to my parents, make them a few dinners so

Dad won't make Mom more miserable, get some clothes, and come back out here."

"I can live with that."

"Good, because we do need to go. I want to be there by noon."

"We ain't gonna be there by noon," Grant informed her a few minutes later as he slung her luggage behind his seat in the truck.

"I know, so please hurry."

"What's in all them little bags?"

"Makeup."

"Honey, you're the most beautiful thing I've ever set eyes on, and ain't nobody that ugly."

She dissolved into giggles, which eased a little of the tension that had settled squarely on his shoulders.

"I like makeup, and lotions, and girly stuff. Buying them gave me this momentary high that I needed to survive. They were the only things I ever bought for myself. If I bought cookbooks or new kitchenware, Dad got mad. If I bought photography stuff or art supplies, Mom complained about the mess. No one cared if I bought new lip gloss or moisturizer and they make me happy, even if only for a minute. I think if I hadn't been so miserable I wouldn't have bought them as often."

"I didn't know you liked to take pictures."

"We've only known each other three days. There's probably a lot you don't know yet."

"Well, tell me. I want to know."

"Tell you what?"

"What're your favorite things to do besides putting expensive shit on your face 'cause you don't need any of it?"

"I like to be with you. Doesn't matter what we're doing."

Well, damn, if that didn't stroke a man's ego in all the right ways.

He laced his fingers through hers after he cranked the truck. "I like that answer just fine. But what about before we met? What'd you like to do then?"

"It's been so long since I did much of anything fun, I honestly don't remember."

"Have to do something about that."

"I love going to the creek. I want to take pictures of the ranch. It's so beautiful here. I like to draw sometimes, too. I love to cook. Oh, my gosh, I want to try new recipes. I've wanted to for so long."

"Then I'm gonna make sure you get to do all of that along with anything else that makes my baby smile."

"I want to understand more about how the ranch works. I want to know more about your land. I want to go with you in the mornings when you leave in your truck. I want to know where you're going."

"You gon' have to get your sexy ass outta my bed before nine in the morning then." He winked at her.

"Isn't there anything you do at a slightly less ungodly hour?" She giggled.

He gave her a grunt and reveled in the fact that she didn't require more than that.

"Tell me about your horse. Dec said your mom named him. Or tell me your favorite things to eat. Or maybe tell me some more stories about Pleasant Glen. What's the Cut 'n Curl?" She was spinning her fingers through the curls just over her left shoulder over and over again. Tug, twist, loop, and release on repeat.

"You just needing me to keep talkin', sugar?"

"Yes. Please. I don't want to think about where we're going."

"I'm gonna be right there the entire time. I ain't going anywhere. You know that, right?"

"I know, but my life never seems to work out the way I want it to."

"You ever met anyone as stubborn as me, peaches? Be honest."

"Probably not, but I like all of the things you're stubborn about."

"I ain't going anywhere. Come hell or high water, we're gonna make this work."

Chapter 29

Everett Camden

Ev supposed he'd carry the regret with him 'til the day he died, and for the most part that was okay by him. His mistakes had cost his son a helping of peace and had done nothing but serve to make Grant all the more stubborn. Ev deserved the remorse.

He wasn't surprised to find Luke climbing up in his truck when he reached his own. "Would you like to ride with your old man, seeing as we're all going the same place?"

"Maybe," Luke considered. "Kaitlyn ain't got a car, and I don't think it's too likely her daddy's gonna be kind about her coming back out here. You and I both know Grant ain't gonna leave her in Lincoln and that he'll give her his truck. I figure he might need a spare. He can have mine. I'll ride back with you."

Ev chuckled. His oldest son was always the cautious methodic thinker. He never did anything that he hadn't planned six ways from Sunday. And, just like Grant and Austin, he expected more from himself than any other mortal man. "I hear ya, son, but your granddaddy's got a spare truck. We'll make do. Austin and Natalie are gonna take care of clearing that corn for Grant today while he's gone. He can't bring himself to do it, and I'll tell ya God's truth I can't stand for him to have to. Keep me company on the drive."

"Yeah, all right, but let's take my truck. It'll get us there a helluvalot faster."

"Fine, but don't be riding that accelerator too hard or we'll catch up to 'em before Lincoln and he'll see us."

"He'd have to admit he's kinda glad we're there and that might gall him more than anything."

"Nah, he ain't gonna be mad we're there as long as we're not needed. Your brother's good at getting himself in neck deep and then figuring out how to swim. Most of the time he makes it, but occasionally he needs a little help. Asking for help ain't ever his preference."

"Tell me about it. You and I both know he needs to be running cattle on that land, but he's clinging to all them good years he had."

"He did have a bunch of good years 'fore the market turned. He put more than his fair share in the business accounts. I can't figure out how to get him to use some of it to get back to rights."

"It ain't just the money. He works my land just as hard as he works his own. He works harder than any of us and nobody would argue that. Every season Austin spent throwing himself off a' bulls, Grant was home running his cattle. Hell, even the weeks it took me to convince Indie to come back to the Glen permanently, he did most'a my work for me. If I were being perfectly honest, I'd say he's the reason Indie's here. He spurred me off'a my own stubborn ass and got me to quit thinkin' and make a move. You should'a seen half the town ready to throw in last night on his behalf. They all know without him the Glen wouldn't be what it is."

"Question is how do we get all that through his thick skull?"

"We could buy Abelkopp's cattle for him."

"Yeah, we could do that, but he's gonna have to have new pens and feeders, too. Also needs a new feed truck. There's a fair amount of work to be done to add in another herd that large, and he's gonna be trying to do all of that work and be out here for Kaitlyn. He does the work of ten men but not even ten men could do all of that."

"Well, we all owe him, so we'll run the ranch in his stead, and he can get things squared with Kaitlyn. You seen the way she looks at him like he hung the moon in the sky just for her. She wants to be out there with him. They'll get it figured. Sounds to me like he's just gotta get her family off her back."

"Damn, son, you gone and got poetic in your old age."

"Yeah, well, my girls softened me up a little."

"Softened you up a *little*? They got you wrapped up so tight around their tiny fingers it's a wonder you can still walk upright."

"Says the man who raised Natalie and Holly Camden and spoilt them up one side and down another."

"Your sisters are doing just fine, thank you very much."

Ev tried to hide his grin when Luke grunted. All of his sons had gotten that grunt from him. It was how cattle ranchers communicated a thousand memories in one quick sound.

"And what do we do if we get him set knee deep in cattle and the markets turn again and corn goes back up? Three years ago we were shitting high 'cause of him and took losses on all our stock."

"There's gonna be good years, and there's gonna be bad ones. All in the world we can do is pray there's more good ones than bad. Try to save during the good to make do during the lean. Other than that, there ain't no guarantees and there never will be. Your brother's finally stumbled up on his one and only. We all knew it would happen eventually, but he's been anxious for it for a long while. I intend to do everything in my power to get them married and give them a life God knows he's worked his ass off for. You and I also know she's real likely to end up with a bun in the oven sooner than later. Your granddaddy says this mess with her ex and her daddy's gonna be a deep bucket of shit. I ain't gonna let him drown in it this time."

"Dad, you didn't let him drown in it when he was seventeen. You were trying to teach him a lesson."

"Yeah, I was, but all I managed to do was make him determined to rely solely on himself and never ask for no help. That wasn't what I was going for and I intend to try and right my wrongs if I can."

Chapter 30

With every mile they progressed, Grant was forced to sit and watch his baby resurrect her shield of armor. Piece by piece, the closer they got to Lincoln the more of herself she tried to morph into something her parents found respectable, he guessed.

"Stop," he finally commanded.

"Stop what?"

"Stop trying to turn yourself back into New Kaitlyn. Just be my Katy Belle. Please."

"What are you talking about?"

"You're sitting over there not listening to me talk, trying to remember how to be something you're not. I pay attention, remember?"

"Grant, I have no idea what we're about to walk into. My mother could be curled up in the bed refusing to eat. My dad could be walking around with a pistol. Seth could be at my house. Kelsey could be there. Josh is most definitely there if he's not out in his patrol car looking for us. And my sister might even be there, though I doubt it because she's never there."

"None of those are reasons for you to try to be something you ain't. It occurs to me that I never said this outright last night so I'm saying it now. I love you. Just the way you are. *My* Katy, not this half version of yourself you show everyone else."

"Wow."

"Yeah, wow. That's what I think whenever I see you."

"I love you too, Grant. Will you just promise me something?"

"Anything."

"Promise you won't let any of them scare you off, but promise if I do ask you to leave so I can deal with all of them, that you will."

"I'll make good on the first half of that but not on the second."

"I have to deal with them carefully. I may need to do it on my own."

"I have to know you're safe and secure and that you know you're loved, so we may be at an impasse, sugar."

"So stubborn."

"Guilty as charged."

"My father is … well … really, he's kind of an asshole lately. He's just extremely controlling. Wants everything done his way because his way is the best way in his mind. Might have to lay off the tying things around my wrists. He's a complete prude, and he was a detective so he notices everything."

"You got marks on your wrists?" Guilt pricked his resolve, but she'd loved every minute of being bound for him.

"They're barely even noticeable."

"I'm sorry, sugar. Didn't mean to pull it too tight."

"No, don't apologize. That was the hottest thing ever. I've never been so turned on. Just keep my father in mind."

"I'd much prefer not to have your father on my mind when I'm getting down and dirty with you, but I'll refrain from mentioning to him that you call me Daddy now, too." He winked at her as her cheeks streaked the color of a ripe raspberry.

"Oh, my God, I can't hear myself all that well when we're having sex. Please tell me I did not actually call you Daddy."

"You didn't yet, but now I have a new goal." His deep bellowed chuckle filled the truck cab. God, he wished he felt as jovial as he sounded.

"Turn here. The gate code is 1631.

"Here? You live *in* the country club?" Grant's stomach turned as he recalled the sheer number of times he'd flipped off this very entrance. Just how much money did the chief of police make? An impending sense of failure took a vicious blow to his already battered sense of self-worth.

"On the ninth fairway, but we don't live close enough to have golf balls come through the windows or anything."

"Guess that's handy."

"What's wrong?"

"Nothing."

"You swore you'd never lie to me."

"Didn't mean to exactly. It's just I ain't ever gonna have this kind of money."

"So?" Kaitlyn's shrug bolstered him far more than he should have allowed.

"Just wondering what the hell you're doing with someone like me."

"Do you really think that little of me?" She sounded good and pissed suddenly. Fuck it. That wasn't what he'd meant at all.

"That came out all wrong. I'm just pretty sure I don't deserve you. Feelin' a little off-put, I guess."

"That was a pretty good recovery there, cowboy. I've dated the rich asshole, remember? I'd much prefer a cowboy with honest intentions and an unbelievable work ethic, even if he can't buy me fancy things. I don't need fancy things. I don't even *want* fancy things. I want you."

"I'm right here, sugar." He lifted her hand to his lips and brushed a kiss between her knuckles, earning himself that sweet grin that always did him in.

Dread slithered over Kaitlyn with every inch Grant's truck progressed. Nausea roiled in her stomach. Bile singed her throat. Josh's squad car was in the driveway. She couldn't see the numbers on the one parked on the street, but it would be a safe bet to say it was another one of her father's lackey cops who would do anything he said to try and win his favor.

It was after 1:00. The warrant had already been issued, and they all knew he would bring her home. They were driving into a trap. Pure unadulterated hatred filled her. "Stop the truck," she demanded frantically.

Grant slammed on the brakes. "What?! Why?"

"They're waiting on you. Just let me out here. I'll run. You drive away fast. I'll call you when I get them calmed down."

"What do you mean they're waiting on me?"

"They assumed we'd be late. Mark my words, there's already a warrant out for your arrest. Just leave me here."

"I ain't leaving you period. They want to arrest me on trumped up charges they can go right ahead and do it. I'm far from being a lawyer, but wouldn't you be the one that would have to say I'd kidnapped you and not let you go? I'm doubting you're planning on doing that, so they got nothing on me. Now, simmer down and breathe for me. It's all gonna be fine."

"It's not going to be fine, but you're right on the charges not being held up in court. You're really smart. Did you know that?"

"Trust me, sugar, I ain't. I do what I know's right."

"You haven't ever committed a crime have you?" Another surge of panic swept through Kaitlyn. If they had him on something else, a kidnapping charge wouldn't be necessary to arrest him.

"Not that I've ever been caught doing. Did a fair amount of underage drinkin'. I've always seen the speed limits as more of a suggestion than a rule, but that's about it."

"Okay, good." She tried to breathe. Her heart broke out in a sprint, robbing her of a little more of her hearing as he turned into the driveway.

"Come here to me." He threw the truck into park and drew her into his arms. "It's going to be fine. If you get scared just look at me or squeeze my hand tighter. I ain't going anywhere. I'll be right beside you the whole time. If I do get arrested, which I ain't, my daddy and probably my big brother are already on their way here to get me out. And as soon as I'm out I'll be right back beside you again."

"How do you know they're on the way? Did they tell you that before we left? Your phone hasn't rung the whole time we've been driving."

"I know 'cause I know my daddy and Luke. That reminds me." He reached into her purse and grabbed her cell phone. "Feels weird to be putting my number in after all this, but on the off chance they do cart me to the jailhouse you might need this."

Clinging to the last fragment of her sanity, she took his cell and entered her number as well.

"Now, you ready? We can sit out here as long as you want."

"Let's just get this over with. So help me God, if they put cuffs on you, I will end someone."

"There's my little hellcat. Come on, Katy Belle."

"Just Katy with a y, remember?"

His answering grunt said it all. The Belle portion of the nickname was going to be sticking around.

Chapter 31

Irked with himself for being nervous, Grant ground his teeth while Kaitlyn slowly slid the key in the deadbolt. Judging by the cop cars parked everywhere and the sheer number of other cars in the driveway there were clearly a house full of people waiting on them. One of them could've opened the door. Choosing to focus on his annoyance about that instead of the gnawing fear that he was about to be arrested, Grant massaged the back of his neck.

You could have cut the tension in the fancy-ass entryway of the mansion with a dull blade when they walked in. Josh and some other cop in uniform headed their way.

"Are you aware there's a warrant out for your arrest, Mr. Camden?" A man a half-head taller and a few decades older than Grant followed the cops. He looked like hell with red-rimmed eyes and a mask of pure rage chiseled in his greying beard.

Her sister coward behind him.

"I'm guessing you're Mr. Sommerville." Grant sighed. "I'd say it was nice to meet you, sir, but I ain't much on saying something I don't mean."

"I am Chief Sommerville. And you would be wise not to be insulting."

Kaitlyn narrowed her eyes. "Daddy, so help me, if you so much as mention the idea of arresting him, I will walk out of this house and I will never come back. Ever! I'm done with all of this ridiculousness from all of you. *I* left the wedding. *I* left Seth. I never want to see him again. I also keyed his car because he's just such an epic asshole. I went with Grant. I intend to stay with Grant. And none of you will have anything to say about any of it, you got that? If you're determined to arrest someone, go ahead and arrest me."

Grant lowered his head, hoping the brim of his hat covered his smirk. His girl had a hearty dose of sweet and innocent, but clearly she could tap right on into that red-headed hellcat status at a moment's notice. That was yet another thing he loved about her.

"You don't even know the half of what you have done to me and to your mother, Kaitlyn Michelle Sommerville. What you've done to our home. The shame you've brought on our entire family. I'm thankful your brother didn't have to see you behaving this way."

Grant's head snapped up. "Say shit like that to her one more time, sir, and I'll make damned sure you never see her again. Where the

213

hell do you get off wanting her to take the blame for being cheated on?"

"Grant," Kaitlyn hissed through her teeth.

The cops stirred like nervous cattle on sorting day. All watching for her daddy to tell 'em to take a piss, he supposed.

"We did not know where you were!" Her father raged in her face. Grant stepped between them, easing Kaitlyn behind him.

"I'm sure you were worried sick about her. I would'a lost my mind if I didn't know she was safe, but she couldn't do anything about the storm or the downed cell towers. And you did know she was safe as soon as she called her sister."

"I wasn't speaking to you."

"I won't stand here and let you blame her for shit that ain't her fault. She's probably the strongest person I've ever met, but she's been strong long enough. Don't seem to me that any of you are man enough to stand up for her and be strong beside her, but I am. And I mean this with all of the precious little respect I can muster for you, sir, back the hell up."

"Arrest him," her father menaced.

"Daddy, no!" Kaitlyn screeched so loudly her own voice ricocheted through her head. No one had ever stood up to her father on her behalf. To her knowledge, no one had ever spoken to her father the way Grant had just talked to him.

In that moment, she lost any semblance of doubt. She loved him. They had terrible timing. He was going to jail all because of her. It was too quick. It made no sense, but she loved him with every fiber of her being.

"Langston, you will do no such thing."

Kaitlyn's mouth hung open stupidly as every head in the foyer of her parent's home snapped to the top of the staircase. She couldn't remember the last time she'd heard her mother speak with any authority or strength. "Mama?"

"Clearly, it is high time I stop hiding inside this ridiculous house and allowing you to make everyone's life miserable because no one will stop you. Now, you," she turned to Officer Harrington. "I have no idea who you are, dear, but if the only reason you are here is so my husband will give you a promotion for kissing his ass, leave. And Josh, darling, you were my precious son's best friend and you will always be welcome in our home, but if your intention this evening is to arrest my daughter's new friend, you can go as well."

No one spoke. No one even breathed. Evelyn Bellamy Sommerville appeared to be making a triumphant return. Kaitlyn refused to hope. She wasn't strong enough to live through watching her mother come apart again.

"Langston, you cannot arrest men simply because they have balls enough to stand up to you. Now, my daughter is back and she is safe, and for those reasons we are going to celebrate some way this evening. I'm sorry, sweetheart, I missed your name." She extended her hand to Grant.

"Uh." He whipped off his cowboy hat. Kaitlyn couldn't help but grin. "I'm ... Grant Camden, ma'am. It's a pleasure to meet you."

"Yes, you as well. Now, Grant is going to be staying for dinner with all of us. Kaitlyn, sweetheart, would you mind cooking us something, anything you want. If I can help, you tell me."

Kaitlyn's trembling hands steadied as her mother gripped them. Certain she was dreaming, she pulled her mother in for a hug. "Thank you," she whispered.

"Evelyn, what do you think you are doing?" Chief Sommerville's shocked gasp lost a little of his earlier fury.

"I am telling you to sit down and shut up, Langston." Her mother drew Kaitlyn into a warm embrace. "Thank you for coming back. I thought I'd lost you, too." Her mother squeezed her tighter and Kaitlyn drank in the hug, one she hadn't experienced in three long years.

"Um, Grant's father and brother are on their way to Lincoln. They live a long way from here. We could invite them for supper as well." In for a penny, in for a pound, Kaitlyn figured.

"Excellent. We'll be happy to have all of them. Grant, why don't you call your father and brother and give them directions."

"And your grandfather, too," Kaitlyn added, mostly to gall her father.

"I'm much obliged, ma'am, but they wouldn't want to intrude."

Her father huffed but seemed to think better of making another retort to her mom.

"It's no intrusion at all. I get the impression we're going to be seeing a great deal of you. And I would like it to go on the official record, Langston, that Seth Christenson never once in the two years you subjected our daughter to him referred to me as ma'am." She turned back to Grant. "I was born and bred in Charleston, South Carolina. Manners go a long way with me. Speaking of manners, please allow me to apologize for my husband's absurd behavior. We were worried, naturally, but this all got way out of hand. Now, Kaitlyn, why don't you show Grant where to put your luggage. You can take my car and pick up anything you'd like to make for supper. Is it terribly clichéd to assume cattle ranchers like steak?"

"Might be clichéd, but it's also the truth," Grant assured her. "I'll take Katy grocery shopping, ma'am. Anything else I can do to help?"

"Katy, oh, I used to call her that when she was a baby." Evelyn patted Grant's cheek. "I like you. I think this whole thing might just have been exactly what we all needed. Langston, if you can't find it in yourself to apologize for being a jackass, go play golf."

Fishing around in her head trying to remember how to rejoin her lower jaw with her upper, Kaitlyn refused to blink, terrified if she closed her eyes the image before her would somehow disappear.

"I'm quite certain I'm dreaming," she confessed as she climbed back up in Grant's truck.

"I take it your mama ain't always that ..."

"With it? No. Well, she used to be. I haven't heard her talk to Daddy like that in years. They used to fight a lot. I think they kind of liked it. She'd argue with him just for the sake of arguing. The only thing they ever agreed on was how perfect my brother was. But I haven't seen her like that ... not since ... well, you know. What if it doesn't last? What if tomorrow she goes back to sitting in his room and not speaking? I don't think I can go through that again." Preemptive disappointment threatened her resolve. It wasn't safe to hope for any other alternative.

"Hang on to the good times, sugar. 'Sides, I'd say we could use all the favors we can get. I thought I was done for before she came flying down them steps."

"Me too. I don't know what to make of any of this. It's too good to be true. It's going to get bad again. It always does."

"Hey," Grant squeezed her hand as he made his way out of the country club. "Good, bad, ugly, I'm right here. We'll figure it out. Let's just take this moment by moment. We still gotta get through a meal with three wool-dyed cattle ranchers and your daddy."

"Four wool-dyed ranchers, cowboy. Your father and grandfather and brother aren't the only full-blooded cowboys who'll be at supper tonight."

"All right, fine, I'm a rancher through and through. That don't mean supper's gonna pleasant."

"Is there a difference between a cowboy and a rancher? Should I not call you a cowboy?" Kaitlyn had been meaning to ask him this for the past few days. Now seemed as good a time as any and it was a welcomed distraction from the insanity of her life.

"You can call me most anything you want, peaches, so long as you call me. But kinda."

"What's the difference?"

"It ain't a big deal and you'd have to have come up ranching to even care. I get called a cowboy plenty. It's an honor really. No big deal."

"Grant, just tell me the difference."

"Cowboy generally refers to a rodeo cowboy. Kinda like my brother Austin. Now, he's a real deal rancher, too, so he ain't a good example at all. But the unspoken code of the Midwest is a cowboy gets himself thrown offa bulls and broncs to impress the buckle-bunnies. A rancher is a man who takes care of his wife, his kids, honors his land, and cares for his animals. He's out there freezing his ass off when it's twenty below because he ain't worth nothing if he ain't taking care of everything and everyone that depends on him. And if he don't wanna work that hard and be the man that stands between his babies and the world, in my opinion, he oughta just go on and sell his saddle cause he ain't worth a pile of cow shit."

"Wow."

"You know what a buckle bunny is?" The concern in his eyes when he was afraid she might not understand gave weight to his expectations of himself.

"Yeah, that one is kind of self-explanatory. You're amazing, by the way."

"Nope, I'm not, but I am a rancher, sweetheart, and I will always stand between you and anything that's out to hurt you, even if it's your family."

An hour later, Grant stood in a kitchen half the size of his entire house watching Kaitlyn prepare rib-eyes and chop potatoes. His mouth had been watering for the last fifteen minutes. She came alive in the kitchen. Not quite to the extent she did when she was in his arms, but her entire being seemed at peace.

Her shoulders were back, her expression fierce. The pink glow in her cheeks said she knew what she was doing and to stand back and watch. He'd offered to help, but she'd told him just to keep talking to her so he was doing his best.

"You're so damned beautiful. Have I told you that today? I shoulda already said it if I haven't."

217

"You tell me that all the time, even though I need to lose like thirty pounds or more."

"Who the hell told you that? I ain't interested in dating a shovel handle in a dress." Catching her hand before she added salt to the potato pot, he jerked her to his chest. "A real man wants something soft to hold onto when he's driving himself in hard and fast." Latching his hands on her delectable ass, he squeezed to make his point. "Wants something to jiggle when he swats her backside. And I must'a done something right in my life at some point, 'cause darlin', them titties spilling through my fingers when I grab you make me harder than a steel pipe." Her teeth sank into her bottom lip as she stared up at him, producing a low growl from him. "I could do that for you, peaches."

"Have I told you today how much I like being yours?"

"Nah, I don't think you have, so go on with it." He rocked her back and forth in the kitchen. The steam from the pots providing a slight screen to their flirtations. The heavenly scents of the food had nothing on the perfume of her.

"I love being with you. I love *you*. And I know it's too fast, and there's all of this craziness, and I still haven't dealt with Seth but I just do. I love you."

"I love you too, peaches."

"Do you think it's okay?"

"To tell me you love me?"

"That we said it before and didn't mean it. How do we know we mean it now?"

"I just know. I told you I ain't much on deeper thinkin'. I just know."

"You're a lot smarter than you think you are, Grant Camden."

A distinctive sound of someone clearing their throat ripped them from the moment. Given the fact that Kaitlyn was still nuzzling her face against his chest and rubbing her hands along his ass, Grant assumed she hadn't heard her sister's entrance.

Patting her backside both in an assurance that there would be more touching later, and to alert her, he took a slight step back and gestured to her sister.

"Since Dad's stalking around the house like a caged animal, you might want to keep your good ear off of his chest so you can hear him coming. Can I talk to my sister please?" Sophie cast a glare on Grant that could've frozen a hot summer day.

218

He grunted his disdain. "That ain't my call, but it's a little easier on her if you stand on her left side. And if you're lookin' at me like that 'cause you think I'm backing off and leaving her alone with you to talk, you're crazier than a half-drowned cat."

"Grant," Kaitlyn scolded though the broad grin on her face spoke much louder. "What do you want Sophie?" She went back to the potatoes. Keeping his vow, Grant stood his ground right beside her.

"I just ... I want to apologize." The word sounded like it tasted mighty bitter. Grant eased his stance.

"For?" Kaitlyn clearly wasn't going to let out any more rope.

"That's my girl," he whispered in her ear. That mischievous smirk formed on her features again. He mentally tallied the time it would take her to finish supper, for them to eat, and then for him to get her back to his bed. Too damn long.

"For not being here," Sophie choked on her admission. "I just ... I didn't know how to deal with Mom not being Mom and with Dad being insane. It was like all of the truths we'd ever learned growing up added up to nothing but a big huge lie. And you, you're so much stronger than I am. You knew how to keep it all together. You're good at this." She gestured to her sister slaving over the hot stove. "I'm no good at taking care of people. I didn't know how to deal with Keith's death. I didn't understand any of it. It was easier to not be here so I was a coward and refused to deal and I'm sorry. I left it all to you."

"And then you ...?" Kaitlyn demanded hotly. For a moment, Grant wasn't certain if the steam around her face was coming from the pot of boiling potatoes or from her ears.

"And then I treated you like a child and was stupid enough to actually believe that you needed me to tell you what to do. And I also let myself believe that your hearing issues were affecting your thinking. The night we didn't know where you were I've never been so scared in my life. I was over here, and I couldn't handle it. On some level, I knew what you were living with every day, but I pretended it wasn't as bad as it was. When you called me at my house, I'd just gotten home. I couldn't be over here anymore. I don't know how you did it for so long. I'm so sorry, Kit-kat. You did deserve a break, a long, long break."

Clearly, sisters could read each other's minds or something. Grant had no idea how Sophie knew what to say when Kaitlyn had prompted her.

"Thank you, and don't call me Kit-kat anymore. I hate that name."

"You used to love it."

"No, I always hated it. I just endured it because you all loved it, and I wanted to make you happy."

Pride swelled throughout Grant's musculature. His little hellcat finally located her voice.

"What's going on with you and Josh?"

"Oh, basically I used him to get to you because I was terrified if you were really gone I was going to have to figure out how to deal with Mom and Dad on my own. I'm a terrible human being."

"You're not a terrible human being," Kaitlyn sighed. "But I could use your help."

"I'm too afraid to hope that Mom's really making a comeback," Sophie tried.

"Me too," Kaitlyn lost a little of her wrath fueled irritation.

"I love you, *Kaitlyn*. I'm sorry I was a lousy big sister. I'll be here from now on."

"I love you, too, and I forgive you, but you better be here."

Suddenly, Grant was stepping back because the girls were hugging and laughing and crying in a ball of insanity in the middle of the kitchen. Women. He shook his head. What the hell?

"You know, if I get mad at one of my brothers, I usually just hit him. He hits me back. We beat the shit out of one another. Then it's over," he commented, though he was fairly certain only the potatoes were listening.

Kaitlyn turned her head to give Grant the grin he was clearly after. It felt good not to be mad at her sister anymore. Sophie hadn't been there, but she was the only other person who understood how much Keith's death had forever altered their entire family.

"She's pretty amazing, isn't she?" Sophie released Kaitlyn and offered Grant a smile.

"I've been saying that since I first laid eyes on her. Pretty sure you all forgot that part though."

"I did forget, and I'm sorry. Have you ever had her mashed potatoes? They're delicious."

Kaitlyn watched a wicked smirk form on Grant's face. His left eyebrow lifted in challenge until he was certain both girls knew what he was thinking. It had everything to do with what he thought was delicious and nothing to do with potatoes.

All of the terror and sadness and anger the day had held and then the fresh air that had been swept into the house when her mother had come back to the land of the living suddenly came out in an eruption of hysterical giggles.

"Why are we laughing so hard?" Sophie joined her. Doubling over, laughing at the expression Grant sported for them both. They laughed until their sides ached, and Kaitlyn was quite certain she'd hadn't felt this good inside her parent's home in three long years.

When they wiped the tears of laughter from their faces, Sophie shook her head. "Okay, so we won't discuss how good her cooking is or what you find delicious about my sister. But seriously, she always wanted to be a little mama. Look at her. It makes her so happy."

"Little mama, huh? I can sure as hell take care of that right now." Grant came right back, waggling his eyebrows this time.

"Oh, that was not better," Kaitlyn continued giggling as she laid the steaks on her favorite iron skillet. The sizzling crack of the meat lit through the air. The sound thrilled her.

"Geez, when you wreck your car you really know how to do it, Kit … sorry. All I meant was I'm glad you're happy, finally. God knows you deserve to be happy. And he's clearly crazy about you. But you better take good care of my sister. I'm still plotting my revenge on Seth."

"You need any help with that, you let me know." Moving behind her, Grant wrapped his arms around Kaitlyn's waist and planted a kiss on top of her head. "I can get you loads of horse and cattle manure if that'd be of any use to your cause."

"Ohhhh, that is good. I'm with Mama. I like you, too. I'd say we could dump it in his precious car, but that seems a little redundant since Kaitlyn keyed the hell out of it already."

"You two will do nothing else to him. God only knows how he's planning on getting back at *me*. I don't need either of you adding more fuel to the fire," Kaitlyn ordered.

"He can't get back at you. You have the text. He cheated. He's screwed. You should forward that text to me and Mom and Dad, just in case, by the way." Sophie pointed out.

"That's a good idea. I'll do that." Kaitlyn wished that would take care of everything. Seth never liked to lose. They hadn't heard the last of him. She was certain.

"I need a little bit of whiskey for the sauce. Mom and Dad only have Gin and Vodka." Kaitlyn searched her parent's cabinets but came up empty. Neither one of them drank all that much.

"I got a bottle of Crown in my truck, sweetness. I can grab it." Grant came to her rescue once again.

"Thank you, just never, ever, ever mention to my father that you had an open bottle of whiskey in your truck."

"Your daddy wouldn't last ten minutes in cattle country, but I'll keep my mouth shut."

She was giving the sauce one final stir when the doorbell rang. Another round of nerves twisted in her stomach. She prayed they weren't about to witness some version of the Hatfields and the McCoys in her parent's dining room. If the McCoys had been wealthy city officials who were largely unaware that beef came from ranches and not packages in the grocery store.

This is gonna be a shit-covered clusterfuck. Grant followed the ridiculous number of hallways in the Summerville's home until he located the front door. His father, brother, and grandfather all looked just as uncomfortable as he felt.

"And the cavalry has arrived, I see." Evelyn was trying, bless her heart. Grant offered her a forced smile.

"Mrs. Sommerville, ma'am, this is my daddy, Ev, my granddaddy, Henry, and my brother, Luke."

"It's lovely to meet you all. Come on in."

"Ma'am," Luke nodded and quickly jerked his Resistol off of his head. His father and grandfather followed suit.

"Let me get you all something to drink. Gimlets?"

"What the hell's a Gimlet?" Luke spoke through his teeth.

"Beats me," Grant mimicked his brother's tone. "Beer's fine, Mrs. Sommerville, or water. Water's good."

"Oh. Okay, I'm not sure we have beer, but I'll ask Kaitlyn."

"Next question, what the hell are we doing here?" Luke spoke with slightly more volume.

"Oh, it's been a ride, trust me. Just try to go with it. Soon as dinner's over we'll all go home."

"Kaitlyn too?"

"I ain't leaving her here."

"Good."

Like a storm with something to prove, Kaitlyn's father made an appearance in the living room they'd been directed to.

"Dad, this is Katy's father, *Chief* Sommerville," Grant sneered.

"Nice to meet you. It's, uh, nice place you've got out here." Ev gestured to the expansive golf course behind the house.

"Do you play golf?" For a moment, her father forgot to be an ornery cuss.

"Nah, I imagine it'd make the cattle real nervous like if we sent golf balls sailing out in their fields. They wouldn't much like it."

The Camden men, at least, laughed.

"How many acres you figure all that takes up?" Granddaddy Camden tried to smooth over the awkward silence that had ensued. He gestured to the golf course. Grant shook his head. You could take the rancher off the ranch, but you sure as hell weren't likely to take the ranch out of the rancher.

"Golf courses are not measured in acres, they are measured in yards." Mr. Sommerville retorted. "That is a par seventy-one Crenshaw and Coore course. It's one of the finest in Nebraska."

"I got no clue who Crenshaw and Coore are, but it seems to me you could run several dozen pairs out there, Pops," Grant wasn't going to let Kaitlyn's asshole of a father make his granddaddy feel stupid.

"That's just what I was thinkin'." Granddaddy slapped Grant on the back.

"Pairs of what?" Mr. Sommerville demanded.

"Cows, obviously, Langston." Mrs. Sommerville returned with a tray of what appeared to be sparkling water with limes in it. "They're *cow*-boys."

"Actually, they're cattle ranchers. There's a difference," Kaitlyn corrected as she made her appearance. "Hi, Mr. Camden," she squeezed Grant's daddy's neck and then his grandfather's.

"Good to see you again, sweetheart. Looks like my grandson's been taking good care of you. That's a mighty pretty smile you're wearing."

Kaitlyn's smile widened. "He's been taking excellent care of me."

"Uh, I didn't know what you wanted done with that dress that was in the bathtub. It kinda started to stink, so I put it out with the trash."

"Oh, I completely forgot. I'm sorry. The trash is right where it belonged," Kaitlyn assured him.

"Your wedding gown?" Her father fumed.

Panic broadcast from Kaitlyn, and Grant drew her back into his arms.

"It was ruined, Daddy."

"That gown cost me eleven-thousand dollars."

"Holy shit," Luke spat the water back in his glass. "Sorry," he cringed.

"It was a ridiculous gown that *you* picked out," Kaitlyn came to Luke's defense.

"Why don't we eat?" Sophie came to her sister's rescue this time. "The food smells amazing."

As everyone headed to the dining room, Ev stared at his water glass. "Fancy golf course house comes with fancy bubbly-water with limes, I'm guessing," he whispered to Grant.

"Suppose so, Dad."

"Wonder how long he'll scour the earth looking for shiny things that don't mean a damned thing. Assurances don't come with a price tag, and we all end up in the same sized box at the end."

They made it through the salads Kaitlyn had prepared. Grant raved about it, though he was itching for the steak.

"All right, Grant, if you've decided to date my daughter, I feel her mother and I deserve to know a little bit about you. Where were you educated?"

Kaitlyn watched shame darken Grant's eyes. Her father already knew he hadn't graduated from high school. She was certain every kind of background check available had already been run on him.

"He's a rancher, Daddy. He works harder than any man I've ever met, including you," she spat. She debated hurling a tomato from her salad at her father.

"Yes, but I'd like to know where he went to school, Kaitlyn, and you mind your tone with me, young lady."

Tension weighted the entire room. Luke glanced constantly from Grant to his father. "Uh, Grant went to UN with me," he lied.

Kaitlyn's eyes closed in defeat.

"And does he also lie outright like you do as well, Mr. Camden?"

"Come again?" Luke huffed.

"He already knows I dropped out." Grant rolled his eyes. "He's just being ornery."

"I agree." Kaitlyn's mother narrowed her eyes. "Langston, they are not here for you to give them the third degree. They are not criminals. Clearly, you've already checked him out thoroughly, because you're you, but I will not sit by and allow you to treat our guests this way. If you can't be polite, go eat in the kitchen. Grant, darling, why don't you tell us all about being a cattle rancher. I've never even seen a ranch."

Clearing his throat, Grant managed a nod. "Uh, we mostly run a cow-calf operation. Biggest ranch in Lincoln county. Third biggest in the state. We got a lot of stock and several dozen prize bulls for breeding. Occasionally, we also background some calves. That means we turn 'em out in a good pasture with good hay and grain to fatten 'em up before we sell 'em off to a lot. When the market's up we'll lease a wheatgrass property down in Oklahoma for the purposes of backlotting. Other than that, I'm pretty sure we're mostly in the business of selling grass." He attempted a joke but her family had no idea what that meant.

"To feed the cows," Luke explained.

"It's beautiful there, Mama. I've honestly never seen anywhere that's prettier. It's peaceful and quiet. The baby cows are adorable. Maybe you could come out there one day when I go."

"I'd love that, sweetheart."

"Me, too," Sophie offered sweetly. Kaitlyn had no idea how her mother was managing to be so strong so suddenly, but she'd never been more thankful in her entire life.

"You'd all be welcomed most anytime." Ev smiled.

"You will not be returning to that ranch," her father huffed.

"Oh, yes, I will," Kaitlyn came right back.

"Langston." Her mother glared viciously.

"No college degree, not even a high school diploma, no military service. Your entire life has been spent on a horseback and yet you seem to somehow believe that you're good enough to date my daughter."

"Daddy, please."

Grant's father stood. "I will not sit here and listen to you insult my son, Mr. Sommerville. Now, I'm real sorry life didn't quite work out just the way you thought it ought to, but Grant had nothing to do with that. And it's not your daughter's job to make you happy."

"He's right, Langston. I'm very sorry to all of you. Please sit down and ignore him."

But it appeared Grant had reached the end of his rope. He stood and tossed his napkin on his plate. "I'm sorry, ma'am, but ignoring him don't change the way he feels, and I ain't gonna sit here with anyone who thinks I ain't even worth the gunpowder it'd take to blow me to hell. Katy, baby, I'm sorry. I tried. I'm done. Let's go. I'll get you dinner on the way."

Disappointment scalded Kaitlyn's entire body. Embarrassment clawed under her skin and clogged her throat, but she would not stay and give her father the satisfaction of thinking he won. No way. Not

225

anymore. "Okay." She hated how frail her own voice sounded. "Just let me pack a few things."

"You are not leaving this house," her father roared like a circus lion on a chain. He already knew he'd lost.

"Yes, Daddy, I am, and the sooner you understand that you don't get to run my life for me anymore, the sooner we can move past all of this."

She saw the gloating grin Grant tried to hide. Her father saw it, too.

"Well, Mr. Camden, it would appear you have not only my incredibly naïve child under your thumb, but my wife as well. So, why don't you stay and enjoy a steak meal I doubt you could even afford. I'm leaving."

"I am not naïve," Kaitlyn matched him decibel for decibel, but this time it was her father's ears that were deaf. He slammed the door to the garage on his way out. She barely made out the roar of his car engine as he drove away. "I'll just get the steaks." She bolted from the room, praying no one would follow her.

Grant was in the kitchen a half second after her, however. "I'm so fucking sorry. I had no business demanding you leave like that. I should'a kept my mouth shut."

She fell into his arms. "No, you shouldn't have. He should have. I'm sorry he set you up like that. I don't know why he's being so awful. He didn't used to be like this."

Chapter 32

Grant wondered if that were true or if Kaitlyn had ever really looked good and hard at her old man in the broad sunlight. In his experience, men rarely changed all that much. Once a shitlicker, always a shitlicker.

"I need to apologize to your family." She lifted her head with that same determination alight in her eyes.

"You don't need to apologize to anyone, sugar. He does. Now, come on. Getting good and pissed off makes a man hungry." He grabbed the platter of steaks while she lifted a bowl full of potatoes.

Luke cut into his steak, clearly anxious to fill his mouth with something besides his own boot. Grant knew he felt bad. He'd been trying to save him. But all of that would have to be communicated later, more than likely through a series of grunts and several shots of Crown.

"Damn, that's good. You oughta go on and buy her a ring," he moaned.

Everyone at the table laughed. "Might be a little quick for all that," Grant winked at Kaitlyn.

"Taste the steak."

Grant obeyed his brother's orders, mostly to keep the momentary relief that Mr. Sommerville had left going. Luke wasn't exaggerating. The meat dipped in the whiskey sauce melted in his mouth. She'd prepared it perfectly. The sauce was incredible. "Okay, maybe I should go on and get down on one knee. Best steak I've ever eaten, peaches, and that's sayin' something."

"Thank you," Kaitlyn's beaming grin made his whole night.

"You know, I proposed to your grandmamma after she made me her lasagna. She made the best lasagna."

"Maybe I'll try that next time," Kaitlyn teased. Grant wished she were ready for another ring, but he knew there was no way for that to be true. Three days ago she'd been engaged to someone else. Her life was still a mess and her daddy hated the scorched earth Grant rode in on. He was going to have to be patient and that wasn't something that had ever come naturally to him.

With their bellies full of rib-eye and the best potatoes they'd ever eaten, Grant and Luke did the dishes. Kaitlyn and Sophie stood and watched them like they were some kind of science museum exhibit.

"What?" Grant finally demanded.

"Daddy never does dishes," Kaitlyn explained.

"There's a whole lot of stuff I do real different than your daddy, darlin'. Please tell me you already figured that."

"Well, yeah, I know, it's just a weird thing to watch in this kitchen."

"Does he have any other brothers that aren't married?" Grant overheard Sophie whisper. He downed the last of the sparkling water in his glass to keep from chuckling.

"Nope, they're both married. His wife's the one who threatened to skin Josh alive."

"That was his wife?"

"Yep."

"Okay, never mind. I do not want to take her on."

Grant caught Luke's smirk, so he wasn't the only one eavesdropping.

"All right, sugar, go get packed up. I gotta get up early and clear a ton of corn tomorrow," Grant offered up a legitimate excuse for why they needed leave as soon as the dishes were done.

"Um, Grant, darling, I know you're anxious to go," Mrs. Sommerville started. "It's just ... I don't get a night with my daughters very often, and there are some important things I need to discuss with them. Langston won't be back tonight. He'll stay up at the station. Would you mind if Kaitlyn stayed here tonight?"

"'Spose that's up to her, ain't it?"

"Right." She turned to Kaitlyn. "Your father and I both need to remember that you are perfectly capable of making your own decisions. But please, there's something I need to tell you and Sophie ... alone."

Grant prayed she'd tell her mother no. He didn't even know how to sleep without her lush curves curled up in his arms where he knew she was warm and safe. He couldn't do it. As soon as Kaitlyn shot him a pleading gaze, he knew she was staying. Every curse word he could think of and a few he made up on the fly formed on his tongue. He refused them all. He would not make her feel guilty about this. He would not be another person in her life who told her what to do, outside of his bedroom anyway.

"Do you mind? I could maybe figure out a way to come back to the ranch tomorrow," she urged quietly.

"How about you just stay with me tonight, son? You'd only be 'bout twenty minutes from here. You can come right back over here

228

whenever she's ready tomorrow," Granddaddy Camden offered him a lifeline. Twenty minutes beat two hours any day of the week.

"Fine," was all he could manage. He dug in the pocket of his Wranglers. "If you need to get out of here, you call me and head out. I'll meet you wherever you are." He pressed the keys to his truck into her palm.

"I'm sorry," she mouthed.

"Here," Sophie sidled up beside them. "You keep your truck. I solemnly swear if he comes home and acts even half as bad as he was at supper, I will personally make certain I get her to you."

"I can get myself out if I need to," Kaitlyn reminded both of them. "Just come here." She took his hand and led him to a side porch off another room he hadn't even seen yet.

"How damn many rooms does this place have?" He was being an ass. He just couldn't quite manage to shut his mouth. Her staying and him leaving wasn't the deal.

"Too many, and for a very long time every single one of them was filled with nothing but misery. I don't know what she wants to tell me, Grant, but it must be important. You don't know what it's like to live with two different people all inside one woman. I'm terrified of what will happen when you all leave. She always managed to act sort of normal when people were over or when she was out at the club. But then she would crawl back inside this shell of her former self as soon as it was just the three of us again. I haven't seen her this adamant in years. I need to know what she wants to tell me. I owe her that. I owe *me* that."

"I know. Okay, I know. I'm just gonna miss you like crazy and it tears me up to leave you here." Unable to keep his hands off of her, he crushed her against his chest in a hug meant to last the rest of the night.

"It means the world to me that you'll miss me. I'll miss you, too. You better be back over here tomorrow morning at the same time you normally get up to do whatever it is you do with all of those cows."

"Soon as I get you back to the ranch I'm gonna teach you what we do and why we do it."

"Good."

Cradling her chin in his callused hand, he memorized the hungry look in her eyes. He'd need that just to get through the night. His thumb caressed over her lips tracing her perfect cupid's bow and their heated abundance.

Slowly, forcing himself to pause and retain the way her eyes reached half-mast and the way her breath whispered across his lips, he leaned in and consumed her mouth like he was receiving his last meal.

She opened for him. A grunt of raw pain wrenched up from his gut as his tongue memorized every flavor of her mouth. Her lips were soft and craving the perfect answer to his rough eager need.

Grant lost himself in the kiss, wishing the sunlight would make a rapid appearance, and this night would forget the debt of time it was owed. His hands gripped her backside. Taking what he wanted, he pressed his rapidly stiffening cock into the cradle of her hips.

Her tender moan slipped down his throat and wrapped itself firmly around his heart.

"No," finally took flight from his tongue when she moved her ministrations to his neck.

"You don't want me to do that?" Hurt confusion played malevolently in her eyes.

"God, no, that ain't what I meant. I want your lips on me most anywhere you want to put them anytime you want to put 'em somewhere. I meant, no, I ain't leaving. I'll go sit out in the damned truck and wait on you to talk. I'll sit out there all night, but I ain't leaving you here alone."

"Grant, I love how stubborn and relentless you are. I really do. It makes me feel things I never even knew were possible, but tonight, I need you to go. I'll be miserable without you, too, but I need to do this on my own."

"I love you and I hate this." The bitter taste of defeat erased her flavors from his mouth. He hated it all the more.

"Right back 'atcha, *rancher*." She gave him a grin. The stars dotting the city skyline had nothing on the light dancing in her eyes.

"Kinda didn't mind *you* calling me cowboy so much."

"I just want to call you mine."

He dove back in for another kiss like a man possessed.

Eventually he forced himself to climb up in his granddaddy's truck. She'd claimed she wasn't sure she could even reach the pedals on his truck, but he wasn't leaving her stranded there with no way to leave.

"You aren't abandoning her, son," his grandfather soothed over the chug of the old Ford-motor.

"Bullshit."

A grunt Grant recognized as the same one all of the Camden men shared, reached his ears as they backed out of the driveway. "It's what I tell myself every time I drive away from that damned nursing home. Thought it might help."

Doubling down on the hatred he held for himself in that moment, he sealed his lips shut. His granddaddy had to sleep without his grandmother every godforsaken night. He had no right to bellyache about being without Katy one night.

Tired of the sound of his own voice, he reviewed the events of the last three days instead of talking to fill the silence. How had his entire life gotten turned upside down in less than a week? Life was a bitch and there was nothing else to it.

Suddenly he remembered the last conversations he'd had with his granddaddy. "You knew," bellowed from his mouth. "You knew who she was. You knew who her daddy was. That's why you were telling me about Great-Granddaddy Miller not liking you and why you said her daddy was hurt and angry."

"Yeah, I knew who she was the moment you showed up with her in a gettin'-married dress in my storm shelter."

"Why didn't you say something?"

"What was I to tell you, son? You kids oughta quit gettin' your news off a' that internet thing and pick up a local paper now and again. Engagement and wedding been in the Star for months. Every time I saw her picture, she looked miserable. Plus, your grandmamma was a red-head spitfire with a miserable old cuss for a daddy. Kinda had a feelin' about you two. I knew about her brother, too. It was in the paper for weeks. Tore the family apart. I got no use for rich politicians sending our boys out to die for no other reason than to make them richer."

"You served in Ko-rea, Pops," Grant drawled.

"Yeah, I served. That's why I'm telling you what I'm telling you. I'll tell you this, too, I know you feel like you're in heaven when she falls asleep in your arms at night. Because you're a man who ain't afraid to be what he's supposed to be, and you're a rancher who knows how to take care of what he's been blessed to have. But love ain't always about walking through heaven, Grant. Sometimes it's about walking straight through hell together. And this time in this case it ain't real likely to be heaven on the front side. That man's gonna keep putting her through hell until he realizes it ain't her he's mad at. It's her brother."

"What kind of sorry-ass shitsack gets mad at a kid who's dead?"

"Oh, son, there are lots of people angry at the dead and buried. That's why they're so angry. Cause that person they loved so much can't be there to defend themselves and that just pisses them off but good. He thinks it's his fault his son ain't here no more. That's a deep hurt. That's a wound I ain't sure you ever get over. The thought of Kaitlyn leaving and going with you to the ranch scares him shitless, and he's taking it out on her. He's terrified to lose her too, and all he's managing to do is push her away so he blames that on you."

"Hey, Pops, you never told me what happened to you and Gran after you got married and you got her out to the ranch."

"I don't tell that story too often 'cause I don't like to relive that hell we walked through those first few months, but I 'spect it's time you heard the truth. For what it's worth and while I'm thinking about it, I took one of them pictures of Kaitlyn from the paper to your grandmamma for her to see. She likes her."

"She tell you that?" His grandmother hadn't spoken the past few times Grant had been in to see her. It killed him to go almost as much as it killed him not to.

"Nah, I just know."

Chapter 33

"Mom, you sound so much better," Kaitlyn tried.

"Well, I feel a little better, at least until I tell you two this, then I'm not sure how I'll feel."

Kaitlyn and Sophie shared a worried glance.

"We don't have to talk, Mama. We could all watch a movie or something," Sophie pled.

Kaitlyn shook her head. Sophie had to stop running from all emotion, she had to stop being afraid of it. Emotions were a part of life, the good, the bad, and the ugly, just like Grant said.

"No, I need to apologize and explain several things to you girls. First of all, I am very sorry for the way I've acted these past few years. I couldn't seem to claw out of the hell of depression. When I did come up for air, I did it for everyone but my children, and I'm so sorry for all of it."

"Mama, we were all depressed and shocked about what happened," Kaitlyn offered her mother a sacrament of empathy.

"Yes, well, that's not all that happened, sweetheart. That's what I need to tell you."

"Okay, just start at the beginning maybe."

"Unfortunately, the beginning was supposed to be an end, just not my son's," her mother stated cryptically.

"What happened?" A brick of suspicion knotted in Kaitlyn's stomach. Her intuition shifted into overdrive.

"First of all, I've been seeing a therapist."

"You have?" All of the fights Kaitlyn and her father had gotten into lately had been about her mother seeing a therapist. "How did I not know this?"

"Probably the same way your father and I had no idea you were working for Chully's Iron Skillet instead of the law firm."

"Does Daddy know you've been going?"

"Oh yes, he knows."

"Well, it seems to be helping," Sophie vowed.

"In some ways it has. It's helped me to face some things. When we realized you'd left the club and run out on Seth, part of me was so relieved because I knew you were headed straight to misery with him, but most of me was terrified I'd lost you, too. And I'd already felt like I'd lost you."

"Mama, I was running away from Seth and from Daddy mostly, not you."

"But, baby, after your brother died, my feisty little girl who tried so hard to prove herself to everyone went away, too. You were here but my Kaitlyn wasn't. You tried so hard to do things the way you thought Keith would do them. It broke my heart. I just couldn't find it in myself to try to tell you to be whoever you wanted to be. I wasn't strong enough to deal with my own pain to help you with yours, and I wasn't strong enough to stand up to your father anymore. I let both of you down."

"I'm sorry. I was trying to make everyone happy, but you never let me down. I just wanted you to be okay."

"I know, sweetheart. I don't really think I'll ever be okay, but I need to be stronger. When I heard your father threaten to have Grant arrested and you threatened to leave and never come back, I realized what my weakness could cost me. Of course, it might cost me that still."

"Whatever you're not saying, please just say it." Kaitlyn couldn't stand it anymore. Waiting on whatever was coming was surely worse than anything her mother could possibly say.

Sinking down in a Henredon chair by the fireplace, her mother drew a visible breath. She faltered. Tears sprang to her eyes and terror ripped through Kaitlyn. No. She couldn't do this again. She couldn't watch her mother dissolve before her very eyes.

"Mama, please," she begged. "You don't have to tell us. Just don't cry."

Scrubbing her hands over her face, smearing her mascara, Evelyn stared her children down. "I'm all right, Kaitlyn. Just give me a moment."

Sophie scooted closer to Kaitlyn on the couch.

"The day before we found out about your brother, I'd filed for divorce."

"What?!" Kaitlyn and Sophie both gasped.

"I was just so angry at your father."

"Oh, God." Kaitlyn's head fell into her hands. Somehow, some way she knew the divorce wasn't the actual confession. The steak she'd consumed threatened to make a rapid reappearance.

"You know how difficult he is to live with. I was so furious at him for putting all of those ridiculous Army stories in Keith's head all the time. I blamed him for Keith joining. I knew I was supposed to be proud of my son and his sacrifice, but I wasn't, I was furious. There, I said it, and I'm so ashamed that I felt that way. And instead of confronting your father or sharing the way I felt, I just got angrier and angrier. I didn't think I could stand to fight with him one more time. He was just so stubborn about everything. Everything has to be done his way and receive the Langston Sommerville seal of approval. I couldn't stand it anymore."

"Oh, God," Kaitlyn managed again, but her mother just kept going.

"That first year that you were in New York and Keith was off fighting it seemed all we did was fight. One day, I was supposed to meet Sylvia and Tori at the club for drinks, but they both cancelled at the last minute. Before I left, I ran into a friend of mine from law school, Max Chislern. I hadn't seen him in years. He asked how Keith was and offered to buy me a drink. I never meant for it to go as far as it did. I just … it had been so long since someone listened to me."

"Oh God, oh God, oh God." Kaitlyn began rocking back and forth. How could her mother have done what was inevitably coming?

"It didn't go on but for a few weeks. I felt so guilty. Nothing like what I feel now, but before that day that everything changed, I thought I'd finally figured out what I wanted. When I filed those papers, I was so sure. God's retribution came mighty fast."

"Wait. What?" Kaitlyn's head lifted as the weight of realization tried to pull her back down. "Retribution? What … Keith? You think it was your fault?"

"Seems fairly obvious it was, Kit-kat." Her mother's sigh was weighted with shame and exhaustion.

"Please, don't call me that."

"Mama, I don't think that's how God works," Sophie finally spoke.

"That's what my therapist says, but you're both wrong. And on top of all of the hell Keith's death put your father through, I'd filed for divorce. I begged for his forgiveness. He moved out of our bedroom. He'll be furious I told you. He never wants to talk about it or for anyone to know, but I needed to apologize and try to explain why I just cannot accept that your brother is gone. It's entirely my fault. I am so sorry for every selfish horrible thing I did that tore our world apart. I don't expect you to ever forgive me. I will never forgive myself.

"But today when I thought you were going to leave and never come back, I just couldn't allow another one of my children to be hurt because of my mistakes. And I will try with all of my might to be stronger from now on. I won't allow your father to ruin what you've found with your cowboy, sweetheart. I want you to be happy, and even more importantly, I want you to be you."

Kaitlyn's entire world tipped off of its axis. The room spun. She reached her hand out for something to steady her, but Grant wasn't there this time. She'd sent him away. The roar in her ears blocked out her mother's voice. She had no power with which to continue to listen.

She had to get out of there.

"Kaitlyn," Sophie grabbed her shoulders when she stood. "It's okay. We'll get through this together."

"What?" Kaitlyn demanded.

"Here." Her mother poured her a shot glass of something horrible that seared from her throat to her stomach. A moment later the warmth began to spread. A hazy fog dulled a little of her fury. She managed breath.

"It's okay if you hate me. Trust me, you couldn't possibly hate me more than I hate myself."

"I don't hate you. I just don't understand why everyone has to cheat. Even me. Why can't things just work out the way they're supposed to? Don't wedding vows mean anything? What's the point of falling in love at all? It clearly doesn't last. It just hurts."

"That isn't true," her mother vowed adamantly. She lifted Kaitlyn's face in her perfectly manicured hands. "I loved your father from the moment I laid eyes on him, and I still love him to this day. I don't like him very much most of the time, but I will always love him if for no other reason than for the fact that he gave me my children. He doesn't have it in himself to forgive me and he shouldn't have to, but that doesn't mean that I regret loving him."

"I should certainly have given you other reasons to love me, and I sure as hell should've given you reasons to like me," Her father's voice vacuumed the room of all other sounds.

"Langston, what are you doing here?"

Kaitlyn concentrated. Her mother's question didn't ring with vengeance. It carried a note of hope.

"I went to the station and couldn't get anything done, so I went out to talk to Keith, or talk to that blasted headstone. I realized he would have given me hell for the way I'd acted and the way I treated your *cowboy*. I just ... when I walked in that room expecting to walk you down the aisle and you were gone ... I came unglued. I know I haven't been the easiest person to live with since your brother died."

"I told them why." Evelyn sighed.

"I heard that, too, Evie."

Evie.

Kaitlyn sank back down on the sofa. Racking her brain, she tried desperately to remember the last time she'd heard her father refer to her mother by his nickname for her. Shaking off a little of the weight that had been placed on her, she drew a deep breath. "Wait, Keith used to argue with you about me?"

She had no memories of any such things. Keith was perfect. She was broken. He never did anything their parents didn't like.

"He argued with me on your behalf constantly whenever he didn't have his tongue down that girl's throat I couldn't stand."

"Caroline?"

"Her, and the ones he cheated on her with," her father threw a nasty glare at her mother.

"Keith cheated on Caroline?" Disbelief crashed through her. How had she missed all of this?

"That has nothing to do with *you* right now, young lady. I thought you were finally making an effort. I thought you were actually going to make something of yourself. Then I find out you'd just walked away from a job I handed you and had taken up with some cowboy."

"I cannot marry Seth." She clung hard and fast to the only thing that she knew was certain.

"Fine, but does it have to be him?"

"I didn't say I was marrying Grant either."

"I saw the way you looked at him, Kit-kat. Your mother used to look at me that way before everything went straight to hell."

"Girls, would you mind going upstairs for a few minutes? I need to speak to your father alone."

It had been many years since Kaitlyn and Sophie had been sent up to their rooms, but just like always, they took a seat on the top step just out of sight and listened.

"You know, I wouldn't mind trying to look at you the way Kaitlyn looks at Grant again." Kaitlyn swore the tremor in her mother's voice shook her to the core. Her breath stalled in her lungs.

"She has marks on her wrists. I don't know how you could have missed them. He bound her hands at some point."

Sophie jerked Kaitlyn's hands out of her lap. Her mouth hung open. "At some point I want to hear about this." She mouthed slow enough for Kaitlyn to read her lips.

"Yes, well, as I recall, the first time I took you back to Charleston to meet my parents I had cuff marks on both my wrists and my ankles. You and I both know it wasn't because I'd been arrested."

"Ew, ew, ew," Kaitlyn and her sister cringed.

"I've tried, Evelyn. I have tried my damnedest to get it out of my head, but I can't. I can't *not* see you with him. I can't. And every time I try that image gets tied up with those men walking into my office."

"Then please, can we try therapy together? I think it would help."

"It would do nothing but alert the entire city to the fact that we haven't been able to move on after our son's death. It makes me look weak, and I won't have that. I'm the Chief of Police."

"At some point, Langston, our family has to mean more to you than your reputation. I don't even think it's me you're still so angry at, and it certainly isn't Kaitlyn or Grant. You're mad at Keith, and until you can make some effort to forgive yourself and to forgive him for disappointing you none of us will be able to go on."

"This wasn't how it was supposed to be." Her father's roar had Kaitlyn covering her good ear. "He was supposed to come home, and not in a damned bag."

Simply unable to listen to any more, Kaitlyn raced to her bedroom. Nothing made sense. The world around her wasn't hers. She had no truths. The pillars of her youth disintegrated around her. Everything but her bed and nightstand was stacked in boxes on the floor. She was supposed to move into Seth's apartment. The rock-like enclosure in her throat sealed off her air supply.

Fishing her phone out of her purse where Grant had laid it with the rest of her luggage, she touched his name.

"Hey, peaches, I was hoping you'd call. Everything okay?"

"No." Her voice had no volume.

"I'm on my way."

"Just please talk to me."

"I'm gonna talk, baby, while I come back to get you."

Chapter 34

Mindlessly, Kaitlyn threw every single thing in her suitcase into the back corner of her empty closet. Tearing open the boxes on top of the piles, she located every pair of jeans she owned, a half-dozen shirts, and a few pairs of ratty pajamas. Hurling them into the suitcase, she paced.

"I'm almost there, sugar. Deep breaths for me, okay?"

She tried. God, she tried, but breathing meant crying, and she refused to do that anymore. She refused to feel anything at all. The air in her lungs burned in an effort to escape but she refused it. She didn't want to breathe, or to think, or to feel. She only wanted to leave. Empty. She was completely empty with nothing left to give. What she couldn't seem to understand was how anyone could simultaneously feel so empty and so heavy.

"I'm here, baby. Want me to come in and get you?" Grant's smooth sleepy tone gave her something to cling to.

"No, I'm on my way out." She ended his call and raced out of her bedroom, almost toppling over Sophie.

"Where are you going?" Her sister demanded.

"Back to the ranch or anywhere Grant wants to go. Anywhere that isn't here."

"You can't just keep running away."

"I'm not running away."

"Yes, you are. Look, I know you've been the one dealing with everything for a long time, but we have to deal with all of this new stuff, too. Mom and Dad are in her bedroom talking. I can't hear what they're saying."

"I don't care what they're saying. I don't care about anything anymore. I'll call you later."

Grant met her at the door, relieved her of her bags, and flung them in the back of the truck. "I'll take you anywhere you want to go."

"You look exhausted. Can we just go back to your grandfather's house? We can come back and get your truck in the morning."

With a single nod, once again, he became her getaway.

He asked no questions. She had no answers to give. Nothing made sense anyway. When she fell into his arms in the guest bedroom, he took her in, holding her in the sanctuary of his body, and became a drug to numb the pain.

Grant walked the length of his grandfather's lawn twice, debating running his fist through the metal shed on his left. Dammit, he needed more land to walk. This half-acre shit was insanity in a box. How did his granddaddy stand this?

He assumed the sun was somewhere under the thick covering of clouds pressing in around him. His own personal sunshine was still curled up in bed, a beautiful broken disaster. He'd expected tears the night before, but she'd given up none. Too strong. She'd been through too much. Confusion was the only recognizable emotion drowning in the blue oceans of her eyes.

Stomping back inside the house, he poured another cup of coffee.

"You could just wake her up," his grandfather tried.

"No. She's exhausted mentally, emotionally, and physically. Let her sleep."

"She give you any idea what happened last night?"

Grant shook his head. "She didn't want to talk. She wanted to run."

"You gonna take her back to the ranch?"

"I swear I've got half a mind to put her in my truck, point it due west, and just drive. She needs to be done with the whole lot of 'em. All they do is hurt her. I won't have it anymore."

"Careful there, son. It ain't about what you will or won't have, it's about what she wants to happen when it comes to her family."

"I know that. Don't mean I have to like it."

Suddenly, Grant sensed her presence. That sweet peach smell of the lotion she'd taken to wearing lately clung to his lungs as she made her appearance in the kitchen.

"Hey, baby, you sleep okay?"

Her hair hung in a cloud of red curls sticking out every direction. He'd put her in the t-shirt he'd been wearing when he'd gotten her back to the house. Her ample curves tugged at the faded cotton. Sheet marks streaked the freckles on her cheeks. Her eyes were clear and fervent as she stared up at him like he was the only thing in her world that made a damned bit of sense. That was all he needed, for her to believe in him.

The anger and irritation he'd felt for the past three hours bled from him in an instant. "Thank you for letting me stay here again, Mr. Camden." Her tender sleepy voice gripped Grant's soul. It was perforated with a sadness he had no idea how to erase.

"You are welcome over here anytime, darlin'. Can I get you some coffee?"

240

"I got it, Pops," Grant handed her a mug and watched over her as she downed a long sip.

"I didn't mean to sleep in. I know you need to get back to the ranch."

"Hey, come here to me." When she set the mug down, he drew her into his arms. "I'm fine. We'll do whatever you want to do. I ain't in any hurry."

"He's got a bunch a' brothers and sisters and a daddy who'd be more than happy to help him out with his chores. Let him take care of you." Granddaddy Camden winked at her. Grant tried to locate his customary irritation that he was going to have to ask for help, but came up empty. She was worth him swallowing a little of his pride.

"Yeah, I know, but he hates to ask people for help." She gave him a grin that didn't quite reach her eyes.

"Truer words may never have been spoken, but love changes a man." Granddaddy Camden shot Grant a goading grin.

"I'm not so sure that's true, Mr. Camden. I can make breakfast. You must be hungry."

Grant and his grandfather shared a quick puzzled glance as she busied herself in the refrigerator pulling out eggs and bacon.

An hour later, Granddaddy Camden drove them all back to Kaitlyn's parents' home to pick up Grant's truck. The knot in his gut just wouldn't quit. Gall sizzled through his veins. Something was coming. He could feel it. His fists clenched and unclenched constantly. His muscles tensed of their own accord. His jaw was locked so tightly his molars ached.

"I'm sorry," she apologized again.

"You didn't do anything to be sorry for."

"I haven't told you why you came to get me last night."

"You talk whenever you're ready, sugar."

"Thank you." The heat of the kiss she brushed on his jaw eased his strain until his grandfather keyed in the gate code and headed back to the house that had hurt his girl. Bile and fury made a biting cocktail in his stomach.

As they neared her house, the anger located its target.

"Oh, no," Kaitlyn whimpered.

A red Audi with the epitaph of their relationship carved in the hood sat beside Grant's truck, and leaning against the hitch of his brand new GMC like a fool with a death wish was Seth himself. His smug expression made Grant want to remove his sac via his throat.

"What is he doing here?" She withered in the seat beside him.

Grant watched her attempt to summon courage from the air around her and come up empty, but she wasn't fighting this rat bastard. Not this time. "You stay put. Do not let her out of this truck," he ordered his grandfather.

"What are you going to do?" Kaitlyn demanded.

"Might talk to him, might kill him. That remains to be seen." Letting the spurs on his boots jangle, Grant seethed as he marched forward. "If I was you, I'd get your ass off 'a my truck lest you want me to cram my tailpipe up it and twist."

"You're the new guy?" Seth laughed. "You. She chose *you* over me? How quaint."

Impudent little asswipe was playing with fire. Unadulterated rage seared up Grant's spine.

"You ain't the sharpest tool in the shed are ya? She's sitting in my truck. Slept in my arms last night. Been keeping my bed nice and warm for days. Sure as hell seems to me she's mine."

A flashfire of pure hatred formed in Seth's eyes. His nostrils flared. He stalked forward but then seemed to think better of it and retreated. Grant stood almost a head taller than him and the weakling city-boy didn't look like he ever lifted more than his finger.

Grant chuckled. "Maybe you do have a few brain cells to rub together, but you're still mighty close to my truck, meaning I'm mighty close to beating the ever-lovin' shit outta you. Been lookin' for a reason since I found out what you did to her."

"What I did to her? She's the one whoring herself out with some dropout with more debt than good sense. I have several friends in the police department, I did a little ..."

He didn't get to finish. Grant had him by the collar of his fancy-ass shirt. With one slight turn of his wrist he shut off the little bitch's air supply, watching his face turn as red as his ass was gonna be. "What did you just call her?" he snarled.

"Grant! Don't hit him. He'll have you arrested. Let him go," Kaitlyn was beside him in a hot minute. "What do you want, Seth? Why are you even here? When I told you to go to hell that's precisely what I meant."

Seth coughed and Grant eased his grip. "Answer her," he growled.

Shaking himself loose, a crazed look came over Seth. "I came to hand deliver this." He thrust a thick envelope he produced from the back pocket of his slacks into Kaitlyn's hands.

If she'd rolled her eyes any harder, they would have lodged themselves in her skull somewhere. Grant kept his malevolent glare on the douche-nugget before him.

Ripping open the envelope, she narrowed her eyes. "You're suing me for public humiliation?" Her laughter shocked Grant. Being sued didn't sound good. "You work for the D.A. You know public humiliation suits never go anywhere."

"I'm also suing you for damages to my car." Seth reached for the paperwork, but Kaitlyn whisked them away and Grant caught his hand.

"You ever put your hands anywhere near her again, I'll break every single bone in your body, slowly."

"Why are you really doing this? I have the text, Seth. It's on my phone and I already forwarded it to lots of other phones, including my father's. All I have to do it is show it to whatever judge you try to bribe to get this to even go to claims court. You'd be the laughing stock of the entire district attorney's office."

"You want me to go away so bad, Kaitlyn. You want me to leave you so you can go off and be a baby making bitch for him, because let's be real, we all know that's all you really wanted and you're not capable of anything else. I'll be happy to leave you to your hillbilly loser as soon as you pay me back for ruining everything."

"I'm gonna kill you," Grant drew his fist back but Kaitlyn stepped between him and Seth.

"No. Don't. Please, Grant." She spun and faced Seth. "So, you don't actually want this to go to court. That's it right? You think I'll pay you off. You're dumber than you look."

"Don't be an idiot, Kaitlyn. You won't be paying me anything. How would you? You gave up the job your father handed you and went to work as some low-life short order cook. But we all know your father won't let this go to court. He'll write you a check to get me to keep my mouth shut. Didn't take me long to figure out how to fix everything you broke. This is perfect. Mighty Chief Sommerville can't ever let anyone know what a stupid excuse for a daughter he has or that his wife is just as much a whore as his little girl."

"How dare you?!" Kaitlyn lunged at him, and in that moment Seth's fate was sealed. He drew his hand back and whipped it across her face.

Grant clobbered him, bringing him to the ground a half-second later.

Stumbling backwards, Kaitlyn gasped as Grant pummeled Seth. She cringed. The sound of shattering bone was loud enough for her to hear.

"Grant, please. Stop! You don't know what he can do." Hot tears singed the raw skin on her cheek.

Seth didn't have a prayer. Grant's knee dug into his groin. His fists flew so quickly, they were a blur. The man hauled hay and cattle for a living. He'd grown up with brothers who were just as muscular as he was. He played football. Seth had done none of those things.

His groans and gasps were gut-wrenching. Another pop of broken bone made its way to Kaitlyn's ears.

The reminder of why he wasn't likely to leave the front lawn of the Sommerville's home unless it was on a stretcher burned on in Kaitlyn's face.

"Grant, stop. You're gonna kill him, son." Granddaddy Camden's voice reached through the haze of terror swamping Kaitlyn's hearing. He gently eased her further away from the fight.

Grant stood and jerked Seth off of the ground, trying to make him stand upright for another round. His head hung oddly to the side. He was barely conscious.

"Grant, please," Kaitlyn screamed.

"You ain't even worth it, you pathetic piece of shit," snarled from Grant as he dropped Seth back to the ground. He reared his boot back. Before the heel collided with Seth's chest, Kaitlyn heard another voice.

"Grant, stop." It was her father. Gracefully, he managed to lower Grant's leg. Everything around her was muted. She could couldn't fully understand her father's voice. All she knew was Grant was going to end up in jail on an assault charge that could ruin his life. It was inevitable now. And it was all her fault.

"There's only so much I can get you out of. Go. Take Kaitlyn with you. Don't make another appearance in Lincoln until you hear from me."

Chapter 35

"What did Daddy say to you? I couldn't understand him." They'd been driving for a half hour. Kaitlyn couldn't stand the silence anymore. It hurt her far more than Seth's hand had.

"Uh, he said to take you with me and not to come back to Lincoln until I heard from him."

"He said that? He told you to take me with you?"

That only got her a nod.

"I'm so sorry about your hands. They look awful. Do you want me to drive? You're bleeding."

"I'm fine. Had far worse."

"You have a scratch on your cheek." Tenderly she touched the cut on his cheekbone, wishing she could heal him the way he always managed to take everything away that hurt her.

"Pansy ass shitstick fights like a bitch. What kind of grown-ass man doesn't know how to take a punch?"

"The pansy-ass shitstick kind, I guess."

This time she got a half smile.

"Your daddy also said there was only so much he could get me out of. Any idea what that meant?"

Kaitlyn's heat refused her another beat. Oh God, oh God, no. She knew what that meant. There was no stopping him now. "He said that? I mean, obviously he said that or you wouldn't have said that he said it. I'm just …"

"Hey, come on, I'm fine, sugar, okay? Feel a helluva lot better, actually. Been wanting to do that for near about a week now. Deep breaths for me. It'll work itself out. Things almost always do."

"What if he presses charges?" Whether he did or he didn't the outcome would be the same. She'd never get to see Grant again. "I still can't believe he hit me. He's never done that before." She tried desperately to fill the void with her own voice.

"And he'll never do it again."

"Thank you. I'm so sorry for all of the trouble I've caused you. I have no idea how you don't hate me."

"I could never hate you. Kinda goes against loving you."

"I don't deserve for you to love me. Love never works out right anyway."

"What's that mean?"

"Nothing. My dad's going to try to get Seth not to press charges. They have to work together a lot. It matters to Seth what my dad thinks. His job depends on it."

"Didn't sound to me like he cares what your daddy thinks anymore since he's trying to get money out of him."

"Daddy can't stand for anyone to think there's anything wrong with our family. He's using that against him." *He'll use it against us, too.* "And knowing Seth he'll probably get what he wants. I can't believe he actually went with a public humiliation charge. That's ridiculous. No one ever wins those."

"He knows that."

"I know he does. I swear I have always hated him. I have no idea how I managed to pretend to be mildly interested in him for two years."

"You tell yourself you're not who you are long enough, it takes hold."

"I'm so sorry about everything."

"Stop. We'll figure this shit out. Let's just get back to the ranch and settle in. Austin and Summer are riding in that local rodeo tonight for charity. I promised I'd come help with the boys. After that, I want to get lost for a good long while."

"That sounds perfect." *If only it were that easy.*

"Wish you'd tell me what happened last night."

The man had just beaten her ex's face in and stood to go to prison for her. If he'd asked her to set herself on fire, she probably would've done it. "Apparently my mom had an affair after Keith left for Afghanistan."

"Come again?"

"Yeah, and she filed for divorce the day before he died. She thinks it's all her fault. Every time I think things can't possibly get worse, they do. Dad came in while she was telling me and Sophie. He almost apologized. And then they started arguing about Keith and I just couldn't stay there anymore."

"That's what he was talking about."

"Who?"

"The motherfucker I just beat into the ground. He figured out about the affair."

"He must've somehow seen the papers Mom filed at the courthouse or something, and that's also how he knows my dad will pay him off."

246

Vomit and bile continued to swirl in Kaitlyn's stomach. She watched Grant try to process everything going on and waited for him to finally decide she just wasn't worth the trouble. That seemed inevitable, too.

"So, that's blackmail, right? Or extortion or some other legal word I don't know."

"They fall under the same law here in Nebraska, so you do know what you're talking about. Usually with extortion something is being stolen or someone is being coerced and willingly pays money to keep something bad from happening. Blackmail is what he's doing. Threatening to reveal information if he isn't paid."

"You think your daddy will arrest him for that?"

"No."

"Why?"

"Because not arresting him for that is the only way he could possibly get Seth not to charge you with assault, and the sentence for assault could send you to prison for years."

"Oh."

"And I don't know if my father even heard anything before the fight. I bet he just heard Seth screaming and came outside. He doesn't know what Seth knows."

"Yeah, didn't think about that."

"I swear, I will do anything I can even if I have to go back to him to keep you from getting into any trouble over this."

"Don't ever say shit like that again. You understand me? You ain't going back to him. I don't give a damn what happens to me."

"Well, I do care."

"I'll be fine."

"I wish I knew why he keeps saying I ruined everything. Surely, he isn't talking about our marriage. He ruined that. Actually, it was doomed from the moment Dad brought him home to meet me. I just don't understand what he's talking about. His daddy owns half of Lancaster county. It's not like he needs the money. And he would never want the D.A. to see that he'd even filed a lawsuit he was guaranteed to lose even if it's not going to claims court. He's just being an asshole as usual."

"Can we talk about anything else, sugar? Please."

"Sorry. You talk. I'm not doing a very good job." Defeat tightened the vise seizing her heart.

"That ain't at all what I said. I just want to get back home. City makes me crazy. Bunch of bullshit I don't understand everywhere I look. Never going back suits me just fine."

Kaitlyn wished it were that easy. If she could simply erase her existence in Lincoln altogether, maybe she could figure out how to believe that they weren't doomed.

Chapter 36

"And my daddy's gonna ride that big huge bull, ain't he Uncle Grant, 'cause he ain't scared of anything. Ain't that right?" J.J. demanded that night as they circled the dusty lot that had been set up for the purposes of the Western Nebraska Stampede Rodeo for Kids in Need.

"Yep. He'll be up in a few minutes, little man. You want another snow cone?"

"Grant, he's already had three, and two bags of popcorn, and a corn dog. If you let him have one more of those it's not all going to stay down. His tongue is already purple and blue from the last two." Kaitlyn beamed at him while she balanced Hank on her hip. He was half asleep on her shoulder and seemed quite content.

"I figure it's my job to spoil 'em up right. If he pukes, Austin can clean it up," he tried to tease her, but with every passing hour she pulled further and further away. He watched the proverbial blade slip slowly into his chest. Inch by inch, she convinced herself she wasn't worth it and that love wasn't even real.

He couldn't get through to her. A million unspoken fears haunted her eyes. Checking his watch for the tenth time that hour alone, he willed Austin to get on with his ride. Grant wasn't going down without a fight. He'd throw all he had in to save this. He'd figure out how to make it work, come hell or high water. He wouldn't watch her walk away because city folk were nothing but a bunch of chickenshit who were incapable of keeping their word when they said I do.

"I can't believe Austin is going to ride one of those." She gestured her head to a bull being loaded into a chute. She was trying. God, she was trying so damn hard to pretend the weight of her life wasn't crushing her. It killed him. "I'm sorry. I know he's your brother, but that's insane." She mouthed while J.J. was playing in a pile of sand nearby.

"He was the champ a few years back, darlin'. He knows what he's doing."

"Coach Camden, Coach Camden," rang from behind them.

Halting, Grant forced a grin as Colton Pearce skidded to a halt before he crashed right into Kaitlyn. The dust he kicked up flew in her face. Grant tried to shield her but hadn't done any better with that than he had managing to keep anything else from hurting her.

Her cheek was still red from where that limp-peckered motherfucker hit her.

"Whoa there, hoss." Grant knelt down to Colton's height. "You okay?"

"Yes, sir, I'm good. Sorry 'bout that, ma'am."

"It's okay," Kaitlyn gave him one of her sweet grins.

"I wanted to tell you I've been practicing every day after my chores. I'm gonna do what you said and go out for quarterback this season."

"Sounds good to me. You almost had it last year. If you wanna come by the ranch some time, get your daddy to drop you off and I'll help you with your long pass."

"Thanks, Coach. I'll do that." Colton's eyes roved over the scabs on Grant's hands. "Hey, what happened to you? You get in a fight, Coach?"

"Nah," Grant lied through his teeth. Kaitlyn cringed and brushed another kiss on Hank's sweaty head. "You know nothing good ever comes from fightin'. I just forgot to wear my gloves when I was working today."

Colton was eleven. He'd grown up helping his parents and his big brothers run their ranch. He knew Grant was lying through his teeth. "Come on, Coach. You even got a mark on your face. Who'd you beat up? Bet they were eating dirt fast weren't they? Pow. Nobody can take on Coach Camden."

Kaitlyn winced at Colton's admiration.

Some part of the universe must've still been on Grant's side. The announcer saved his ass. "Up next, legendary barrel racer, Summer Camden will be turning and burning for us on Whirlwind, ladies and gentlemen. You might remember her when she was barrel racing title bearer Summer Sanchez. Straight up out of Camden Ranch from right here in Pleasant Glen, let's hear it for Summer and Whirlwind."

"That's my mama. That's my mama! I want to see," J.J. raced to the chutes.

Grant hoisted him up on his shoulders and pretended to be too distracted to answer any more of Colton's questions.

"I'll see ya later, Coach," Colton called as he faded back into the crowds.

A quick gasp of breath left Kaitlyn's mouth when Summer's horse burst onto the dirt like he was flying. Summer rode low, leaning over his neck. Fierce determination broadcast from both the horse and her rider.

Kaitlyn had never seen anything like it. Summer rounded the first barrel like a shot. Her power and agility were awe inspiring. The ground shook to the rhythm of the horse's hooves. Kaitlyn wished she could hear him gallop. She couldn't make anything out over the roar of the crowd.

Summer reminded Kaitlyn of all she would never be. Strong. Powerful. Someone who could fight for what they knew they wanted. A cowgirl. Someone who could actually help her husband do things on the ranch where she belonged.

The city didn't make any sense to Grant because he didn't belong there. He was a cattle rancher through and through. Kaitlyn had no idea where she belonged. Sophie was right. Every foundation they'd been raised on had crumbled. Every truth stacked up to one big lie. The only place she felt at home was in Grant's arms, and she was going to have to give that up as well.

Sheer determination to make certain Seth didn't hurt Grant in any way was all that kept her firmly planted on the dusty ground. That and being beside Grant, feeling his gentle caresses, and the kisses he continually whispered in her hair, absorbing him. Eventually this was all going to fall apart just like everything else in her life. He would get sick and tired of the turmoil she constantly brought to his life. Seth would see to it that Grant paid for what he'd done. Her father would get his way. He always did. Nothing lasted forever.

Her father had been right, too. She was naïve to have ever believed anything would. But she would do everything in her power to make certain Grant didn't lose his ranch or his freedom because of her.

"Can you hear me, peaches?" His voice in her ear jerked her back to the present and out of the bleak future she'd knew was coming.

"Always." Keeping little Hank cradled against her, she laid her head on Grant's chest.

Summer was no longer rounding the barrels. Her ride was over. The raucous applause was fading.

"There's Mama." J.J. tugged on Grant's hand. Summer's broad grin as she made her approach stung Kaitlyn's soul. Quelling the jealousy proved futile. Summer had everything Kailtyn had ever wanted, a loving husband, and a beautiful family, and a home to raise them in.

She'd been terrified to admit that was exactly what she wanted until she'd been on the precipice of having it all, only to have it jerked away.

"Mama," Hank roused suddenly and leaned towards Summer.

"Here, I'll take him. I know he gets heavy. Why don't you both go get good and lost for a while. Long truck ride on a dirt road solves most any problem."

"You sound like Austin," Grant sighed.

"Just never tell him I was quoting him. I'll deny it six ways from Sunday."

"We can hang around and keep up with them," Grant offered. "That way you can hand Austin his ropes."

"Nah, I've handed him his ropes more times than I can count. You two look like you could use a night off. Go on. I've got them."

"You looked amazing out there," Kaitlyn vowed. She may have been envious of Summer, but she'd never begrudge her anything. "I've never been to a rodeo before but I know that was one heck of a ride."

"Thanks. I need to leave it to the youngins coming up now. I'm getting too old to do this. I probably won't be able to walk tomorrow. But every time she rounds that money barrel I get to remember who I used to be, and all the shit I went through to get where I'm standing, and why I'm so damn glad Austin refused to give up on me even when I didn't think I was worth saving. It's worth remembering." The kiss she planted on Hank's plump cheeks drove home her point.

"You sure you don't mind if we go?" Grant asked again.

"Don't you want to see your brother ride?" Kaitlyn didn't want him to miss anything. If Seth got his way, he may not be able to see Austin bull ride for a very long time.

"I used to help him train. I've seen him ride hundreds of times. I'd rather go get lost somewhere with you."

"What was Summer talking about?" Kaitlyn asked him as he helped her up into his truck.

"The money barrel? That's the first barrel in the pattern. How well she makes that first turn sets up her whole run." That wasn't what she wanted to know, and he had no idea why he didn't want to tell her Austin and Summer's story.

A shot of jealousy he'd been trying to kill most of the day over what his brothers had made him loathe himself all the more. Dammit, he should have done everything differently. He had no business belting her up and spanking her. She was too innocent. He'd fucked everything up. He should never have taken her home in the first place. And he sure as hell shouldn't have ever let her within striking distance of Seth. Raw regret churned through his veins.

"I meant about the hell she'd said she'd gone through to get where she is."

"Yeah, I figured that's what you meant."

"Do you not want to tell me?"

"It ain't that. I'd just rather you tell me why you look ready to run every single time you think I ain't looking atcha. I'm sorry I scared you. God, tell me you know I'd never lay a hand on you ever. All that stuff we did, I was stupid enough to think that's what you wanted."

"What on earth are you talking about? What stuff?"

"On my couch night before last."

"Grant, that was what I wanted. It's *exactly* what I want. You smacking my ass drives me wild. I almost came as soon as you had my hands behind my back. I am not weak. My deafness does not mean I don't want to experience sexual things that some people might not like, but I do."

"I never said it had anything to do with your hearing. I just kinda lost it this morning with Seth. Then Colton talking about me fightin'. I just … I lost my temper and I scared you. I am so sorry. When he hit you, I lost my fucking mind."

"I am not scared of you Grant Camden. I am in love with you and *that* scares me to death."

"Why?"

"Because Seth won't back down. Because my father would rather have me home and away from you. Because I don't have any idea how to be a cowgirl. Because all I want is to be married to you, and to have babies with you, and raise them, and cook suppers for you, and have Christmases, and birthdays, and a life with you. I want to have really dirty sex with you every night. And I can't ever have any of that. And I'm not sure I can survive the pain of never being in your arms again or never getting to hear you call me peaches or tell me you love me. I'm not sure I'd even want to survive it."

Her vows brought life breath back to his lungs. Stomping on the brakes, he pulled over on the side of the road. "Why can't you have that? That's exactly what I want, too."

"Because I know my father. He'll pay Seth off to keep him quiet in exchange for me not being with you. And I'll let him do it because it will be over my dead body that I let you go to prison for me. And because I'm supposed to want more than to be a wife and a mom, but Seth was right, that is all I want. It's not all I'm capable of by a long shot, but I'm not allowed for that to be what I want."

"You're allowed to want anything in this world, Katy, and I will do everything in my power to give you everything you're after. If it's money he's wantin', I'll sell my land. It's worth a fortune. I don't need your daddy's money. All I need is you."

"Oh, my God, Grant, you are not selling your land. Are you crazy? I am not worth this."

"You are worth everything to me."

The dread he'd tried to keep at bay all evening slithered over his skin. His stomach turned. Searching the desolate road around them, Grant ordered his pulse to slow from its frantic pace, but it was no use. Sweat trickled down the back of his neck despite the cool blast of his air conditioning. Every hair on his body stood on end. Something was coming. He could feel it. His gut never lied.

Headlights bathed them in the cab of the truck as a car came over the hill. Kaitlyn shielded her eyes. Grant blinked the flare of lights from his eyes as the squad car passed them by.

"Was that ...?"

"They're probably headed to the rodeo make sure no one that's been drinkin' tries to get behind the wheel. Let's just get out of here. There's somewhere I want to take you that no one will be able to find us anyway."

Bile churned in his stomach. He eased the truck back on the road and prayed like he'd never prayed before. But it seemed his luck was up. The squad car made a turn in the middle of the road and hit the blue lights.

Chapter 37

"I swear I'll figure out a way to get Daddy to get you out," Kaitlyn repeated for the third time. Certain she was going to vomit, she tried to order her thoughts. She'd offer never to see him again in exchange for her father making this all disappear. Her father would win yet again.

"Here," Grant thrust his phone and keys in her hands. "Call my brother. Tell him to come get you and then to come to Lincoln. Tell Dad to get me a lawyer. I love you, baby, and I swear I will figure out some way to be with you."

"Step out of the vehicle with your hands up," Josh's voice echoed in the cab of the truck.

"Grant, do what he says. Don't lose your temper. Don't give them anything to add to your charges. I'll make this go away, but you cannot fight with him. They have guns, and they'll use them."

"There's a pistol under your seat," Grant sighed.

"Then don't give them a reason to search this truck. Just go."

Kaitlyn flung herself out of the passenger side. Fury burning in her soul. "What are his charges?" she demanded hatefully. "I'm his representation. You have to tell me."

"Get in the car, Kit-kat. You're safe now. I saw what he did to Seth. I won't have you with someone like that."

"Seth deserved everything he got and then some. Why are you doing this, Josh? You know as soon as you leave I'm calling my father to undo this."

Narrowing her eyes, Kaitlyn was certain she saw a niggle of worry twist in the blue reflection of lights in Josh's cold black eyes. "Who do you think ordered his arrest?"

She continued to press. "You tell me exactly what he's charged with."

"You have the right to remain silent," Josh ignored her completely. The clink of the handcuffs on the silent road shook through her. She had to fix this. Now.

"Get in the car, Kaitlyn. I'll ride back there with him. You sit up front," Josh's partner sounded concerned.

"I would rather set myself on fire than get in that car with either of you. You can all go straight to hell. Grant, I will be right behind you. I will fix this. I love you so much," she screamed as they shoved him forcefully in the back of the car. She saw fury burn in Grant's eyes and prayed he'd somehow manage not to kill Josh before she got to her father.

Throwing herself in his truck, she pushed the driver's seat as close to the steering wheel as she could get it and cranked the massive engine before touching Luke's name on the phone.

"Luke?" she concentrated to be able to hear his brother.

"Grant? That you? Hang on I can't hear ya."

Kaitlyn could just make out the low murmurs of the rodeo crowd. Good, they hadn't gone home yet. They were close. The beat of her pulse double-timed the passing seconds. She pressed the peddle harder.

"Okay, try now."

"It's Kaitlyn. I have Grant's phone. He's been arrested. They're taking him to Lincoln. I'm on my way there. Can you meet me at the police station?"

"Of course. Deep breaths, okay? We'll get this sorted. I thought he just got in a fight. What'd they arrest him for?"

"Because in Lincoln it's assault, not just a fight. I'm so sorry. It's all my fault."

"We're on our way. We'll meet you there."

He ended the call. Leaning across the seat to reach her purse, Kaitlyn almost drove the truck off the road. Jerking herself back up, she ordered herself to get it together. She was Grant's only hope and she would not let him down. Reaching again, she successfully located her own phone and managed to keep the truck driving straight out of Pleasant Glen.

Touching her father's name on her contact list, she debated the words to say that would make this go away. That she'd never see Grant again, certainly. That she'd do whatever her father wanted, even get her graduate degree and get a job at a law firm. It didn't matter what, she'd do it.

The phone rang endlessly. No one answered. Rage consumed her. She touched his office number instead. No answer. She tried again with the same results. Hurling her phone in the seat beside her, she swore once she got Grant out of this, she'd never speak to her father again. "This is low even for you, Daddy," she huffed to the ether. "Ugh, why won't you go faster?" she shouted at the truck itself this time.

Remembering that the truck wasn't meant to have any speed, it was meant to haul cattle, didn't make her feel any better.

Seeing no other choice, she swallowed back bile as she located her phone once again and touched Seth's name this time. She'd give him back the ring, sell everything she owned, give it all to him if he'd just drop the charges. But again she was denied. No one answered.

One final idea sprang to her mind. She called the precinct.

"Chief Sommerville's office," a woman's voice she didn't recognize answered. His regular assistant must've already gone home for the night.

"Yes, this is Kaitlyn Sommerville. I need to speak to my father, now."

"I'm so sorry, dear, your father's in a locked door meeting. He said not to interrupt him for any reason."

"This is his daughter. It's an emergency."

"Yes, I understand, but his orders were quite clear. Perhaps you could phone someone else, or I can give him a message as soon as he's out of the meeting."

"Who exactly is he in this locked-door meeting with?"

"The District Attorney, ma'am."

"You know he hit her, right? Any man with half a functioning nad would've beaten the shit out of him. Guess that's not something you'd understand." Grant couldn't help himself. God, how the hell was this even happening? The fact that Kaitlyn was going to throw herself at her father's mercy made him crazy. She would offer to never see him again to keep him from going to prison. He had to stop her. There had to be another way.

"Women really get off on that kind of shit don't they?" Josh huffed indignantly.

"What?"

"That whole big badass cowboy that's gonna save 'em from whatever story they made up in their little head and ride her off into the sunset. What a load of shit. Just look where you're sitting now. Good luck playing her hero from your cell. Those conjugal visits are a bitch."

"Oh, I get it now. Sophie figured out what a douche you really are and told you to take a long walk the opposite direction and you're taking it out on me and Katy."

"Her name is Kaitlyn."

"Shows you how much you know. Mark my words, she'll always be my Katy Belle and she won't go down without one hell of a fight. Strongest woman I've ever met."

"What's she going to be able to do? She can't even hear."

Chapter 38

Kaitlyn burst through the doors of the Lincoln City Police Precinct. Grant was standing at the desk still in cuffs. Josh was arguing with the officer working the desk. He hadn't been booked. He wasn't behind bars yet.

"Katy, don't do this," he pled. When he started to walk towards her Josh grabbed his shoulder.

"You stay put."

"Fuck off," Grant jerked away.

"No," Kaitlyn was in his face a moment later. "You promised me you wouldn't give him anything to make this worse. I have to do this. I love you so much, but I have to do this. Just do what he says."

He jerked at his restraints trying to get to her. Raw pain stabbed through her chest. She couldn't breathe. Mentally, she stopped concentrating. He called out her name but she chose not to hear him. If she listened to him, if she let his voice carry her back to him, he was going to jail.

She shoved a cop out of her way and took the stairs two at a time.

Sprinting to the end of the corridor, she flung open the door to her father's office. Both of her parents gasped at her entrance. "You win. Okay, you fucking win."

"Kaitlyn, mind your language and your tone," her father scolded. "I told you not to come back to Lincoln until I contacted you. Why are you here?"

"I'll never see him again, okay? I'll come back home. I'll go work at whatever law office you want me to. I'll do anything, just please, do not let them lock Grant up."

"What?" Her mother appeared stunned. "Lock him up?"

"What on earth are you talking about?" her father demanded.

"Like you don't know Josh just arrested him. I'm not a fool, Daddy. Grant's downstairs waiting to be booked."

"On whose orders?" Her father stood and marched towards the door.

His words brought her up short. "Wait. You didn't issue the warrant? Why are you both in here together? What's going on?"

"We'll explain everything in just a minute, sweetheart," her mother soothed. "Come on. I need to speak with Josh."

"As do I," her father growled.

Fury radiated from her father as Kaitlyn and her mother followed in his wake. "Where is Officer Anderson?" he shouted at a passing traffic cop.

"He's over there arguing with Lassiter, Chief."

Her father had Josh by the scruff of the neck and up against the concrete brick wall in the next second. "Who signed the warrant for his arrest, and far more importantly, who ordered it?"

"Uh, well, Seth said ..." Josh stammered.

"Get the cuffs off of him, immediately," her father's roar welled inside of Kaitlyn. Relief washed through her making her dizzy. She swayed. Her mother reached and steadied her.

"It's okay. We're going to get everything put back together. I promise you. Your father and I owe you much more than this, and there's quite a bit you don't know."

"False arrest is a very, very serious charge, Officer Anderson. Internal affairs will have a heyday with this. I could have your badge for far less. You would do well to remember who runs this department and who signs your paychecks. Being my son's best friend growing up does not give you carte blanche approval to go about imprisoning anyone you please. If you do not have a warrant that I ordered to be issued and you had signed by a magistrate judge for Mr. Camden's arrest, you have a great deal of explaining to do," her father menaced.

"Seth said he hit her. I was saving her," Josh pled.

"Yes, well it would appear Mr. Christenson wouldn't know the truth if he tripped over it and landed on his sorry ass. In fact, why don't you go get me Seth. I *am* ordering a warrant for his arrest. Judge Stevens is working tonight. He will sign the warrant."

"What is he arresting Seth for?" Kaitlyn asked her mother. Watching Grant shake his arms out and flex his wrists broke what was left of her heart.

"You'll see. Just wait."

Before Kaitlyn could process that, Ev, Jessie, Luke, Austin, and Holly burst onto the scene.

"Do not say anything else," Holly commanded her brother. "He has representation and I demand that he be released to speak with his lawyer."

"He's not under arrest, ma'am," Officer Lassiter looked genuinely humored at her vehemence. Grant rolled his eyes.

"He's not?"

"No ma'am. He's free to go."

"Not just yet. I'd like to see all of you in my office. I have a great deal to apologize for and to explain." Chief Sommerville directed the Camdens upstairs.

It wasn't until Kaitlyn raced into his arms that Grant allowed himself to believe he wasn't actually going to prison. Folding her into his chest, he held onto his saving grace for all he was worth.

"You know what's going on?" he finally managed to ask.

"I have no idea. All I know is Josh arrested you without a warrant and that they're out getting Seth. I can't believe any of this. I'm just so glad you're not going to jail."

"Yeah, that makes two of us."

"I'm so sorry, Grant."

"Stop it. Let's go figure out what the hell is going on. My head's spinning."

Leaning up on her tiptoes she brushed a tender kiss across his lips. "Does that help any?"

"Maybe just a little. Do it again and let's see if it keeps getting better."

He swallowed her sweet giggle as he took her lips with greed, still not quite able to believe he wasn't going to have to go years without having her in his arms.

Grant's father cleared his throat. "All right, you two, maybe you should save that for after whatever her daddy's about to tell us."

"I thought you were supposed to be getting' thrown off a bull?" Grant asked Austin as they climbed the precinct stairs.

"Man, at some point you're gonna realize that there ain't nothing more important to any of us than this family, and there ain't nothing I wouldn't do for my big brother. Soon as I heard they had you, I headed this way with my checkbook in hand. Nothing I ever won is worth anything without my family. And I wouldn't have anything at all if it weren't for you."

"That goes for all of us," Luke cuffed Grant on the neck.

"Thank you," Grant weighed the words on his tongue. The flavor wasn't too bad. He should've been saying it for a long time now.

The slam of the office door jolted through him. Grant clung to Kaitlyn. The office was way too small with so many people and having spent the last two hours trying to imagine life in a cell made him desperate to be back in wide open spaces. He couldn't breathe. He could barely think.

"I'd like to save the explanation for all of this until after Seth is here, so I'll start with my apologies." Her father began to pace. "First and foremost I am very sorry for my incredibly rude behavior while you were in my home. It was unforgivable. I've done a lot of unforgivable things the past few years.

"That probably wouldn't even make the top ten, but I do apologize none the less. Kaitlyn, sweetheart, I owe you the biggest apology of all, save perhaps the one I owe your mother. The divorce papers she filed three years ago came across my desk maybe two minutes before two men I'd never seen before and never want to see again marched into my office to tell me my son wouldn't be coming home." He shook his head. His raw explanation quelled a little of Grant's anger. "The only thing that made sense to me in those first few hours was the way this precinct worked. I somehow stupidly allowed myself to think that if I'd just held on tighter, never allowed anyone to do anything I didn't dictate, just the way I do here, that I could fix it all. But I couldn't.

"And I can't. And police precincts and families aren't one in the same. I blamed everyone else for Keith's death, but no one more than I blamed myself. I took it out on you and your mother because you were available and he wasn't. Again, I am so very sorry. Your mother has been asking me for years to go with her to counseling. Every time you brought it up, I felt like you were taking her side and I acted deplorably. We will be going to counseling as often as we need to go to put this back together stronger than it ever was before."

Kaitlyn blinked back tears. Grant wiped them away and wrapped her up in his arms. "Through hell or high water." He whispered in her good ear. She managed a slight nod.

"I was on my way outside to tell Seth to leave when you pulled up this morning. I heard everything he said about the lawsuits, and I assure you when I saw him slap you if Grant hadn't done what he did I would have. I realized then that my insistence that no one ever know that the Sommervilles have some things they need to work through was holding all of you hostage. When his hand came across my little girl's cheek, it was more than I could stand. And it was all my fault. My chokehold was crushing my family, and I will never let that happen again. I can change. I just hope you'll give me a chance."

"Daddy." Kaitlyn raced out of Grant's and into her father's. "Thank you."

"It's us that should be thanking you, sweetheart," her mother vowed. "You held us all together for three long years. You gave up everything you ever wanted to try to save us."

"You did, and as screwed up as I got everything, please know how proud I am of you." Her father squeezed her tighter. "Your whole life I never knew what to do with you. You wanted to do things I didn't understand. It scared me. You're my little girl and I just wanted so badly to protect you. You wanted to go off to New York and be a chef. It finally occurred to me this morning when I saw your cowboy decimating the man I'd chosen for you that you don't need me to make any decisions for you. The ones you make are far more sound than any I've ever made on your behalf. You never really needed our help at all, and we had no business using your hearing issues to try and control your life. So, if you want to go back to New York, your mother and I will support you completely."

"I don't want to go back to New York." Kaitlyn's gaze found Grant's. Her teeth sank into that bottom lip and he was done for. Suddenly, he was drunk with possibility and relief.

"Come here to me."

She raced back into his arms.

"I had a feeling." Her father offered Grant a humble smile. "If you want to move out to a ranch half way between here and Wyoming, your mother and I will do whatever we can to help you do that as well."

"What about Seth, though?"

Like it had been written into some kind of movie script, someone knocked on the door.

"The idiot did always have impeccable timing. Let him in," her father ordered.

"Damn, you didn't hold back none, did ya?" Austin spoke through his teeth as he viewed Seth, swollen, hunched over, and bruised, being escorted in the office in handcuffs. Josh and a man in a suit Grant had never seen before sandwiched themselves inside as well.

"Never have, never will. Not when it comes to her," Grant vowed.

Kaitlyn whispered another kiss along his jaw. "Maybe don't beat anyone else up on my behalf."

"I'll try to make that my general policy, but I will always keep you safe."

"I know."

"I don't know what you're up to, Chief, but he's going down for what he did," Seth spoke around his busted lips.

"I doubt that, Mr. Christensen. Did you convince one of my police officers that you could get an arrest warrant for Grant Camden and that all he needed to do was go and pick him up?"

Seth turned his head and refused to answer.

"That's what I thought. Listen up. I was standing in my garage this morning when you explained how you intended to blackmail my family. I was there the entire time. I saw your hand strike my little girl, which caused you to fall down my front steps."

Seth's head snapped upward. He opened his mouth to protest, but Chief Sommerville held up his hand.

"I am the Chief of Police, and it is my word against yours."

Grant couldn't believe his ears.

"Yes, and I haven't been in the courtroom defending anyone in so long, I'm anxious to return." Her mother smirked. "If you'd like to continue to harass and abuse my daughter, I'd be more than happy to represent my family. In fact, there is nothing I will ever fight harder for. I've been wallowing in my own pain long enough. It's time I learn to fight back. I owe them more than that."

"They used to call her Evil Evelyn when she was the prosecuting attorney. I fell in love with her the first time I saw her in the court room. Consider your options carefully, Mr. Christensen."

"It was a really bad fall. I was standing right there." Kaitlyn taunted as she and her father shared a conspiratorial grin.

"But probably not as bad as this one." Her father slammed several thick file folders down on his desk. "I used to be a damn good detective. Your mother helped me put all of the pieces together today. I knew there had to be some reason he needed me to pay him to keep quiet other than vengeance. Vengeance will make a man do a lot of stupid things. Treat his family like they're worth nothing at all, for one. But blackmail reeks of desperation. It seems Seth, here, has been anxious to get a job paying more than he was making at the D.A.'s office. He was after something with a substantially higher paycheck, ever since his father cut him off because he discovered Seth had a gambling problem.

"When he figured out that state nepotism laws would not allow him to continue to work there and be married to you, he saw an opportunity and decided to auction off his upcoming position in our family to the highest bidder. Kaitlyn, when you decided to quit working at Baylor, Holsten, and Brown and to keep what happened to you a secret, you gave him all he needed.

"I support your decisions, sweetheart, all I ask is that you tell me about them from here on out. Anyway, you showed your strength yet again when you threatened Morris Holsten with a harassment charge. You told Seth what happened, and he immediately went to Morris to make him an offer. He would keep you from telling me about what happened if Morris would make him a partner in the firm. He agreed as long as Seth promised to pull strings with the police department using his perceived influence with me. When you left him standing at the altar in front of every member of the law enforcement of Lincoln, he assumed his deal making was over. If he had no access to our family, he was worth less to the firm."

"Conspiracy is a second degree felony in the state of Nebraska, Seth," Ms. Sommerville drawled. "And that will be weighed on top of your blackmail charges, and I don't think it would be too difficult to add collusion and intent to illegally gather evidence for your clients from the police. I could put you behind bars for a very long time. And this morning you decided to hit my daughter. That alone makes me want to see you in orange." Mrs. Sommerville spelled out exactly how this would work.

"You don't have proof of any of this," Seth voice shook.

"Oh, but I do. Morris sang like bird before I even got him in the interrogation room. He thought Kaitlyn had finally told me about the deal he wanted to make with her. He would have copped to most anything to keep me from going to his wife. And District Attorney Kelly was more than happy to turn over your computer from her office where your online gambling appears to be a very serious issue. And this afternoon, another witness came forward."

Kaitlyn wasn't certain she could take any more surprises. Her mouth hung open when her father returned to his office with Kelsey.

"What are you doing here?"

"I'm so sorry about everything, Kit-kat."

"Don't call me ... never mind. What are you here to say?"

"Sophie called me this morning and told me she'd seen Seth after uh, he *fell*. She said he was going to have your new boyfriend arrested. I couldn't let that happen. Not after what I did to you. I will testify that everything your father found out about Seth I knew about and even helped him plan to get the partnership so he could get out of debt. I thought I was helping him. I was delusional. He swore to me he wasn't gambling anymore, and that his parents wouldn't help him because of you. I thought he loved me, but he was just using me because I've been paying his rent and his credit card bills. I went to his apartment and got his laptop. He's still racking up debt. I was stupid and jealous of you, and I knew you didn't really even like him so I thought it was okay.

"It wasn't okay. I was so angry your dad got you that job and then you quit. And I'd had a crush on Seth for a very long time. It seemed to me you had everything I wanted. But I want to try to make this up to you. With my testimony, the case is open and shut." She turned to Seth. "Unless you agree to get some help. Chief Sommerville is offering not to pursue charges as long as you no longer work in law anywhere, and you go to Gamblers Anonymous on a regular basis, and really deal with this. And you have to leave Kaitlyn and the Camden family alone."

"And if I don't?"

"Then you will be arrested on conspiracy and assault charges," Kaitlyn's father stated succinctly.

"You're seriously going to arrest me on assault charges after what he did. I have broken ribs, and look at my face."

"A very intelligent young man told me a few days ago that no one else seemed willing to stand up and be strong beside my daughter. I'm standing up. My strength will never rival hers, but I will not let my family go down while I'm at the helm. And my wife is right, it is high time that she and my children were more important than my reputation. Besides, I'm married to one hell of an attorney and juries are far more sympathetic to the person who, pardon my language, beat the shit out of the man who hit his ex-fiancée than they are to the man that abused his intended. Might not be fair, but it's the way it works."

"I can still tell everyone about her affair," he jabbed his finger at her mother. Kaitlyn almost wished Grant would hit him one more time for good measure.

"You do as you see fit. I had a long talk with Grant's grandfather after Grant and Kaitlyn left this morning. He explained to me that angry people want you to see how powerful they are. I know you're angry, Seth. And I know more than anything you want to feel like you're still in control because that means you don't have a problem and it makes you feel powerful. I know that hurt people hurt other people, because I was hurt and angry for so long. All I wanted was to believe that I was in control because that made me powerful. I'm still hurt and angry, I suppose, but I will not continue to hurt my own family. If you want to tell people what happened, I won't try to stop you. You can also mention to them that it was largely my fault and not Evelyn's. If we're going to survive my son's death, and put our family back together, we have to look forward and not back. Mistakes were made, and I made most of them."

Unable to believe what she was hearing, Kaitlyn shuddered. Grant was right there, running his hands up and down her arms, enveloping her in his strength. She didn't have to be strong alone anymore, and it wasn't just going to be him standing beside her.

Chapter 39

"Kelsey," Kaitlyn stopped her in the hallway outside her father's office.

"I'm sorry, Kaitlyn. I really am. I know you have to hate me."

"I don't hate you. I wanted to give you this." She dug in her pocket and handed Kelsey the ring. "I don't know who to give it to. You can give it to his parents if you want. I don't want him to sell it and gamble the money away. It sounds like he's been living off of you for a while, so you keep it. All I know is I don't want to have anything to do with it. And Kels, you deserve better, too. He's an asshole, and he always will be."

"Yeah, I know. I'm not so great at picking out good guys. I was really in love with him. I wish I could figure out if he really loved me too, or if he was just using me for money."

"Piece of advice, figure out exactly who you are and what you want. Figure out if you and Seth are worth fighting for and worth working through his gambling addiction, because that won't be easy. But the right road and the easy road are very rarely one in the same."

Grant winked at her when he heard his grandfather's advice coming from her lips. "Figure out what you need to make your life everything you want it to be and then go get that. Sometimes, you end up driving your car right into the life you always wanted. Sometimes, you have to work a little harder for it."

"Yeah, I need to do that."

Kaitlyn accepted Kelsey's awkward hug.

"Kaitlyn, wait." Josh chased after them as they made their way to the parking lot. Absolute shock and complete exhaustion competed for attention in Kaitlyn's psyche.

"What do you want?" Grant kept his arm around her, never wavering.

"I wanted to apologize to both of you. Seth said Grant had hit you and that he'd beaten up Seth when he tried to stop him. He told me he had someone getting a warrant. Like an idiot, I believed him."

"And you believed him because that's what you wanted to be the truth, Josh," Kaitlyn refused to sugar coat anything anymore. She wasn't going to give Josh or anyone else a free pass to think she was weak.

"You want to tell her what you said to me while you had me illegally locked up in the back of police car or shall I?" Grant demanded.

Mutiny flashed in Josh's eyes. His hands drove through his hair. Whatever he'd said it must've been bad. Kaitlyn sighed. The desperate desire to run coursed through her yet again, but she remained steadfast right beside Grant. She had to stop running from people who thought she was weak. She had to stand and show them how powerful she was.

"Look, Keith asked me to look out for you and Sophie before he left. It was kind of weird. Like he somehow knew he wasn't going to come back. I was trying to do right by him."

"Bullshit." Grant rolled his eyes. Kaitlyn couldn't help but giggle at Josh's shocked expression. "You got a hero complex a country mile wide and you thought while her big brother was off fighting you'd get to come in and play her savior. If that got her right on in your bed, well, that was okay too, 'cause she needed someone to look after her. She don't need anybody lookin' after her, but if she needs a little help now and again I'll be right there every single time. You, on the other hand, need to get your head outta your own ass, and for God's sake stop lickin' other people's. Figure your shit out and stop dumping it on my baby."

"That's pretty much it in a nutshell." Kaitlyn grinned. She also had to stop viewing people she'd perceived as strong as being perfect, her brother included. No one was perfect. That didn't mean they were worthless any more than it meant her hearing loss made her weak. People were complicated messes, sometimes trying to do what was right, sometimes giving in to things they shouldn't. Josh had a lot of work to do. Everyone did, she supposed.

"So, you're just gonna go off and marry him. Not live in Lincoln anymore. Have his babies or whatever," Josh pouted.

"Not sure where you got the idea that we needed to run our plans by you, cityboy. She don't need your help making decisions." Grant wasn't taking Josh's crap anymore either, it seemed.

"Bye, Josh." Kaitlyn tugged on Grant's hand and guided him out to the parking lot.

As soon as his eyes landed on his truck, he doubled over laughing. "Sweet Jesus, peaches, remind me to teach you to drive, and more importantly how to park my truck."

"It's a huge truck and I was kind of in a hurry saving your ass and all." Kaitlyn tried with all of her might to be irritated with him but had no luck. She broke out in hysterical giggles.

"Mm-hmm. And I'm much obliged to ya, but the truck will fit in one parking space if you park it straight, and I'm pretty sure that bush that's under the front wheel ain't gonna make a recovery."

"Would you just shut up and take me home."

"Like you calling the ranch home more than I should," he confessed.

"Grant, you've driven from Lincoln back to the ranch and then back to Lincoln. And you got in a fight this morning. Don't you want to just stay at my parent's house? Or we could maybe go back to your grandfather's."

"Pops is staying up at the nursing home with my grandmother tonight. Something he said he needed to do. Unless your parents aren't gonna mind me tucking your sexy curves up in bed with me completely nekkid then we're going back to the ranch."

"So stubborn."

"Yeah, I changed my mind about that."

"You don't think you're stubborn anymore?"

"Nope. I've heard people call Seth stubborn and your daddy stubborn and I ain't ever gonna be anything like either of them, so I decided I'm determined."

"I see. Well, you are very determined, and I'm pretty sure it's the motivations behind the stubbornness that can make it go from healthy to unhealthy."

"And you'll let me know if I'm getting too big for my buckskins."

"I'm not even completely sure what that means, but I'm definitely not complaining about your size." She wondered if she would ever get tired of flirting with him. Her parent's marriage dampened a little of her enthusiasm, however.

He gave her a hungry growl as the truck bounced down from the curb she'd driven it up on. Shaking his head, he turned to study her. His goading grin disappeared in an instant. "What's that look for?"

"Do you think if we ever got married that it would really be forever? Is forever even a possibility?"

"I think your parents are gonna put it back together, sweetheart. Sounded to me like they're fighting to get back to where they're supposed to be."

"I know that, and that makes me so happy for them, but I just wish I understood why everyone cheats. Why can't people just stay together forever? Isn't that how it's supposed to work? Unless the person you marry is awful or something? My dad was difficult to live with, but he wasn't necessarily awful. And my mom is a wonderful person. I don't understand how that happened and look how much pain it caused, even years after the affair. How do we know it won't happen to us? And what if I'm a terrible rancher's wife? I don't even know what buckskins are. Not that you've proposed or anything, I'm just thinking ahead."

"You just talking this out or do I get a say?"

"You get a say." Kaitlyn sank her teeth into her bottom lip to make herself shut up.

"Don't do that. I gotta drive all the way back, and I'm already hard up just having you in my truck talking about gettin' married."

Curious and almost drunk with the giddiness that he wasn't going to prison and her parents were going to help her put their family back together, Kaitlyn snaked her hand down the front of his jeans. The man truly never lied. There was a distinctive bulge behind his zipper line. His left eyebrow cocked upwards.

"You really are impressive and relentless and *determined*."

"Nah, sugar, I'm just a cattle rancher. Now, listen to me a minute, I ain't ever understood a single thing about politics, or war, or trying to outdo your neighbors, or cheatin' for that matter. It just don't make no sense to me. Maybe it comes from growing up down a long dirt road and working my tail end off for as long as I can remember. But here's what I think, I figure people get all caught up on having the big things. On the big house, and blowing a shit ton of money on a vacation, or buying a fancy-ass car, although I do love my truck. God in Heaven, help me, I love this truck, but anyway, seems to me they cage themselves in all these things so they can post about it on all them sites where people put pictures of their life so it looks good on the outside. Nobody seems to think they might wanna thank their lucky stars for all the little things they already got going on the inside.

"It just don't make any sense to me. You can chase pots of gold for the rest of your life, but that ain't much of a life, in my book. People take on a whole lifetime from the outside 'stead a working on it one moment at a time from the inside. There had to be several dozen moments when your daddy and your mama could 'a done a thousand things differently. When he could of put away his pride. When she could of spoken up about needing him to chill the fuck out and listen to her. When he could of taken up for his kids instead of putting on a show for Lincoln. When both of 'em could have worried more about what was going on inside than what people on the outside thought. But they just kept reinforcing that cage. Eventually the door slammed and they were trapped.

"I plan to take life on moment by moment from the inside. Just like my daddy and my granddaddy and my great-granddaddy and my great-great granddaddy, before them. Every single moment of every single day I'm gonna love you. Be right beside you. Make babies with you. Be there to raise 'em up on horseback just like I was raised. Be home every afternoon, put you in my lap and love up on you. And take you to bed every single night and make certain you're satisfied.

"If there's something fancy you want, I'll do my damnedest to get it for you. I don't want you wanting something you don't have. But from what I've seen the cityfolks ain't got nothing on that long dirt road that raised me. They mess everything up. Too much stuff, too many people, too much keepin' up with who's got what and what they're doing with it. I don't give a shit what anyone else is doing. I just have to know my babies are warm, and fed, and content, and loved. That's all in the world that will ever matter to me. If I convince you to marry me, I ain't got nothing else to prove but that I'll love you 'til my dying breath and that I'll be waitin' on you at them pearly gates."

His vows slipped through her one hearing ear, gently wrapped themselves around her heart, and took up residence in her soul. If there had ever been any doubt at all, it disappeared altogether. She leaned over the console between them and brushed a kiss on the cut on his cheek from his fight with Seth. She'd been through hell since her brother's death so she certainly recognized heaven when it was laid out right in front of her. And she was going to hold on for dear life.

"When I first met you almost a week ago, you told me you weren't much for deep thinking. You were wrong. You're the smartest man I've ever met. And I keep telling you I don't need anything fancy. I've lived that life and you're right, all of the lies everyone tells themselves will never add up to the truth. I think every single thing I never even knew I was searching for is two hours from here in those huge prairies I don't know much about yet."

"Then let's get you home and plant us some roots."

By the time, Grant parked his truck by the house, she was sound asleep. Unable to believe all they'd been through, he just sat and took her in bathed in moonlight, safe and content right beside him.

Suddenly, nothing else even mattered. Not being arrested, or beating the shit out of her ex, or her daddy being an ornery SOB one minute and then trying to make amends, or her mother's affair, or the downed corn, and lost cattle, and the debt. Even with all of that, Grant considered himself one lucky bastard.

He gently eased her lax body into his arms and shut the truck door with his shoulder. She roused.

"Shh, it's okay, baby. I gotcha." With a sweet sigh, she tucked her head on his shoulder and let him carry her inside.

Easing her out of her jeans, he pulled the covers over them and cradled her on his chest. This would always be the only thing that ever mattered to him.

Chapter 40

The next morning Grant held her hand while he stared out at blackened ground as far as he could see. Austin and Natalie had burned back the dead corn for him. He supposed he appreciated it. Didn't make looking at it much easier.

"How long does it take the grass to come back?" Katy asked softly.

"Few weeks."

She squeezed his hand. "I'm so sorry, baby."

"Ain't that my line?"

"Not anymore. Can I do anything to help?"

"A week ago this would probably have killed me. Just having you here makes it better."

"I'm right here. Remember last night when you told me to let you know if you got too big for your buckskins?"

"Yeah." Grant wondered where this was going.

"If it means what I think it means, then I'm supposed to tell you when you've gone from being determined to being stubborn."

"That works."

"You might be stretching the buckskins just a little. Why don't you go talk to your dad?"

"Mama get you to tell me that?"

"You said yourself she's always right."

"Yeah, okay. Got something else I need to ask him about anyway. You okay at the house for a little while?"

"I could unpack a few of my suitcases if it's okay with you. Hope and your mom said they'd take me to the grocery store because you have the saddest refrigerator I've ever seen."

"That mean I ain't gotta eat Hungry Man meals no more?"

"I don't know. You gonna ask me to marry you anytime soon?"

"I've got plans, sugar, don't you worry."

"Thought I might make lasagna tonight. It worked for your grandmother."

"You ain't gotta work that hard, but if that's what you've got a mind to do I ain't gonna try and stop ya."

Grant located his daddy and his brothers and sisters in the office. Well, at least he wouldn't have to ask everyone individually.

"Look like you got something on your mind, son." God love him, his daddy tried to hide his smirk and failed miserably.

"Yeah, I do. First off, thank you for coming to Lincoln last night."

"They made me stay here," Natalie fussed.

"That's just 'cause you're 'bout half a hair less stubborn than Holly."

Both of his baby sisters glared at him.

"And I didn't know how long we were gonna be out there and I knew you'd get all the cattle fed this morning," Ev explained. "You can outride any of the boys and they won't deny that."

"I know you were there in spirit, sis. Anyway, I was thinkin' maybe I'd borrow some money from the joint accounts and buy Abelkopp's stock and equipment, if it's okay with all of you."

"Nope," Luke shook his head.

That took Grant back. "But I thought you all wanted me to run cattle and give up on the corn?"

"We do, but you ain't *borrowing* it. You put a shit ton of money in it so you can *have* it. None of this borrowing shit."

"Agreed," Holly crossed her arms over her chest and narrowed her eyes.

"Oh, you know better than to argue now," Austin chuckled. "She's about to go cowgirl all over your ass."

"All right fine. I was also thinkin' maybe I'd *take* a little money and buy an engagement ring."

"You always were smart," Grant's daddy offered him his hand and then pulled him in for a hug. "And I already told Abelkopp we'd be out with trucks next week."

Before Grant could contend with that, his father's cell phone buzzed. His brow furrowed as he answered. "Hey, Dad, everything okay?"

Sudden tension stirred in the wind. Grant braced for the worst. His brothers and sisters all moved closer together. They felt it too. Ranchers lived by their gut. They always knew. Natalie laid her head on Grant's shoulder. He brushed a kiss on his sister's head. Thankful for the first time in far too long that his family was standing beside him, helping him.

"We're on our way," his father's voice was haggard. It chafed at Grant's soul. Ev ended the call looking like he'd aged ten years in the past three minutes. "They've taken Mama to St. Elizabeth's with heart failure. It ... uh ... it doesn't look good. We need to head on."

The hours stretched on, timed by the blinking light on the morphine injector. The knot in Kaitlyn's throat wouldn't budge. She was a welcomed intruder on his family's pain that somehow she felt as well. She'd never even met Grant's sweet grandmother, but she was so thankful that they all had a chance to tell her goodbye as she slowly slipped away.

Glancing from Grant to his brothers to his daddy and granddaddy, it struck her how humble cowboys looked without their hats, how when life was its most ugly and horrible you took off your armor and let it have you because there was nothing else you could do. Grief was a part of life. You never even got a chance to try and negotiate, to beg it not to take what you were so certain you could never live without.

All of the Camden men refused tears. She knew they would come eventually out in the middle of a field when they were all alone, where no one would bear witness to their grief. Stronger than any men should ever have to be.

For the third time that week Grant drove them back to the ranch in the middle of the night. This time Granddaddy Camden rode with them. Too lost to return to his home. He belonged on the ranch anyway.

"So, I'm just going to talk and if you want me to stop, just tell me." The words took flight from the fissures in Kaitlyn's heart. "It's like there's always this hole right in the middle of your chest. It doesn't go away. It's there, and it's staying. And it hurts. God, it just ... hurts so bad. And you can't run from it or pretend it doesn't exist. But eventually, you can draw a breath without it stinging the hole. And then you feel guilty about that, but she wouldn't want you to. Because she wants you to learn to rebuild yourself around the hole, and you don't want to go back to normal, and that's okay. You figure out a new normal and that's okay, too.

"She would want you to do that. I know she would because Keith wanted me to learn to breathe without wishing I wouldn't. She would want that because she loved you all so much, just like Keith loved us so much. It never goes away but you learn. And then you take another breath, and you take a step forward, and you never ever forget that the hole is there. Believe me, I know what I'm talking about. It's always with you, but you just figure out a way to feel it without letting it consume you. It takes a long time. But you can do it because this family is the strongest family I have ever seen. And I will be right here to help you learn how to take each step you have to take. Grief just sucks but you have to keep on breathing around the hole." With her words, she knew the way to deal with her brother's death was to help other people deal with all of life's blows. That's what families were supposed to do.

"Grant, son," his grandfather's voice was drenched in pain. "If you don't never do another thing in this life that's right, know you got life's most important decision right. And just never let her go."

Kaitlyn turned in her seat and hugged Granddaddy Camden for all she was worth.

Three days later, Kaitlyn stood in the Camden graveyard between Grant's sisters watching his shovel dip rhythmically into the dirt. His brothers and fathers and brother-in-law dug beside him. Silent tears she'd swear she never saw as long as she lived marred every face.

Necessary moments no one wanted to live. Her parents stood off in the distance. They'd wanted to show their support. Indie balanced both twins crying in Savana's hair. Her father stood steadfast beside her.

"I want to help Daddy dig," J.J. pled with Summer again. Her chin trembled as she shook her head. No one was strong all the time. No one should have to be.

Life would go on, different but the same, the cycle would continue, and for the first time in Kaitlyn's life she believed that death was a part of life. She both hated that and understood it.

"Feel like getting lost for a good long while?" Grant voice was raw after the casket was lowered into the ground. Kaitlyn threw her arms around him.

"I will go anywhere in the world with you any time, Grant Camden, but the last time you said that to me you got arrested, so maybe just ask me if I'll go up to the creek with you."

"Fair point. You wanna go up to the creek with me and my brothers and sisters and live life a little?"

"Sure. But I thought we were helping your granddaddy move into the cottage by the front gates today." Kaitlyn wondered if his grandfather shouldn't stay with his parents a few more days just until he could feel the sun and make sense of it again.

"Tomorrow. He don't want to do it today."

"I know you're glad he's moving back out here. Now we'll only have to go to Lincoln to see my family."

"He belongs on the ranch, and if we invite your folks out here enough I can keep you right here, which is where I prefer us to be."

"Me too."

There were already a dozen trucks circled up around the creek. The Camdens and their friends were ready to shed just a little of the grief and take a step forward. The spring day seemed to agree. Sunlight glittered across the truck hoods and skated across the lapping water.

Grant helped his brothers arrange logs and kindling in the old firepit.

When he retrieved a bottle of Jim Beam from his truck, Kaitlyn followed him to the pit. "I thought you liked Crown."

"I do, peaches, but I only build whiskey-bonfires with the cheap shit." With a wink, he handed her the matches. "The sound and the smell means something good is coming, right?" he asked as she reveled in the spark both from the match and the one in her belly.

"Definitely."

"Then throw it in, sugar, I'm ready for good stuff."

The next time Grant took Kaitlyn up to the creek the weather was scorching. He'd rushed his chores but had gotten caught up helping one of their new heifers calve. They were later getting up there than he'd intended.

"You're awfully quiet. I miss hearing you talk." She hadn't stopped grinning all damn day. Prettiest thing he'd ever seen.

"I'm nervous." He swore he'd never lie to her and he had no intention of starting now.

"Nervous about what?"

"I 'spect you know, peaches."

"You don't have to be nervous."

"Okay, then I'm excited. Little dizzy to be honest with ya."

"You usually tell me dizzy is good."

"Dizzy after I fuck you senseless is good, but this just kinda makes me feel woozy. Guess love does that to a man." Throwing the truck into park, he hopped out and half dragged her out of the truck. He caught her before she could stumble. "Come on."

"This is so romantic," she gushed.

"Pretty sure it's kinda hillbilly romantic, but it's the best I could come up with. You love this creek so sit here." He positioned her on the hitch of his truck right over the scratch she'd left on it with her car.

Hysterical giggles overtook her. He swore there wasn't a sweeter sound on the planet save maybe her moaning out his name. "This hitch got us in a whole lot of trouble."

"The best kinda trouble." He got down on one knee and fished the ring box out of his pocket.

Chapter 41

Grant paced in the waiting room at the auditory therapist's office in Lincoln. Why hadn't she just let him go in with her? He should have insisted.

She'd been exhausted lately, and she couldn't hear him as well. She was so dizzy that morning he caught her before she tumbled face first on the kitchen floor. He'd driven her straight to the doctor. She'd cried all the way. Terrified she was losing more of her hearing and for some reason because they were driving back over the street where they'd first met.

She was losing it. The nurse had been called in fifteen minutes ago. She'd gone in with some kind of supply box and she still hadn't come out. Desperate for something to do, Grant pulled out his phone and practiced sign language some more. A week ago when she'd first confessed that she wasn't hearing him as well, he'd started trying to learn.

So far, he had the most important things down. He knew how to tell her he loved her. That was a start.

Ordering himself to be patient wasn't working. He knocked on the door where they'd taken her and then barged in.

The doctor, the nurse, and his fiancée all snapped to attention.

"Is it getting worse? Just tell me. We'll figure it out," he demanded.

The doctor grinned as Kaitlyn nodded her head. "The hearing in her left ear has actually improved since I saw her a year ago. The nerves that were agitated after her brother's death have soothed and are healing themselves. I would say that's due to her new home and adoring fiancé. She will never be able to hear out of her right ear, but we've known that. There is a great deal of fluid in both ears, however, and that's why she's struggling to hear us currently. That, coupled with her dizziness and emotional responses made me curious, since they're all common signs of pregnancy."

"We might want to move the wedding to the end of summer instead of this fall." Kaitlyn beamed at him.

Grant sank down in a nearby chair. "Because you're ...? There's nothing wrong with your hearing. It's that you're gonna ..."

"I was thinking maybe if it's a boy we could name him after my brother, and if it's a girl we could name her after your grandmother."

"Damn."

280

By the time they were back in the truck, he'd processed what was coming. He sported a smug grin for the next hour. "What'd you say to me that night about a month ago?" he goaded.

Laughing, she rolled her eyes at him. "I told you to get me pregnant."

"And what did I do?"

"Are you gloating, Grant Camden?"

"Maybe a little."

"I guess you deserve to gloat. You okay getting married next month sometime?"

"Let me get the hay in and then I'll vow to love you even during calving season."

"Aww, you say the sweetest things."

"I love you, Katy Belle, more than life itself."

"I love you, too."

Epilogue

Kaitlyn tried not to remember the last time she'd been standing in a room in a wedding gown. This time was certainly different. Last time all she'd wanted to do was run away. This time all she wanted was to rush down the aisle. Last time, the earth itself had violently protested her upcoming nuptials. This time the sun was high in the sky over the ranch. The incessant summer heat had even eased for the day. Hay bales cast shadows over the endless prairies and calves dotted the landscape, the most picture-perfect morning she could imagine.

"Hey, Sophie." She'd put this off for way too long.

"Yeah?" Sophie checked her hair in the mirror again, hoping to attract one of the Pleasant Glen cowboys who were still unattached.

"I'm sorry I kept running away. That night I left Mom and Dad's I should have made sure you were okay."

Her sister gave her a kind grin. "Well, I should have made sure you were okay for a long, long time, Katy, and I didn't. So we both screwed up, but I don't think you were actually running away."

"You don't?"

"Nope. I think you were trying as hard as you could to run to where you know you belong." She gestured to the sanctuary of land surrounding them.

"Yeah, I think I was, too." Running her hands over her tiny bump, she thanked God for all he'd blessed her with.

"I told you months ago, Sommervilles do not run away. We always run towards things, and that's the third time you've rubbed that little pooch you have." Her grandmother's smirk said she already knew. Sophie squealed and threw her arms around her sister. "When will my great-grandbaby be making *his* arrival?"

"We don't know what it is yet."

"I know, darling. I always know."

"Late February."

"I take it Langston doesn't know."

"He's doing good with counseling and working on everything with Mom. And she's been out of bed more than she's been in it. They're doing really well. I thought I'd share this with them after the honeymoon."

"Smart girl. A father's heart can only take so much." Her grandmother reached up and tugged on her good ear. Kaitlyn did the same.

"I'm going to be an aunt!" Sophie proceeded to dance around the room.

"What was that?" Their father opened the door.

"Nothing Daddy," Kaitlyn and her sister shared a quick conspiratorial grin.

"No offense, sweetheart, but I hear just fine. I'm not going to think about what I just heard for a little while, though. Are you ready?" This time when her father made his appearance, she was waiting on him.

"So ready."

"Your belly or your sweet little ass," Grant asked his wife as soon as he got her inside the hotel room in Denver.

"What?"

"Which do you want me to rub first? I know you're tired and wanting a nap, and I have plans for you all night, Mrs. Katy Camden. I'm gonna put you to bed for a while first. I can always get you to sleep when I rub your ass, but you get all sweet, and cuddly, and sleepy when I rub your belly, too. I didn't know which you wanted."

"I'm sorry I'm so tired all the time."

"You're growing my baby in there. That's hard work."

"If he's as stubborn as his daddy, it might be," she laughed.

"Determined, and he?"

"Nana says it's a boy."

"I don't care what it is."

"Me either, and rub my belly." She spun and directed him to the zipper than ran the length of the wedding gown.

"Trying not to remember the first time I took you out of one of these."

"I tried that all morning, but we can't have a future if we don't have a past."

"Yeah, I know. Thank you for being my future, peaches."

"There is nothing else I've ever wanted to be."

Another Epilogue

Ten Years Later

Staring down at the massive bump that prevented her from seeing her feet, Katy whimpered. "I'm too fat to reach the mixing bowls in the cabinet. How am I supposed to pack them?"

A loud crash sounded behind her. Spinning quickly, she shook her head. "You helping Mommy pack up the house, Kade?" She scooped up their sixteen-month-old son from the pile of pots and pans he'd successfully yanked out of the box on the floor.

"No, no, no." Kade wriggled until Katy set him back on his feet, just as determined as his daddy. He promptly climbed inside the box and sat on the cookbooks she'd lined along the bottom.

"Fine, sit in the box." She sighed.

Before she could decide what to work on next, Grant flung open the kitchen door carrying a soaking wet three-year-old Barrett inside. Keith and Dallas followed him in, and the guilt written all over their faces said whatever had happened had been their fault.

"What did you do to him?" Katy demanded.

"He said he wanted to go swimmin', Mama," Keith pled. "I promise."

"They dunked him in the stock tank again," Grant sighed. "Get on back outside. Stop bringing mud and manure in the house we're trying to move out of. Your mama just cleaned the floors. The both of you can muck the stalls in all four barns for this."

"Keith Langston Camden, how many times have you been told not to dunk your brothers in the tanks?" Katy huffed.

"It's hot outside. We was bored. We didn't hurt him none," Dallas pled on his big brother's behalf.

"No. Don't say we was bored to Daddy," Keith pled through his teeth.

"Oh, I'll take care of you being bored, son. That won't happen again. There's six dozen hay bales of you can stack after you get the stalls clean. And the front porch the new house needs painting. Now, get," Grant ordered. The boys marched back out to the front porch. "I was gonna put him up in the combine with me, see if I couldn't at least get one of 'em to nap so we can get some more stuff up to Mama and Daddy's."

"Are we always going to call it your mama and daddy's house?" Kaitlyn grinned as she grabbed a roll of paper towels and handed them to her husband so he could mop up Barrett. "I already took all of the towels up there, of course."

"I know. I'm sorry. Dakota and Savana were supposed to keep an eye on 'em. Dad's got most of their stuff packed up. Mama and Holly are heading down here in a little while to help with the house trade."

"It's okay. The boys are excited they get their own rooms. I'm a little sad, though," Kaitlyn took in the house, remembering the time she'd stumbled in the kitchen on her first night at the ranch and then each and every time Grant had eased her inside carrying their newest baby in his capable arms.

"Yeah, it'll be different, that's for sure, but sugar, we're all outta room." Stripping Barrett out of his soaking wet clothes, he located a pair of Batman underoos from one of the laundry baskets nearby. "And I know you're excited to cook in that kitchen."

"I do it!" Barrett proceeded to pull on the underwear backwards.

"I ain't even gonna fix that right now." Grant shook his head and then paused to give her that sexy-as-sin grin that always got them in trouble. He guided her to his chest.

"Every time you give me that look, I end up pregnant again."

"That ain't exactly the way this all works, peaches, and you know it. It is probably a bad sign how often I thank the Lord up above this one's a girl, though." He rubbed his hand over her bump.

She giggled. "After five boys, I'll believe it when I see it. Where's Brady?"

"He's out with Dad checking cattle."

"You mean he's out with your dad talking him into convincing me to let them get another puppy."

"One in the same, ain't it?"

"Five boys, three dogs, and another on the way, it's a good thing I love you, Grant Camden."

"It's a real good thing, but if you weren't so damned sexy we wouldn't have this problem."

"So damn sexy, so damn sexy," Barrett repeated as he scampered to his half-empty room.

"Grant!"

"Sorry," he cringed. "It's the truth though."

"Yes, well, I fielded everything the last time they were down at the front of the church for children's time and Brady informed the pastor that he wasn't allowed to point with his middle finger even though his daddy and his uncles do it to each other all the time. If he tells Pastor Jenkins he's so *damn sexy*," she mouthed, "it's all you, cattle rancher."

"That's only fair. Now, what can I do to help?"

"You can keep Kade from unpacking everything I pack."

"Sweet Jesus, he ain't supposed to be mischievous yet."

"Yes, well, he is his father's son. Hey, instead of making them clean horse stalls why don't we get the older boys to carry boxes up to your parents?"

"We could, but your cookbooks ain't likely to survive, and I'm scared to think about what might become of the good dishes of my grandmama's you love so much."

"Good point."

"How about we wait on Mama and Aunt Holly to get down here to watch these youngins, and I put you up in my truck, and we go spend the afternoon at the creek. Trust me, I can't get you more pregnant. I know. I've tried."

Dissolving into a fit of giggles, Katy shook her head. "I thought we were moving today."

"We are, but I miss you, peaches. Just for a little while."

"Grant Camden skipping out on work. I must be a terrible influence."

"I've been telling Mama and Daddy for years you were nothing but trouble. Nobody believes me."

Katy rolled her eyes, wishing the offer wasn't quite so intriguing. They had so much work to do. She couldn't help herself. He was and would always be her everything and spending a few hours all alone with him sounded like heaven. "That sounds so fun, but I don't think I can get in the back of the truck anymore."

"Come here to me." Before she could protest, Grant scooped her up in his arms and tried to hide his slight strain from her. "See, I still gotcha, peaches."

"Put me down. I'm too heavy for you to do this. I'm seven months pregnant."

"Keep talking like that. I'm counting strikes."

"Are you now? Well, trust me, my ass is plenty big enough to…"

"That's good for at least ten, Katy Belle."

"It's a good thing you're so damned sexy," she quoted back.

"And this right here is how we ended up with six kids, just so you know. I sure do love you, Mrs. Camden."

"Oh yeah? Well, I kind of think I love you, too, Mr. Camden." The twinkle in his pale green eyes said he remembered all too well.

"What's a guy got to do to make you damn sure?"

"Give her every possible thing she ever wanted and put her up in the back of his truck out by the creek."

From the Author

Thank you for reading "Title." I hope you enjoyed it! If you did, and you would like to know more about The Gifted Realm or my writings, there are several ways for us to connect.

1. Leave me a review on Amazon, Barnes and Noble, or Goodreads
2. Visit my blog http://jillianneal.com to learn more about my writing, my family, my favorite products, recipes, and more.
3. Sign up for my newsletters and emails on my site. Be the first to know about the next "Realm" novels and other exciting news.
4. Like my fan page on Facebook. http://facebook.com/jilliannealauthor
5. Follow me on Twitter. @jilliannealauth
6. Follow me on Pinterest. http://pinterest.com/readjillianneal/

Thank you for your support of my books! I so appreciate it!

About the Author

Bestselling author, Jillian Neal, was not only born 30 but also came accessorized with loads of books and adorable handbags in which to carry them, at least that's what she tells people. After earning a degree in education, she discovered that her passion could never be housed inside a classroom. A vehement lover of love and having maintained a lifelong affair with the awe-inspiring power of words, she set to turn the romance industry on its head. Her overly-caffeinated, troupe-spinning muse is never happy with the standard formula story. She believes every book should be brimming with passion, loaded with hot sexy scenes, packed with a gut-punch of emotion, and have characters that leap off the page and right into your heart.

Her first series, The Gifted Realm, defines contemporary romance with a fantasy twist. Her Gypsy Beach series will leave you longing to visit the sultry shores of the tiny bohemian beach town, and her erotic romance series, Camden Ranch, will make you certain there is nothing better than a cowboy with some chaps and a plan. The sheer amount of coffee required to keep all of those characters dancing in her head would border on lethal, so she unleashes their engaging stories on page after page of spellbinding reads.

Jillian lives outside of Atlanta with her own sexy sweetheart, their teenage sons, and enough stiletto heels, cowgirl boots, and flip-flops to exist in any of the fictional worlds she brings to life.

For more information on the author and her stories, check out her website, at http://jillianneal.com

Made in the USA
Middletown, DE
23 July 2021

44654234R10177